1

ISBN: 978-1-894936-71-2
Author: Brian T. Seifrit

Cover RT
Saga Books
Sagabooks.net

Dedications.

Dedicated to all those who waited patiently for the second printing of this title, and all those who read it the first time.

To my wife Tracy and son Dayton, to my daughter Desarae, and sons Christopher, and Garett, a special acknowledgement to each of you.

"One."

Beaten for three days they tried to get him to confess to the murder of Andre Fischer, but he stood firm. "I saw nothing. Nor did I kill anyone. I jumped our borders and attempted an escape that is all."

"Stand up." The general demanded. "Your ride has arrived. You will be taken back to the border. If I see you in this domain again, you will be shot." He led Hayden to the front entrance. "They," he started as he pointed to two men, "have been ordered to kill you if you try to escape, understood?"

His first thought was to run. It was dark and if he made it to the tree line, he might get away. He hesitated for a moment, then nodded, and opened the rear door of the black sedan. The smell inside was that of stale smoke and coffee. Sitting in the back seat, he took notice of the two men up front. One of them held an AK-47 in his black leather gloved hands. From above his left brow, a scar ran its course down his cheek and to the base of his jaw.

The driver wore a fur cap and on the dash board in front of him was a holstered .45. He looked back at Hayden through the rear view mirror, flashing him a grimacing smile that exposed his silver-capped teeth. The conversation between the two men as they drove toward Poski helped him learn more about Andre Fischer. Apparently, Andre was a cleaner, a professional hit man. He tried to listen more intently to the conversation. However, leaning forward brought him that much closer to death as the muzzle of the AK-47 was shoved into his face. "Any closer and I will blow your brains out. Sit back." The gunman ordered.

Raising his hands, Hayden sat back. He ran his finger over the puffy lip he received during the previous three-day beating. His mouth ached, as did his blackened eyes. He felt dizzy and nauseated from both the beating and sleep-deprivation. There was nothing more he wanted than to be back in his dank one bedroom, apartment. Like everything in Poski, it was overly priced and not very well maintained, but it was home. Born and raised there he lived his entire life under the scrutiny of both the Poski Militia, and the Communist Party Army a militant secret police organisation commonly known as the CPA. This wasn't by chance.

In 1970, the Russian Republican Army, a new political party was on the rise. They stood for freedom, equality, and peace. In 1976 at the age of ten, he was forced to watch as the CPA put his father to death for being one of the founders of that political up rise. Unfortunately, this forever, sealed his fate. Even now, twenty-seven years later that memory haunted him. And for twenty-seven years, his desire to escape the communism he and many others were forced to live with grew. With three unsuccessful attempts, his luck hadn't changed. In fact, it had got worse. Now at 31 he was a marked man by the Balcov Officials, any further attempts would be suicide.

There was one other option available, one he thought about often. He could follow in his father's footsteps and join the ranks of the Russian Rebel Army, a more elite and deadly political underground movement than the once reputed Russian Republican Army. The Russian Rebel Army known as the RRA stood for all the same reasons as the Russian Republican Army of old. With one distinction, the ability to kill was a perquisite. The problem he always wrestled with and what held him back from joining was his unwillingness to kill.

The Tangera River came into view, it divided the two domains, the border, was straight ahead. The border guard was his old friend Vlavidov, which meant only one thing—he was in for another beating.

The car came to a stop and both men up front stepped out. The passenger opened the door and motioned to him as he too exited, "You are back where you belong. Heed the warning the general gave you. Do not attempt entry into our domain again. Now, go, before I shoot you."

As he crossed the bridge from Balcov to Poski to his surprise, Vlavidov only gestured to him to continue walking. "So, Hayden Rochsoff…You are the man who has taken the life of one of the KGB's most wanted, huh?"

"I have killed nobody."

"No? Maybe I shoot you dead now for jumping the border, no?" Vlavidov chuckled. "Ah, if you did kill this man or if others believe you did you will be dead in one week. I do not want to waste a bullet on a dead man. You go. Stay clear of this bridge, next time I shoot."

"Two."

One year later standing in the shadows, the cross hairs of his Remington Sniper Rifle on Vlavidov's forehead stood Hayden Rochsoff a now reputed RRA member. Smiling, he slowly squeezed the trigger, and Vlavidov's limp body fell to the ground. Retreating to the dinghy left for him on the river-shore by the RRA. His instructions were to approach Balcov by way of its east shore. Once there, he would meet up with another RRA member and together they would attempt to rescue Monique Farell, a high-ranking member of the RRA and his long-time childhood friend. Monique was in custody of the Balcov Officials and was being held as a political prisoner.

Paddling the dinghy out of earshot, Hayden fired up the trolling engine and proceeded eastward. The water reeked of dead fish and it wafted up his flared nostrils. He squinted, slowly crossing the Tangera River into the unsettled fog. In the bleakness, he heard the sirens from the border; obviously Vlavidov's body had been discovered. Although killing the border guard was not part of the plan, when the opportunity rose, he took it and he had no regrets.

Through the murky darkness he looked towards the shore, but saw no one. Where could his associate be? The glowing needle of his compass confirmed he was headed in the right direction. The person he was to meet should be coming into view anytime.

Carefully, he flipped the switch to turn off the engine. Apprehension tugged at his gut. Without any sudden movement, he glided onto the shore. His first step off the dinghy brought the bite of a bullet that ripped through his left shoulder. Falling to the ground, he reached into the craft and retrieved the sniper rifle. Taking careful aim he pointed the weapon in the direction of the gunfire, through the night vision scope he saw nothing.

Again, there was a burst of gunfire, this time from the opposite direction. Hayden inched into the frigid waters. A retreat to the dinghy was out of the question. By now the shooter, or shooters, had the craft in their sights, waiting for him to try an escape.

Drifting into the river, he realised his only chance would be to find another place where he could swim to shore. It would be an hour tops, before the entire shore crawled with the Balcov Officials and the Poski Militia. To try to swim back to Poski was out of the question not only because of the distance, but the fate that awaited him there. No, he needed to find a place on the Balcov shore where he might have a chance.

The cold water numbed his body and he felt the weight of each stroke in the icy water. He was now without the survival gear and explosives the RRA supplied him to liberate Monique. However, the

Glock was in his waistband, the compass in his pocket and the rifle was shouldered. Not much of an arsenal but he was determined and that was all that mattered.

He swam aimlessly for what seemed like eternity before spotting a place where he could go ashore. It was scattered with rocks and bramble and provided him at least with some obscurity. He pulled himself out of the freezing water and sat on the shore. He began to shiver uncontrollably. Although his left shoulder ached the bullet exited clean. The cold water for now slowed the bleeding, but he knew it was only a matter of time before his body temperature rose.

This process began quickly when he noticed a slight glow in the bush. He repositioned himself, barely able to discern the outline of a man and a dog. A tracking dog no doubt. *Great. If he catches the scent of blood, I'm dead.* His only recourse was to re-enter the frigid water.

***

An hour later he found a dilapidated boathouse a short distance away from the murky lapping waters of the Tangera. Inside found an old jacket and blanket hanging on the wall, removing his wet clothes he wrapped himself up. The manhunt for Vlavidov's killer was well on its way and the Poski Militia were on full alert.

Contemplating his next move he realised the RRA would be of no help to him now. He didn't have a clue how far down river he travelled in the darkness, or how close he was to any town. What he did know is that he couldn't be caught, not by the Balcov Officials and especially not by the Poski Militia. He had to make it out of both domains, and he had to do it fast. A difficult task with no identification, his only hope would be to cross the Atelic Mountain Range into the domain of Seka. It would take him at least a week to cross the mountains, but it was his best option. He sat up with his back to the wall. The wind outside caused the frame of the boathouse to sway from side to side. The little shack creaked and cracked sounding its age. He checked his weapons and ammo. He counted fifteen rounds for the pistol and thirty-five rounds for the rifle. It would have to do.

"One bullet, one kill," he whispered.

As his body temperature rose, so did his spirit. He no longer shivered and his clothes were almost dry. He tore strips from the old blanket and made a tourniquet for his shoulder. The bleeding was not as bad as he first anticipated. He would be able to move sooner than the three or four days he expected to stay.

***

Early the next morning Hayden peered cautiously out the boathouse door. He saw only forest and an old ramshackle cabin off in the distance, its occupants gone. Exiting, he walked over to the cabin and searched for anything he could use in the days to come. He found a long length of hemp rope about half an inch thick. He rolled it up and tucked it into the back of his pants. Further searching produced an old dull hatchet, an old pair of woollen pants. Most importantly in a cupboard he found a list of canned goods, their labels faded or missing altogether. Hungry as he was he opened one of the cans to test its contents. It was pickled herring. Not something he often ate or for that matter even liked. He counted seven cans, and could only hope that not all of them were herring.

Finding an old burlap sack, he added the cans, woollen pants, jacket, and old blanket. The contents of the bag weighed a couple of pounds and he hoped it would hold. With his rifle slung across his good shoulder and the burlap sack in hand, he headed for the Atelic Mountains with one thing on his mind; escape. Once he was over the mountains, he would be safe enough in Seka. The Balcov Officials and the Poski Militia had no jurisdiction there. His only concern would be keeping his eyes peeled for any CPA. They tended to pop up anywhere. They knew his identity and were likely ordered to shoot first and ask questions later.

He travelled south in the shadows of an old dirt road that lead from the outskirts of Balcov. The road was rarely travelled except for an occasional farmer or woodcutter. It was the most direct way to the Atelic Mountains and although it was risky, it was the quickest route. Resting briefly at a brook to quench his thirst, he heard the sound of a vehicle as it stopped. He heard the doors close and then gunfire. Cautiously he released the safety on his rifle and waited. Then crawled closer to the edge of the road and looked in the direction of the vehicle. A man dressed in a brown, green, and red Balcov Official uniform stood beside the truck and at his feet sprawled another man begging for his life.

Hayden raised the barrel of his rifle and looked through the scope at both men. The man on the ground wore civilian clothes and couldn't have been older then twenty-five or twenty-six. The man with the AK-47 was definitely a Balcov Official. His first thought was to fire; however, he knew if he did the unique sound of his rifle would alert others of his presence. Instead, he decided he would try to get close to kill the Official with the pistol, a much quieter weapon with no reverberation. With the Official out of the way he could take the truck and drive to the Atelic Mountains.

Crawling within a few feet of the Official, the man began to turn in his direction. He rose and fired. "You weren't expecting that were you?" He scoffed as the official spun around from the impact, his body smashing against the side of the truck and sliding to the ground, leaving a smear of fresh blood behind. Observing the young man on the ground Hayden knew he had little chance of surviving.

"Please, please help me," the young man stuttered, clenching his stomach in agony.

"I wish I could. What is your name?"

"My name is Cam, Cam Hellin."

"You have been gut shot Cam, there isn't much I can do for you. Let me help you into the truck. Perhaps I can get you into Balcov, to a hospital."

"No, I mustn't go to Balcov. If they discover I'm alive they will kill me."

"Why do the Balcovians want to kill you?"

"I am in possession of some footage… activities of the CPA…" With that said, Cam passed out, slumping to the ground.

Hayden carried the dead Balcov Official to the back of the truck and lifted Cam into the seat of the old dodge. He took the official's AK-47 and put it behind the seat. It wasn't one of his favourite weapons but it might come in handy.

Starting the truck, he paused to look at his passenger. Dark blood oozed from his wound indicating he took a bullet to his spleen. It would take a miracle for the young man to pull through. There was one doctor in Balcov who was an RRA member; however, Hayden could only hope he was still around.

***

Daylight was beginning to fade into night. It would be his best chance to get Cam to the doctor and the sooner the better. He drove to the outskirts of Balcov, the official bouncing around in the back of the truck like a sack of turnips. Parking the truck, he unloaded Cam from the passenger's seat. A half-mile of walking lay ahead before they would reach the Doctor's residence unless they blatantly drove through Balcov. Storing his gear in the truck he threw Cam over his shoulder and began the distance.

Doctor Chernowski met the two at the door and helped Hayden set Cam down on a cot. "How have you been?" the Doctor asked.

"About as well as can be, under the circumstances."

"I thought you perished with the others. It is good to see you."

"Thanks. It's good to see you too. This is Cam. As you can see, he needs your help. A Balcov Official tried to end his life."

"He has done a pretty good job. I don't think this kid will make it through the night."

"Don't give up on him yet. He's taken a bullet in his gut, but he's still breathing. That's got to count for something."

"It does, it does. Perhaps there is hope, albeit only a little. Wounds like these usually kill."

"I know. Please do what you can for him. He claims to have some video footage of the CPA. If this footage can help the RRA and its cause then his life is worth saving. Don't you agree?"

"I do. But, his wounds are dire. If I can save him, his recovery cannot be done here. The officials are sweeping houses and one never knows whose house is next."

"How long before he can travel?"

"I'd guess five days."

"All right, in five days I'll return and take him to a safe house where he can recover completely. I feel responsible for his life. The video he claims to have can only, further our cause. Are you with me?"

"I am."

"Good. Then I'll see you in five days," Hayden said as he turned to walk away.

"I think tonight you'll be safe here with me. Get a good night's rest, have some food. You can go tomorrow. How does that sound?"

"If you think it's safe. I have no quarrels."

"Good. Help yourself to whatever you want and feel free to use my facilities," Doctor Chernowski replied.

"Thanks. It will give me a chance to work out arrangements for our friend." He pointed at the limp figure lying on the cot. "You said that the Balcov Officials are sweeping houses, what is the reason for that?"

"They need no reason. All they are doing is bullying those that put them in power. Striking fear in most." Chernowski sighed as he cleaned Cam's wound to have a better look. "He'll live. The bullet exited, he is going to need surgery though. Come, help me get this cot into the clean room."

"Of course." Together the two men rolled the cot into a back room that boasted nothing more then crude medical apparatuses and large sink. Hayden watched as Chernowski positioned himself next to Cam's side, "Am I still needed?" he asked.

"There is nothing more you can do. Keep watch so that no one interrupts without us knowing. The Officials travel in threes, they cannot find you here."

"No, that wouldn't be good. What should I do should someone come?"

"Let me know. I will talk, you will hide."

Hayden nodded and stepped out of the room closing the door. Sitting down nearest the front entrance, he looked around. The flat was well kept with tangerine painted walls and a wood stained floor. A bookcase sat in one corner and a TV was next to that. There was one couch and one chair in the living room. The flat was scattered with medical journals, certificates, and degrees. Compared to life in Poski, those living in Balcov were better off, they always had been even though all that separated the two domains was a bridge and river. It was pathetic. He shook his head.

The night passed without incident. Chernowski was able to put Cam back together and the kid's prognosis was good. In the early morning, Hayden left the Dr.'s flat to arrange further housing for Cam until he completely recovered.

"Three."

Four days later, returning to Dr. Chernowski's flat before dark, Hayden found the place to have been ransacked. Disarrayed furniture and linens greeted him when he opened the door. He wondered if the two were imprisoned or executed. It didn't look like the work of the Balcovian Officials. This was confirmed when he noticed a note tacked to the wall. It read. "Hayden, meet me in Lengstin. Flat 6. Both Cam and Chernowski have been imprisoned. I am in possession of video. If you want them to live, come quickly."

There was only a two-letter signature at the bottom, and it simply read EL, but he knew who wrote it. "Ellis," he muttered. Ellis was an ex-member of the RRA who was now a CPA informative. Other than the few pictures, he saw of him that was all he knew and all he wanted to know. But there was more to Ellis than that. Setting fire to the letter, he tossed it into the sink. If he were going to Lengstin, he would need food and gear. He stocked up on non-perishables from the Dr.'s cupboards, luckily finding extra cartridges for his pistol and rifle. Taking one last look around he exited into the cover of night.

He walked in the shadows the distance to the outskirts of town where he stowed the truck. Only a few hours remained until dawn and he knew he best use it to his advantage. It was about fifty clicks to the Atelic Mountains and he was now more determined then ever to get there.

In dawn's early light, he watched as the Atelic Mountain range came into view rising before him like a mirage that meant freedom. Freedom though for him would have to wait. He had a destiny to fill. Parking the truck on an incline he removed his gear then released the parking brake. The truck picked up speed as it crashed unmanned, mowing over small saplings on its route to the jagged bluffs of the Tangera River. Looking in the direction of the mountain he was going to have to cross he tied the burlap sack to one of his belt loops, tucked the pistol into his waistband, shouldered the sniper rifle and held the AK-47 in his hand. It was early morning, if he could manage he would be deep in the mountain by noon.

The Atelic Mountain range led into the Domain of Seka and the little town of Lengstin. It was twenty miles across and around 3400 m at the highest altitude. Snow remained on the peaks well into summer. Crossing wasn't going to be an easy feat. What drove him was that by the end of the week, he would only be a short distance from freedom and the mysteries that the video held.

The sun was an orange ball overhead when he rested for the first time. His throat was dry, the little bit of moisture that was in the air dissipated as he ascended the climb. It seemed as though the sun sucked the moisture out of the air and he thirsted for water. He was this far once before and knew that over the next crest was a brook. Parched, he stood and walked to where it flowed. Taking a long refreshing drink his thoughts turned to Dr Chernowski and Cam. He felt responsible and in a way, he was. *If only I minded my own business then perhaps at least Dr. Chernowski would still be a free man,* he thought.

Looking in the direction of the two domains, he realised how much he hated them and the misgovernment that reigned. He would never understand how two regions in the same country so close in proximity were so different yet the same.

***

Ellis was sipping on Vodka in one of the Taverns in Lengstin, anticipating his reunion with Hayden. He had no video. That was only a ploy to get Hayden to come to him. However, he did plant a video to see if Hayden could retrieve the fake tape. If he could, then Ellis would put forth his master plan.

Again, he was turning his back on a political party that he believed in, much like when he belonged to the RRA. Even then, Ellis was only looking out for himself, sure he put on a good act when he was amongst his peers. But everyone who knew the man—knew that he was yellow.

Ellis looked at his watch, noting it was 5:15. Calling over the waiter, he requested more Vodka and some food. "What is the special this evening?"

"Tonight is the same as every other night, sir."

"Well then, I'll have what I had last night."

"Sir you weren't here last night."

"No kidding. Give me a menu and get lost." Ellis replied.

The waiter quickly handed him a menu and briskly walked away.

He decided on lamb chops and mashed potatoes with a side of fried onions. "Hey waiter, take my order would you?"

"What is it I can get for you?" a different waiter asked.

"I'll have the lamb chops, mashed spuds and a plate of fried onions. And bring me another Vodka, no ice."

"Not tonight sir. Go sober up and come back tomorrow if you want those lamb chops. And we will not be serving you any alcohol either. You've had enough I would say."

"What, what are you saying? You're not going to serve me, huh, is that what you are saying?" He tried to stand taking a clumsy swing at the waiter and fell onto his back. The waiter escorted him out into the street.

"If I come back here I'm gonna burn this place down." He slurred as he strode off to the next nearest liquor establishment. By 3:00 a.m., he'd been thrown out of more establishments than he was allowed into. Now he was trying to climb the stairway to his rented flat, with not much success. He walked up four stairs and stumbled back three almost tumbling on more than one occasion to the bottom. Help arrived in the form of the waiter. He had been watching Ellis's antics from across the way for the past couple of minutes. Ellis looked into the waiter's eyes and tried mumbling something but in his drunken state could only produce a slurring of words that sounded more like a gurgling then anything else.

The waiter only shook his head, "That's right. I'm your fairy Godfather."

"I knew it. I knew you were that," slurred Ellis pointing at him.

"What room number are you looking for?"

"I haven't got the slightest idea. I think I got a key in one of these here pockets."

The waiter stood and watched Ellis put his hand into the same pocket repeatedly. "Try the other pocket man, the one on your left," he finally offered.

Ellis reached into his left jacket pocket and pulled out the key. "You are a Godfather fairy ain't ya?" he slurred.

"That's fairy Godfather, not Godfather fairy. What number does the key have on it?"

"If the numbers would stop moving around, I'd be able to tell ya." He tossed the key to the waiter. "What number can you make out of that squiggly mess?"

The number on the key read six. The waiter helped him to the door and opened it for him. "There you go. Here is your key and sleep well."

Ellis stumbled to the bed and collapsed. The waiter looked at his pocket watch 4:00 a.m. w*hat a night*, he thought as he crossed the street in the direction of home.

***

At 11:00 a.m. the following morning, Ellis finally began to stir. His head ached from the binge the night before and the taste in his mouth was foul. On top of all that, he couldn't remember a thing. Sitting up he noticed he slept in his clothes and on the soles of his shoes was a scat of dog shit, which he'd unknowingly smeared all over the foot of the bed. With no time to stand and make it to the bathroom, he puked inside the wastebasket beside his bed. *Great way to start the day. I've got to quit drinking,* he thought.

Kicking off his shoes, he headed straight for the shower. He looked deeply into the mirror and shook his head. "You look like crap my friend," he said to his reflection. Removing his clothes, he turned the shower on. The nozzle sputtered a few times and then finally began spitting a trickle of pale yellow water. It took almost fifteen minutes to lather up and by that time the water was cold. Cursing aloud, he heard a knock at the flat's door.

"Who is it?"

"Maid service, can we clean your room now?"

Ellis shut off the water. Reaching for a towel he realised there weren't any hanging on the towel rack. "It's going to be one of those days I can tell," he said, stepping out of the shower stall as he slipped on the tile floor. He was able to keep his balance by grabbing a hold of the bathroom sink and vanity. He looked everywhere for a towel, but found none. He steamed out of the bathroom, pulled the blanket from his bed, and used it instead. "Look, you're going have to come back or better yet, I'll let you know when you can clean up in here."

"We'll be next door then, let us know when you're decent and we can tidy up."

"Yeah, yeah." He listened as the cleaning buggy creaked on by. Picking up his bag, he took out some clean clothes, his razor, and the .45 calibre pistol that he always brought with him whenever he shaved. He didn't know why he always brought the gun with him. It was habit. Perhaps it had to do with the fact that his life was always in danger. From all the people he miffed it was a wonder he still breathed today. Returning to the bathroom, he turned the sink on. Of course, there was more water pressure than what the shower had. Looking into the mirror, he shook his head.

Shaved and cleaned now he left the hotel room. Seeing the chambermaid, he whistled to let her know that he was awake and that she could go about cleaning the place.

He walked over to a nearby coffee house, ordered a large black coffee and a breakfast bagel and sausage. His stomach wasn't up to the task of eating and when the bagel came he pushed it to the side and ordered more coffee. Sipping the hot beverage, he began to reminisce about the CPA and of course the RRA. He smiled at the thought of conning Hayden. Moreover, after Hayden retrieved the video and followed through with his next plan he would take pleasure in putting a bullet between his eyes. Less queasy now he leisurely picked at the bagel and sausage. As a rush of workers from the different mining outfits arrived for lunch, he stood and paid his bill.

"Thank you, come again," said the cute cashier behind the counter.

Ellis nodded and tipped the young woman. Opening the door to leave he looked back again, smiled, winked, and walked outside. The noon air was stuffy. Taking a deep breath he spit and proceeded to the hotel. Entering the office, he asked for a telephone.

"No phone here," said the old man behind the front desk.

"What do you mean you have no phone?"

"No phone here."

"I'm a guest and I need a phone."

The old man looked at him and shook his head. "No phone here."

From the back room came an older woman. "What is the problem?" she asked.

"I need a phone."

"We have a phone but it is only for our guests."

"I am a guest and this guy says there is no phone."

"Pay no attention to him," said the woman. "He is simple and hasn't spoken a word of brevity in almost twelve years. What is your room number?"

"Six."

"Mr Ellis Leroy."

"That's right."

"The phone is through that door and to your left. By the way, it only stays connected for five minutes you'll have to be quick. Or pay again."

"Why is that?"

"If it weren't on a timer I wouldn't know how to bill my guests."

"No problem, it'll be a quick call." Ellis entered the phone room and dialled Andre Fischer's direct line. After the fourth ring a voice answered at the other end.

"You got me. Who is this?"

Ellis had to remember exactly what the dialogue was that he had agreed to use. "This is Yorel Sille, is the jack on the mound?" This essentially was asking if Hayden was on his way.

"That is affirmative. The jack is on the mound." The voice from the other end responded.

"Chernowski and Hellin what is the word?"

"Both bent the bars." In other words, they somehow managed to escape. There was silence on both ends of the line for a minute.

"All right, clear their names. I'll send flowers their way," replied Ellis.

There was a short pause on the other end followed by a snicker. "The jack will be in your deck in three, maybe four days. The two missing cards will be found shortly thereafter."

He knew this meant that Hayden would be getting into Lengstin in three or four days and that the missing cards were Dr. Chernowski and Cam Hellin. They would be lead directly to him and assassinated as well.

"Remember Yorel, this number will no longer exist after this call. You will have to meet with my associate again in order to receive the new number."

"I'm aware of that. I'll meet him in Fanshaw say mid August," he suggested.

"That works Yorel. However, if you hear from me before then…" at that moment the telephone went dead. Looking at the timer on the box he realised his five minutes were up. He quickly dialled the number again but it didn't ring. Slamming the receiver down he exited the hotel office and stepped again into the dirty streets of Lengstin. *So, the jack will be in my deck in three or four days*. Ellis smiled.

The only thing about the call he didn't like was that Andre never got to finish whatever it was that he was trying to say at the end. He could only wonder what Andre meant to say. He never met Andre. No one had that he was aware of, and instead he always met with the bad breathed Moroccan. He did however, converse with Andre by way of telephone. Andre always paid him well for the few jobs that he did.

This time however, he was playing outside of Andre's court. Andre wanted that video as much as both the RRA and CPA. Only thing was he didn't have it. Still, he was going to squeeze Andre as much as the RRA and CPA letting all of them believe that he did. He had no desire to meet anybody in Fanshaw. That too was a ploy to get Andre out of the way for a short while. He knew Andre's reputation, but because of ignorance or stupidity, he didn't care. It was all about money.

His plan was simple. Once he was in Canada, he would contact either the CPA or RRA. Once either one of them was contacted, he knew the others would notify him and make him an offer. The first to place one hundred thousand US dollars in his hands would receive the fake tape. Hopefully he would be able to slip out of sight before anyone got a chance to view it. It was a plan that he was certain he could pull off.

"Four."

Hayden was huddled beneath a spruce tree his feet badly blistered. He walked almost to the summit by now and the hike was beginning to take its toll on his body. Earlier in the day he heard a Helicopter and thought it would be best to settle in earlier than usual. Five clicks from his position, almost directly in front of him in a parallel line was an army camp set up. It wasn't a military camp. It was the CPA. Due to a malfunction with one of the rotors on the craft, they were forced to land. They had no idea he was even in the vicinity.

They radioed ahead and parts were on the way, but not until the following afternoon. They were ordered to stay close to the chopper because of the cargo it held. Any other time they would've been picked up and a new pilot and crew along with a mechanic would've replaced them. The helicopter had been coming from Kamchatka, and it was loaded to the hilt with munitions and a prisoner. The prisoner's name was Alex Farell an ex-member of the RRA, and a man wanted for numerous crimes as seen deemed by the CPA secret police.

Alex was picked up trying to get into Canada, via Alaska. A higher up official of the CPA working out of Alaska and Kamchatka received a lead that someone whom was wanted by the CPA was poking around, trying to secure save passage into the Canadians. The CPA picked him up not twenty-four hours later. He was boarded onto the cargo helicopter, tethered and shackled to a middle seat, two guards on either side sat next to him. When the craft began having problems, the CPA loosened his shackles in case he had to jump. He probably would have remained in the craft his chances of living then were somewhat greater than if he were to jump. There were only six parachutes in the craft and of course six CPA.

He was relieved when the pilot was able to maintain control and gently land the chopper. He was even more relieved when they let him out under guard when the thing finally quit smoking, not before, but after. The CPA chained his leg to a tree where he now sat. Settling in they lit a fire to cook some army issued tack and biscuits. It smelled good from where Alex was sitting and he anticipated that one of them would bring him a feeding of it. It was better than having to eat grubs and slugs, but he had eaten those before as well.

Instead, the guard brought him a cup of black coffee and a biscuit. Apparently, there were only six cans of tack as well. He was not surprised.

Before dark the guard returned and threw him an old woollen blanket. It reeked of dirt and mildew with a slight tainted smell of urine. There were stains on it from years of not being cleaned, regardless, he thanked the guard and nodded his thanks.

"It's not much, but it's better than a kick in the groin with a frozen boot." replied the guard.

Alex chuckled, "You got that right." He wrapped the blanket around his shoulders, leaned upright against the tree, and watched the flickering fire. He couldn't feel the warmth from the flame. It didn't make much difference to him, the blanket would do. He watched the fire until it was only a pile of glowing embers. The others had crawled into the cab of the helicopter and were by now sleeping. He looked at the chain around the tree and his leg. If only he could break one of the cold metal links, by morning he'd be long gone. He looked at the chain trying to figure out if it was possible. "Nope. I'm not getting out of this." Making himself comfortable, he closed his eyes.

The guard came over in the morning and handed him another biscuit and coffee for his breakfast. Alex sat up as best he could and took the meagre offerings. "Much appreciated," he said. The guard nodded and walked away. Looking over to where the CPA gathered, he shook his head. *Here I am eating a stale biscuit, drinking burnt coffee and they're feasting on more tack.* The smell of the cooking food was soon overtaken by the scent of human excrement and urine. As the six men took care of their daily business not less then ten feet behind the tree he was chained to.

He looked up to the sky to take a guess at what time it might be, the sun was slowly creeping into full view, he guessed the time to be around 8:00 a.m.

One of the younger men walked over to him and unlocked the chain. "Get up. We are putting you back into the chopper."

"What for?"

"I'm just following orders."

"Do you think you could let me take a piss?"

"Make it quick and don't try anything stupid. I'd hate to have to shoot you, I'd rather you face what's coming to you in Poski."

Alex smiled. "Yeah and exactly what is that kid?"

"I'll tell you this much, I'm going to live longer than you," replied the young guard.

"I wouldn't count on it kid. I say three, four years tops and the CPA will only be a memory and so will you if you don't get out now."

"Just do your business. Hurry up."

"It's kind of difficult with you standing over me like a vulture."

"Let me help you along." There was a report of gunfire. Alex jumped. The kid had fired at his feet.

"You're crazy do you know that?"

"I've been told that before, now hurry up."

Alex did up his fly and the two of them walked back to the helicopter.

***

Hayden looked towards the rock bluffs that he would be crossing. They were a few hundred yards away but he could tell from where he rested as he looked at them that they were steep. As he approached closer, he began to pick out the route he would take once there. The eastern bluff looked to be his best bet. However, the closer he got the harder it looked.

He stumbled with the gear a couple of times as he ascended, hoping not to have knocked the scope out of kilter. He didn't care much about the AK-47, as for the sniper rifle it was important that it didn't bounce around. The accuracy of the scope had to remain true. If it didn't it could prove to be deadly not to an enemy, but to himself. He rehearsed in his mind what all snipers were taught. 'A snipers scope must remain true; it can be out by one hair, but not by two.' That little ditty always brought back memories.

Ascending the last few feet he rested and looked over the sniper rifle. The scope's end caps remained on, as did the muzzle cap. He removed the end caps and looked through the 10X scope. He couldn't be sure if the cross hairs were jarred or not unless he fired a shot. Instead, he decided to depend on his expertise. Judging on how well the rest of the rifle fared, his expertise told him that the scope was unaffected.

Putting the caps back on he set the rifle down and reached around back for the AK-47. He gave it a quick look over and decided that it too suffered little if any damage. The burlap sack on the other hand was another story. It tore open on one side and was now short four cans of food. He used half of one of his bootlaces to mend the hole. Hopefully, it would survive the rest of the trip. Standing, he loaded himself up with the gear once more and began the final lag of his climb.

Within the hour, he was looking over the other side down into a valley. There was a speck on a clearing about a mile away. Walking along the top of the ridge, he kept the distant object in view. As he approached closer, he could make out the distinct shape of a helicopter.

Heading off the ridge as quickly as he could, he travelled in that direction, towards the helicopter. It was imperative that he got out of view and stayed hidden until he could ascertain their friendliness. At what he thought to be the same parallel of latitude as the helicopter he stopped and took a compass reading. He was still going north east, perhaps a little bit more east then north, but not enough to matter.

The helicopter was now about 700 yards away directly in front of his position he guessed. It would be easy enough for him to circle around. Before he did that though he wanted to be sure that they weren't friendly. If it were the RRA, all his worries would be over. It was possible, but unlikely. Most of the RRA members except for the ones in Poski were in different chapters all across the country and as faraway as

Canada. A short distance away a clearing in the thick wall of trees came into view. He stayed well hidden in the shadows of the overgrown forest as he approached, careful not to move too fast or too slow. Finally, the helicopter came into view. He put everything down except for the sniper rifle. He pulled back the bolt and set it on semi-automatic. Unlocking the safety and in the prone position he crawled on the forest floor until he was within 400 yards of the helicopter. Looking through the scope, he focused in on a man standing near the back of the craft. Unsurprisingly it was the CPA.

Moving the rifle slowly, from left to right and back again. He counted six men on the outside mingling closely together and what appeared to be another man sitting inside. He crept a short distance north to get a better view of the inside. Kneeling, he rested his elbow on his knee and scoped in on the object. "What the…" he began to say rather loudly, catching himself before finishing the sentence. He couldn't believe what he thought he saw or for that matter who he thought, he had seen. Looking again quickly through the scope, he shook with anticipation. He tried to focus on the person in the helicopter but to no avail. He was too excited and excessively jittery. Taking a moment he inhaled deeply and exhaled slowly. In control now he held the rifle steady and again focused in on the man in the back seat.

"My God," he said beneath his breath. There, sitting inside was Alex. Chained and cuffed, but alive and breathing. He hadn't seen Alex since they both tried to escape out of the country a year earlier. Everyone thought for sure that he was dead. Taking a moment to gather his thoughts, in a brief moment, he knew what he had to do. There were six CPA operatives and he knew he could fire off that many shots in as many seconds. And without a doubt make that many kills.

He dry shot the men to make sure he used the right speed and knew the distances between each. He counted "one, one thousand, pull the trigger, two, one thousand pull the trigger..." and so on. He studied this until he knew the exact fluid motion he would use. Taking a deep breath he got his first kill lined up in the crosshairs. Counting to three, he slowly squeezed the trigger. His first shot went wild shattering the front window of the helicopter, the CPA began running this way and that pointing in all different directions.

Unable to move Alex slid behind the seat in front of him. With only a second to compensate for the overshot, Hayden fired again, and seven seconds later no one was standing. Quickly he ran out of the bush hollering, "Alex. It is me, Hayden." He sprinted the distance to the helicopter. "I can't believe it. You are alive."

"Thanks to you I'll stay alive, these guys were returning me to Poski to face a judgement by the CPA on some outlandish and trumped up charges. The firing squad was all that was in my future."

"Everybody thinks you are dead. Which one of these creeps has the key for those chains that they got you in?"

"I can't tell anymore, they aren't too recognisable without faces."

"Head shots tend to do that."

"I think it's the guy with the brown over coat on. If you can't find the keys then you'll have to shoot these chains off cause we haven't got much time. The only reason this chopper is here is because the rotor calved on it yesterday. The CPA radioed ahead and parts are being flown here sometime today. We have to hurry."

He didn't even make the distance to the man in the brown jacket before he found the key ring lying on the ground a few paces away. The chains left deep impressions in Alex's legs and wrists as he removed them. They were tight enough that the blood circulation throughout his limbs was slowed. He couldn't feel his legs and when he tried to stand, he fell forward. Hayden managed to catch him and helped him over to where the fire had been.

"Thanks. By the way what are you doing out here?"

"The RRA's old friend Ellis is behind this." He explained to Alex what had taken place.

"And it's because of him that Monique is imprisoned?"

"I can't say for sure. After I popped Vlavidov, the RRA's plan was to break her out. She was being held in Balcov at the old triplex building. I was one in a party of two that was suppose to rescue her."

"What happened?"

"Like I told you, when I reached the east shoreline of the Tangera in Balcov an official or maybe the CPA were waiting for me. It was obvious that my RRA contact in Balcov had been discovered. Or, on the other hand was part of the assassination attempt on my life. I had no recourse but to get out and get out fast. I considered going after her myself until all this other stuff took place. Now, if I even get glimpsed by the CPA, the Poski Militia, or even the Balcov Officials I'm as good as dead."

"I don't blame you. I blame these pigs." Alex pointed at the clutter of dead bodies. "These pigs and that yellow piece of work Ellis. He has been a thorn in every organisation that would have him. For now, we have to deal with one problem at a time. The other chopper is scheduled to be here around three. What time do you got now?"

"It's 11:30 a.m."

"Good. We have enough time to hide the dead."

"Hide them. What do you mean hide them?" Hayden chuckled.

"What else do you suggest?"

"Load them up into the helicopter and blow the thing sky high. The only problem with that is when the others arrive they'll find only six bodies. They will know that you got away."

"No they won't. You know why? We picked up an extra guy, some high ranking CPA and I don't recall the pilot mentioning it when he radioed ahead. They maintain radio silence all the way from Kamchatka. The only time they made contact was when we landed here." Alex grinned from ear to ear.

"Good we'll load them up and send them to hell."

"First let my legs get their feeling back, then I'll give you a hand. Besides, if we have time I want to check out the cargo. There may be some stuff in there that we might be able to use."

Hayden shook his head. "The cargo might be useful or some of it. But, the arms they got are pitiful. I have an AK-47 back in the bush that is better than any weapon these guys have."

"You have an AK-47? Perfect!"

"I also have some canned goods, which, to me it looks like you could use."

"Food. I'd love some food. I've eaten only two biscuits since yesterday."

"I'll go get the gear. You sit tight and I'll be back in a couple of minutes."

"I'll be here," said Alex. "I'll be here."

Hayden walked back to where the gear was stowed, thinking about the childhood Alex and he had. For over thirty years, they were the best of friends. Both his and Alex's father grew up together as well. They were the ones who first started the Russian Republican Association and both died fighting for its cause.

It wasn't until Alex's Uncle took over the Association that it eventually became the Russian Rebel Army. During that time, he and Alex always said that they wanted to be a part of the RRA. His mother though refused to let him join. To grant his mother her wish, he quit pursuing it until she went to her grave.

For the next few years he tried to join and for years he was turned away. Until finally, being successful only a year ago. Monique swore him in. Now, he was on the lamb and Monique was a political prisoner in Balcov. The good thing was that Alex was alive and well, Vlavidov was dead and the CPA were six members short. Returning to the helicopter with the gear, he was surprised to see Alex up and about. He was rummaging through the cargo that the chopper held. Hayden opened a can of fruit and handed it to him. "Anything worth keeping in there?"

"Nothing."

"I assumed as much."

"Man. You wouldn't believe how good this fruit tastes."

"I would. I lived off of sauerkraut and pickled herring for almost a week."

"Sorry to hear that. I think I'd rather eat biscuits. Yuck." He tossed the now empty can into the helicopter. "Let's get these guys loaded up. I have a plan. Since you can't been seen in Balcov and everyone presumes I'm dead. I'm going back to get Monique. She's the only family I have left. You go to Lengstin, find Ellis and put a bullet between his eyes. Monique and I will meet up with you in Lengstin. There is a little place called the Bear Cove. It's east of there on the outskirts. It's a good place to hide out for awhile."

"I know the place." Hayden assured.

"Good, then we'll meet there."

"The Bear Cove it is," he replied handing the AK-47 over to Alex. Taking the weapon, Alex punctured the helicopter's fuel tanks. They walked a distance away and took cover behind a mound of dirt and rock. Taking aim at the spewing fuel tanks, they fired in unison. Instantly the helicopter exploded sending debris in all directions. Black smoke billowed in the sky. It could be seen for miles but they didn't care. By the time the CPA Territorial reserve arrived, they'd be long gone.

It would take Alex four days to get into Balcov and then he would have to find out for sure where Monique was being held. If everything went well, they would be on their way to the Bear Cove in a week. Meet up with Hayden and together they would head for Canada. Hopefully this would give Hayden enough time to take care of Ellis and to be in possession of the videotape.

The two men agreed it would take three weeks. If in three weeks Alex and Monique hadn't showed, Hayden would be on his own. As the CPA Territorial helicopter became audible in the distance the two friends shook hands and went their separate ways.

"Five."

Arriving in Lengstin three-day's later, Hayden wasn't surprised that the little town hadn't changed much since his last visit back in his late twenties during one of his futile attempts to escape. It was still a gathering place of riffraff. The dirty streets were scattered with debris from a nearby landfill. The wooden sidewalks were warped and twisted from the many days of rain the place got. Today the ground was dry and dust billowed in the air.

He squinted from his position looking to see if any Balcov or Poski Official's were around. Not seeing any he laid down the rifle and burlap sack and covered them with some cedar bows. He checked the pistol to make sure the clip was full. Then coursed his way to the hotel that Ellis told him to meet him at. Hayden wanted that video and he wanted it bad. If the Balcov Officials were ready to kill for it then it was worth killing for.

If the CPA were to get it before the 'RRA', then whatever it might reveal about the CPA's organisation would surely be lost. Ever since he helped Cam that's all he wanted to get his hands on. Then he could have the revenge he longed for since being a child. The tape would bring the NSA down on the CPA quicker then one could say jack sprat. Then, finally the people of Poski and Balcov could rise again. And a proper government could be elected.

He walked into the darkened lobby. He hadn't shaved or bathed in two weeks, so he fit right in. He went over to a red high back chair that sat in a darkened corner and sat down. He looked around the lobby that was filled with cigarette smoke and stale air. He wanted to see Ellis before he spotted him. Then he would follow him around for a bit, checking him out. It would be just like Ellis to turn him in. Or at the least lead someone to him that he'd rather not see, such as a Balcov Official or someone from the Poski Militia.

He waited for two hours until finally spotting Ellis on the other side of the room. He hadn't change since the last time he was pointed out to him. They had never been face to face or even spoke. Hayden saw him a year ago when he was taking money from one of the high ranking CPA Officials for turning Monique along with five other RRA members in. At that point, Hayden wanted to run over to him and put a bullet in his head.

Nevertheless, he also knew patience would be a virtue. He would kill Ellis there were no two ways about it. But not before he knew where Cam Hellin and Dr. Chernowski were being held and definitely not before, the video was in his hands. He watched Ellis jostled his big size and high-class look around in the small pub. He was as noticeable as a nun in a whorehouse. Hayden looked at his watch and noted the time to be 2:00 p.m. He figured he'd let him slug back a couple before he followed in after him.

At 3:15 p.m., Hayden walked into the pub. Ellis was sitting at a table nearest an old dartboard that hung on the wall, one dart stuck in its bull's eye. The smell of beer and smoke as well as human flatulence hung in the air. It was a dirty place and Ellis fit right in. Hayden could tell by the way Ellis, was swaying as he sat at the table. And by his blood shot eyes that he was drunk. He pulled up on a stool at the bar and ordered a beer. "I'd like a cold one please." The bartender reached into the cooler and pulled out a Seka Peva. Hayden twisted off the cap and took a long swig. The beer tasted good taking away the dryness in his mouth as it went down his throat. He tossed the money on the counter that would pay for the beer and walked over to another table that was closer to his friend Ellis. The guy was so tuned that he didn't even recognise Hayden.

However, then again, Hayden didn't recognise Hayden. He smelled bad and his hair was all matted. The skin on his face was greasy and covered in dust and dirt. And he had a face full of whiskers. Ellis probably thought he was one of the mineworkers. For now, this suited Hayden. The closer he could get to him the better—the RRA had always stressed. 'Keep your friends close, but your enemy's closer'. Hayden was following this school of thought now. He sat at the table until Ellis stood and went to relieve himself, Hayden watched as he closed the restroom door. Then he stood and followed behind. Ellis stood at one of the urinals pissing all over his own hand. Sauntering over to one of the urinals himself, he pretended to piss. "Sure hot out today," he said trying to get a conversation going with Ellis. He walked over to the double sink and washed his hands.

"Don't worry the rain's will be on us b'fore ya know it. Then we'll all be c'mplaining." Ellis slurred.

"I suppose you're right. Are you from around here?"

"Hell no. Hey, do I know you from somewhere?" Ellis tried to focus his eyes.

"Nope. I'm new here. Pulled in last week." Ellis looked a bit closer at him with one eye closed. Then he swayed back.

"I guess I don't know ya. Ya kinda reminded me of someone is all." Ellis swaggered over to the sink. Hayden took that opportunity to slip out of the restroom. He went and sat at the bar and ordered another Peva. Then he waited on Ellis again to either leave or pass out. Ellis swaggered out of the restroom and slumped down at his table. He ordered more vodka and a liverwurst sandwich. "I want lots of onions too. You got that." he said belligerently to the server. Who then scurried off like a frightened animal. He noticed Hayden looking at him and hollered over to him. "What the hell ya doin' way over there? C'mon over here and have a vodka with me, wouldja?"

He stood and walked over to his table. "Nice of you to invite me over."

"Well believe me guy that ain't my intention. I ain't trying to be nice to ya. I simply wanted to ask something of ya. I have a friend whose suppose to meet me here in the next little while. Ya look like ya could use a couple of American dollars. I figured I'd ask you to do something for me." Ellis slurred.

"What would that be?"

"I'm about as drunk as I'd like to be. I was hoping that if I offered you fifty bucks you would keep your eye opened for that friend of mine. His name is Hayden Rochsoff, probably be here in a few hours. What do ya say? That way I can hustle up to my room and sober up a bit before he gets here."

"I'd like to help you but, I don't know what your friend looks like." Hayden said coyly.

"Yeah ya do. After all, it is you Hayden. I might be drunk but I ain't stupid. How long have you been here?"

Hayden was perplexed that Ellis guessed who he was. "I've been here for about four hours. Do you always get this drunk during the day?"

"What is it to you."

"I don't know it's just that I can't believe how yellow you really are."

"Yellow. You think I'm yellow."

"What would you call it? What kind of man turns in his own people to gain a few bucks?"

"A few bucks. You don't know a thing. I've made more money turning on guys like you then you'll ever make in your lifetime. If you haven't noticed money talks and bullshit walks. You and all the other radicals will be trying to make enough money to feed yourselves and I'll be up in Canada swilling Canadian beer and living the way the free world allows. Don't be calling me yellow. I'm a businessman looking out for my own interests nothing less. Got it?"

"Do you really think your going to make it to Canada? Do you think I'm stupid enough to let you get away that easy?"

"You ain't going to have a choice, Mr. SS Tycat. For now, follow me to my room. We'll talk business there."

"You want to talk business. Do it here."

"It isn't going to happen like that. What I have to tell you puts both our lives in jeopardy. If you don't want to know where Cam Hellin is and the good Doctor Chernowski as well as that videotape…that, well, has some rather unorthodox and disturbing practises by the CPA on it.

Then go ahead and sit here. Better yet, get the hell out of Lengstin. I'm going to my room and since you're here you know what room number that is." Ellis stood up and stumbled out of the bar. He called Hayden's bluff. Hayden knew he would have no choice but to meet him in his room. He waited a few minutes and then headed up. He could only hope Ellis hadn't set him up. Room six was at the end of the darkened hallway. As he knocked, Ellis simply said, "The doors open. Come in. Decided to see things my way huh?" he blithered. "I knew you would, come on, sit down." He gestured Hayden to a chair.

"What kind of business do you want to talk about?"

"In time, in time. Relax for a bit. Tell me what's new with the RRA?"

"As if I'd tell you anything like that."

"Why not. Don't you trust me?" Ellis questioned sarcastically.

"From what I've read and know about you, you're a lying two face back stabber, might even be because of you that my father was killed way back when. I don't even like being in your presence. Why would I trust you."

"That's too bad. I'm about to put a lot of trust into you and your abilities. You want that tape don't you?"

"Of course I do. But from that question I'm assuming you want it too?"

"Maybe. What do you want more the tape or the lives of your friends?" he asked coldly.

"Quit toying with me. I think you know the answer to that question. What are you proposing? That you'll help free my friends?"

"Not at all. I'm offering to tell you where they are. I'm not going to help you free them. What do I care if they are executed? And in return I want you to help me retrieve the tape."

Hayden was only a few deep-breaths away from pulling the gun from his waistband and killing him then and there. "What are you telling me? That you aren't in possession of that tape?"

"Do you think that if I was I would give a damn about your two friends, who if questioned and tortured enough will undoubtedly mention your name? Perhaps they will even reveal your little click of RRA members. Wouldn't that be a tragedy? The entire organisation brought down because you hesitated to help me out. What would the others think of you?"

"Listen, I'm this close to ending your existence. Tell me what this deal is all about before I end it and you right now."

"Do I detect a little bit of hostility? Or is that animosity? Go ahead put a bullet in me. You wouldn't make it out of this building without meeting me in hell. You'd be dead before I hit the floor. Do you think I'd invite you here if I didn't have my ass covered?"

"Here's one for you do you think I'd come all this way without notifying the RRA? Do you think I'd be here alone? I have to cover my ass too." He was lying through his teeth of course. But, who was to say that Ellis wasn't either?

"Fair enough. Are you ready now to talk business?"

"I'm ready to listen to what you have to say if that's what you mean. As for talking business, I think I'll wait to hear what you're offering. So go ahead."

"It was revealed to me that this tape your friend Cam claims to have is back in Balcov. He has an uncle there who happens to be an old friend of yours, goes by the name of General Liwwet. Can you say that, Hayden? Liwwet, sound familiar?"

"I don't know any General Liwwet. What are you talking about?"

"Such a short memory. A year ago you were interrogated when you and Alex tried to defect from the domain of Poski. Am I bringing General Liwwet back into your memory? Can you see his face now? He's the general who threatened to kill you if he ever saw you again. Is that a coincidence or what?" Ellis began to chuckle. "What I expect you to do is retrieve that tape and bring it back to me. If you agree, I will let you know where your friends are being held. But, first I want that tape in my hands."

"You're an idiot. You know I can't go back to Balcov. There is a bounty on me. The first Balcovian that sees me will blow the whistle. Not every day are they offered such a deal, they report me, and reap the reward. Not one of them would do anything different." It was the truth and Ellis knew it.

"That's too bad. That is my offer. Use your wits. Use all those great techniques that the RRA has taught you."

Hayden could tell by his tone that there would be no way in swaying him. He was confident in himself that he could and would retrieve the videotape. He wanted to add another equation to the deal. He figured if Ellis would guarantee safe passage to Alaska for himself, Alex, Monique, Cam, and the Doctor. Then he would agree. If not then he was going shoot him right there and then. "One question Ellis. What do you want with the tape?"

"Like I said earlier I'm a business man. That tape will easily fetch me a hundred thousand American dollars and perhaps more. If you decide to do this, be forewarned that if you try and to copy the tape…I will know. What is your answer? Are you going to retrieve that film for me or are we both going to walk away from this little meeting empty handed?"

"Put it this way. I'll get you that tape. I will guarantee it in your hands in less then three weeks but only if you will guarantee me something."

"Seems to me that you really can't request a thing from me. I'm the one with the knowledge of where your friends are and yes that does include your friend Alex's sister, what's her name…it evades me, oh yes, Monique."

"What do you know about Monique."

"Obviously, more then you. I find it quite humorous that you can guarantee that tape in my hands in three weeks. Chances are you'll never even get close." Ellis taunted.

Chances were he was right.

"I'll tell you what. You deliver that film to me and I will fill you in on what has been going on with Monique. How they have drugged her and made her act inappropriately, you know, as a two bit whore."

Hayden's mind raced, he had to remember whom it was coming from. Ellis from what he knew of him was trained in, psychological warfare. He couldn't be sure if he was pulling his chain or not. "I'll get the film. But, first I want you to guarantee and fund a safe passage to Alaska for me and four friends."

"As I stated to you earlier I don't think you're in a position to request anything from me."

"You're wrong. If what you have implied has happened to Monique, then chances are that she's already been killed. Or has been so drugged that she is no longer the woman she once was. As for Cam and the Doctor, who's to say that they too haven't already been executed? In which case I haven't got anything to gain. Do I?" Hayden questioned. Using the same technique Ellis used. He had Ellis's attention and he stared at Hayden in his half-soberness.

Hayden continued, "Yet, on the other hand you've already told me where the tape, film or whatever you want to call it is. I guess I could turn my back and walk out, retrieve the tape and hand it over to the National Security Agency (NSA). Or for that matter the CIA. Couldn't I? On the other hand, better yet, I could take your life and take my chances that whoever you claim is watching us isn't nearly as good of a shot as I am. What do you have to add to that?"

"You have some valid points. I admire your attempt to sway me. In fact I admire your attempt so…that I will offer you and four of your friends safe passage…to Alaska, only." Ellis said sinisterly. "But, you must deliver that film to me intact in three weeks, like you have so passionately claimed you could do."

"It isn't going to happen like that either."

"Tell me then how is it going to happen?"

"You're going to write down the location on where, Monique, Cam and the Doctor are being held, if not at the same location. Then, you and I are going to the local Postal Outlet and you're going to purchase a stamp. I will write the address on it to where the letter is going to be sent. We are going to find a local mailing box and send off the letter. We're going to watch that mail box with our lives, until it is picked up. Once the postal service has it I'll head back to Balcov and retrieve the tape. The letter should arrive there before or only days after I arrive. Either way I will wait for the letter. And when I open it, it better contain the locals. If it doesn't I'll hunt you down and you won't like what I'll do once I find you." Hayden said with sincerity and conviction.

"There seems to be a few discrepancies in your plan. If I write down the locations where your good friends are and you receive that information before I have the film in my hands who is to say that you wouldn't forfeit our deal? Then again who is to say that I would write down the proper locations anyway?"

"Perhaps, I should word it like this. If I open that letter and the places you have mentioned in that letter turn out to be different places that come out of your mouth when I deliver the tape, you'll still be dead." Hayden was as candid as possible.

"I see where you are going with this. Either way you will have to return here to be sure that what I write down are the proper locations. Because, you aren't going to be sure, now are you?"

"That's right, but on the same token you aren't going to be sure that I don't retrieve that tape and use it for my own benefit. You see the way I have it figured is we can make this little deal benefit both of us or we can screw each other. I doubt you want to be screwed and neither do I."

"You talk good business. I only hope you follow through. Otherwise, I'll guarantee the downfall of the RRA."

Hayden looked at him and nodded. "And I guarantee that I will kill you if you do not follow through with your part of this bargain. Which is telling me where my friends are being held and providing us with a funded and safe passage to Alaska."

"I'm a businessman. I'll keep my end of the bargain." Ellis assured.

A few minutes later Ellis wrote down the locations on a piece of blank paper and folded it. The two of them picked up an envelope from the front desk of the hotel and went to the only Postal Outlet in Lengstin where they purchased a stamp from the machine outside. Hayden wrote the address to where it was going on the envelope and handed it back to Ellis so that he could affix the stamp. Returning to the hotel, they slipped the envelope into a mailbox on the other side of the street. They sat in the hotel lobby monitoring it from the big window until the mail was picked up that following morning at around 4:00 a.m. Then looking at one another one last time with hatred in their eyes, Hayden slipped out of the dank hotel into the cool morning. His destination the town of Balcov.

He retrieved the sack and his rifle then coursed his way again through the Atelic Mountain Range. He travelled for four days until finally coming across the helicopter that Alex and he left in ruins. The CPA scavenged what they could from the wreckage. All that remained was the twisted charred metal frame. Taking the opportunity to take a break, he sat in the little bit of shade that the helicopter's remains provided. He rested for a little over an hour, then again headed deeper into the Atelic.

***

Two days later he was looking from a top of one of the higher mountain ridges down on the town of Balcov. He tried to come up with a plan on how he was going to get close enough to General Liwwet to be able to pull off the caper. His beard and stringy hair he knew were a good disguise. He hoped that the general wouldn't have a clue on, who he was when he finally showed up. After all, it had been over a year since the general interrogated him for jumping the domain border in one of his futile attempts to escape. He thought back to the three day beating he received. As the general tried to get him to confess to killing, some hit man named Andre Fischer. Hayden could never figure out why the two Governments cared. After all Andre Fischer was an assassin. He remembered that beating as if it were yesterday. Standing, he headed towards Balcov.

He made it to the dirt road that would lead him into the town. Hiding the sniper rifle and making sure his pistol was locked and loaded. He took a compass reading then stepped out of the forest and onto the road. The few people that past never even regarded him, he probably looked like the numerous other vagrants and homeless people that they'd see on any given day. He walked the three miles into town. Then checked into a below the belt hotel under an assumed name.

He tossed the old burlap sack on the bed, and pulled out the Glock from his waistband and set it where he could reach it in a quick second. Removing his boots, socks, and smelly clothing, he rinsed them out in the little sink. He contemplated, but decided against cutting the beard that now covered his face in it's matted form. He felt better but still looked ragged. He adopted the look for his concealment. Tonight he would sleep. Tomorrow he would retrieve the footage.

"Six."

May 24, leaving his room around 7:00 a.m., he proceeded towards the down town core. The street vendors and markets were coming to life, and Balcovian Officials were beginning to go about their daily hassling of its citizens. Walking over to a man who was selling bread and bacon, he ordered a serving. The vendor put a piece of fresh bread on a plate and smothered it in butter and bacon grease then loaded it with the sizzling hot pork and handed it to him. Paying, Hayden traipsed over to one of the benches that lined the street. He knew it would only be a matter of time before one of the officials noticed him. He also knew that they would want to question him simply because they had never seen him before. Sure enough, as he was about to take a bite of the bread and bacon one of the officials approached. "You, vagrant, what you got there?"

"Bread and bacon."

"Some bread and bacon? It's probably the only thing you've eaten in a while, isn't it vagrant?"

"Yes sir, it is."

"How about I do this?" The official smacked the food out of his hand. Hayden looked at him and shrugged. "What's you name vagrant?"

He knew from experience that if he didn't answer the official's question the interrogation would go on. Which, was part of his intent, he needed to get close to General Liwwet. He couldn't remember what he looked like or for that matter if he was even in charge anymore. Hayden figured he could lie his way into finding out if the general was deployed there, by keeping the official who bullied him talking. If he were, his residence would be the same used by the Balcovian Officials for last fifty years. "My name is…before I say sir what is it of your concern. I have committed no crime. I'm simply passing through. My stay in Balcov has been a pleasant one but the unemployment level is too high. I've heard that Vuctin to the north may be looking for labourers. I will be leaving here today."

"Vuctin. What have you heard about the domain of Vuctin?"

"I was told early this morning by a passer-by that Vuctin is in need of workers in the logging camps. Isn't that true?" Hayden questioned with pathetic fallacy as if he were concerned.

"It is true vagrant. I suggest if that is your destination that you pick up and go, before I decide to bring you to the general for vagrancy. Perhaps, I should bring you to him anyhow. What say you?"

"I will leave sir. I wouldn't want to disturb the general."

"No, you would not want to disturb General Liwwet. I suggest you leave as quickly as possible. If I see you, again I will apprehend you. Now go—get out of here vagrant, Balcov doesn't need the likes of you."

Hayden turned and walked back to his hotel where he retrieved his gear and headed out of Balcov. He ducked into the nearby forest and walked amongst its shadows until he was in a gorge that was obscured by large trees. Over a little knoll was the building that was used as the Balcovian Officials Command Post. The building sat right on the shore of the Tangera River and was only about five miles to the Poski border.

For seven hours he laid in wait, keeping his eyes peeled for when the general left. Finally a Balcov Official vehicle approached and pulled up next to the front doors of the command post. The driver exited the big car and opened the door for the general who slipped into the back seat with two bodyguards. Hayden watched as they drove in the direction of the Poski border and then out of sight.

The direction they travelled answered his question that the general's residence was indeed the same one used for high-ranking officials for the past fifty years. It lay between the border and Balcov. It was a big house and said to be impenetrable.

A truck drove up and two officials jumped out of the back and two more jumped in. It was obviously a shift change. He waited for the truck to leave and then proceeded in the direction of the general's residence. Following the road, he stayed alert for oncoming vehicles, passers-by, and the like. He could smell the water from the Tangera as he walked and could hear the crashing waves as they pummelled the rocky shore. Rounding a corner and looking up he could see the big house as it loomed down on the road and the shores of the Tangera. The light emitting from it looked like a big star in the dark horizon. The big gate at the bottom of the hill was locked tight. The twelve-foot fence lead to a sheer rock bluff in one direction and up and over a ridge in the opposite direction leading away from the house.

Hayden followed the fence to where it stopped at the bottom of the bluff. He looked up and considered an attempt in ascending it. That is until he noticed a few odd looking protrusions. They were obviously sensors of some sort, perhaps even land minds. Instead, he followed the fence up the grassy ridge to where he was able to see the dirt road leading up and to the eastside of the general's mansion. There he waited until dawn.

As the morning sun began to rise, he knew it would only be a matter of time before the general and his bodyguards would be leaving for the command post. Patiently he waited, staying hidden amongst some undergrowth. Finally an hour later he saw dust rising. Looking to the gate he watched as the general's car headed west towards the command post. Clocking how long it took the gate to close. He was surprised that it took a full fifteen seconds. If he couldn't find another way in he'd have to use the gate when the general returned that evening and fifteen seconds was enough time for him to do it.

He walked east along the fence for five hundred yards, stopping he took notice of a building on the other side, it was the heart of the electric fence, from the sound of the transistor he guessed it was ten thousand volts, enough to weld metal to metal. He knew now that he had only one option. Walking back to the grassy ridge, he sat beneath a birch tree. He had hours to wait. It gave him enough time to put together and rehearse a plan. It would be dark when the general returned and it would be unlikely that he would be noticed under the cover of darkness. Once the car entered he would count to five and rush the gate. Leaving ten full seconds to enter before it locked and completed the electric-circuit like a big switch. Timing and obscurity would be the key.

Inside he would wait for morning before advancing. He would have to travel vigilantly and cautiously. If he were sighted, no matter who he pretended to be he would die. Once he made it to the fortress he needed to get to the second floor. The footage he was suppose to retrieve was in a second floor bedroom, with purple velvet wall covering. There was a large brass vase with turquoise highlights. It sat in the corner of the room near a large dresser or so he was told. It was in that vase underneath a thick piece of Styrofoam that an assortment of dried plants and flowers were inserted, that he'd find the elusive video.

He sat in cover beneath the tree the entire day. Never could he remember it being so peaceful. It was almost unnerving. He drifted in and out of sleep lulled by the birds and warm sun. He awoke when the first drops of rain drizzled through the leaves of the birch tree. Looking up at the sky, he watched the clouds as they billowed in the atmosphere. There was a storm brewing. Deciding to head to the cover of a large evergreen that would keep the rain off better then the birch he was under, he stood and ran towards it. By the time he made it to the cover of the tree, the downpour was ferocious. The pine swayed this way and that as the wind whistled.

Moving around to the other side and protected from the wind he found some relief. He ducked his head into his knees. He was being pelted now, not only by the cold rain but also by pieces of dirt and debris. Branches that were blown off nearby trees slammed against the fence. They gathered there like branches in a beaver dam. Something metal flashed by that he could only guess was aluminium.

There was a loud zap and flash of blue light, followed by another zap. The aluminium shorted out the fence. He quickly picked the smouldering piece up and tossed into the fence to be sure, satisfied, he took the opportunity immediately to scale it. Standing on some of the debris that gathered he climbed up and over. The bramble he stood on gave him that extra boost he needed to reach the top. As he landed with a thud to the ground on the other side, he heard the audible buzzing of the again activated fence. Had he attempted to climb the fence a tenth of a second later he would have been stuck to it like paper to glue.

Noticing that his pistol was lying on the ground on the other side in plain view, he shook his head. He figured he could chuck a few pieces of wood or something over the fence and cover up the weapon. He'd retrieve it when he headed back to Lengstin, if he had the chance.

Finally managing to toss an old rotted log over the fence on his fourth try it landed on the hard earth spewing it's red rotting wood in all directions and by chance covering up the Glock. It was only by fluke that happened, but he was relieved it had. He was without a gun but the hatchet remained tied to his waist. Vigilantly he headed east towards the dirt road that would ultimately lead him to the fortress on the hill. He was definitely ill equipped without the Glock, but his training with the RRA taught him many ways to kill. His only hope was that he wouldn't have to.

The storm that erupted earlier finally gave way to a magenta sky and a distant rainbow. Walking along the fence to the dirt road, he paid close attention to the ground he stepped on. The Balcovians were famous for the way they strategically placed land mines and booby traps. The last thing he wanted was to become a victim. He walked until he unexpectedly came to another fence that bordered the big mansion. This one however was fifteen feet high and topped with razor wire. On the other side metal skewers protruded from the ground. It was a lethal set up. Beyond the skewers was a moat of glass shards and more razor wire entwined with pieces of lumber loaded with nails and spikes covering an area of about thirty yards. Beyond that, it looked to be clear sailing.

Trotting back to the undergrowth, he tried to figure out how he was going to get inside. The only feasible thing to do was wait for the general to return or watch for someone to leave and then rush the gate before it closed.

The opportunity came at dusk when finally the general's car pulled up to the gate. The only thing was as soon as the car approached, floodlight's elucidated the dark making everything visible. Taking cover, he waited for the lights to shut off. They illuminated the front gate long after it closed. His only recourse was to wait until morning. An attempt in daylight would be bold and perhaps the general and his staff would be less suspicious that someone may try exactly that. Finding an uprooted tree that the wind that day toppled over Hayden curled up in the big hole.

He slept little that night. As dawn rose so did he. Crawling back up the embankment, he again waited for the general's car to leave. An hour later the big black car rolled up to the gate. As the car slowly crept away he stood and ran the distance across the road and in through the gate. Crouching by some shrubbery, he looked down the yard. The shrubbery he was crouching beside led all the way down the black topped driveway on either side. Staying hidden while he attempted to get closer to the big house, he approached within fifty yards of it when two big Bouviers des Flandres darted in his direction barking viciously. Standing, he ran as fast as his legs would carry him towards the gate. What he was going to do once he got there he hadn't a clue. Surprisingly the two dogs stopped abruptly turned and headed back towards the house.

Catching his breath, he looked down the long yard. The dogs were no where in sight. Here he was locked inside an electrified fence with two huge dogs that wanted undoubtedly to kill if not maim him. He was certainly in a predicament. It wasn't until his second attempt did he realise that the dogs were either trained to go a certain distance, then retreat. Or there was an electric wire imbedded in the ground that only allowed them to go so far before their collars gave them a zap. The latter he hoped.

He noted the area where they always seemed to stop. Then he crawled over to it like a snake in the grass. When he was near what he thought to be the area, he began to dig with his fingers, searching for any underground wire. In only a few minutes, he found it. All he had to do was cut it get the dogs to cross and hopefully be quick enough to join the two ends before they could cross back. That was the difficult part. Before he cut the wire, he crept back to the gate. He had to get the dogs to go at least that far.

He removed his boots and socks. Figuring it would be a good idea to leave them somewhere and hopefully the dogs would get confused and search them out. Giving himself that extra second or two before they realised they were socks. It was a wild hunch and one he hoped would work. He thought about tossing the socks onto the fence. That way if it were electrified the dogs would kill themselves. However, that would alert anyone in the house, he was sure once the fence went off so would numerous bells and whistles. Instead he tied them to a branch on a nearby pear tree.

Returning to where he exposed the thin wire he used the blade of his hatched to peel two inches of the insulation away getting a zap in the process that numbed his hands momentarily. He walked in the shadows of the shrubbery until he heard the dogs running in his direction. Standing, he ran towards the pear tree then jumped, and rolled in the direction of where he cut the wire. Like planned the dogs darted towards the tree and jumped up at the socks. Quickly he brought the two ends of the wire up and twisted them together making the circuit complete. Running over to the shrubbery again he waited to see what the dogs were going to do. Finally they gave up on the socks and turned back towards the house, but stopped on the other side of the wire. *Thank God for electric collars,* he thought.

Standing in the shadows at the rear of the big house, he looked up at the second floor trying to figure out how he was going to get in. Finally, peering in a first floor window he noticed it was unlocked. Pulling himself up and through he entered. The clanking of pots and pans from a nearby room confirmed that he was near the kitchen. Silently he opened the door and looked toward the end of a long hallway. At the end was a set of stairs that he would have to ascend. He closed the door and listened to the sounds. He waited impatiently for a few minutes then darted to the end of the hallway. Silently he took the steps two at a time, until he was standing in another hallway lined with four doors. One of them he knew was the room he was looking for. Creeping along the wall, he came to the first door. Putting his ear against it he listened to be sure no one was inside. Slowly he turned the knob and looked inside, but it was the wrong room.

The next door he checked proved to be the room he was looking for. He crept inside and over to the brass planter that held the so-called footage. He removed the dried plants and piece of Styrofoam. Obviously Ellis hadn't lied. At the bottom of the planter was a container that held a videocassette used in Camcorders. Putting the film in his pocket he replaced the plants and exited the room. Descended the stairs he cautiously darted back to the room on the first floor where he gained entry. Silently he slipped out the window into the warm afternoon.

He fooled the dogs the same way, retrieved his socks, and stuck them into his back pocket. He had the tape. The dogs were back where they belonged and now he was faced with how he was_going to get out. Obviously, he'd have to get out the same way he got in. He found an area on the grounds with a couple of fruit trees and decided to wait there until the opportunity to slip out the gate arose.

Two days and two fences later he was standing on the grassy ridge where he left the sack. He retrieved the Glock, which hadn't suffered any from the pieces of rotting log that covered it. He rested for a bit before heading back towards Balcov and over the Atelic Mountains. Removing the tape from his pocket he looked it over for damage from all the ducking and rolling he had done. God, how he wanted to know what was on it. He looked it over one last time and put it back into his shirt pocket. In time, perhaps he would know what it revealed. Standing, he walked down the embankment and onto the dirt road. To his back were the two borders of Balcov and Poski and in front of him lay the Balcov command post and Balcov itself.

When the command post came into view he ducked into the forest and stayed hidden as he continued. On the other side of Balcov, he rested for a bit. Then headed back into town where he retrieved the letter

Ellis and he sent to an assumed person in care of general delivery. The clerk wasn't going to give it to him until he had shown identification. Already anticipating this he timed it so that when he got there it would be close to closing time. Pulling out the Glock, he placed it to lips of the post office clerk. "Is this enough identification?" The clerk reached for the alarm. "Don't even try it. Give me the letter and I'll be gone." Sweat broke out above the clerk's brow and he slowly handed Hayden the letter.

"Good. Now come around here." The clerk walked around the counter while Hayden kept the barrel of the Glock pressed to his lips. "My intentions are not to hurt you providing you do as I say." The clerk looked at him and nodded. "Lock up." Hayden followed the clerk across the floor and over to the steel door. The nervous clerk pushed the doorknob in locking it. "Very good. I'm going to have to tie you up. You'll be found soon enough so please don't fight me on this. Where is the parcel tape?" The clerk was about to say something but Hayden shook his head. "Don't speak. Take me to it." The clerk turned and Hayden followed him behind the counter and to a drawer. "Open it." The clerk slid the drawer opened and Hayden nodded for him to grab the two-inch wide sticky tape. "Fold your hands together and put them up in front." The entire time he held the Glock to the clerk's forehead.

With his empty hand he wrapped the clerk's wrists together then he made the clerk lay down and finished by he taping his mouth shut. Finding an empty mailbag he slipped it over the clerk's head and pulled the string taunt. Locking the clerk in a back room, he made his way to the staff room and scrimmaged for some food, he was famished. Finding a couple of oranges a half sandwich he exited the post office making sure the door was locked. It was beginning to get dark as he continued walking along the dirt road to where he ditched the rifle and where he would again head into the Atelic Mountains. He slipped into some undergrowth and rested. He was overcome with hunger and tired from the past four days excursions but he succeeded. He had the tape and the letter.

"Seven."

May 29, he awoke at first light. Not having the opportunity to look at the letter the night before, he opened it. The locations mentioned were genuine locations, and the RRA did have knowledge of them. Although they were old addresses and as of lately he knew they weren't active, he couldn't say for sure if the Balcovians wouldn't hold anyone there. It was an old army base that lay near the border of Seka, if the addresses weren't the ones that came out of Ellis's mouth once he handed him the tape then he'd shoot him, that simple. Putting the letter into the envelope, he slipped it back into his pocket. Looking up to the morning sky he stood with rifle in hand and headed in the direction of Lengstin.

***

On June 6, he was seated across from Ellis. His sandy blond hair now short, and his beard shaven.

"Congratulations."

"Never mind the formalities. I want to hear you repeat the locations you wrote in that letter."

"I have yet to see the film. How do I know you have retrieved it?"

Reaching into his pocket, he set the cassette down on the table. "Does that answer you question?"

"It proves nothing to me. Except that you have a videocassette in your possession. I would like to view the footage so that I know it is authentic." Ellis reached for the tape. Hayden quickly grabbed it.

"I don't think so. Give me the locations first."

Ellis glared at him. "I do hold the knowledge to where your friends are being held. A sum of money, fake identification done professionally by my hand for you and your four friends as well as the name of the cruise ship that will take you and your friends to Nome Alaska. I have kept my end of the bargain."

"Really, show me the items you have mentioned."

Ellis pulled from his inside pocket a manila envelope that held five ID's and a sum of cash. "Now hand over that tape," he said gesturing to it.

"Nope. I want the names of those locations. These ID's mean nothing if you're lying. And that sum of cash is an insult." Hayden threw back the envelope.

"Perhaps this will convince you otherwise? Seems someone attempted to rescue your lady friend. Unfortunately for her would be rescuer he was apprehended. Apparently, he almost died during the interrogation. I've been told that the lad's name is my old nemesis Alex Farell. Does that ring a bell?"

"Why should I believe that crap spewing from your mouth?"

"You don't have to believe it. But remember that the longer you try to delegate with me. The greater their chances are that they will all be executed before you can liberate them." Ellis said with mirth and antagonism. "I'll give you a few minutes to decide, then this whole deal is off. Your friends can be executed for all I care. Make the right decision or live with the consequences."

He left Hayden with no other choice but to submit. "Add another grand to that envelope and I'll hand over the tape."

"That could take me a few hours to culminate. I would think you wouldn't want to waste anytime."

"You're right about that. That's why you're going to sit up and pull the cash out of your big thick wallet. If you haven't got it in your wallet then I'm going to take my chances and blow your brains out right now." He declared as he pushed the chair out from the table and stood with the Glock in his hand pointing it at Ellis's head.

Ellis stood and removed his wallet pulling out two five-hundred-dollar bills. Slipping them into the envelope, he slammed it down on the table. Hayden picked it up and shuffled through it. And in turn tossed Ellis the tape.

"Give me those locations." He demanded as he put the Glock closer to his head.

"You're flirting with disaster. I already explained to you that I wanted to view this tape to verify the authenticity. But, with the cold steel of that gun against my head I guess I haven't a choice do I?"

"Apparently not."

"Your friends are being held at the old Vuctin 409 military post. They are under guard by officials who are under the command of Captain Rezoctin. In case you don't know or have never heard of Captain Rezoctin, I assure you he is as ruthless if not more so then General Liwwet. You're going to be up against a baneful assemblage and I pity you. Now our business is done. You have the name of the ship and the fake ID's that will get you into Alaska. I offer you nothing more. Except that the ship sails in ten days if you miss it you'll be on your own."

"I won't miss the ship. However, if you're lying about these locals and I don't find anyone there. I'll hunt you down until my dying day and simply shoot you. And if I see you again between now and when my friends and I arrive in Alaska, I'm going to leave you with bruises and contusions in some back alley because I blatantly don't like you. Either way be prepared for nothing less then a beating you'll never forget." Hayden proclaimed with honesty.

"So hostile. Honestly, can't you come up with something unique? Your empty threats are only a mere few from the hundreds I've got. Yet, here I am. I'm afraid that in all actuality I will out live you.

Once you liberate your friends, you and they will be hunted like the other radicals that both the Poski Militia and the Balcovian Officials put to death on a daily basis. The CPA will undoubtedly get involved putting an end to your entire caper."

"The only way I see that happening is if you leak something. If you do I guarantee your death." Hayden said with intent.

"Look. I assure you that I wouldn't do such a thing. What do I care about the CPA, Poski and that hell hole Balcov? Or for that matter the RRA? You should worry about them…not me. I dislike all of the above and care little for the outcome. It means nothing to me either way. You kill them. They kill you or for that matter you all die is irrelevant to me. I'm a businessman my goal is money. And with this tape I'll have plenty." Ellis held up the videocassette.

"You'll have plenty of money all right but, you'll have to live with the fact that one day someone is going to blow your yellow guts out. And you know what it might be me." Hayden turned and walked out of his room not giving Ellis any time to respond.

He had to come up with a plan to get over to Vuctin. He decided that his best bet would be to stay in Seka and take a bus to the Bear Cove east of Lengstin. It was where Alex and he agreed to meet. He would secure a room and then in the morning bus over to the town of Beriliski which bordered the domain of Seka and Yakutsk where the town of Vuctin was occupied. Once he crossed the border, Vuctin was only a few miles west and it would take but a few hours to get there.

Hiding in the shadows, he dismantled the rifle and put the barrel down one pant leg, he tucked the stock down his waistband in the back and put the smaller pieces in his pockets. Then he boarded a bus at 4:00 p.m. at 5:15 he was sitting in his room at the Bear Cove. The bus driver informed him that the bus the following morning to Beriliski stopped at the Bear Cove at 7:00 a.m., and arrived in Beriliski at 10:00 a.m.

Being tired and exhausted he took a long hot bath, shaved, and washed his clothes in his bath water then he hung them to dry. He wrapped a towel around his waist and lay on the bed. His mind filled with hatred for Ellis, the CPA, Poski, and Balcov. He hated those two municipalities not to mention the two domains that they occupied. Seka was the only domain with any kind of humanity. Still it too was an arduous territory to live in. Hayden closed his eyes and dreamt of the freedom that he was determined to have.

***

June 7, he awoke when the first rooster began to crow in the distance. He felt good today, he was clean his clothes were fresh and the sun was shining. Walking over to the bus station, he purchased a ticket to Beriliski. The clerk never even gave him a second look as he paid for the ticket. Outside he sat on a bench, his one leg revealing to all the barrel of the rifle as it made his pant leg stick out. Realising how conspicuous it looked he decided to stand in wait instead. Finally, the bus arrived. As he boarded the driver punched holes in his ticket, handed it back, and told him to grab a seat.

The bus arrived before 10:00 a.m. As he stepped off Hayden briefly looked around the dirty town. It's main industries were textiles and steel forging. It was a town full of hard workers and heavy drinkers. Even the women looked rough. He walked his course through the little town and eventually came to the sign stating the Seka border was two miles south-west. Passed by only one vehicle he walked for a short distance then darted up one side of the road and into the bush. To get caught with the collection of weapons on his person would mean nothing less then being introduced to a firing squad.

Finding cover, he removed the barrel of the rifle tied to his leg and pulled the stock out that was tucked down his backside. Putting it together he loaded it and headed west to the town of Vuctin. He crossed the parallel near noon and stepped into the domain of Yakutsk. He had only a short distance to travel before he'd be safe in the outskirts of Vuctin. His destination was the Vuctin 409 Military Post and Prison Camp that lie in the Tangera Mountains, south-east of Vuctin and south-west of Seka. Firstly, he wanted to get into Vuctin and acquire some gear. He didn't know what kind of shape Alex and the rest would be in. It was safe to assume they were not to fit.

As he walked, he made mental notes of the items he would purchase in Vuctin from an underground mercenary post he knew of. Arriving a short while later he located the people from whom he could purchase the gear. "What are you looking for old friend? Long time no see. Where have you been hiding, Hayden?" asked Peter Michelovich. Hayden was glad it was Pete running the store. He reached out his hand and shook Pete's.

"It's been a long time. How have things been going?" he questioned.

"I imagine as good as they ever have. Business picks up now and again, then dies off. I hear that our old friend Vlavidov has met his demise. Too bad, huh?" He smiled. "What brings you all the way here?"

"I need some things."

"What kind of things do you need?"

"I need a good army surplus backpack, some non-perishables, water tablets, a first aid kit and any small arms you might be able to provide me with. I also need a couple pairs of pants, large, medium and small sizes as well as a few shirts and I would like it if you could make all those camouflaged."

"I don't see a problem with that order. I do have a couple of Glocks on hand, but that is it. How are you set for ammunition? I see you got an M-40 sniper rifle, great accuracy those. I have only fifty rounds for that calibre, but I have thousands of rounds for the Glocks. I could probably come up with a .9mm Calico if you are interested?"

"For sure, I'll take the Calico and the two Glocks. The fifty rounds of ammo for the M-40 and I guess a couple of hundred rounds for each of the Glocks and say three, maybe, four hundred for the .9mm Calico."

Pete looked at him and smiled. "I always like doing business with you. Are you billing it or paying cash?"

"What's the total?"

Pete began punching some digits into a calculator. "Is it personal or business?" he laughed.

"Both."

"All right so you'll get twenty-five percent off." He went back to his calculator. "I'm going do one better. I'll throw in the clothes and backpack you pay for the guns and ammo. How does that sound?"

"I'll let you know once you give me a price." Hayden chuckled.

"Hang on. I see you already have a three thousand-dollar credit with us. Been a while since you've done any shopping, eh? I'll let you have the guns and ammo for two thousand seven hundred and fifty. We can use the credit if you want or part of the credit or whatever you want."

"I'll pay cash. I like the idea of having a three grand credit." Reaching into his pocket, he fished out three grand. "Do you got change for that?"

"Three hundred and fifty bucks? Sure do." He gave him the change and went into a back room. Hayden did a quick calculation, he still had three thousand two hundred and fifty dollars out of the measly six grand Ellis gave him.

Pete returned with the gear. "Here you go. Everything you ordered."

Hayden looked his purchases over. "Thanks a lot. By the way are you guys still operating out of Alaska?"

"Is that where you're heading."

"I never said that, just wondering if you still operate out of there."

"Of course we do."

"Would my account stand there as well?"

"You are heading there aren't you?" Pete chuckled with goodwill.

Hayden looked at him and nodded. "Yeah, I have some business to tend to there. So what about the account, will it be honoured there?"

"I'll contact the post myself. There is a new guy running it and their location has changed. Nevertheless, the deals are the same. I don't think I want to reveal the locations to you in person or the new guy's name. It cover's my ass. What I will do is mail it to an address in Nome, it'll probably take a month to get there, but it will get there. How does that sound?"

"It works for me. It is fail-safe. Where can I retrieve the letter?"

"I'll send it to the Viscount Motel. What name would you like to pick it up by?"

Hayden pulled one of the ID's out that Ellis had given him. "How about Ryce Lennskov."

"Ryce Lennskov it is. I'll send this off directly." He assured. The two shook hands and bid each other farewell. Hayden stepped out into the early evening and proceeded to the west side of Vuctin. From there, he headed into the Tangera Mountains. The date was June 7. He had nine days left to free his associates and to make it back to Lengstin and the ship called the Hilroy that would take them to Alaska and freedom. This time though they wouldn't have to go back to Vuctin nor Beriliski, instead they would head directly west and cross the parallel east of Lengstin, close to the Atelic Mountains. From the 409, it would take three days providing Alex and the others were in sound shape. He accounted for a five-day maximum excursion it was all they could afford, leaving them with one day to make the ship.

"Eight."

On June 10, he was looking down from a ridge to the Balcov 409 Military Post and Prison Camp. From where he stood, he could see that the place was operating. There were a few vehicles in the compound and from what he could see of people, he counted fifteen officials. That didn't including the ones that might be inside the building.

Hayden cautiously hiked down the ridge until he was a few hundred yards away from the compound. There were four guard towers and two were manned. He removed the backpack and set it down. Crouching behind a fallen log and using the sniper rifle, he scoped in on the compound. It appeared the guards in the towers were also armed with M-40's. They were obviously Balcovian sharpshooters. They were regarded as the worlds most adept. Concealing himself he shook his head, he was going to face quite an opposition.

Grabbing the backpack, he headed for the tree line. Finding a place where he could buy some time, he rested. His best chance he decided would be to slip into the base in darkness. He figured if he could get by the two towers using the cover of darkness that he would be able to perhaps release and arm Alex and the others. With luck they could slip out without a confrontation and make it into the Tangera's before the officials noticed that they were missing. If it turned out differently every passage in and out of Russia would be blocked.

Retrieving a Military Food Pack also known as a MFP, he heard the audible snapping of a twig. Turning he faced the barrel of an AK-47. "You, stand up." Demanded the official behind the gun, slowly, Hayden stood and raised his arms. "What is your purpose of being here? Who are you?" he questioned with infuriation. Whether or not he answered, he was as good as dead. It didn't matter what he did next. Quickly he bolted forward knocking the gun from the officials hand and before his foe could cry out, he had him by the throat and squeezed with such force that the officials eyes bulged and turned blood shot.

"My name is none of your business. Now, using your fingers how many of you are wondering around out here?" The official counted off five digits.

"The compound. How many there?" The guy was slowly losing consciousness. Hayden eased off a bit from the hold around his neck. He gasped a couple of times and then counted to twenty-five.

"There are thirty of you. Is that correct?"

The official nodded yes with the same rhythm Hayden used to break his neck. His limp body crumbled to the ground as his last breath expelled deep from within. There were five more to find and exterminate before it would be safe to continue the assault on the compound. He dragged the dead man to some undergrowth and hid his body from view.

Then started a one-man crusade eradicating the remaining officials scattered about the outside perimeter of the compound. None of the men discharged a shot. He killed each as the first by disjoining their heads from their spines. It wasn't something he embraced with pride or joy. It was simply something needing to be done.

Returning to where he left the gear, he finished the MFP he started. Then waited in silence and anticipation as evening approached. As the sky darkened, he cautiously made his way to the compound carrying with him the Calico and Glock. Peering from behind a large rock protruding from the ground he watched as the compound lit up with exterior floodlighting. The compound illuminated with the rotating lights making it almost impossible to converge upon without being noticed.

He needed to get in and get out and he needed to do it tonight otherwise they'd definitely be behind schedule, possibly missing the Hilroy. He wasn't enthusiastic about that. There would be other ships, but sometimes they never made it to port for months at a time. Hayden decided that he'd impinge on the compound in the early twilight before dawn. By then, the officials would be in a sombre and penetrating the base at that time would play in his favour.

From where he was situated, he could faintly make out that only the front tower was now occupied. This was a plus and would definitely work in his favour. He also noticed that one of the vehicles was missing. He counted three earlier and now he could only see two. The big army deuce was missing. He couldn't help but wondered what that might imply. Did it imply that the base was now less five or six-men? Did it imply that they transported Alex and the others? Hayden's mind quibbled with the possibilities. He knew he couldn't withdraw. If they were moved, he'd be learning about it soon enough.

He was either leaving with his friends or he was going to kill as many of the Balcovian swine as possible. With four hundred rounds for the Calico and two hundred fifty for the Glocks, he wouldn't go down without a fight and certainly not without killing as many as he could.

He studied the shadows that were cast by the tower lights as well as the shadows cast by the big floodlights that continually revolved. He watched them attentively until he could visualise the movements he'd have to make to successfully gain access into the compound without being observed. As time went by the lights inside the building blacked out until only three rooms remained lit.

He waited for a few revolutions from the floodlights. Then made his first daring move and darted directly below the first tower. He could here the floorboards above as they creaked while the guard changed position. His heart pounded and felt heavy in his chest. Sweat formed on his face, as he stood motionless waiting in nervous anxiety. The lights came around again.

As they continued circulating he swiftly dashed to the cover of a jeep and lay down on the ground hidden by the vehicle and its shadow. There was one more move to complete before he'd be in the shadows of the building. If he made it that far without being spotted, it would be clear sailing from there. Taking a few deep breaths, he waited for the floodlights to again circle the compound. Then he crawled the distance to the building and around the corner until he was concealed from the guard in the tower. Standing he hotfooted to an opened window he noted earlier. Peering in he made certain it was empty. He removed the screen and silently hoisted himself up and in.

"Of all the rooms in the building I slip into a lavatory," he silently complained. Opening the door an inch or two, he eyeballed the building's layout. There was a big metal door across the way locked tight with a paddle lock. It had to be a prisoner's cell. Two chairs on either side of the door were now empty— thank God. *I guess my selection of windows to slip into wasn't that bad after all.* Waiting a few minutes to make sure the coast was clear he pranced up to the door. "Pssst, pssst, anyone there?" Tapping a couple times on the door, he asked again if anyone was there.

"Who's that," he heard a weak voice reply.

"Alex, is that you?"

"Hayden."

"Yeah, it's me. Are you okay? Where are the others?" he whispered.

"We're all here.

"Are you all okay? Can you travel?"

"We can travel but we're not all doing so well."

"Hang tight for a minute I hear someone coming." The pitter-patter of feet slowly approached almost echoing in the silent corridor. He went back to the lavatory and loosened the light bulb in case whoever it was wanted to use the can. He stood behind the door and patiently waited for it to open. Hearing the clanging of keys and then the door across the way open up he set the Calico down in the corner and prepared himself to pounce.

"Come to me now woman." He heard a voice say. Opening the door a crack, he spotted the two men. One held a brown bag in his hand and he brought it up to his mouth, he took a long swig from the bottle hidden inside. At that precise moment, Hayden rushed the two men pushing them into the cell and slamming them to the floor. One guy's head bounced off the concrete floor and was knocked out instantly. "What the..." The other began as Hayden pulled out the Glock and pressed it to his head.

"Don't say a word." he threatened. "Or there will be a bloody mess all over this floor. Understood?" He kept his knee firmly planted behind the guy's head keeping him pinned. He began to speak, but Hayden smashed the butt of the Glock into the back of his head. He looked over to Alex and the others. "Are you guys okay?"

Monique darted forward to his open arms and began to sob. "Hayden, it's been terrible," she cried.

"I know, but I'm going to get you out of here. Alex, Cam, Doc are you ready to roll? I'll explain this whole thing once we get out of here." he promised.

"We're ready. Let's get before these guys come to." Alex rose to his feet pointing at the two officials.

"They aren't going to come to." Hayden dragged one of them over to the stainless steel toilet that sat in the corner and shoved his head into it. The official kicked and gurgled a bit as he gasped for air beneath the surface of the water. When the bubbles stopped he became silent and his body slumped to the floor. "One down one to go." Hayden said as he grabbed the other official. This one put up more of a fight, but he too eventually fell silent.

He laid the two blue faced bodies out on the floor for display. Then the five of them exited the cell and locked the door. "Follow me." Hayden led them to the window that he gained entry from. "Remember, once you get outside pull up as close to the building as you can. Stay hidden in the shadows. The front tower is manned." As the four of them dropped to the ground on the outside, Hayden grabbed the Calico that he leaned up against the lavatory wall. Then he followed suit.

Putting the screen back, he gestured to the others. "C'mon." he said as he slid along the wall. Stopping at the edge of the building, he looked up to the first tower. The guard was definitely there. He could see his silhouette against the horizon. "Were going to have to do this one at a time. You're going to have to do exactly as I do. I'll go first and you guys follow suit when I wave you on. Okay." The four of them nodded. Hayden fell to the ground and crept back to the jeep. He waited for the right light then signalled the next person to proceed. Ten minutes later, the five of them were out of the barracks. Hayden led them to his backpack and where the other gear was hidden. "I have some MFP's if you guys are hungry." he replied.

"Food would be nice. How did you know where we were?" Alex asked. Hayden explained to the crew how, when, where and why. And that once they got back to Lengstin they had a ship to board that was going to take them to Alaska.

"Problem is, can we trust Ellis? He's as yellow as a canary." stated Alex.

"Not only that but…" Cam began to add before all hell broke loose. There was a succession of gunfire, yelling voices, and running feet. They had been spotted. They tried to jump for cover but it was too late Cam and the Doctor fell to the ground riddled with bullets. Neither one had a chance as blood spurted from their wounds. Hayden stood with the Calico seeking retribution and ran firing rapidly in the direction of where the bullets had first come from. Alex and Monique followed on his coattails. Each of them armed with a Glock. The sound of gunfire echoed in the forest as flashing light was expelled from the barrels. Bullets whizzed by in all directions and the evening air filled with the smell of smoke and gunpowder.

As their opposition fell to the ground wounded or dead, they made their break to the nearby forest. The officials retreated to regroup and request more manpower. Quickly the three friends headed east into the Tangera Mountain Range. It would only be a matter of time before the area would be crawling with their foe. There was no denying that. They hiked for five miles then rested as dawn approached. "What do you suppose Cam was about to say before he was shot? Did he ever say anything to you guy's about a tape?" Hayden asked.

"We were all held separately until last evening. We had only been together for an hour or an hour and a half before you showed up. During that time he didn't say much." replied Alex.

"I'm more concerned about the officials right now. They ever see us again its lights out. We have to get into Alaska one way or the other and then into Canada. That's the only thing we can do." expressed Monique.

"Do we risk boarding the Hilroy? Or do we find another way?" Alex queried.

"For now we better head into Lengstin. The only one we have to worry about there is Ellis and his henchmen. The Hilroy doesn't sail until the sixteenth. Today is only the eleventh. That gives us five days. If we can get into Lengstin before then, we'll certainly check out the ship and our options. If anything looks suspicious then we'll seek another and that could take months." Hayden replied. However, he and the others were prepared to hideout for as long as it might take if they were forced to miss the ship. They'd be in the domain of Seka, the Balcovians as well as the Poski Militia had no jurisdiction there. The CPA worried them the most. They had a tendency to pop up anywhere. Avoidance and stealth until they were on their way to Alaska would be crucial in their survival. That was a given.

"I figure if we hike straight over those passes and avoiding the Atelic Mountains. We'll make it to Lengstin in less then three days. The problem with that is I know the Balcov Officials will be watching that route. But, it is the quickest and most direct way. What do you figure, do we go that way or head south-east into the Atelic's? Either way we'll make it to Lengstin before the ship sails. But we'll only have a day to scout it out." Alex remarked.

"I'm indifferent. How about you Hayden?" Monique asked.

"We're well equipped I think to take on a small platoon or regiment. I don't think it'll come down to that, I'm sure we can slip right by. I like the idea of getting into Lengstin two days early it would give us more time to do some reconnaissance. The more intelligence we can get on that ship the better. I could see Ellis setting us up. Especially now if what he was hoping was on that tape, isn't or wasn't. Then again, maybe he knows something that none of us do. With that, I think a reconnaissance mission is in order and we couldn't pull one off in less then a day. I say we go straight over those passes as you have suggested Alex, to hell with the Atelic's, and kill any Balcovian that tries to get in our way." Hayden answered half heartily.

***

In the early twilight, they crossed the parallel that divided the domain of Yakutsk and Seka. Their battle was half won. They walked the distance into Lengstin and by midday they were hiding in the shadows cast by trees that surrounded the little town. "Almost free at last." Hayden gazed into the streets of Lengstin.

"Key word 'almost', but so far so good." Monique added.

Alex nodded his head. "Come on let's head to the Bear Cove." They followed the tree line to the outskirts of Lengstin and then travelled along the dirt road that led to the Bear Cove. They spent the evening recuperating. Lulled to sleep by the howling winds that blew in from the north and the perpetuating pitter-patter of rain as it pelted the exterior walls of the hotel.

From their room, they could also hear the crashing from the Bering Sea as it lashed out at the shore with angry waves of destruction. They awoke in the early grey of dawn. Clouds hung in the sky sinisterly. "Looks like we're in for more of the same as last night." replied Monique.

"That's good. Not many people will be out and about. We'll have a better chance of checking a few things. The Hilroy should be docking sometime today. I say we find out when it's scheduled to land and try to be there when it does. It might be delayed now because of the storm last night. But, we need to watch who treads off and who trots on." stated Alex.

"Good point. How about you and Monique go ahead and do that? I'll head back into Lengstin and snoop around a bit. If there are any CPA creeping around then we're gonna have to be extra diligent when we board. It will only take one of them to identify anyone of us. They'd undoubtedly inform the Seka Guard and then look out."

"I don't think Monique and I have a problem with that. What do you say Monique?"

"I really don't want to hike all the way back to Lengstin. The only problem I have is can't you be identified by Ellis? He hasn't seen Alex or I in over a year. What do you suppose he'll do if he sees you and that tape you did acquire for him is useless? I think he'd turn you over quicker than any CPA who thought you were Hayden Rochsoff."

"That's valid. The CPA, are more inclined to recognise two of the RRA's most authoritative members, then a guy whose only been with the organisation for a short while. I think I'm more partial to being recognised by an official or one of the Poski Militia then the CPA. Since they haven't got any authority here in Seka, my chances of being pursued are slimmer then either yours or Alex's. I'm not denying the threat isn't there. Chances are our friend Ellis is long gone and if he so happens to be kicking around Lengstin, then at least we'll know where he is. My greatest concern is that the CPA may have been informed about your guy's escape, and the death of all them officials back in Vuctin. Chances are some of them have been discharged this way and they'll be watching the ports like hawks."

"By the same token Hayden, what if Ellis is hanging around and he spots you? Monique is right he'd turn you over to the CPA or the Guard before you'd have time to react. Maybe I should go to Lengstin. You and Monique check out the port and find out as much as you can on the Hilroy."

Hayden looked at Alex and shook his head. "It's better that I go to Lengstin. Whatever is between Ellis and I will remain that way. He isn't interested in our escape nor does he care how many officials we've slaughtered. If, that tape had no monetary gain he'd have pulled the plug on us a long time ago. Probably the first time he viewed it. He isn't going to be our problem, not yet at least. The CPA on the other hand...they're a threat. They're the ones we have to watch out for."

"I suppose you're right. Either way it is a risk." replied Alex.

"I'm glad you've come around."

"Just be careful we're only a few stages away from freedom. I wouldn't want you to miss that." Monique said with honesty and reluctance as a dreary smile crossed her face. Hayden momentarily lost himself in her words knowing that 'yes' if he were sighted or identified as the man who helped liberate two of the RRA's most influential and sought members, death to him was probable.

"Not to worry. I have every intention on experiencing freedom. I'll make that boat and I will see Alaska with both you and Alex at my side." He said as he exited into the cool morning. He had two of the Glocks and both were loaded with thirty rounds each. If he had to use them there would be no reservations, he would. He'd go down fighting even if it meant death.

The town was quiet except for the music coursing out of the many different pubs that lined the wooden boardwalk. The smell from the cafés emitted scents of sausage, eggs, and coffee. Hayden's mouth salivated with hunger, he wanted to stop at one and indulge himself. Coursing his way down the boardwalk, he entered the door that led into the swanky hotel. The smoke filled lobby was full of miners who had the day off. They played shuffleboard and threw darts, argued and yelled. It appeared to be a typical day in the lives of the Lengstin inhabitants. Venturing into the bar he ordered a Peva, keeping his eyes peeled for any sign of the enemy.

By 2:00 p.m., he staked out most of the pubs and coffee-houses. No one even batted an eye at him. Nowhere, did he see Ellis or any CPA. Throughout the day radiobroadcasts addressed the escape. Yet, Lengstin residence never even gave the news a second thought. In fact, some of them cheered when they heard it. There was no love loss between the Lengstinians and the Balcovians. Returning to the Bear Cove before 6:00 p.m., Alex and Monique were both waiting for his return with grave looks on their faces. "What's up?"

"The dock is swarming with CPA plus Ellis is onboard." replied Alex.

"That's why there weren't any CPA in Lengstin they've congregated here at the dock. Are you sure Ellis is onboard?"

"He and three of his henchmen. He even spoke with a couple of CPA before he boarded. I think he's setting us up."

"He doesn't want to do that. I don't know what the deal is there, but I'm sure he isn't setting us up."

"We're going to have to board that ship one-way or another. It's the only one scheduled for three months." explained Monique.

"How many CPA did you count?" Hayden asked.

"At least ten of them." answered Monique.

"Those are only the ones we saw. We can't be sure how many if any are onboard. Also, the Hilroy sails at 5:00 a.m. tomorrow morning. We have to be on it by then otherwise we're gonna have a long wait for the next one." said Alex sternly. "Any suggestions?" he added.

Hayden had a few suggestions all right. Nevertheless, he knew they couldn't walk down the dock shooting. No, they had to come up with a more elaborate plan, one that they could pull off without too much upheaval. As they sat in silence contemplating they heard footsteps approach their room. Hayden pulled out his Glock and undid the safety unaware of what was going to take place. Then the knocking came.

"Yes, who is it?" Alex questioned, as Hayden slid into the bathroom armed and ready. Monique crouched behind one of the beds also armed with a Glock.

"Lengstin Dry Cleaners. I have your uniforms ready." Came the reply. The three looked at each other not knowing what to expect.

"Uniforms?" Alex repeated.

"That's right sir, the uniforms Commander Ellis Leroy requested that we wash. He said when we were finished to bring them to you."

Alex looked over to Hayden shrugging his shoulders, his eyes big. "What do you suppose this is all about?" he asked softly pointing his chin at the door.

Hayden shrugged. "I don't have a clue."

"Ah yes, yes, that's right. I'm in my bathrobe, could you please hold on a second?" Alex asked of the person behind the door.

"Yes, sir." Came the reply. Alex approached the door cautiously and slowly opened it with a Glock behind his back.

"Here you are sir." The young man said as he handed Alex three uniforms and strolled off.

"Thank you," Alex called behind as the man got into his van. "Check these out. They're Seka Guard military uniforms." Alex laid them out on the bed. "No CPA would ever question anyone wearing one of these. I think we have found the way onto the boat. Thanks to Ellis. What do you suppose his intentions are?"

"I have no idea." Hayden looked over the uniforms.

"He obviously wants us on that boat. But, how did he know that there were only three of us?" questioned Monique.

"None of this makes any sense to me." Hayden replied dumbfounded. "The only thing we can assume is that Monique is right, he wants us on that ship. What's in store for us when we get there is beyond me. Monique brings up a good question too how did he know there were only three of us? That alone makes me suspicious. But, I'm not going miss the opportunity to board that ship. Whatever it is he's up to we'll deal with when that time comes."

***

Ellis sat behind the table in his cabin pouring his fourth vodka and lime. He knew it would only be a matter of time before he got the call that the uniforms were delivered and he smiled. He set the entire thing up. The video was nothing except a ploy to get Hayden to fall for his master plan. Now, in only a few hours he would be face to face with the three of them. *How, gullible they had been*, he thought.

He didn't care about the CPA or for that matter the RRA. He despised both creeds. What he was truly interested in were Hayden's abilities. As for Monique and Alex, death would find them both. He chuckled again as he thought about how he played Hayden as a puppet and at what he was going to request of him next.

He looked at the news paper clipping he had and read it over. It was from the Alaska Times, apparently the United States D.E.A, had confiscated a large undisclosed sum of money in both Canadian and US currencies which was destined for Europe. Ellis's contacts in the US supplied him with the information on where the currency could be located and the amount, which was sixty four million.

That's, where Hayden and the others fit into his plan. He swilled back the last of his vodka and lime then slammed the glass onto the table smacking his lips as he did so. "In time Hayden, you will be of no use to me and I will enjoy watching you die." he said to himself as he poured another drink.

The three boarded the Hilroy that evening. It was June 16. They managed to tear down the M-40 sniper rifle as well as the Calico and smuggled them onboard. The Glocks they kept on their person. Knowing that they would be taken away once Ellis's henchmen padded them down. The uniforms prevented any unwanted looks as they boarded giving them enough time to ditch the rifle and Calico. The cabin numbers supplied to Hayden by Ellis at the beginning of the whole charade of course didn't exist. Five minutes after boarding they were approached by two of Ellis's henchmen. "Hayden Rochsoff?" Hayden heard the deep voice say from behind. Turning he recognised the man standing there. He had seen him in the presence of Ellis before.

"Yup."

"Good, you and your friends follow me." The man demanded.

The three looked at each other and shrugged their shoulders. "Where, are we following you to?" Alex asked.

"Keep quiet or I'll have a bullet put into your head."

"Don't talk to my friends like that." Hayden pulled his Glock out and put it to the man's temple. "Now answer my friend. Where are we following you to?"

"As if you don't know."

"Regardless on whether or not I know, I want you to answer my friend." Hayden pushed the barrel of the gun harder into the man's temple.

"Ellis has requested your presence. He'd like for the three of you to meet him in his cabin." the man replied.

"See, was that so bad? Next time one of us asks you a question, answer. I don't care who you are or whom you work for. I'll kill you with my bare hands." Hayden quickly put the Glock back into his waistband.

The man looked at him and smiled. "You're as good as dead, as good as dead." He replied as he led the three of them to Ellis's cabin.

Stopping in front of cabin twenty-three on the upper deck the man knocked a couple of times and then motioned them to come in.

"Here's the three little pigs you wanted me to fetch." The man said as he walked around behind Ellis.

"Excellent. How are you Hayden, Monique and of course old friend Alex?" Ellis asked. "I'm surprised the three of you have survived for this long."

"Cut the crap and get to the point of this little meeting." Hayden retorted.

"What, you're not going to thank me for the uniforms? Or the first class ride to Alaska."

"Not until we're well on our way will I thank you for anything. Now, what's your point, why are we here, and why am I looking at your ugly face? Do you not recall what I said the last time we met if I ever saw you again."

Ellis raised his hand. "Always so hostile, always so hostile. I do have a business proposition for you again. This one entails a large sum of money which, I will graciously, split with you. Now, before you say no, let me inform you that will not be acceptable. Not only do I have knowledge about this large sum of money but also some interesting facts about the RRA. The information I have will surely be the cause of the RRA's demise and the rise up of the CPA, now wouldn't that be grand?"

"What are you talking about?" Alex asked. Ellis looked at the three of them and smiled.

"In time Alex, in time." Ellis kicked back the drink in his hand. He motioned to the man standing behind him to escort the three out. "Show them to their cabin."

The man led them outside to the middle deck and then to their cabin, number fifteen.

"Here's you cabin, and here's your keys." The man said as he tossed them at Hayden. Turning he walked away. Hayden handed the keys to Alex who unlocked the cabin door and they entered. The cabin consisted of two permanent beds and a cot sat in one corner. There was a head with a shower and sink, in the middle of the floor there was a metal table with two benches. The lighting was dim and bothersome, but it would be home for the next few weeks until they finally landed in Alaska.

"Who gets the cot?" Monique asked with a smile.

"I'll take it." Hayden said. That evening, the three of them stayed in their cabin. They talked amongst themselves, wondering what Ellis was up to. Chances were he wasn't going to tell them a thing until they were somewhere out in the middle of the Bering Sea.

"I guess we might as well make the best of it," replied Alex. "I only wish I knew for sure if Ellis did know something about the RRA.

He's lied so much in the five years I've known him." Alex was right of course. Ellis was as yellow as they came. However, there was a time when he could be trusted. Then, as he grew older he became arrogant and two-faced. Everything became money to him, money this money that. He also turned his back on friends and associates more then once. How he managed to stay alive was beyond their reasoning.

Nevertheless, here they were again under his influence. Hayden would have put a bullet in his head along time ago had he not somehow manipulated him. But, that's what he did and that's what he was trained in. It was probably a good thing that he was not involved with the RRA anymore. They would have probably all been to war more times then not with that crazy at the wheel. Ellis received top honours in psychological warfare. You could never tell if he was telling the truth about this, that, or the other thing until it was too late. Did Hayden personally think he knew something about the RRA? Yeah, at that time he did. Everything he said to him about where Alex and Monique were being held, to where the video was, etc, everything he said had all been true. Hayden thought about this as he stared out the porthole window.

"What's on your mind?" Monique asked.

"Just thinking about Ellis. What did the RRA ever see in him anyway?"

"He was involved with the RRA years before Monique and I were introduced to it. When the CPA shot my old man and your old man, Ellis was next to command. For reasons unbeknownst to any of us, one day resigned his post. He turned against what he once stood for and that was the RRA. Personally, I think he left because he got tired of trying to make a difference. There is something else about Ellis that you obviously don't know."

"What's that?"

"He is your uncle. I know that probably comes a shock but, it is true."

"You got to be kidding. That yellow belly is my uncle. You cannot be for real. Are you? Please tell me you're not for real." Hayden said with hope.

"Its true." Monique answered.

"I never knew that? I don't recall anyone telling me that he was my uncle, I can't ever remember seeing him. Both of you know my family was tight. Are you sure that he is my uncle?" He was hoping for a different answer.

"Sorry, it's the truth. He also knows who you are." Alex said as he slapped Hayden on the back. Hayden found out from Alex later that Ellis changed his name way back in the seventies around the same time the RRA were getting established. Since his operative role entailed a lot of reconnaissance, he had many different names and finally he settled on

Ellis Leroy. There wasn't much else. He did suggest that there was more to it than that, but that it was all history. It didn't change the way Hayden felt towards the guy, he hated him even if he was his uncle.

"I never want him to know that I know." Hayden said with conviction.

"Nine."

June 19, three days after the Hilroy set sail for Alaska, Ellis again called the three to his cabin. "How has your trip been so far?" Would either of you like a vodka and lime?"

"How about telling us why we're here?" Hayden questioned demandingly. Ellis finished pouring himself a drink then he turned and sat down in front of them.

"Tell me, what would you do with one million three hundred and thirty thousand dollars? Or, for that matter what would either of you do with that kind of money?" The three looked at each other and shook their heads.

"What are you trying to pull now Ellis? You know neither of us will ever see that kind of money."

"On the contrary, Monique. It is within each of your grasps. I have a business proposition that will ultimately net each of you that amount. One million three hundred and thirty thousand dollars." Ellis was dangling a bone in front of them and he knew it.

"What does this business proposition entail?" Hayden asked. "Because, I'm not going to kill anyone for you if that is what's required."

"There may be blood shed. However, it will have nothing to do with me. Would you like to hear more or would you rather die now?" He snapped his fingers signalling to the five men hidden in his room, who now stepped out with guns in hand.

"I guess, we're gonna be forced to hear what you have to say." Hayden said with hostility as the one man that was nearest Monique grabbed her putting his pistol to her head.

"I suppose, so. Take her and lock her up."

"Wait. We'll listen." Hayden said, as Alex was about to pull out his Glock. That's all they would need is for a bunch of guns going off. The three of them would have definitely lost the battle. The man holding Monique let her go and she slapped him across his face.

"Don't ever touch me again." Turning she pranced back to where Alex and Hayden were. The whole time Ellis grinned.

"Are we ready to listen now? All right. As I was saying, I have a business proposition for the three of you. To make it worth your while I am offering each of you a large sum of money. More than either of you will ever see in your lifetime. For the record, it is not a movement against the CPA or the RRA in fact neither of them is involved. It involves the D.E.A, the US Navy and sixty four million dollars in both Canadian and US currency. Have I got your attention?"

"You have our attention all right. If it involves sixty four million dollars, how do you figure a million and some change a piece between the three of us is enough?" Hayden knew a million bucks would definitely be more than he would ever see under different circumstances. Still, if it involved the US Government and the three of them decided to go for it he wanted a lot more than a million and some change.

"Exactly, there is no way I'd want to even attempt playing with the US Government, not for a million bucks. No way." said Alex.

"You haven't even heard the rest of the deal. Or, how easy this deal can be pulled off."

"Yeah, well I heard six words, Drug Enforcement Agency and United States Navy. None of which anyone in their right mind would want to infiltrate. Not for a million dollars, come up with something better Ellis or take a hike." Monique said. "We're not soldiers of fortune," she added.

"For now this meeting is over. Get the hell out of here. And be grateful I don't kill each of you where you sit." The three of them stood and exited his cabin.

"I guess we know now why he made it easy for us to board." Hayden replied.

"What are we suppose to do? There is no way he is going to let us leave this ship. It doesn't even dock in Nome for another three weeks." Monique stated.

"Personally, I say we play him a while longer. He's greedy and if he thinks he can get his hands on sixty four million dollars and that we're his only hope of pulling it off...he'll raise our stakes." Hayden was sure of that. Looking towards the bow of the big ship and the eastern horizon where freedom waited he smiled. "Here's a plan that we ought to consider. What if we were to accept the next offer that he makes, then keep the entire sixty four million ourselves?" Monique and Alex looked at one another, then back at Hayden. He could tell by the expressions on their faces that they thought he was crazy. Yet, the glint in their eyes told another story.

"I like the idea, but I'm sure he's gonna want some kind of guarantee that we will return with the cash." Alex explained.

"That's why we got to come up with a plan. Come on think about it sixty four million. We could supply the RRA with anything it needs to infiltrate and expose the CPA for what it really is." Hayden replied.

"Alex, I say Hayden is onto something. Besides, if the D.E.A have confiscated the cash, chances are it was for a major drug or arms deal. We'd only be taking money away from some cartel." Monique responded.

"True enough, but do we want some cartel on our backs? Let's not forget how the US Government might react." Alex said with thoughtful perceptiveness about the idea. Shaking his head he added, "That is a lot of cash."

"It is, and to think we could have it all. All we got to do is make sure the three of us aren't separated. In other words, if Ellis say's one of us has to stay behind until the cash is in his hands we tell him no way. Instead, I say we play the same game he's playing with us. That is to say we'll offer him something else, I don't know what…but, I bet we could come up with something." Hayden added.

"We haven't got a thing though."

"That isn't necessarily true, Monique. We could certainly come up with a bullshit story and offer him information on one thing or another. We know what his interests are and that's money. We could try to convince him that we too have information about the same money, but that our information is totally conflicting with his. I know it will take a lot of bullshitting. But couldn't we pull something off like that?" Alex questioned ideally.

"With a bit of adlibbing and rehearsing. I think you might be onto something. What if we tell him that the amount he mentioned isn't the same amount we've been told. Lets tell him we heard through our undertakings that it is closer to eighty or ninety million in currency. The only way we can pull it off is to wait for him to offer us something else again, accept it, and listen to what he has to say. Then we can go on about the fact that we heard something totally different. We might be able to convince him…if not, then, we follow through with what he asks. When we meet up with him to make the transaction, we blatantly kill him and take the cash. Either way I say if we do this, we do it for the entire amount. If we can pull it off without killing him then that's even better, cause then he'd have to live with the fact that we screwed him this time." Hayden said with hilarious delight and conviction. Monique and Alex chuckled a bit.

"Let's do it."

That evening, a storm blew in from the north-east. The cold green waves from the Bering Sea smashed at the ship's hull, putting the entire ship on high alert. Until early twilight, the storm relentlessly tried hammering the Hilroy into submission, but the big ship powered on sustaining no damage. That day the Hilroy's schedule was to dock for the last time at a nearby Island port for fuel and to transfer passengers. From there it would travel directly to Nome Alaska, a two-and a half-week course through one of the coldest parts of the Western Hemisphere.

The three remained onboard and in their cabin when the ship docked. The storm from the night before made each of them queasy. They did some minor maintenance to the rifle and Calico and restored them to their full capacity. The saltwater air made their firing pins bind causing their triggers to quit operating smoothly. It took a couple of hours to maintain them, but, when they were done they operated as smooth as a vanilla milkshake. Hayden took a quick inventory of the rounds they had for each gun.

There were two full Calico clip's with a hundred rounds each, not including the eighty or ninety rounds it was loaded with now. There were five clips containing twelve rounds each for the M-40 sniper rifle, their Glocks which surprisingly Ellis had not demanded they hand over had about sixty rounds each. Not a bad onslaught of weaponry, but the arms were not enough to take on the D.E.A, or the US Navy. Stealth would be their only ally. "Do you guy's feel like heading out to the deck. Maybe some fresh air will clear our heads?" Hayden was not sure that he even felt like stepping out.

"Couldn't hurt I suppose. The sun is shining, why not?" Monique replied.

"Might as well, probably wouldn't hurt if we headed to the dining room. I feel fatigued and wouldn't mind having a bite to eat," said Alex. Hayden folded up the cot and put both guns between it. Keeping their Glocks on them, they exited the cabin and headed up to the top deck to get some fresh air and a bite to eat. The sun shone with penetrating brilliance making Hayden's eyes burn and water from the sheer brightness. The salt air was distinct, but so was the everlasting smell of diesel fuel from the ships that had come and gone. Along the shore one could see the fuel slicks on the water as the waves lapped up against the dock and rocky shore of the Komandor Island, where the Hilroy sat waiting to exchange passengers and refuel.

"Wow is it ever bright out."

"Hot too. It feels good. Better take it all in because in a week we will be near Alaska and in one of the coldest climates in North America."

Before he could reply to Monique, they were again approached by on of Ellis's henchmen. He was dressed in a three-piece suit and had a mop of red hair. "Ellis is expecting your presence. He would like for you three to meet him again in his cabin."

"Listen here Red, you tell him that the three of us will come to his cabin after we have a bite to eat. We'll get there when we get there."

"You must be Hayden? Ellis told me you'd try to resist. I am afraid though he is expecting you three now. Not later, but right now." The man said as he pulled out a .45 magnum with the same lightening speed Hayden could and pointed it at them. "Now, get moving. And don't even try to pull out those Glocks." He pointed towards three more men standing above on the top deck with submachine-pistols hidded in their overcoats.

"I guess we do it your way this time," Hayden replied. The gunman motioned to Alex to take the lead keeping Hayden in the back and the .45 in his kidneys. They walked up to the top floor and entered Ellis's cabin.

"It's good to see you all again. I hope you have had enough time to make a decision on the proposal I have offered. I am even going to up the ante for you. Perhaps, my last offer was stingy. What I propose now is thirty percent of the take. Quite a sum, I'd say for such a simple task. Nearly twenty million dollars that the three of you can divide amongst yourselves any way you see fit. Does that offer seem more substantial?"

"Tell us more. And by the way, it's eight hundred thousand short of twenty million. Why not make it twenty million even?"

"Always the critic Monique. Nothing is ever good enough for you. Fine we will make it twenty million not a penny more." replied Ellis.

"I'm afraid you're both wrong. Thirty percent of eighty million is a lot more then twenty million." Hayden replied.

"What the are you talking about, eighty million. Have you forgotten the total sum Hayden? It's sixty four million. Not eighty."

"That's where you're wrong. We have heard through our associates that the confiscated currency is near to eighty million plus, not sixty-four like you've been told. I think you knew that all a long and have been pulling our chains. The three of us have talked and we will consider the proposal for thirty percent of the entire take. If it turns out to be the sum you've implied we want a minimum of twenty million." Hayden was, trying to sound convincing enough to lure Ellis into finishing the deal and revealing the whereabouts of the booty. He hoped Ellis wasn't going to question them, if he did, he'd know right away that they were pulling his chain not vice versa.

"How could the three of you find out such information? My associates have never been wrong on things as this."

"Never mind how we found out. Do you still want to deal or do we walk out of here and you can go and find someone else to pull this thing off."

"I am confused, Hayden. If, the three of you have information on this, why are you onboard this ship and not trying to take the money for yourselves? Could it be that you actually know nothing? Perhaps, you are trying to gain something, perhaps the location where the goods are held? I am not a stupid businessman, if you think you have fooled me, think again lad. I've been in this type of business for a long time. I know when someone is toying with me. If you can provide me with the information on where the money is, then, and only then, will I believe what you said. So tell me where is the money?"

"I'm not going to lie to you, Ellis. Our associates were unable to give us that information. However, the person who obtained the amount down to the decimal is a US Customs officer and an associate of the RRA." Hayden was lying like a sidewalk but he had to convince Ellis one-way or another.

"A US Customs officer and an associate of the RRA. I find that amusing. You haven't fooled me. Since, when does the RRA have an associate in the US Customs?"

"Say, I was pulling your chain what difference does it make? Say we accept your offer of twenty million and subtract that from sixty four million, what do you come up with? Exactly forty four million right? So, out of the eighty million we'll make sure you get at least that amount. We'll walk away with thirty six million and you'd never know it would you? Or you can believe me when I say the amount you have been informed about conflicts with what we know. And seventy percent of eighty million for you is a lot more than a measly forty four million. It's more like fifty-six.

And we walk away with twenty-four million, you see Ellis, either way you know that we are your only hope. If you no longer wish to negotiate then we'll carry on. Forget the whole thing." There was a complex look on Ellis's face. He was tossing the information around in his head contemplating what Hayden said. Perhaps he befuddled him? The only reason they decided to play with him was so that he'd reveal the location, without saying something like, "before I reveal the location…blah blah blah." The three of them wanted to be together when the deal went down and they knew that Ellis wasn't going to reveal the location unless one of them stayed behind. If he fell for Hayden's tale, then they would have some negotiating power.

"I need to think on this a while. The three of you can leave my cabin. I will inform you of my decision after the ship sails. I'd be foolish to give you more information right now while we are docked."

They stood and exited the cabin. "Figure we fooled him?" asked Alex.

"Hard to say. We certainly got him thinking." Hayden replied as they made their way to one of the cafes on the ship. At 3:00 p.m., the ships big horns blew and again the Hilroy set sail. Its next stop was Nome Alaska.

"Ten."

For close to a week they never saw Ellis or his henchmen. They were out on deck one cool evening as the sun was beginning to take leave of the day and the dark cool waters of the Bering Sea, lapped up against the big ship's hull rocking it gently to and fro. The sky was an assortment of colours, magenta, pale blue, yellow, pink and orange. The breeze that blew tousled their hair and filled their lungs with salt air.

The scent that lingered from the dark water in a minute way reminded Hayden of the cold Tangera River except the smell of rotting fish was replaced with the scent of diesel. As they stood on deck, looking at the spectacular view they could feel the temperature change as the Hilroy continued getting closer to their destination, chiselling through huge waves that crested near twenty-feet. "Seven, maybe eight more days and we'll be docking in Nome. It feel's pretty good to be that close to freedom, doesn't it?" Monique pointed out.

"It does. I wish I knew for sure that we're going to see it. I'd like to know what is going on with Ellis. We've been sailing now close to a week and we don't know for sure what he's up to." Hayden replied.

"That could be a good thing. Maybe he's decided to find someone else who can possibly pull off that heist. It wouldn't bother me at all if we never saw him again. Yeah, it's a lot of money to give up, but at what cost would we have obtained it? Who is to say how many people would have died? Not to mention perhaps either one of us?"

"Good point Monique. Maybe it is for the better. We've struggled before and freedom alone would suffice." stated Alex.

"It would, but you both know that Ellis isn't going to let that happen. Even if he has decided to find someone else which, is unlikely. He's going to make sure that we don't make it to Nome without some kind of effort to screw us. Maybe we should shoot him." Hayden said with humour trying to lighten up the conversation. Alex and Monique smiled and shook their heads.

"You're probably right. I can't see him trying to get someone else to pull this thing off. His associates are all too stupid. He's probably waiting for the right time to pounce, you know, seal the deal." Alex replied. The three grew silent for what seemed like hours and stared without cause to the beautiful sunset painted on the horizon. Chilled they returned to their cabin.

***

Ellis sat holding the clipping from the Alaska Times. His thoughts were of the eighty million dollars and the idiot who supplied him with the false information, that the confiscated amount was sixty four million. He crumpled up the clipping and tossed it on the floor. "You're an imbecile Nottingworth," he said to himself in a muffled breath. For the past six days the only thing he thought of, was what Hayden told him. He knew that he could very well be lying. Then again, maybe he wasn't.

It pissed him off every time he thought about it. When he finally got his hands on Nottingworth, the little puke, he was going make him squirm. How could he have mistaken eighty million for sixty four million? Nottingworth was a bit of an idiot he knew, but not a complete imbecile. Hayden had the upper hand now and Ellis knew that if he didn't conform to what he requested, then he'd never see the money. His face was red with madness as he slammed his fist into the table.

Might as well get on with it, he thought after taking a few deep breaths to calm down. He had no choice now except to offer Hayden and the others thirty percent of the entire sum. However, how could he be sure that the threesome would return? He couldn't expect one of them to stay behind, nor could he now force one of them to stay behind, not now they'd tell him to hit the road. The only thing that seemed feasible was to make one of them sick.

Food poisoning was an option. He was tight with one of the cooks onboard. He sat there chewing the inside of his lip. "Yeah, that's it. That's exactly what I'm going to do," he said to himself. He could only hope that, Cookie the ships daytime cook would help him out. Cookie did owe him a favour since that night in the casino when he covered the cooks bet. It was a small one, but still he covered it. He figured the cook owed him at least that. He didn't want to make either one of them too sick, just mildly enough for one of them to have to stay behind. That way he could be assured that the others would return.

The obvious person of course would be Monique. He recalled reading in her private folder when he was an RRA member that she was allergic to nuts. Timing would be everything. What he had to do was convince the three to have dinner with him the night before they docked. If they accepted then he would have Cookie do the deed. Standing he looked at his watch, it was almost 7:30 p.m., Cookie would be getting off shift in about thirty minutes and by 9:00 p.m., he'd be down at the casino.

Ellis exited his cabin, locked it, and headed to the Hilroy's Golden Nugget Casino. Stopping off at a smoke shop, he picked himself up a package of Havana Platinum's, but not without first complaining about the price. "What do you mean thirty five ninety-nine for a measly four Havana's? What is this world coming to? How much is that per single? Thirty-five ninety-nine doesn't go into four, no way no how." he bellowed as he tossed the man behind the counter a fifty. "I want all the change back."

"Yes sir," the store clerk began, "And thank you for your patronage," he said as he handed Ellis the change. He hated guys like the one on the other side of the counter, the man bought Havana's from him six or seven times already and the price never went up. And every time he stopped by to pick up his cigars, he always bitched. The man was an asshole and he didn't like him one damn bit. *I hope you choke on one of those,* the store clerk thought. Ellis turned and exited the little store tossing the wrapper from the cigar tin onto the floor. Biting the end off one, he put it to his mouth and fired it up. The cigar smoke tasted good in his mouth and he nodded, *now that's a Havana,* he thought as the smoke billowed from his mouth.

Arriving at the Golden Nugget he took his usual spot at the Black Jack table, he bought five hundred dollars in chips and began to play a few hands. In the first hour, he doubled his money. He was always good at Black Jack. He cashed in the first five hundred and began playing with only his winnings. That was how he played, and that's probably why he never lost more then what he had won. After a few more hands he cashed in again and began to look for Cookie. He stopped off at a few different tables, playing a hand here, rolling the dice there.

The Casino hummed with people. The big circulating fans in the ceiling exhausted the smell of cigar and cigarette smoke outside. The Casino itself smelled of salt air, seafood, and every now and then you'd get a whiff of perfume and cologne. Ellis squeezed his way through the mingling crowd and up to the long bar. Knocking on the counter to get the barmaids attention, he ordered a lime and vodka. Looking to the far wall he spotted an empty table, paid for the drink, and sauntered over.

Sitting he fired up another Havana and waited. It was almost 10:00 p.m., and still there was no sign of Cookie. He didn't mind he was seven hundred dollars richer than he was at the beginning of the evening. *Not bad,* he thought to himself, *not bad at all.* By 11:30 p.m., Ellis consumed probably a little more alcohol than he wanted. He was trying to cut down and now here he was near obliterated. He shook his head, "Damn it Cookie, where the hell are ya?" he muttered in a slur. Seeing one of the waitresses, he waved her over. "Bring me another lime and vodka wouldja, and I don't want any ice. Oh yeah little lady suppose you could help me out. Could ya tell me if Cookie has been about?"

"Cookie? Cookie who?"

"You know, the cook. Cookie."

"You mean Gustov from the morning shift. Yeah he's come and gone already. Won't be seeing him again until tomorrow."

"What time was it…when he was here?" Ellis said between belches.

"Same time as always, he comes here usually around 9:00 p.m."

"Uh, all right then. Can you hurry up with my drink I'm getting dry. By the way, thanks."

"That was lime and vodka, wasn't it?"

"That be it." The waitress smiled at Ellis and pranced off.

Unable to sleep, Hayden took a brisk walk down to the pub and have a drink, it was 11:30 p.m., and the bar he hoped would be quiet. The pub was called the Bear Claw. It was small for a ship as big as the Hilroy but it was also only one of the many pubs onboard. The Bear Claw could sit maybe twenty or thirty people and that would be crowded. Usually there were never more than twenty-five people when he had visited before. Tonight however, there were only six patrons. Pulling up to the bar, he ordered a beer. "What's with the silence? Usually there are a few more people kicking around?"

"It's two for one night in both of the Casino's. Plus there are a couple of live shows going on." The bar keep continued wiping down the counter. Hayden finished the beer and ordered another. He walked over to one of the tables and lit the candle in the middle. Eventually, curiosity got the best of him as he heard roaring laughter coming from the Casino down the corridor. Finishing off the brew he left a tip on the table and proceeded to the Casino.

The big room was filled with laughter and the sound of spinning wheels and slot machines. Looking at how many people were actually inside, he felt claustrophobic. Making his way deeper into the crowd, he thought he spotted Ellis, his head bobbing up and down. Standing on his tiptoes, he looked over the heads of people who obscured his view. Sure enough, there was Ellis stumbling through the crowd.

He watched, as Ellis pulled up to a table of old women dressed in their pick me up clothes. Actually, for their ages neither woman looked unappetising. It was obvious to him that Ellis was trying to score. He chuckled silently as he made his way to the bar and ordered a lime and vodka. "I'd like to send this over to that table with the three women near the Black Jack table. I want it to go to the old man sitting with them, the big guy with green eye's." he said above the humming of the crowd. The waitress nodded.

"Who would you like it to be from?"

"Tell him it's from…umm." he thought for a moment then blurted out, "AF." Hayden was standing a short distance away, hiding in the crowd. As the waitress brought the drink over and handed it to Ellis, he could faintly make out what the waitress was saying.

"This is for you sir…a gentleman said it was from AF."

"AF. AF who? Was the guys name Alex, Andre or what?" Ellis replied nervously.

"I don't know sir; he just said to bring this to you."

"What did this guy look like. Was he big, tall, short or small?" It didn't matter; he had never seen Andre before, which is who he thought of as soon as he heard the initials. He figured if the lady described someone he knew, it wouldn't be so bad. Even if Alex was hanging around some where. It wouldn't matter. If it was someone he didn't know, he better start watching his back.

"I never got a very good look at him sir…sorry."

Ellis looked around quickly trying not to be conspicuous. "Well ladies, I'm afraid I have to get going. Would either of you like to join me in my cabin for a night-cap?"

The one lady he was trying to score on looked at him and smiled. "Perhaps another time. When you are not so drunk…" she said coyly with a snicker.

"Probably for the best. I wouldn't be much fun. All right ladies I bid you goodnight." The three women giggled in their chairs. Ellis stood up and proceeded to his cabin. His mind racing with the possibility that Andre Fischer was on the ship.

Hayden walked over to the table where the three ladies sat. "Hello. Shame to be alone on this fine evening? I sent a drink over this way to an old friend I saw sitting with you. Why did he leave?"

"You must be Alex?" one of the ladies said.

"No ma'am, I'm not."

"Of course then you're Andre?"

"Andre?" Hayden questioned.

"Yes, Ellis asked the waitress that brought the drink over if your name had been, Alex or Andre. When she couldn't answer him, he decided it was time to go. He did seem a bit edgy though. We were all having such a nice time up until then."

"I'm sorry I scared him off. I guess I'll catch up with him later. Thank you ladies and have a nice evening." Hayden said as he turned and walked away. What could Ellis have meant, the only Andre he ever heard of was Andre Fischer how popular was that name anyway? The only reason he was thinking about that was because he realised then that both Alex and Andre Fischer had the same initials. Hayden never even thought about that.

Could it be the same Andre he had been interrogated for possibly killing? But how could that be, Andre, was suppose to be dead. Hayden decided that he wouldn't mention anything yet. If Ellis was some how involved with this Andre fellow and it turned out to be the same Andre, then something else was going on. Perhaps, there was a bounty on Ellis's head? That was quite possible, and Andre was trying to take him out. Was Andre Fischer still alive? Hayden's mind raced. It seemed he inadvertently ruffled a few of Ellis's feathers. He figured he'd let the thing run its course. He wouldn't even tell the others. Hayden hadn't a clue on what he started.

Making his way out of the Casino into the galley and up the flight of stairs that led to the middle deck he walked over to the railing that skirted around and gazed to the horizon. The sky was laden with stars and they looked like a million candles flickering. He smiled at what the torment might be that Ellis was going through, not knowing who it was that sent him the drink. *He did leave in a heated rush*, Hayden thought.

***

Ellis stumbled out of his little bathroom after puking his guts out. *That's it. That's it. I don't ever want to take another drink.* His head ached, but not from a hangover that wouldn't be until after he woke up. No, his head ached with the possibility that Andre Fischer was onboard. He had nothing to hide from Andre other than the fact that the video he was suppose to have didn't exist, nor did he have any incriminating evidence against the CPA, or the RRA.

Finding his way to his bed, he slumped into it, .45 in hand. If anybody dared come through his door or otherwise break in, he'd be ready. He felt as paranoid as a little kid getting caught looking at girlie magazines. The booze coursing through his veins wasn't much help either. He easily drank a dozen vodkas and limes. That thought alone made him stand erect and dart to the bathroom. This time he stayed behind making sure he wasn't going to have to puke again. He waited until he finished heaving then stuck his finger down his throat making himself spew the entire contents of his stomach.

***

Hayden looked over the edge of the deck at the cold black Bering Sea. His hair blew freely in the wind. *I've never been so close to freedom, yet, I'm not free,* he thought as he inhaled a lung full of sea air. He knew without a doubt that this would be his last attempt. If he and the others didn't make it this time there never would be a next, they'd be dead. He wasn't ready to give up the fight by any means he'd never be ready for that, but he was beginning to question if he'd ever be free. Turning he headed to cabin fifteen.

***

The way the ship heaved this way and that is what finally woke up Ellis. It was 9:00 a.m., and he felt sick from the night of booze. They were obviously in choppy waters. Ellis looked out his porthole window to a dark and dismal morning. Outside the ship was being pelted with rain and in the sky lightening cracked and snapped. He rolled his eyes into the back of his head. *How pleasant, the weather outside is quite fitting for the way I feel.* Making his way into the bathroom, he turned on the shower.

The lukewarm water washed away the odour of sweat and bad breath. His tongue felt like it was growing hair and he reached for the mouthwash sitting on the shower shelf. Today, he needed to finalise the plan and seal the currency deal with Hayden and the others. It would give the threesome time to figure out how to pull it off. All he was going to provide them with was the information on where it was located. The rest would be up to them to figure out and if they did pull it off all four of them would be rich.

If Hayden wasn't pulling his chain, in a matter of days he'd be looking at his percent of the cut of whatever the sum. If it were eighty million then he'd have at his disposal fifty six million. *What would I do with all that cash,* he thought, as he dried himself off and put on some clean clothes, sure, he owed some of it out but not enough to effect the amount.

Looking into the mirror he thought about the amount he owed his five men, a cool fifty thousand. He offered that amount when he swayed them to join his little escapade. Ten thousand dollars each, with a possible ten thousand dollar bonus to keep him alive long enough to make it to Canada. So far, they were doing exactly what he hired them for, and that was protection. There were numerous other debts that he owed but once he made it to Canada, he wouldn't owe a thing to anyone. Cause no one would be able to track him down. Not when he had that amount of money to play with.

He might head to Mexico or for that matter any other destination in the world where money bought anything one desired. If he went to Mexico, he could buy himself an entire army. He thought about this as he sat down at the table and lit his last Havana. In a bit he'd head down to the restaurant where Cookie worked to have a couple of words with him. As he sat there enjoying his morning cigar, he thought about the possibility that Andre Fischer was onboard. What did it mean? He hadn't burned him yet, as far as he was concerned Andre had no reason to do anything to him. Maybe he was freaking out about nothing. Maybe it was Alex after all that shot him the drink the night before. The only way he would be sure was to ask him. *First things first,* he thought as he stood and exited.

He walked down the galley until he came to cabin twenty-eight, then he knocked. The door swung opened and Ellis entered. "Hey big guy." The man nodded his head and gestured him to sit. "No, no, I haven't got time right now Red. Listen I'm gonna need you and the others to watch my back extra diligently, there may be a guy onboard that could cause problems. You may have heard of him. He goes by the name of Andre Fischer. I'm kind of doing a deal with him but it hasn't happened yet. He's the type to shoot first and ask questions later. Have you ever heard of him?"

The man smiled. "I've heard of him. Want me to find out for sure if he's onboard?"

"No, I don't want anybody doing anything like that. If he's here, he'll get in touch with me. I only want you guys aware of the possibility, kapeesh?"

"We got your back. If Andre is onboard and he's looking to cause difficulties, what do you want us to do, kill him?"

Ellis smiled for a few seconds. "That would take care of the problem. Nah, only if he tries something, then I'll expect you guys to act accordingly. If you kill him, you kill him. But, until then hang tight and be ready. I may be able to squeeze him for some cash. I really don't want him to be unable to pay. If you know what I mean?"

"Good enough. You want me to round the guys up and inform them or are you gonna do that?"

"For now I want you to accompany me down to the bottom deck. I need something to eat and I need to have a few words with Cookie."

"Sure thing, I haven't eaten yet either. Lead the way." The two men stepped out of the cabin and headed for the flight of stairs near the back of the ship that wasn't constantly filled with bustling people. "What makes you think Andre's onboard?"

"A little incident that took place last night. Someone, bought me a drink, the waitress said it was from some guy with the initials AF. I know it could've been Alex, but I don't know for sure. Not until I talk to the so-and-so."

"I see. Better safe then sorry, I guess."

"That's right Red, and that's why I hired you. What do you know about Andre?"

"Nothing, I've never met him or even know what he might look like. I know the name. He's definitely not one to piss off. But, I want that ten grand for sure and the possible ten grand bonus. If you're dead I won't get it will I. In other words Ellis if it came down to where I had to kill him, I would. You can rest easy knowing that." replied Red. The two men laughed quietly as they exited the stairwell into the bottom galley. The smell of food wafted towards them, as did the smell of fresh brewed coffee. "Sure smells good."

"That it does. I think I'm gonna treat myself to pancakes and sausage and top all that off with a big espresso."

"Me, I'm going to have eggs, bacon and toast. Maybe even two orders." replied Red. They entered the café and pulled up to a table for two. It wasn't long before the waitress came to take their orders.

"Is Cookie working this morning?" Ellis asked.

"He sure is. Actually," the waitress began, "he should be on his break right now."

"Is there anyway I can see him, it's rather important that I speak with him."

"Sure, go through that door and to your left." she said as she pointed to a pale blue door. "It's only suppose to be for staff, but, the big boss isn't here today, so go ahead. Would you like me to take your order?"

"Please, I'll have pancakes and sausage along with a big espresso." Ellis said as he stood and walked towards the door.

"And what would you like, sir?"

"Two orders of bacon, eggs and toast as well as a tall OJ."

"Okay, your orders will be here shortly."

Ellis walked down the hallway until he came to the first door on his left. Peering in he saw Cookie, sipping on tea and reading some magazine. He lightly tapped on the door. Cookie looked up and smiled gesturing him in. "Dear friend Ellis, what brings you?"

"Having some breakfast plus I wanted to stop in and see how you're doing old friend."

"I am doing well. I missed you last night, I was half expecting to see you around the Black Jack table."

"I was there all right, but I guess by the time you showed up I must have already left. Listen Cookie, I have a great favour to ask of you."

"Anything dear friend. What can I help you with?"

Ellis explained to him what he wanted him to do.

"It would ruin my reputation as a five star cook not to mention the legalities that the Hilroy might be faced with. I'm afraid I can't do such a thing. What if the woman dies? I would be a murderer. Peanut allergies are not something to play with. People have died from such ailments. I find it somewhat offensive that you would even ask me. No. I can't do that."

"C'mon Cookie, who bailed you out when you over bet your hand? The peanut oil thing was only a suggestion. There must be other ways to make the woman ill, so, that she is incapable of leaving her room. It's quite relevant that she does not leave this ship when we dock in Nome. I'm not asking you to kill her. Can you feed her a raw egg or something? You know to give her a mild case of the trots for a day or two. If I was at liberty to tell you why it was so important I would."

"Why can't you tell me?"

"I can tell you this much Cookie. I'm a Russian Disease Control agent and this lady may be a carrier of a deadly micro-organism. The RDC has been tailing her and her companions since Kamchatka." Ellis could tell that Cookie was interested in hearing more, he knew about the old-mans past from the conversations they held that night at the casino. He knew how vulnerable the old man was and that he probably already fooled him.

"What kind of micro-organism?" Cookie asked with great concern.

"Settle down Cookie. It isn't transferable, unless you swap spit with her. It isn't an airborne viral infection either. It can only be spread through human saliva. However, we haven't discovered yet, if it can also be spread through other body fluids. That's all I can tell you. From that bit of information Cookie I hope it helps you in making the right decision to help us keep her on board."

Cookie always wanted to play some significant role in life. But, whiskey destroyed any life he tried to cut out for himself. All he had left were his five star culinary awards and a name that was long forgotten. "It's enough. I suppose no one else is aware?"

"That's right. The RDC doesn't want to alarm the Hilroy's passengers. We're sure that once we have her come to the ship's infirmary we'll be able to run the necessary test to confirm or deny what she might or might not have. That way no one gets suspicious. Once we have her contained and if she is carrying this organism, she will immediately be taken to our facility by way of helicopter. I've asked this of you because I felt I could trust you. We don't want to harm the lady only detain her without her knowing it. You can understand why. The United States would surely force us to stay at sea or turn us back until they could do a complete medical investigation on each and everyone of us onboard."

"I do feel better knowing that if I help I may be saving others. I suppose since this does seem to be a dire situation. I could perhaps give her a bellyache if nothing else. All right, I will do it." Cookie said in a kindly voice as he looked into Ellis's eyes as if hoping Ellis would tell him how heroic he was.

"Good, you have made the right decision. I thank you on behalf of the RDC. I will try to bring the lady and her companions to dinner the night before we are due in port. If the lady and her companions decline then I thank you beforehand for being so accommodative to the RDC. And hopefully we will find another means of keeping her onboard. I have a recent picture of the lady in question." Ellis began as he handed Cookie the photo. "That's her, that's the lady you need to watch for."

Cookie looked at Monique's picture. "This is the woman you want me to give a belly ache to? Quite a looker she is."

"Yes she is and if we can't help her she may die. It is sad. But, with further studies the RDC may be able to trace the virus DNA structure right down to the first person who ever got it. Then we can kick it in the ass." Cookie reached out to shake Ellis's hand as if to seal the deal. Ellis smiled and accepted the shake.

"You are clear on what I've asked you to do?"

"Sure am Ellis. Don't worry. I'll be certain to slow her down if not incapacitate her for a day or two."

"Excellent. Thanks again." Ellis turned and walked back out to his table. *Problem solved,* he thought as he sat down.

"How did it go with your friend?" Red asked.

"Perfectly. How was breakfast? Or hasn't it come yet?"

"Hasn't come yet. Soon I hope. The smell of food is making me feel weaker by the minute. What time you got?"

Ellis looked at his watch, "Near 10:30 a.m. We've been here for thirty minutes, you'd think the eats would've been here by now." No sooner did he finish that sentence and the waitress returned.

"Here's you orders sorry it has taken so long. Now, it was eggs for you," she began, "and flap jacks for you, correct?"

"That's right. Thank you very much."

"No problem. Enjoy your breakfast," she said as she turned and darted away.

"Let's dig in Red and get out of here. Still have to round up the others and fetch Hayden and his associates. Things are gonna start movin' fast now. In a few more days, we'll be in Nome. I've been contemplating also the fact that once we're there I really haven't got any use for probably three of your crew. I want to keep you on and one other guy I've been watching close. When I settle with you, I'll be offering you another contract, a more permanent one. We'll talk when that time comes." Ellis shovelled a forkful of breakfast into his mouth.

"Who is this other guy you are thinking on keeping? I'll tell you if he's any good."

"That's all right. I'll make this decision on my own. Rest-assure Red, I haven't even considered getting rid of you. Once this deal I'm putting together with those three guests of ours," he started, referring to Hayden, Monique, and Alex. "Once that deals done I'll be needing a threatening menace like you. As far as I'm concerned, your position with me is quite secure if you decide to stay on. For now lets focus on the job at hand." Red smiled his pearly whites showing a tattoo on one of his top teeth. Ellis noticed it for the first time and had to take a second glance to see if what he saw was there. "What is that all about? How did you ever get a tattoo there? That must have hurt. You must be crazy." Ellis said as he gestured to the tattoo with his fork, slopping the food he on it onto the table.

"You like that? I had an old lady that was an oral hygienist and a tattoo artist. It's actually quite painless. They've been doing this kind of body art in different parts of the world for at least a decade now."

Ellis was still looking at him befuddled, shaking his head in disbelief. "What is it of anyway?"

"A bullet."

"A bullet. What kind of tattoo is a bullet?"

"Actually, it's a bullet that enters the left side of my teeth and exits the right side."

"So its on both sides of your teeth?"

"Yup."

"Crazy." Ellis finished off the last of his pancakes. At 11:15 a.m. the two men paid their bill and headed back to round up the other hired men, including Hayden, Alex, and Monique. They all gathered in Ellis's cabin before 1:00 p.m. "Well, Hayden, Alex and the ever lovely Monique. I've decided to give you the benefit of the doubt. I will offer you thirty percent of the entire take, but only if it is above and beyond sixty four million. If it isn't I will offer you twenty million not a penny more. I do have a few problems with this arrangement. One being the fact that you might decide not to return. That is why I must ask for some kind of guarantee. Perhaps, one of you might stay behind?" Ellis asked knowing full well what the answer was to that.

"Not likely. It's going to take the three of us to pull it off. We're not toying with Balcovians, or the stupid Poski Militia. We're dealing with the US Navy and the D.E.A. They are far more advanced in tactics then any of the Russian Military and other domesticated establishments including the CPA. You know it's a fact too, otherwise you wouldn't have asked for our assistance.

You know that we're your only hope. But, only if we're together. If you don't like that idea then I guess we all lose. Cause there is no way we're going to be separated. You're going to have to take the risk that we don't return. My word is as good as yours…if I say we're going to return, then we will." Hayden replied. *We'll return all right to blow you away.*

"I was afraid of that. I need more of a policy then your word. I assure you that if one of you, and I don't care which stays behind no harm will come to them. You have my word."

"You're an idiot Ellis. What, I'm suppose to take your word, yet, you won't take mine? This meeting is going nowhere fast. You know how this has to go down. The three of us stay together or you can try and find someone else to help you pull off this charade."

There was a long silence in the room. Ellis knew what he was doing no matter how he played this hand Monique would be staying behind. He already took care of that. "Here is what I propose," he began. "Gentlemen would you excuse us," he said to his henchmen. "All except you, Red. I want you here." The four henchmen made their way out of the cabin and waited outside Ellis's door.

Hayden knew what was going to happen next, Ellis was going to tell them that he wanted this big redheaded chum of his to accompany them. "Before, you say anything Ellis. The three of us aren't recruiting." Hayden said with force and conviction.

"Goddamn it, Hayden. Why are you such a hard ass? You're lucky that you still breathe. Neither of you would have made it onboard had I not graciously produced for you Seka Guard Uniforms. Quit making this difficult. Red has been trained in as much as you have. He received his training in Europe. He is one of the best covert missionaries that money can buy. I'll agree that the three of you will not be separated, but only if Red can join you on your assault. I would request that he sticks to you Hayden like glue and that if you try to double cross me he'll simply kill you. That's all."

"Really. What makes you think I might not kill him." Hayden looked the big fellow over. He was big all right at least six four and near two hundred and ninety pounds. By now Ellis was getting red in the face, he knew that if he did anything stupid the deal would be off. As well, the three of them were aware that if Ellis decided to he could easily grab any one of them and force them to abide. He had enough men paid off to do that. "We're back to square one Ellis. We don't need anyone tagging along. Sorry."

"Hayden, you…" Ellis held back the last part of the sentence deciding it would be better at that point to submit. Leading Hayden and the others to believe that, they were gaining something. "Fine we'll do it your way but you so much as fart in my direction, and I will slaughter anyone and everyone that you were ever close to. I will have every man that has ever worked for me and owes me a favour hunting down every living family member of your two idiot friends as well. I'll put a bounty on each of your heads. So, don't even think about double crossing me."

"You know what, I'm getting sick of the way you are treating us like we are your dogs. Neither one of us has to agree with anything you say. You see—this is a totally new deal. We've earned our place onboard this ship and the tickets that will take us to Alaska and freedom. That was a done deal when I handed over to you that video. The way I see it Ellis your word means nothing, we don't have to follow through with any plan, or business proposition. We're free and clear with you as it stands now. This deal is for the money. I suggest you start treating each of us with more dignity. As it is we owe you nothing nor do you owe us." Hayden explained.

"That is true, however, twenty million minimum in your pockets sure sounds nice now don't it? You want this money as bad as I want it."

"Twenty million or more in our pockets does sound palatable, but, freedom alone would suffice. Remember that Ellis and get on with it. I have no desire to sit in your presence. It nauseates me." There was silence for a few minutes and then Ellis finally filled them in on where the money could be located on the Navy Ship called the Navy Blue. It was under lock and key in the President Suite and guarded by Navy personnel. Also onboard were D.E.A agents as well as Naval Intelligence Officers, the numbers Ellis hadn't a clue. The money was held in one crate. The bills were supposedly in stacks of one hundred and five hundred-dollar bills. Each stack contained between ten thousand and fifty thousand dollars. "It's going to be tough trying to retrieve all that?"

"It isn't my problem. It's yours. Remember that once the Hilroy docks you will have two days before it leaves port again. Also remember what I said if you try to double cross me. And if you don't accept you will not live through the night."

"There you go again, threatening us. Since I don't doubt you, we'll agree to your terms. First, I'm going to repeat them so we all know what it is that has been offered. You are offering us thirty percent of the total sum, if the sum is above and beyond sixty four million. If the sum is only the sixty four million like you've been told it is, we, the three of us will receive twenty million. Most importantly, the three of us will not be separated. Correct?"

"That's right."

"Then, that's all that needs to be said. We'll be in touch."

"Hold on Hayden, since you have agreed. Would the three of you join me for dinner the night before the strike? My treat, a celebration of sorts?"

"I'll tell you what if we decide to meet you, we will. If not we'll be seeing you when this job is done." Hayden stood to exit.

"Very well Hayden, if you decide I will meet you three at the restaurant on the bottom deck say between 6:00 and 7:00 p.m. the night before we dock in Nome. One other thing, I wasn't able to thank you Alex for that drink you sent my way." Ellis said as he tried to fish for who sent it.

"I haven't a clue on what you are talking about." replied Alex, dumbfounded.

"Humph, I guess it was someone else. All right then." There was concern in Ellis's voice.

The three exited. "I think we suckered him, what do you say Alex, Monique?"

"I think we are gonna be rich." Monique sung out.

"Yeah, sixty four million bucks. I wish I could see the look on Ellis's face the day this ship sails from Nome, cause we ain't going to be on it and he ain't going to see a dime."

"Eleven."

On June 26, the day after they accepted Ellis's proposal, they decided to split up and round up magazines, books, and newspapers, anything that might have a picture or story about the Nome Naval Base. They hadn't much time to come up with a plan of attack, if they could get some info on the Base then they might be able to have a better understanding on how it was set up. They needed to know things like, did the base offer public tours? If so how often, on what days etc. Were there guard towers? Was the place surrounded with razor wire? They had to know as much as possible or they would be going at it blind. "I'll do the bottom deck there are a couple of stores down there." Hayden said.

"I'll take the top deck."

"I guess that leaves me with this deck then. Humph, how convenient for you guys. This is probably the biggest one. How many stores do you suppose are on this level?" Monique questioned with humour.

"I would feel better if you're close to our cabin. That way if something goes wrong you'll have a better chance to get away. Especially, if you can make it to the cabin cause the Calico will be waiting. And that's some stopping power. Besides, I have never seen any of Ellis's men on this deck, but I have seen them on the bottom and the top. In short Monique I don't want you to ever have to go through what you did the last time."

"That's sweet Alex. I guess that's why I love you bro. All right, I'll stay close. Do you guys want to meet somewhere in a few hours or what?"

"Good question. Has either one of you ever walked the entire ship? I couldn't guess how long it could take to check out all the stores. I read somewhere on one of those tourist signs, I can't remember what deck it was on. I read that it would take forty-eight hours of store hopping to be able to visit each. That leads me to believe there are at least forty-eight stores." Hayden commented with a grin.

"I wouldn't doubt that for a minute. Let's do what we can and meet back here at around six. My watch says 8:00 a.m., what about yours? We might as well synchronise them." Alex and Hayden looked at their watches and set the appropriate time. "Your guys' watches are now set to eight a.m., right?" They both nodded. "All right then let's do some shopping. We're looking for magazines and stuff that might have information on Nome and its Naval Base, or just its Naval Base. I think we better stick to information on Nome. If we start scooping all the books on the base we might be leaving behind a bit of a paper trail, wouldn't you agree?"

"A couple of good ones probably wouldn't matter. Let's say one book each on the base and whatever we can find on Nome and its ports that sort of thing."

"I'm solid with that."

"Me too," said Monique.

"Excellent, now raise your arms in front." The two of them looked at Hayden with a puzzled look. "C'mon humour me," he pleaded. Finally they raised their arms to meet his and he clamoured with a smile, "All for one, and one for all."

It took Hayden a couple of minutes to get to the stairwell that led to the bottom deck. He could smell freshly brewed coffee and bacon. He decided to follow his nose and stop off at the café. A quick breakfast would make the gruelling task that lay ahead of him a bit more pleasant. He hated shopping, even if it were for only some literature. Walking over to a table that sat vacant, he looked over the menu. The café was called the Pickled Onion. The menu consisted of the usual with the added touch of some Russian classics, like Lubshki, Borscht, Sausages, Cabbage Rolls and of course Herring in three or four different recipes. Deciding on crepes and ham he closed the menu and waited to be served. The café was nicely decorated with a hazy bluish green décor, and was quite clean. There were a few hanging plants. Against a back wall was a quaint water garden with a fountain. It was a nice establishment. The food certainly smelled good, and what he noticed of the servers, they all seemed pleasant. He sat for a few minutes until finally a waitress approached.

"Are you ready to make your order sir?"

"Sure am, I wanted to comment though on your establishment. It's very nice. I've been onboard since Kamchatka and this is the first time I've eaten here."

"Well, we'll make your visit enjoyable. Now what can I get you?"

"Yes, all right. I'll have the crepes and ham, a large coffee and brown toast."

"It's on its way sir, would you like anything to drink before the food arrives? Perhaps you'd like your coffee now."

"Yeah, sure. Thank you." He said as the waitress smiled and nodded.

"I'll be right back then with your coffee." She returned with a large ceramic coffee cup that was more like a bowl.

"That's a large?" He never saw coffee served in such a big mug.

"Yes it is. Would you like a smaller one?"

"Nah, I think I can put it down. Thanks again." He said as he began adding the condiments. Before he looked up, she was gone. Bringing the cup to his lips, he inhaled its bitter-sweetness. It was one hundred percent Colombian there was no doubt about that. While taking a second drink, he heard a commotion in the back followed by loud laughter. Some kid around eighteen or nineteen ran out holding in his hands a picture.

"Cookie has a girlfriend. Cookie has a girlfriend." The kid was saying as he darted towards Hayden. An older guy dressed in a cook uniform with a look of dread on his face darted out behind him. At the same time, the waitress was returning with Hayden's order. It was like a scene from the Keystone Cops. The kid ran headlong into the waitress. The food flew up in the air spilling blueberries, whipped cream, and maple syrup all over the floor. The crepes themselves flew from the plate, they looked like little UFO's flying through air. It was a rather comical sight. The few patrons that were present laughed amongst themselves. When it was all said and done the waitress was the first to rise and she blatantly kicked the kid in the side.

"You idiot, O'Malley." she blurted.

"I'm sorry Colleen. Owww, I think I broke my arm." Hayden sat at the table shaking his head. He noticed the kid dropped the picture and he picked it up to hand it back to the guy who was obviously named Cookie, that is until he noticed it was a picture on Monique.

"How did you get this picture? I know this woman."

Cookie snatch the photo back, "You know this woman?"

"Yes I do. She is a friend of mine. I don't recall her mentioning that she knew any cooks. Especially on this ship."

"We must talk then. Follow me." Cookie gestured for him to follow.

He was aghast at what Cookie told him. "So the guy who approached you said his name was Ellis? And that he was with the RDC?" he questioned with a smile. It was typical of Ellis to pull such a stunt.

"It was not the first time we met. We met in the Golden Nugget a few nights after we set sail."

"That's why you believed him when he told you Monique was carrying some virus. Pretty clever of him I must say."

"Or pretty stupid of me," replied Cookie shamefully.

"Now you know he is a liar and a two bit thug. All he did was take advantage of your friendliness. In other words, he used you. He has been doing that for a long time I'm told. If it benefits him, he doesn't care. Don't let him know that we have had this conversation. Follow out with his plan. I'll make sure he is the first one to take a bite from whatever Monique orders. I kind of figured something was up when he asked us to dinner. Now I know."

"I'll play." Cookie said.

Hayden smiled at the old guy and nodded. "Thanks," he said as Cookie led him back out to the dinning room.

"By the way what was it you ordered Hayden?"

"Crepes and ham, along with brown toast." He answered.

"Good enough, a special order of that is coming up." The cook said as he winked and headed back into the kitchen. Hayden wasn't sure what to think at that point. He found his way back to his table and sat down. The mess on the floor was being cleaned up and the kid who came flying out of the kitchen was standing at the cashier counter holding his arm wrapped in ice. "Is the kids arm broke?" He asked of the guy cleaning the floor.

"Yeah, stupid O'Malley. He's always pulling stuff like that. This time though, he's paying. He's waiting for Mr. Kessler to take him to the infirmary."

"What, the kid can't go by himself."

"Kessler is his uncle and he needs to know everything that happens because of Eddy. Eddy has been causing a lot of crap lately. He's going to be upset that he is still fooling around. We'll probably hear him all the way back here screaming when he gets here."

"Eddy? That's O'Malley's name?" Hayden questioned.

"That's right. The kid will have all this one-day. You know the Pickled Onion franchise. Kessler owns every one of them. All Eddy does is fool around and fool around. A kid like him doesn't deserve something like this. Maybe, if he'd pull his weight a bit, even then I'm sure he'd still be an idiot."

"Some people are born lucky I guess. How about the young lady he ran into is she okay?"

"Colleen, oh yeah. That's one tough chick. She probably broke O'Malley's arm. No one has to worry about Colleen, she holds her own quite well. I remember one time her and I were doing a late shift on the Hilroy's sister ship, if I remember correctly, I think the ship was called the Komandor Queen One or something like that. Anyway, we were sailing from Kamchatka to down south near Vladivostok. These two older guys came into the Pickled Onion both obviously drunk. They ordered some food then they tried to order some vodka. But no way was Colleen going to serve them any. One of the guys tried grabbing her to make her sit on his lap, Colleen levelled him, smack, with the tray in her hand. When the other guy stood up, she kicked him in the nuts. It was awful funny. Both of them lying there, one split-open, and the other sprawled out on the floor clutching his groin. I laugh about that to this day. We transported her back to another ship. In case the two guys came back sober and tried to confront her." Hayden found the story quite amusing and chuckled along with the kid.

"Good for her. It's not every day that you hear a story like that. How old is she?" He knew she must been in her early-to mid twenties. Hayden was trying to keep the conversation going. He was also a bit curious.

"I think she's either thirty or thirty one."

"Really, she didn't look it. I thought maybe twenty-three, twenty-four. Huh, she must be doing something right to look that good."

"She is pretty cute. Isn't she?"

"How long have you known her?" Hayden began fishing for more information.

"I've been working with her for the past three and a half years."

"Both you and her have been working for the Pickled Onion that long?"

"I have. Colleen has been here five or six years I think. This is the only job she's had. She likes it. She says she loves the travel. I think there is more to it than that, but, whatever. She's worked her way up that's for sure. Kessler classifies her and a couple others as Customer Service Specialists. It's his term for someone who can be left in charge I guess. Colleen jokingly calls herself, 'the bitch that knows it all'." The kid chuckled. "She's great people to work with. If the next question is what I think its going to be, yes, she is single." The kid said as he looked at Hayden and smiled.

"Since you are on to my little ploy. What else can you tell me about her." He joked.

"Wouldn't want to give too much away. Besides, if she knew I was talking about her behind her back. She'd probably kick my ass."

"C'mon on kid, tell me something else."

"All right. I'll tell you one other thing. Have you ever heard of the great Taras Bulba? There was a movie about him. Can't remember who stared in it, but I think it was Jamie Lee Curtis's old man. I can't think of his name right now… But anyway, Taras Bulba, the real Taras Bulba, is supposedly Colleen's great Grandfather."

"Get out of here," Hayden said not knowing if he should believe the kid or not. The half smirk on his face told him that the kid was probably bullshitting.

"No, really. That's what I have heard."

Hayden looked at the kid shaking his head in a doubtful gesture. "C'mon kid, you're not serious," he was almost ready to start laughing, not because of the possible fact, but, because the kid may have fooled him. He thought it was rather humorous that if kid was bullshitting he was doing one hell of a good job. The kid had talent.

"Okay. I was fooling with you. But for real this time, her last name is Taras. That's all I'm going to say," he said grinning from ear to ear.

"Thanks kid. I appreciate it." And he did. Perhaps he might ask her out for a night-cap sometime before they docked, after that, he would probably never see her again.

"No problem. She seems a little preoccupied lately anyway."

"What do you mean by that?"

"I don't know for sure, but I'm betting she hasn't been intimate with a man in six, maybe seven months."

"Whoa kid, whoa. That's a bit rude don't you think? It's a little bit more than I care to hear."

"I'm sorry. I suppose it was out of line. It's just that I haven't seen her with a man for probably that long. Sorry again, I really didn't mean to sound that loathsome."

"Forget it. It really has know bearing on anything." Hayden replied. "Just be careful on what you say from now on. Some people could get offended hearing things like that." He looked at Hayden and nodded, then continued cleaning up the mess on the floor.

He certainly has spirit, Hayden thought. The kid put everything he had into making that floor shine again. There was one more question that he wanted to ask, "Say kid, what's your name? I'm sorry I didn't formally introduce myself, but my name is Hayden."

"Pleased to meet you Hayden. My name is Valadimere, most people call me Val." he reached out his hand.

"Pleased to meet you to Val. Not everyday do I run into people as chipper as you. I'm glad I did, its people like you that make the world a friendlier place. Keep it up, Val."

"It's in my blood. My old man use to keep us kids laughing and talking for hours, a lot of the time about nothing at all. He had the gift to gab. God could he gab, funny too. I remember one time, I think it was Christmas Eve or one of our birthdays…anyway, there was paper, you know wrapping paper scattered all over the living room floor. I remember that because my little brother came running in from one of the other rooms. It was only a four-bedroom house and the bedrooms were upstairs…so I guess he must have been running either out of the kitchen or maybe the bathroom. Anyway, he came running in from some where and slid on a piece of this red wrapping paper. He slid right across the floor and smacked into the wall knocking down all of my mother's pictures and knick-knack's that she hung. Am, I boring you with this?" he asked.

Hayden was trying to catch up on the first hundred words he said. But, he didn't want to be rude. "No, no. You're not boring me. Besides, I'm still waiting for my breakfast."

"Good, cause I have a bit more cleaning to do and I hate working in silence. Anyway, like I was saying, that day, whatever day it was, someone's birthday or Christmas or whatever. After my brother knocked down all of my mom's stuff. The old man laughed so hard that he rolled on the floor. When he finally came to his senses. He told us how his little brother, our uncle, had the same thing happen to him. Except uncle Horst, wait a minute…was it Horst or was it Petrovich...yeah, it was uncle Horst. Anyway, he ended up with his feet stuck in the wall.

And I guess my Babushka, or Grandmother, whichever you prefer, had just finished watering one of her plants and it fell on top of his head and dumped out. The old man said Horst sat there bawling his eyes out, mud dripping from his face. I guess he had it in his mouth, his nose, in his ears. Back then the old man told us a lot of the older folk used pig manure in some of their houseplants. Apparently that particular plant, was one of the ones that Babushka used it in. Could you imagine? Boy that would be funny. Well, for that short little story it took the old man two hours to tell. Mind you he did get off track a few times and he did repeat himself. Anyway, I've probably talked your ear off. The mess is cleaned, I guess that's it. Good luck with Colleen and enjoy your breakfast, maybe I'll see you around sometime?"

"You never know Val, you never know."

"Cool. I'll be seeing you." With that he turned and walked away. Hayden sat there with his mouth hung opened trying to comprehend how anyone could talk so much. *Boy, could he rattle on*, he thought to himself. He was certainly an interesting character, one of the more interesting ones he met in a long time. Hayden was still dazed when he heard her voice. "I guess you've met Val?"

"Yes, yes I have. He can certainly talk can't he? And how are you feeling after that collision, I hope you're not hurt."

"Nothing but my pride. Sorry about the way I acted. It wasn't very lady like for me to curse him the way I did or for that matter kick him."

"No problem. It sounds like O'Malley deserved it." Hayden said with a half grin.

"He deserved it all right and if you don't mind me saying I'm glad he broke his arm," she said shyly tilting her head. Hayden could smell the strawberry shampoo she used. He inhaled deeply but softly, she smelled good. Even the smell of cooking grease her uniform gave off smelled terrific on her. He had to stop himself from leaning forward to inhale her scent. She was beautiful, more beautiful then he could remember when she approached him that first time to take his order. Before Eddy boy, O'Malley came running out.

"Some peoples children…" Was the only thing he could say, awe-struck at her sheer beauty. It wasn't Barbie doll beauty either. No, Colleen was more than that. She had long, well-kept hair that she wore in one big ponytail. Her eyes were a beautiful brown, a shade darker than her hair which, seemed to be streaked with a light blonde. She personified to him true beauty in all its natural form. He couldn't tell what was beneath her clothes, other than the fact that her breast weren't too large, nor were they too small. She had the eyes of an Egyptian Goddess their shape, colour everything. A few minutes went by and when she finally began to talk, he caught himself staring at her.

"Are you okay? Is there anything wrong?" she began as she looked at him quizzically.

"No, nothings wrong. I'm sorry if I seem to be staring."

"That's okay. It happens to me lots. It's my eyes right? Yes, one of them is smaller then the other and I've been told before that they are vaguely shaped like an Egyptian's." she replied with a smile.

Hayden chuckled a bit and turned a few shades of red. "Yeah, exactly. All that." he said. Colleen looked at him and shook her head grinning.

"Are you ready to make another order now? Or, do you still want the crepes?"

"Crepes…yeah. I think Cookie is throwing them together." Hayden was trying to stall her so he could get up the nerve to ask if she might consider having drinks with him that night.

"All right then, I guess when its ready I'll be bringing them to you."

She was about to turn and walk away. Hayden's mind raced, finally he blurted out, "You wouldn't happen to want to grab a drink or two later would you?" he asked as gentlemanly as possible.

"You're not some kind of weirdo are you?" she asked.

For a moment Hayden's heart stood still. "By all means no." he felt like an idiot. Here he was asking some woman, whom he never met before to have drinks with him. At least it was gutsy.

Colleen snickered. "I was only kidding. I get off at 9:00 p.m."

He looked at her in disbelief. "Are you serious? You'll have drinks with me?"

"Why not? I figure any man who can sit through hearing Val carry on without telling him to shut up can't be all that bad."

He was awe-struck until he realised that he hadn't even introduced himself. Instantly his moral dropped. *I'm such a moron,* he thought. "By the way, my name is Hayden. I'm sorry I didn't cordially introduce myself before asking if you would consider having drinks with me."

"Not to worry. I heard you introduce yourself to Val. I'll catch you on the flip-flop, Hayden." Hayden sat there watching as she went about her work. His mind whirled with possibilities. *Beautiful and horny,* he thought privately to himself. He had no intentions on trying to score with her. He wasn't that type of a guy on the first date. A few minutes later Cookie himself brought out his crepes. The plate was stacked high. Whipped cream and blueberries toppled down the sides of the stack of crepes, two big pieces of ham sat next to the toast.

"You didn't have to go through all that trouble." Hayden said looking at the plate.

"No trouble at all. It's on the menu. This is the big-man breakfast."

"No doubt, big-man all right. I won't be able to put all that away."

"Ah, everyone who has ever ordered it said the same, but, they each finished it. It looks bigger than it is. The whip cream and blueberries add a deceptive look. Go ahead dig in. And enjoy." He turned and walked back to the kitchen. Hayden looked at the mound full of crepes and whipped cream and berries. The crepes were piled five high and between each layer was whipped cream. It was excellent to say the least and by God if he didn't finish the entire thing.

He left a tip on the table hoping Colleen would pick it up, then paid his bill. He glimpsed at Colleen again and was somewhat touched to see her looking at him. Smiling she waved. Hayden waved back then ducked out of the Pickled Onion. It was close to 10:00 a.m., he noticed. "I better get a move on," he muttered to himself. The morning had certainly been interesting, if he hadn't went to the restaurant he wouldn't have met Colleen, or stumbled across Ellis's dim-witted agenda. *That's okay, he'll be the one that pays.*

The first store he came to on the bottom deck was called the Porthole. The shelves were stacked with magazines, books, and other literature. Looking for one on Naval bases preferably the ones in Alaska, he came across a book titled Naval Bases of the North. It was a two hundred page glossy print filled with pictures and blurbs. *Excellent,* he thought. It seemed kind of strange all these good things were happening to him. He flipped through the book a couple of times not trying to look too antsy then he carried on down the one isle and picked up another book not pertaining to Naval Bases. It was a crime/mystery titled The O'Brien Series. It looked interesting enough if nothing else it would provide him with a bit of a cover. He strolled over to the cashier and set the books down on the counter. "Is there anything else for you today, sir?"

"I was wondering if you might have something on things to do in Alaska? You know a tourist booklet or something?"

"Sure do. We have this one called The Great White North. Its by this journalist fellow named Borg Gustavikin. We sell probably three of these a week. I see you got The O'Brien Series; I've read that one. It's not bad—it certainly is fast paced. I enjoyed it. It's not too bad of a book at all. Apparently, that's one in a series of three or four. The author, what's his name…Brian T. Seifrit, supposedly that's his first work and I've certainly read worse. But, yeah, 'The Great White North' is a pretty good informative type read." Hayden held the booklet in his hand looking it over. It was laced with all kinds of things, even a few Alaskan recipes.

"All right I'll take these three." Hayden reached into his pocket for some cash.

"That's seventeen ninety five, plus twenty three forty, plus eight." The cashier said as he punched the numbers into the cash register. "For a total of $52.80 including taxes." Hayden handed him a fifty and a ten. "Great," he said as he handed back the seven dollars and twenty cents in change due. "Would you like a bag."

"That's all right. Thanks a lot."

"You bet enjoy the books," he said as Hayden turned and walked away.

Back at the Pickled Onion, Colleen was having her fifteen-minute break chatting with one of her friends. "I'm so serious, he's drop dead gorgeous. And his name…I love his name, the way it sounds alone gives me goose pimples. God I can't wait Cee Jay until tonight," she said to her friend as a huge smile crossed her face.

"Tell me again what he looks like. I wish I would have seen him."

"Well, he has dirty blonde hair and these eyes that are cold as ice but they give off warmth. It's so hard to describe. He has this sweetest smile. It is somewhat intimidating, but at the same time comforting. He looked rugged and well kept all at the same time. I'm getting hot and bothered thinking about him. Look my nipples are hard," she said with a snicker.

Cee Jay laughed along with her. "Good for you. I'm happy for you but also a tad jealous. Sounds like he's quite a cutie." Colleen sat transfixed daydreaming. It had been forever since she felt like this. "Come one girlfriend work is beckoning." Cee Jay said as she stood up.

"Yeah." The two companions exited the coffee room and returned to the floor and their gruelling work. The restaurant had filled since they took their break. *Good, the day will go faster,* Colleen thought to herself, giddy as a girl with a new Barbie.

Returning to the cabin before 6:00 p.m., Hayden threw the five books and two magazines he found on Nome on top of one of the beds. He pulled up a chair to the table and waited for Alex and Monique. His mind flooded with Colleen's beauty and persona. He tried thinking back to when he may have felt this way before but nothing came to life. *I've never felt quite like this,* he thought.

He had butterflies in his stomach and sweaty palms. His heart fluttered every now and then when her image crossed his mind. He couldn't get over her eyes. They were so vibrant. He loved her bashing attitude too. She obviously didn't take much crap. She was the perfect woman in his mind. He waited in anticipation. *Three more hours,* he thought. The sound of the door opening tore him away from the fantasy playing in his mind.

"How did it go with you? Did you come up with anything, Hayden?" Monique asked as the door opened again.

"We all made it? Good cause I found this book titled 'The Great White North'," Alex began.

Hayden laughed a bit. "I picked up the same one."

"Me too." added Monique.

"Oh." was Alex's response. "Now each of us can look it over and study it a bit. I've looked at some of it. All the info we need to make this thing work is in it. I even found a post card with the navy ship the Navy Blue on it. Check it out," he said as he handed it to Monique. Her eyes got big.

"It's a huge gun-ship. That's going to prove interesting."

"It's not a cutter?" Hayden asked. "You know a navy passenger ship. They do have a couple of guns on them."

"No, this one is loaded to the hilt with artillery. Take a look." She said as she handed the post card over. "It's going to be tough to infiltrate," she added. Hayden looked at the card. It was definitely a gunner ship. By size, it looked like it could completely swallow the Hilroy.

"Any thoughts? This bad boy is huge." He replied still looking at the picture.

"It's definitely intimidating. But, I don't think it's going to be that hard to infiltrate."

"How's that?" Hayden questioned.

"If you look real close you'll see that according to that picture near the stern there is a ladder. It's hard to see because of the size of the ship but it's there. I figure we can board the ship from that spot."

"That ladder has to be at least twenty-five, thirty, maybe even forty feet above the water. It's hard to tell by the picture. I do see the ladder though." Hayden remarked.

"I figured once we port in Nome we could get some climbing gear and repel up. We'll need a rowboat or something to get close and we'll have to somehow get a rope around the bottom rung but I think we can figure that out. Then we pull ourselves up. That's the easy part."

"We're going to be doing this in the cover of little darkness, right?" Monique gestured.

"Yup. I figured Hayden and I would board it. We're going to need someone to stay on the boat that takes us there. Not only for back up but, also to load up the goods. Remember that we don't want to alarm anybody. This whole thing has to be done in stealth mode. We get in. We retrieve. We disappear into the void. Sixty four million dollars richer."

"Before we make any final decisions on how we're going to pull this off we better look at all our options although I don't doubt your plan, Alex. We better think it through. You have to think that with that kind of bread on board it's not going to be a walk in the park. You're right about stealth. That is the only way. I say we take a day or two to read up on other possible avenues. I mean, if the ship has tours and some of them do. It would be simple to get lost and what an excuse to use if we ever got caught. However, if someone spots the ropes that we'll need to climb that ladder we'll be in a whole lot of hooey."

"Point taken." Alex said as he nodded. Hayden looked over to Monique who had already begun reading.

"Do either one of you need the bathroom?" she asked. "I want to take a hot shower. It was muggy today and I think I've sweated ten gallons."

"I don't need it. What about you Alex?"

"Nah, go ahead Monique."

Monique entered the little bathroom and removed her clothes. She looked at herself in the mirror at her long black hair blowing it away from her eyes. "We'll be free soon," she said to her reflection.

At 8:30 p.m., Hayden began getting ready to head down to the Pickled Onion.

"Where are you off to?" Monique asked. He fibbed that he was going over to The Golden Nugget to shoot some craps. Knowing that neither Monique nor Alex were into gambling he figured it was the easiest thing to come up with that might deter either of them from tagging along.

"The Nugget. Why would you want to waste your money?" Alex asked.

"I don't know. Who's to say that I won't win? What do the both of you have planned for this evening?"

"Nothing really. I don't know. Do you want to tag along with Hayden, Monique?" *Heart be still*, Hayden thought to himself as she waited to reply.

"Nah, you go ahead if you want Alex. I think I'll do some reading." Alex contemplated for a few minutes then declined as well.

Relieved that he and Colleen would be alone Hayden nodded. "All right then. I should be back later this evening." He turned and exited their cabin. There was a spectacular sunset in the sky and he looked at it then smiled. "Almost as beautiful as the awaiting Colleen Taras," he said to himself as he walked over to the stairwell. Going down he met up with Ellis's henchman Red, who was coming up with his arms full of take out food from the Pickled Onion. “Evening Red.” Hayden said. He looked at Hayden and smiled.

“If it isn’t Mister Hayden. How are you doing tonight?” He asked with a mild tone of dislike.

“Not bad. How about yourself?” He shrugged his shoulders not saying a word and continued up the stairs, while Hayden continued onward to the Pickled Onion. The time was 8:52 p.m. Colleen would be getting off shift soon. Nervous, Hayden pulled a chair up to a table and waited. At 9:05 p.m., he heard the voice he was longing to hear all day. “You made it,” she said. Looking at her, he was transfixed by her beauty.

“I sure did. I wouldn’t miss having a drink with someone as beautiful as you.” He replied.

She stared at him batting her eyes. “Where do you want to go?” She asked.

“You probably know this ship better than I, where do you suggest we go?”

“To be honest I wouldn’t mind going to my cabin and showering.”

“All right would you like to meet up later than after you shower?” He asked, her body language telling him something else.

“Nope, why don’t you come with me? I have wine in my fridge you could have a drink while I shower. How does that sound? Then we’ll play the rest of the evening by ear,” she said in a teasingly manner.

“Sure, as long as I don’t make you feel uncomfortable.”

“Not at all.” She took him by the arm. “Come with me Hayden, come with me.” They walked down the galley and to her cabin. Inside it was full of frilly this and frilly that. It was definitely a woman’s quarters. She gestured for him to sit down on a couch that was full of stuffed animals.

“You can toss those guys on the floor. Honestly, they don’t mind.” She said with a cute little snicker. Hayden removed only some of the animals making enough room for himself to sit down. He heard the clanking of wineglasses as Colleen returned.

“Here you go. I’ll be done in about fifteen minutes make yourself comfortable.” She handed him the wine and two glasses. “Go ahead and help yourself its pretty good wine. I’ll see you in a bit.”

“Thanks, thanks very much,” he said as he poured himself a glass. He watched as Colleen entered her bathroom.

“I know I’ve said it before, but damn is she good looking.” He said quietly to self. Bringing the wineglass up to his nose, he smelled the vintage. It was a red medium dry wine a blush you could say called Blizzard Mountain. It was distilled by a vineyard in Canada he noticed, in British Columbia to be exact, in a town called Columbia Gardens. The decal on the bottle portrayed a mountain valley with the focal point being a log structure of sorts. Hayden wondered how Colleen managed to get the vintage from so far away.

He brought the glass to his mouth and took a sip letting the vintage sit there on his tongue until it evaporated. The after taste was pleasant and it made his palate crave another sip. Swishing it around he swallowed letting the aromatic odour escape through his sinus cavity so that he could taste and smell it at the same time. It was one of the best vintages he tasted. Smacking his lips he finished the glass and poured another. *Someday, I might visit this place called Columbia Gardens and its vineyard.*

Colleen stepped out of the shower into the steam filled bathroom, which had fogged up the mirror. Reaching for a towel she wiped away the condensation and switched on the exhaust fan. After drying herself, she brushed her teeth and sprayed herself with body spray. Naked she looked at her reflection in the mirror. For her age, she looked hot. She especially liked the shape of he buttocks it took five years to get this body and she was proud of it.

Slipping on her purple thong underwear she pulled them up in a sultry manner, in the same manner she decided she would take them off. Then she put on her bra the one that perfectly matched her thong. With only the two pieces of clothing on she again looked at herself. Purple was her favourite colour and she did look stunning in it. She smiled, "I'm to sexy for my clothes… I'm to sexy." she quietly sang. She was happier than she had been in a long time.

Now, for what to wear, she thought as she looked through the two sets of clothes she brought into the shower with her. She picked out the pair of pants with the zipper running down the leg but it was too 80-ish. Finally, she settled on a black pair of pants and a blue top, looking in the mirror once more she brushed her hair and stepped out to meet Hayden. "Sorry, I took so long." She said as she walked over to where he was sitting on the couch.

"No problem. You look stunning."

"Thank you. You don't look so bad yourself." She said with that snicker of her's.

Hayden blushed. He could feel the heated rush of blood as it ran up his face. "Thank you back."

"How is the wine?"

"Very good. How did you manage to get it from so far away?"

"I have a girlfriend that lives down that way in a pulp and paper town called Castlebridge. Once a year we get together, she's always bringing me stuff. You see it's her ploy to get me to move there," she said with humour.

"That would entail a lot of legalities wouldn't it?"

"Not for me. I'm Canadian. I'm from the North West Territories. I'm NWT through and through"

"Really? Whatever made you want to work way up here."

"I like to travel and I like testing my limits you could say. Or you could say I'm crazy. I don't know. I like the salt air. I like the cold. I like the beautiful sunsets and rises that you can only see from way out here. I like meeting new and interesting people. But, most of all if I were to really think about it I like the solitude. Someday, I want to…you know…disappear. Live on a mountain somewhere. What about yourself, what brings you way up here?"

"Actually, I'm from Poski."

"Huh," she began, "Where is that?"

"Got a world atlas?"

"Somewhere around here," she said as she stood up and began looking for it. Hayden watched her little body as it bent down here, knelt down there. "Ah ha, found it." She opened the book up to reveal the world map. "I bet I can find it, tell me the name again."

"All right. Poski. It's spelled POSKI," he answered.

"Nope, that didn't help c'mon give me another hint."

"It's in Russia."

"I knew it was I could tell by the name. But, I still don't see it. What's it near?"

"The Atelic Mountains." He watched as Colleen frantically searched for the mountain range.

"Okay I'm going to go to a Russian map. I think that would be better," she said as she began thumbing through the Atlas. "You never did tell me what brings you way over here."

"Just touring. I finally got my passport about ten years ago when I was twenty-six. I take trips once a year sometimes for months at a time."

"How do you afford that?"

"My work involves a lot of travel at times," he paused for a minute, "I guess I'm working most of the time. But, I still try and get away on personal trips. This trip to Nome being one of them, kind of."

"What are you going to do when you get there? Aren't the bears big enough in Russia?"

"Huh, bears. How did we get onto that subject?"

"I figured you for the outdoorsy type and the only thing worth seeing in Nome are the bears," she snickered still looking through the Atlas.

"Do you want me to help you find Poski?"

"No, I already found it. Wow you are a long way from home."

"I know. It's good to get away. Where would you like to go to have drinks?"

"I thought we were having drinks." The smile on her face lit up the room.

"Well, yeah, but…well whatever you prefer."

"I prefer to stay right here. We can always order something in if you are hungry."

"No, I'm okay. I'm still full from breakfast plus the wine."

"Good, then we'll have a chit and chat night. So you are from Poski and your job allows you to do a lot of travelling? What line of work are you in?" She asked as she put her wineglass to her raspberry red lips.

"I work for a government agency out of Poski. I do a lot of data research. I attend UN meetings that sort of thing."

"Like James Bond?" Colleen smiled.

Hayden chuckled, "No, I'm not a spy. I'm a public and international affairs worker more than anything." God how he hoped he wasn't sounding to phoney. He didn't want to blatantly tell her that he was in all actuality a wanted felon by the Balcovian Government on the lamb with two associates. Or for that matter, that he belonged to a revolutionary movement called the RRA. And that he was on his way to steal sixty four million dollars from the US Navy and the D.E.A. He didn't care if she knew his name, the country he was from, or any of that. He was so far away from there and was never going back, it didn't matter. As far as he knew there weren't any Balcov Officials onboard or Poski Militia either. He was free and clear in that aspect. The only threat onboard was Ellis Leroy.

"Sounds like you have a great job. But to be honest with you I'm glad its you and not me. I couldn't handle that kind of pressure."

"I work well under pressure." He chuckled. "Now, how does a Canadian girl work in the US? Isn't it difficult to do with all the legalities and that sort of thing."

"That it is. You have to have a working visa for one. You probably know those aren't cheap or easy to get. Especially with the world being as it is, all botched up. Once you are issued that than you need countless immunisation shots and a passport. You also need a fair amount of cash. Particularly since the Canadian dollar sucks."

"No kidding. That's a farce isn't it." They rattled back and forth like that for most of the evening. They ended up cuddling on the couch watching for the sun to rise. It was pure magic. As the first rays from the big yellow ball in the sky began to gleam bringing forth a new day. It was time for Hayden to leave.

"Will I see you again?"

"I'd love that Colleen. That would be terrific. Same time tonight?"

"Nah." Hayden almost fainted from embarrassment. That is until she continued. "Today is what the twenty-seventh? We aren't due to port until Friday, July 2. That's five nights."

Hayden smiled with relief. "I'll see you tonight then. And every night until we dock."

"Twelve."

It was 5:30 a.m., when he returned to the cabin that the three of them shared. Creeping over to his cot, he unfolded it as quietly as possible not wanting to rouse his roommates, then slid between the sheets and closed his eyes. If he only got a few hours of sleep, it would be better then none. He was tired from lying awake all night curled up with Colleen watching as the sun rose.

At 10:30 a.m., Alex stirred him. "Hey wake up." Hayden tossed the pillow over his head and waved at Alex to get lost. He was tired and wanted a few more minutes of shuteye.

"A few more minutes, c'mon." He heard Alex walk over to the table. Then the room grew deathly silent. He could sense some kind of commotion going on. Dreary eyed he pulled the pillow off his head and at the same time a rush of cold water dumped all over him. "Ahh, what the…" he began as he turned to see Monique standing there with a big smile on her face. Alex was at the table laughing hysterically.

"All right, all right I'm awake. Jesus Christ, Monique that was cold not to mention mean." He looked at her and smiled, "You'll get yours, so will you Alex, so will you." Slipping into his jeans and pulling a shirt over his shoulders, he met them at the table. "What's on the agenda for today folks?" He asked as he pulled up a chair. Hoping they weren't going to ask where he had been all night.

They didn't.

Instead they hammered out a few different ideas on how to proceed with the aggress, they decided that although the books and magazines each of them picked up offered good information they couldn't compare them to the real thing.

"I think its better that we wait until we dock before we confirm on the best way to board and retrieve the goods. The books and magazines offered some good information but it's all past tense. You know. I mean the picture of the Navy Blue on that post card was probably taken in the late eighties. We can't be sure that it even looks the same today. That is other than its size.

Example being, remember that ladder we looked at we can't be sure it's there today. For all we know it could have been a throw over ladder. When we dock, we'll have to get as close to it as we can. That's the best way to plan the assault. I've read and flipped through most of these books last night. After a lot of consideration I came to the conclusion they weren't informing me enough on what I think we really need to know. That is to say as compared to the real thing and up close."

"I have to agree Alex. It's not going to give us much time though. We're going to have to obtain all the intelligence we can on the big-gunner that first day." Hayden said.

"Get me on the Internet and I'll get as much data as I can find in cyber space. I might even be able to pull off the Internet a blue print of the ship if not the Navy Blue then perhaps another Navy ship with the same dimensions, personnel capacity, etceteras."

"That's an excellent idea Monique. Has either of you seen anyone onboard with a lap top by chance?"

"Even if we did what are we suppose to do, steal it?" Alex questioned with a chuckle. Hayden didn't see a problem with that. They could easily return it after they used it. He raised an eyebrow and looked at Monique who was obviously thinking the same thing.

"That would work," she replied.

"Are you saying you have seen someone with a lap top?" Hayden asked Alex.

"No. But, maybe we should all take a stroll and see if we do come across someone who does? There has to be some type of computer on this ship even if it's in someone's office. Breaking into an office is as easy as taking some poor bastards lap top. What do you say?"

"I say we're simple. We should have come up with a plan like this right from the start. We probably could've come up with one of those lap top things ourselves." Hayden said shaking his head.

"I doubt that. With all that was going on. Ellis toying with us, the Balcov Officials and Poski Militia ready to kill us. We didn't have time to come up with something so elaborate. Now is our opportunity."

"You're probably right Monique. We didn't have time. Not until you mentioned the Internet did I even think about how useful it could be or for that matter a computer in general. I guess there is a use for those things after all."

"There will always be uses for them. It's the wave of the future." Monique replied. Deep down Hayden knew she was right but he for one really didn't have much use as of yet to go headfirst into all the new tech bunk. He could pull stuff up on the net. He could format databases that type of thing, but computers were far and between from where they came from. They were virtually a new concept in Poski. Now, more than ever he realised their underestimated value.

"I realise that now. Let's see if we can't track one down."

"Should we split up or do we want to chum around together?"

"Let's do it together Alex."

"All right then pitter-patter let's get at her." They excited the cabin noting the time to be 1:00 p.m. Four hours later they located what they were looking for it was in an office that appeared to be a medical office. They just happened to stumble upon it. It was located below the bottom deck close to the bow and away from the public eye. The door was a big steel one and it was locked tighter than a popcorn fart. Looking in through the window Monique said it was perfect.

"Excellent. It's a Pentium three," she said.

Which meant nothing at all to Hayden, "Does that mean I can't turn it on?" He shrugged his shoulders.

"Funny. It means that the processing chip is a Pentium class. It is one of the most advanced in the entire world. If it's linked up with a satellite, we'll be able to get whatever we need. We only have to figure out how to get inside."

"That is going to be a problem. This door is as heavy as a tank." Alex commented.

"Think about all the locks we picked as kids, Alex, no door was safe. All we need are a few simple things like a piece of stiff wire, maybe a couple of small screwdrivers, a hairpin or two. I think the lock is pick-able it's the only way were going to get in." Hayden pointed out.

"All that stuff is easily enough to get. Maybe the tools we used to tear down the guns will work. Let's go and get them." Monique offered.

"The gun tools are too big we need smaller ones like a jewellery screwdriver. We could probably find a store onboard that would have something like that. If we can pick up a set of them that are from 3 mm down to about 1 mm and preferably all flat heads than we'll be in that room tonight. It would be even better if we could find a set with long shafts. But, anything that size will get us in." Hayden was sure of that.

"All right, let's go find what we need. This time lets split up we can cover more ground. It's Thursday the majority of gift shops etceteras will be open until around 9:00 p.m., we have a few hours to come up with what we need." The three of them walked up the short stairwell and out onto the bottom deck.

"Okay guys. Let's meet back here after 9:00 p.m., with, or without tools." They walked up to the second deck then split up. The air was cool and the winds that blew gently felt exhilarating as Hayden cruised from store to store. He looked for the items they needed to get inside the room for what seemed like hours. Monique and he crossed paths once and she wasn't having any luck either. Out of all the stores that were on the Hilroy, not one of them carried the particular items they were searching for.

Hayden managed to find a tossed away coat hanger in one of the on deck restrooms he used. It could certainly be made to work. He bought a small penknife, a set of sewing needles, a box of safety pins, and five large sized paper clips. Those were the only items he could find that were accessible on the ship. Why he couldn't find a set of small flat head screwdrivers was beyond him but he couldn't and he hadn't. He wasn't sure what kind of luck, Alex and Monique may be having, but he figured it was the same.

With the items in his pocket he headed back to the bottom deck not to meet the others but to let Colleen know that something had come up and that he'd either be late or not show at all. "Awe that sucks. I was looking forward to seeing you again tonight."

"It could happen, just later than we agreed is all."

"All right. My door will be open."

"Thanks for understanding Colleen. Hopefully I'll see you later."

"I hope so." Smiling he stepped out of the Pickled Onion. He walked down the galley towards the bow of the ship making his way to meet the others. From the Pickled Onion, it was a long walk. But, he was able to see parts of the ship he otherwise wouldn't have seen had he went the same route that they used before. Most of the area down here was for the employees of the ship. It wasn't nearly as clean as the middle and top decks.

Opened pipes ran along the wall in the galley and he could hear rushing water pumping through them. There were big conduits that housed miles and miles of wiring that supplied electricity to all the cabins, offices, stores, restaurant's, and the like. Then the galley would open up again to a bigger and brighter foyer that led to more employee residence or cabins. Finally, after what seemed like miles of catacombs he came to the door where the three of them were suppose to meet. It wasn't quite 9:00 p.m., he walked up the flight of stairs that led to the second deck and waited.

It was swarming with people out for their evening walks or coming from here or there. Leaning up against the railing as he had done a hundred times before he looked to the horizon. His mind muddled with dreams and $21.333,333.00. Which was the sum the three of them would have each after retrieving the sixty four million. Granted some of it would be destined for Poski and the RRA but not all of it. Hayden already decided that he wanted only twenty million. The balance he was going to give to the RRA. He didn't know how much Alex or Monique settled on giving them but from him it would be a minimum of one million and change.

Looking over to the deck kiosk he walked over and purchased a Snapple along with a frankfurter and onion rings. Sitting down he noticed one of Ellis's henchmen standing in the shadows. Looking around he spotted the other four including Red. It was the first time he saw them on that deck. He wasn't sure if they were tailing him or if it was coincidental that they were out and about. All that mattered was the fact that he knew they were there and he wasn't going to lose sight of them. He ate the food, finished his Snapple, and then headed back to the railing keeping an ever-vigilant eye on the henchmen.

Finally, Alex and Monique approached. "Over here," Hayden yelled. Monique looked over at him and waved.

"Any luck." Alex asked.

"Some, but don't look now. Ellis's henchmen are out and about and they are on this deck."

"Really? Where are they?" Alex asked.

"Over near the kiosk. I don't know exactly what they are doing or why they are here. They are spread out and it looks to me like they are looking for something. It's hard to say if they have seen me looking at them but I don't think they have."

"Figure we should call this off until we're in the clear?"

"Let's hang out for a few more minutes then we'll head to the door. If they approach, we'll know that they are tailing us. I haven't seen them look this way much, but we can't be sure until we get out of view. If they are tailing us they'll follow." Hayden said.

"What did you come up with in way of tools, Hayden?"

"Not much, Monique. I picked up some sewing needles, a box of safety pins, a pen knife and some big ass paper clips, the real hard metal ones, plus I found a coat hanger. One or the other will get us in. Don't worry you'll be cruising the Internet in no time. What did you guy's come up with?"

"Pretty much the same as you."

"Unreal eh, a ship this size without a thing even resembling what we wanted."

"Not really it's probably a safety issue. After all if some maniacs were to get a hold of tools, who is to say what they might attempt." said Monique with a chuckle, referring to the three of them.

Hayden turned facing the same direction as they were. Together they looked out across the mass of black cold water, each silently reflecting on their journey. Seconds later he turned his head to see if the henchmen were still hanging about. "They're gone. I can't see them anywhere. C'mon lets go." He said as the three headed to the exit that would lead them below deck and to the computer room. Monique and Alex went ahead. Hayden turned to look one last time to see if anyone was following them. "It's clear guys. No one is following."

"Great, let's do this." Alex said. They walked down the corridor and to the first big heavy door. "Excellent it's still open." Alex opened the door for Monique and Hayden and they ducked in. Closing the heavy door Alex locked it from the inside. "Can't have anyone disturbing us now can we."

"Works for me, let's go." Monique replied. A few short minutes later they were standing again at the door that held behind it the computer. Alex tried a couple of times to unlock it but it was futile. Then

Hayden tried and Monique tried but the items they had to use weren't cutting it.

"It's hopeless guys. What do you say? Should we scrap this idea and look for another computer elsewhere?"

"I don't know Hayden this is the perfect spot. There isn't a soul around and no one can get in without us hearing. Let's try a couple of more times first. Like you said, when we were kids there wasn't a lock we couldn't pick."

"Yeah, yeah. All right lets give it another go." He was glad they disagreed with him because a few minutes later they heard the audible click as the lock retracted back into the door.

"We're in," said Alex as he slowly pushed the door opened. Perseverance had paid off. The three entered. Monique went directly to the computer while Alex and Hayden kept six. Hayden watched Monique as she booted it up. She punched a few things in with the keyboard to get around the security and then the screen lit up.

"We're in luck. The computer is linked up with a satellite. We should be able to get on the net without a problem."

The minutes dragged on and Hayden was getting impatient. "How much longer, Monique?"

"Not sure. I'm still trying to logon. I keep getting an error reading, access denied. I'm guessing that there is another security firewall. I got to locate the file. Ah ha, I've got it." Monique punched in a bunch of keys and digits and finally the two words she was hoping for popped up, access gained. "We're on our way now," she said as she logged on. Within ten minutes she located and printed off two different naval ships' blue prints and some literature on the Nome Navel Base. "I couldn't get anything on the Navy Blue, but these will certainly help."

"Damn right they will." Alex said as he handed Hayden the information. Together they looked over the information while Monique shut down the computer.

"This is excellent." Hayden said. He was about to add something else, when Monique interrupted.

"Check this out." Alex and Hayden walked over to the desk where Monique sat. Somehow, she accidentally gained access to a list of cabin numbers on board the Hilroy. There were three long columns and by certain cabin numbers, there were asterisks.

"What do you suppose that means?"

"I don't know should we click one on?"

"Does our cabin have an asterisk?" Hayden asked.

"Nope. But it looks like Ellis's does."

"Really? If anything click that one on." He was curious now. Why would Ellis's cabin number have an asterisk?

"All right here it goes." Monique clicked the number. Instantly the screen flickered and a clear view into Ellis's room showed up.

"Someone is watching his room. Who do you think it could be?"

"I haven't a clue but if they've been watching that room chances are they've also seen us. Is there anyway to find that out?" Alex asked.

"Yeah, there is. But that could take hours. Do either of you have anywhere to be?"

Hayden could only think about Colleen. He told her that he would do his best to meet her again later that evening. He looked at his watch and noted that it was already 10:30 p.m. Knowing that what they stumbled upon would have to take precedence. He made a conscious decision to say no. "I don't. What about you Alex?"

"Nope."

"All right then. If you guys want me to carry on— it could take a while. But, then at least we can be sure that we were either seen or we weren't." She swivelled the chair back to face the monitor her fingers ready to start punching keys.

"I say go for it. Could be someone has been setting him up for a fall. If that's the case and we were spotted in that room you can bet whoever is looking in on him will undoubtedly also be looking for us." Hayden said.

Alex nodded. "Go for it Monique. We have nothing but time." Two hours later she was able to tell that, no, they weren't seen. The three of them were relieved. But now wondered if pulling off the heist would be such a good idea. Finally deciding that since they were not been witnessed in Ellis's room by whoever it was that was watching him, that they would follow through. They weren't planning on coming back onboard anyway. Although in Ellis's mind, they wouldn't have choice.

They gathered the information that Monique printed off the net. She shut down the computer and they exited the office locking it behind. At 1:00 a.m., they were back at their cabin going over the possibilities on who was watching their friend Ellis. They were sure that someone was gathering intelligence on him. They had to avoid him now like the plague.

Eventually they turned their attention to the information they obtained from the net. They went over a slew of different ideas on how to pull the heist off. According to the information, it stated that the Navy ships of Navy Blue's particular size usually had onboard two hundred and fifty personnel minimum. If the ships were used for intelligence operations, which the Navy Blue was, the number of personnel usually doubled. From one of the blueprints, they ascertained that the President Suite was on the very top deck nearest the helli-pad. Of course, it would be. They'd have to board the ship and make their way to the top deck. A feat, that with that many personnel onboard definitely put them at a disadvantage. They settled in for the rest of the evening not knowing how they were going to pull it off. Tomorrow they would thrash out the final framework for the assault.

"Thirteen."

Hayden didn't sleep well that evening. His mind raced with possibilities. What if they were caught? What if they were forced into a combat situation? There'd be no way they would come out of something such as that unscathed. He wasn't sure what it was he was feeling as he lay there. He wanted that money. There was no doubt about that. He also wanted to live. He figured that if he lived he would at least have a chance with Colleen. He wouldn't be much good riddled with bullets lying in a puddle of his own blood or whisked away to some prison in the USA, all for some stupid cash. Sleep finally found him and when it did it hit him hard. Dreams of Colleen, freedom, money, and death palpitated—his sleeping mind.

The three awoke in unison at 10:00 a.m. They took their turns in the bathroom then met at the table. The papers they printed out the night before scattered the tabletop. Alex was looking intently at a blue print. "What seems so interesting with that one?" Hayden asked gesturing to the picture he held in his hand.

"It looks big. I don't want to burst anyone's bubble. In all actuality this heist is going to be tough to pull off."

"I've contemplated the same thing. Maybe we should call it off? We can't be sure that whoever has been watching Ellis knows something we don't. I can't even imagine who it could possibly be. Is it the CPA, CIA, the KGB, the FBI? That's to name a few, the list could go on."

"It certainly could Hayden. We have four days to figure it out. What if we were to do some intelligence work and see what we can come up with? If it turns out to be a government agency watching him then we'll scrap the whole thing. I mean sixty four million is a lot of coin to pass up without first being one hundred percent sure that we can't pull it off. What we should concentrate on for the next couple of days is figure out whom has been watching our friend. If it turns out to be someone insignificant I say we follow through with it." Monique replied. The cabin grew silent as the three of them sat in self-contemplation.

"What I suggest we do in that case is get back to that room and watch who comes and goes. The main room was certainly big enough for one of us to find a place to skulk. We could do two or three-hour shifts each. Until we discover who it is that is lurking onboard and has taken an interest in Ellis."

"That works. What do you say Hayden?"

"It's a start. And it's probably a good idea to deal with one problem at a time. We know that the Navy Blue isn't going anywhere, but we haven't a clue on who has been monitoring our friend. I think it is important to find out."

For two nights, the three of them took turns watching the computer room, but neither observed anyone coming or going. Hayden met with Colleen one last time before telling her that because of his work and some pressing events he would not be able to see her again. It tore his heart out but he didn't want her getting involved. He figured since they hadn't discovered who was watching Ellis that it would be safer if he remained close to Alex and Monique. He knew it meant he wouldn't have the opportunity to see Colleen again.

"When will you be returning? I could probably schedule work on whatever ship it is you'll be boarding to travel back." Colleen said with hope and desire. How could he tell her that he wasn't ever coming back? He realised then that he was giving up one dream to pursue another. He decided to tell her that his business in Nome was probably going to cut his holiday short, that he hoped to be back on board the Hilroy before it headed back to Kamchatka.

His true intentions were simple. He figured that if he survived the assault on the Navy Blue, he would slip back on board and inform her of exactly what had been going on and who he really was. He hoped that she would leave all this behind and together they would head into Canada. It sounded corny since they only met days earlier. There was something about her that he truly fell in love with. He wanted at that moment nothing more than to spend eternity with her.

"The truth is my holiday has been cut short. I have business in Nome, which I hope to take care of in the two days the Hilroy will be docked. If I can take care of things before it leaves port, chances are I'll be on it. But, until she docks, I'm afraid I won't have much time to be sociable. Even if I could, I'd be preoccupied. I'm sorry. I did enjoy our time together and hopefully we'll meet again."

"I understand. If you get done your business before we leave, we can spend the entire return trip back together. That would be nice. Can you spend tonight with me?"

Hayden shook his head. "I'm afraid I can't."

"All right. I guess I'll see you again when I see you." She leaned forward and kissed his cheek. It was a sweet and tender kiss. One he would never forget. He had never fallen so hard for a woman.

"I promise to do my best in getting my business done so that I can be onboard before you sail."

"I know you will. It's going to be hard, knowing that for the next four days until we dock I will not see you. Yet, we'll both be onboard under the same moon. I think that is the hardest part. Knowing you are here and I can not treasure you," she said. Hayden left Colleen's cabin that night with his mind made up. He would return for her. Rich or poor he would sweep her off her feet. For the first time in his life, he was truly in love. This kind of love he knew didn't come around but once in a man's life.

He asked himself how could he have made up his mind so quickly barely knowing the women. When you are in love, you know it, self replied. Hayden returned to his shared accommodations fifteen minutes later. Alex was there, he and Monique just switched shifts. "I take it no one showed up down below?" He said referring to the computer room.

"Not a soul. I'm getting tired of this Hayden. I think I'm getting ship fever. I can't wait until this ship docks it's been so long."

"Yeah, it has been. Don't be losing it this close to freedom. Four more days and we could be richer than we have ever dreamed." Hayden said with a slant of humour.

"Or, plastered to the cold steel of the Navy Blue."

"You know we don't have to go through with it if you feel we shouldn't. We'll have our freedom. Like we talked about earlier that too would suffice."

"I know. Except, there are so many people we could help with that kind of money. We could virtually help the RRA with a completely funded uprise against the CPA. I think about all the children, you know. The ones that haven't got a hope of becoming anything other than a slave to the communism of Poski and Balcov and all the other domains in the great country of Russia. That's what I think about and that's what drives me. I know the risks as I'm sure both you and Monique do. The only thing I ask Hayden is that if anything happens to me I want half of my cut to go to Monique and the other half directly to the RRA."

"Nothing is going to happen to you, me or Monique. We're going to look the Navy Blue over, before we try anything. We've already agreed to that. If it looks impenetrable then we're not even going to attempt it. We'll take the next steps in getting to Canada. Either way in four days we'll never look back again Alex, we'll be free. That alone ought to keep your spirits lively." Hayden said as the cabin door swung open. It was Monique.

"I saw who has been looking in on our friend. You're not going to believe this. It's Red. I think he belongs to some organisation. I can't figure out why he'd be watching Ellis he was there both times when we had meetings. What do you guys suppose he's watching him for?"

Hayden was at a loss for words. It didn't make much sense. Why would he be watching? It dawned on them that he was watching because that's what he was being paid for. Ellis obviously had his guys pull shifts watching him and his cabin. So that he remained safe at all times. It was brilliant. To be sure however, they wanted and needed to test the theory.

"Was Red still down there when you left?" Hayden asked.

"Yes he was."

"Good then here is what we have to do. You have to go back down, Alex and I will go to Ellis's cabin and see if he is alone, once we are sure we'll knock on the door and when he answers, we'll bust in like madmen. If his henchmen show up then we know."

"If they don't then Red is up to something else. In which case we'll have to deal with him in a different manner." Alex stated.

"It'll be another bridge we'll have to cross, I guess."

"I'm game I don't mind heading back down there and keeping an eye on Red."

"Okay. Head down we'll give you enough time to get settled say twenty minutes. Then Alex and I will head up to Ellis's cabin."

"All right. I'll talk to you guys in a bit." With that said she exited their cabin.

Alex and Hayden waited for ten minutes and knowing that it would take them at least that long to make it to Ellis's cabin they headed up to the top deck to confront him. Hayden banged hard on his door three or four times. "Ellis, its Alex and Hayden. We need to talk to you, it's important."

"What do you two want?" Came the response from the other side of the cabin door.

"Open the door and we'll tell you."

They heard some stumbling going on and then Ellis swear as he stubbed his toe. "This better be good. I was in the middle of getting some shut-eye," he said as he opened the door.

Hayden pulled out his Glock and planted it to Ellis's head. "Get over to that table and sit your ass down. I got to have some words with you. You yellow bastard." This was all part of the act.

"What is this all about?" Hayden let the play-acting get out of hand, as he smashed him square in the nose. Ellis grabbed his bloody nose a look of pain and shock across face. "I'm going to have you killed in thirty seconds you son of a bitch."

"Not if I kill you first." Hayden threatened as four of Ellis's henchmen came bursting through his door.

"I ought to have them throw your asses overboard," he said as the four guys surrounded Alex and Hayden.

"I don't think these four idiots can do it."

"Believe me Hayden they can do it. If I didn't have a use for you that's exactly where you'd be headed. Now tell me what is this all about."

"If you don't know you bastard I'm not going to tell you. Especially not in front of these freaks, if you're curious to know you'll ask me another time. But the next time I'm going to break more than your nose."

"The next time you aren't going to have a chance. Get out of here. Both of you," he said with malevolence as he held a white kerchief up to his nose. He gestured to his men to escort Alex and Hayden out. "Get them the out of here."

"That was some pretty good acting Hayden. I guess we know now why his room is being watched. I feel relieved knowing who and why."

"Me too. To be honest though I wasn't acting when I punched him in the face. I've been dying to do that. I figured I might never have an opportunity again. It felt good too." Hayden said with a chuckle. He was enthralled that the computer room dilemma was solved. Today it was the 29 of June, there were two nights, and three days to go before the Hilroy would be docking. And Hayden planned on spending every possible moment with Colleen.

The three of them crashed early. Skulking around for the past two days had been deadening. Now it was no longer a mystery. They could now sit back and wait patiently to dock. Their minds were made up. They were going to pull the heist off providing it was feasible. Then they were going to head straight to Canada millions of dollars richer. June 30 would prove to be an evening Hayden wouldn't soon forget. He met Colleen at the Pickled Onion as she was getting off shift. "Can I see you, tonight?" He asked. Colleen's eyes lit up and her beautiful smile covered her face.

"You've caught up on your work then?"

"Sure have."

"Well then walk me back to my cabin." Together arm in arm they retreated to her cabin.

"Fourteen."

Monday July 1, they were now only twenty-four hours away from their destination and the Navy Blue. And tonight they had a little dinner party to attend. He had yet to tell Alex or Monique, about Ellis's little plot to make Monique sick. Nor did he tell them that for the past while Ellis was scared by someone with initials AF. As for Colleen, he was sure that they knew something was up. Why else would he be disappearing until the early hours of predawn. Maybe they thought he was gambling all those nights.

Whatever they thought or didn't think, they never quizzed him. Soon enough they would know. As they rose from their slumber, they felt the thrill of the chase building up. They were more ready and more focused on the assault then ever before. The fact that also freedom was only hours away made them elated and intoxicated. Even if they didn't pull the heist off. They were on their way to freedom. "How do you guy's feel this morning?" Hayden asked.

"I can't believe how close we are, I'm so excited. Freedom is only hours away."

"Yeah, and sixty four million bucks we hope." Alex said. "If I had to chose between one or the other I'd most definitely take the freedom. If both are attainable then by God I'm going to have both. Ooh-yeah." He said in his Macho Man Randy Savage voice. Whenever Alex did that, it meant he was fully committed and ready to proceed. "And tonight when we sit down at the table with Ellis to break bread. I'm going to order the biggest steak and lobster dinner that restaurant has. If he's going to pay for it then I'm going be sure that he pays." Alex laughed.

"I'm with you buddy."

"That's for sure. I wonder what the Hilroy has onboard in way of expensive champagne?" Monique questioned with spunk.

"Ooh-yeah."

"Here, here." Hayden said as he rose his hand. They were definitely in good-spirits and nothing was going to bring them down. Either way freedom was only nautical miles away.

***

The morning shift for Colleen was progressing slowly in her mind. All she thought about was Hayden since he left her bedside early that morning. Tonight would be the last night they could spend together for a long time and maybe forever. He promised her that if he did get his business done before the Hilroy set sail again for Kamchatka that he would definitely be onboard.

If he misses it, I'll probably never see him again, she thought as she wiped off her fiftieth table of the day. She thought about their lovemaking and how it felt right. She had never been swept away like that before. She was thirty-one and knew that her biological time clock was ticking away. Most of her friends of the same age had husbands, houses, and children. She wanted to be with him. She longed to be with him. The things they shared with one another were things that neither one ever shared with another. That spoke volumes to Colleen. *Could I really be in love?* She thought. Self's reply was, yes. She wondered if Hayden felt the same way.

He did.

She took her fifteen-minute break at her usual time with her usual companion.

"I saw you and that handsome guy, what's his name…?"

"Hayden."

"Yes, Hayden. I saw you guys leave together last night. How did things go?"

"I haven't felt this way since I was a teenager. He's gorgeous isn't he?" She smacked her lips. Her heart beat fast as she spoke about him.

"I'll say. My God you are lucky. What does he do?"

"He said he was an international affairs worker. He's from Russia, can you believe that. And he speaks perfect English. I guess it was a perquisite for his work." Colleen's mind raced as she thought back again to the previous night.

"An international affairs worker from Russia? Sounds like a James Bond movie and you got a cameo appearance."

"Funny you should say that cause I said the same thing to him."

"Tell me more. How old is he? Does he have a brother?" Cee Jay chuckled.

"I don't know about that. I know he is thirty-six. He never out right said it. He clumsily, I think, mentioned he got his passport ten years ago when he was twenty-six. He's the perfect age. I've fallen hard for his personality not too mention his great looks."

"You're not in love with him are you? You've only known him for a week."

"I don't know. If love means you don't want to be with anyone else and you can see yourself beating your mate in the head with a cane when you are both in your sixties. Then I'm in love."

"Come on Colleen are you sure you're not infatuated with him. After all, he's a very good-looking man. If I was in your shoes I'd probably be as confused as you are."

"No. I'm not confused. I could honestly live out the rest of my life with him. I don't get it myself but there is something more between us than animal magnetism. I think I'm crazy in love."

"If that's the case than I wish you the best of luck. You're not stupid. If you say you feel this way, chances are, it's real. People fall in love everyday. Sometimes though, what they thought was love turns out to be plain old craving for carnal knowledge. You know what I mean. Be careful. Get to know him better before committing anything. That's all I can say. Since I've been through something similar not too long ago with that idiot, I was involved with. And remember I met him on a ship as well."

"Thanks Cee Jay. It means a lot to hear that from a friend. Come on, coffee break is over."

***

The three of them exited their cabin together. Monique was heading to the pool to suntan and to do a couple of laps. Alex decided on heading to a pub on the top deck called Ye Old Pub. "Do you care to join me Hayden?"

"Nah, I'm not too fond of that English beer. But thanks for asking. I think I'll head over to the Nugget and see how badly I can do in couple of rounds of crap's."

"All right. We'll see you later."

"You bet talk to you later. Oh, hey, Alex. What time are we suppose to meet Ellis for dinner?"

"I think he said 6:00 or 7:00 p.m. Let's meet back around 5:00 p.m."

"Okay." Hayden turned and walked away. He headed in the opposite direction to the middle deck. He watched Monique do a couple of dives and laps around the big pool. God she was stunning. He thought of their history, they went steady for almost two years when they were fifteen and sixteen. Then one-day Monique was whisked away to some private school. They never saw each other again until in their twenties. They tried rekindling their relationship but it was lost in the years that passed. They had casual sex on more than one occasion hoping to find what they lost, maybe spark the fire. Then the sex stopped and instead they became fast friends.

Hayden finally made it to the Golden Nugget near 2:00 p.m. the place was hopping with patrons. Worming his way into the swarm of people and over to the craps table he played three rounds, lost some coin, then headed to the Bear Claw. He would have stayed longer if the Nugget wasn't swarming.

He couldn't believe how many people were out gambling at 2:00 in the afternoon and to think the majority would be there at 4:00 a.m., especially tonight since the Nugget was staying opened until one hour before docking tomorrow. Pulling up to the bar at the Bear Claw, he ordered a beer, then another. He realised after his third that it was getting on to 4:30 p.m. Standing he exited and headed for the cabin. Monique was already showered and Alex was stepping into the bathroom, when he opened the cabin door. "Did you win any money?"

"Not a cent Alex. Not a cent."

"Well one good thing. This time tomorrow we'll know for sure if we'll all be rich." Alex said as he closed the door to the bathroom.

"How was the pool, Monique?" Hayden asked.

"Exuberant. Although the weather was chilly, the pool was warm. I don't think I could swim in it everyday. It has a lot more chlorine in it than any other pool I've swam in."

"They probably have to do that. So many different people using it and all."

"Undoubtedly. Yuck, that's why I prefer the open waters."

"I hear you. They can get dirty. Especially with people urinating and such in them." Hayden said teasingly.

"What a horrible thought."

"It's the truth though." He replied as Monique sat on her bed her nose wrinkled up.

"Thanks. I'll never swim in a pool again," she said jokingly. "By the way when do we get to meet your lady friend?"

"Lady friend?" He questioned. "What are you talking about?"

"Come on Hayden. I smelled her perfume on your clothes," she said coyly.

"All right. I have met a lady. And tonight you'll get to meet her."

"Tonight?" Monique was intrigued.

"Yup. After we meet and have dinner with Ellis. She works at the restaurant we're going to. I told her however not to serve us because the guy we were having dinner with was a womaniser. And that I didn't want him being rude to her, which he is prone to do. It protects her. Also if what I do for a living comes up I told her I was an international public affairs worker."

"Good thinking. What's her name? And Hayden, don't feel badly about you know…what we use to have. I'm glad you've found a lady friend. I hope you find happiness. It doesn't matter that you and I could never find happiness, some things aren't meant to be. I had you long before she did." Monique said teasingly with a smile.

Hayden too smiled at her remark and nodded. "Yeah, we had each other long before anyone else did. Do you think of those days?"

"Yes, I do. I also know that what we had way back when we can never have again. Anyway, what we have now is probably the greatest gift we could give each other and that's friendship. And friends want friends to find happiness and true love. That's what I wish for you."

Hayden smiled at her. She was right. They had to carry on in search for that person they wanted to spend eternity with. Fortunately for him, he already found that in Colleen. "I wish nothing less for you as well. I hope someday you also find happiness and all that comes with it."

"I will. I'll find what I'm looking for one day."

Hayden walked over to her and kissed her cheek. "We'll be pals forever Monique. Nothing will prevent that."

She looked at him and smiled. "Pals," she said as a small tear welled up in her eye. Her mind racing back to when they were teenagers sitting on the banks of the Tangera talking. Hayden had always been so polite, not like most guys who wanted one thing. He had always been gracious and never forced the sex issue with her. They had their moments too. Like the time when Hayden and his mother were fighting over the fact that he wanted to join the RRA. He called his mother a list of names and threw a few things around and then he slipped into the mountains for two days. When she found out what had gone on, she went up one side of him and down the other. She finally convinced him to return and to apologise to his mother. He never brought the RRA up again until she passed away. Other thoughts and things they did stirred in her head. Her daydreaming was interrupted as Alex stepped out of the bathroom.

"Saved you some hot water buddy if you want to have a shower."

"Thanks Alex." Retrieving clean clothes, he stepped into the steamy bathroom and showered himself. At 6:30 p.m., they headed to the bottom deck and the Pickled Onion. Sure enough, Ellis was sitting there with Red at his side. His four other henchmen were seated at a table behind him. He was wearing a nose brace his eyes were blackened. He gave Hayden a dirty look. "See what you have done to my nose."

"It looks good on you."

"You think you are pretty smart don't you? Pull up a chair and sit down. For now, I will forget about my nose. We are here to talk business and to have a celebration of sorts." The three pulled up chairs and sat down. "So here you are the three musketeers. I hope things have been going well. Hard to believe that in less than twenty-four hours we will be docking in Nome."

"It's hard to believe that in less then seventy-two hours the three of us will never have to look at you again. Except for that last time when we divvy up the loot. After that, I hope for your sake I never see you or your henchmen again nor will I ever submit to another one of your proposals." Hayden said with intent.

"I wouldn't count on that. As you go about your life, you'll soon discover it's a small world. I am sure our paths will cross again after all this is said and done." Hayden knew he was right. He might not like it or care to admit it but this yellow bastard in front after all was blood.

"Keep your dreams to yourself Ellis. I don't see the likes of you in my future. If by chance our paths do cross don't expect me to come over and shake your hand."

"I would never expect that from such an arrogant person as yourself. You remind me of your old man."

"Don't bring up my father. From what I know of you, you cheated him how many times? Not to mention Alex and Monique's father. You've cheated and back stabbed your way to the riches you now have and in the process, you screwed both of our fathers. You haven't got the right to even mention them."

"Say it's so. It doesn't matter. I have kept both of their successors alive. Or have you forgotten it is because of me you are on this ship after all. It is because of me, the three of you will soon be richer than either of your fathers ever were, or would have ever been. Perhaps I did make some poor choices in life but I had nothing to do with the death of your fathers. I may have conned them, cheated them, but I had nothing to do with their deaths. The fact that you say that insults me. But for now forget it. I asked you here to have dinner with me and too make sure we are clear on what is suppose to take place."

"We're clear. How about we get on with dinner. You repulse me and I don't like being in your presence."

"I know. You have stated your dislike for me in the past. This is more than a dinner it's a business meeting. I would hope you would demonstrate sounder manners. Our deal was you three would receive thirty percent of the entire take only if the said sum was more than sixty-four million. If the amount is only sixty-four million you will receive twenty million to divide between the three of you any way you see fit."

"That's right. Has something changed?"

"Nothing has changed Hayden. I am only trying to refresh everyone's memory. Now that I have let's order." Their table grew silent as those sitting at it looked through the menu. Hayden settled on prime rib, escargots, salad, and a baked stuffed potato. Alex ordered the New York steak and lobster as well as all the fixings. Monique ordered the seafood linguine and a Caesar salad. Requested that the seafood not be cooked in peanut oil, as she was allergic. They settled on sodas and coffees to drink rather than an expensive wine. Still, what the three of them ordered easily added a hundred and some odd bucks to Ellis's bill. Hayden could tell by the way Ellis, looked at them that he wasn't impressed. He kept his mouth shut though.

Hayden smiled at the thought that Ellis had no idea that he knew what his intentions were. He was going to have Ellis eat from each of their plates. Leaving Monique's for him to taste last. She could then order another or something else. As they sat, he scanned the floor for Colleen. He finally located her sitting behind the food warming counter gazing back at him. She smiled and waved.

Hayden nodded in her direction as inconspicuously as he could. He caught a glimpse of Monique eyeing her. Looking at Monique, he smiled. She returned his smile and nodded in a 'not bad, not bad' gesture. They sat in silence none of them saying much. Finally, their meal's arrived piping hot. The smell of it all was tantalising. Hayden purposely noticed Ellis eyeing Monique's plate. When Ellis caught Hayden looking at him his eyes evaded his. "Hold on a second Monique don't touch that, you either Alex." Hayden said as he caught them both in mid stride with their forks going to their mouths. "What's up with eyeing our food like that Ellis?"

"What the are you talking about?"

"Do you think I'm stupid. I seen how you looked our plates over."

"And that means what?"

"I have no idea. You tell me."

"I was simply admiring the cook's preparation of the food brought to us. I looked at every plate brought. You are paranoid."

"Really." Hayden cut a piece of his steak off and set it on Ellis's plate. "Eat that then."

"Whatever for?"

"Humour me," he said gesturing to the piece of prime rib on Ellis's plate.

"Very well. If it'll make you feel better."

"It will. Now go ahead." They watched as Ellis put the piece in his mouth and swallowed. Hayden did that with a piece of everything that was on his plate as well as Alex's. However, when he came to Monique's helpings Ellis suddenly became quite evasive.

"I can't stomach sea food linguini. Besides, I ate a piece of something from both yours and Alex's plate? I know what you are thinking Hayden, and I would never consider that. I need all three of you healthy and fit."

"Then I guess you'll have to find someone else to pull off this heist. Too bad for you that it's on such short notice."

"What are you trying to pull. We made a deal. You can't back out now." Ellis responded with exasperation. He knew that he was going to be forced to eat something from Monique's plate. He could only hope that he didn't get too sick with the trots. He contemplated standing up and leaving in a huff but that would certainly prove his guilt. He sat there waiting for Hayden's response.

"We made a deal all right. But if you recall a conversation, we had. You owe us nothing, as we owe you nothing. We are free and clear with you. We agreed to this proposal not as a favour to you or because we owe you anything but for the money. The way I see it, you either eat some linguini or we're through. I mean really. So what, if you don't like linguini. I'm sure you'd eat something worse for perhaps say forty-four million." Hayden replied. "Now go ahead, eat up."

"Whatever. Give me some of that linguini. I'd like to get on with what's on my plate." Ellis didn't care at that point if he got the trots or not, it was no different from waking up with a hangover and sour stomach. Plus he was counting on Monique to eat it. The two of them might be sick for a day or two, big deal. Red would then be with Hayden and Alex and he'd have his insurance that they would return.

Hayden scooped up a fork full of Monique's linguini and slopped it on Ellis's plate. He looked at Hayden with hatred and disgust. Hayden smiled. When he put the last bit in his mouth Ellis smiled back. "There are you satisfied? Go ahead Monique there is nothing wrong with your linguini." He said with hope.

"I think not. I'll feel safer if she orders another."

"Why would I want to do that, Hayden? He ate some of it and I'm hungry." Monique spoke out. He looked at her and shook his head.

"Trust me Monique. Order something else." He used a tone in his voice that he knew she was familiar with. The tone that told her, he knew something she didn't. "I have a feeling someone may have done something to your linguini. You see I've seen you eat linguini before Ellis and when you said you didn't like it something clicked."

"I said I didn't like seafood linguini."

"My mistake. Go ahead Monique order again."

"You..." Ellis began.

Hayden could swear that there was steam coming out of his ears. He and he alone had turned a plus for Ellis into a minus. "Whoa, what's the matter. What do you care if she orders again?" Hayden asked as a matter-of-fact.

"I don't care. She is quite welcome to do so. Go ahead Monique feel free." Ellis said knowing now that he was going to be the only one sick. Hayden called his bluff—he had outfoxed him this time.

Alex and Hayden were finishing their steaks when Monique's second order came. "Thank you." she said to the waitress who set her plate down. "It smell's good." The waitress nodded and pranced away.

Hayden put the last piece of steak into his mouth and savoured its flavour. "Man that was excellent. Thanks for the treat." He said with hubris.

"I hope you enjoyed it." Ellis snootily replied.

Hayden looked at him and nodded with a big devilish grin. "I did." A few minutes later Ellis and his men left the Pickled Onion he paid on his way out looked back at Hayden and glared menacingly. Then he turned and disappeared. It was almost closing time when the three of them finished with their coffees. They left another tip for the waitress, stood, and headed for the exit. On their way out Hayden introduced Colleen to his friends. Alex looked dumb founded.

"How come…what, why didn't I know about this? That's where you've been slipping off. I must be blind as a bat I hadn't a clue you found yourself a little honey," he said nudging Hayden with a big smile. "It's certainly nice to meet you, umm 'Colleen'…it is, right?" Alex asked.

"Yes, that's right. It has been nice meeting you as well. And you too Monique."

Monique smiled, "It's nice meeting you Colleen, too bad we weren't introduced earlier. Hayden is a bit of a stickler. Anyway, I'm sure you two would like some time alone. Come on Alex let's leave these two love birds alone." Monique said with sincerity and approval. Hayden caught Alex looking back at Colleen, checking her out both up and down. Hayden smiled and shook his head as brother and sister disappeared down the galley leading to the stairs.

"Your friends are nice."

"Yeah, they are the best friends I've ever had."

"Thanks for introducing us. I appreciate it. What should we do tonight? It might be the last time we see each other for a while."

"I know. Rest assured I'm going to do my best to be back onboard before…before you leave port. What do you say Colleen would you like to take a walk on deck and talk some?" Hayden asked.

"Yes…yes lets do that."

"Fifteen."

Ellis had been sitting on the toilet since returning to his cabin after having dinner with Hayden and his associates the night before. The waste paper basket was now between his legs, sometimes he was plagued with the trots other times he had to puke. He was in desperate shape. His only thought as he sat there his rectum a ring-of-fire, was the cash he'd have in the next couple of days. That alone made up for the agony his gut was in. He felt this way on more then one occasion. This was the first time it was caused by food poisoning. Usually it was from the amount of booze he consumed when he drank.

He was bitter towards Hayden. Yet, at the same time he admired him. He outwitted him, fouled his plan. Now, there was no insurance, that, the three of them would return. All he could hang on to was Hayden's word. Ellis thought about this as he reached over and opened the little porthole window to let some air into the bathroom. His own stink was making him queasy. He had even flushed a few times.

The effort he to use to open the window made his stomach burble and wrench with contractions. He didn't even have to push, the cold water splashed up tickling his balls. At the same time he leaned forward and upchucked into the garbage can between his legs on the floor. *Thank God, for that,* he thought. He wasn't sure if he was getting better or worse. He was in and out of the john all night. Finally deciding at 6:00 a.m., to sit on the throne until he was certain he was done.

Cleaning himself up after being held hostage to the bathroom for the past two hours, he exited the foul-smelling room. He pulled up to the table holding his stomach. He had nothing left to expel and now he was experiencing painful stomach cramps. He found it uncomfortable sitting on the hard wooden chair his rectum screaming with strain. It felt as though he had severe case of hemorrhoids. Standing he wobbled over to the bed and rested.

***

The three rose at 8:30 that morning on the final leg of their journey. The Hilroy was due to dock at 2:00 p.m. In the distance they could see land as the Bering Sea closed in between the domain of Kivak at the north-east tip of the country of Russia and the continent of Alaska. They were getting closer to the Bering Strait, the Arctic Ocean and freedom. The air even smelled different this distance east. Hayden longed now more than ever to step on to solid ground. The three-week cruise had definitely been tenacious and wearying. "Look at that, isn't it beautiful?" Monique was referring to the land they could now see.

"It certainly is. I can hardly wait until we dock. It's been a long haul and I long for solid ground."

"I hear you. I can't wait either. What about you Alex how do you feel knowing this trip is soon going to end?" Monique questioned.

"I feel fine. I'm getting antsy about the Navy Blue and it's riches. I wish I were in Nome right now checking it out. I guess another five hours to freedom and all that cash isn't as bad as five days though. I feel good guy's I really do." The three stood in silence looking back in the direction they had come. Back there, way back there was the country they left behind and all its stupid little domains. Alex was once this far and even then he had been captured and returned to Russia. They knew they weren't out of the CPA's reach yet. Not until they were in Canada, maybe then they would at last find the freedom they were looking for. To be this close was the greatest feeling ever. It was true that the CPA might even pop up in Alaska they had before. They felt certain this time however that once they pulled the heist off—if they could they'd never look back nor would they ever get mixed up with the likes of Ellis Leroy again.

They retreated to the open food court on their deck and pulled up to a table that looked eastward in the direction of Alaska and the days rising sun. They ordered a round of coffees, bacon and eggs, some toast and three large glasses of OJ. The wind blew softly as the three ate their breakfast bringing with it the scent of the Arctic and the industrialised world. Hayden noticed a couple of killer whales swimming in the distance and he smiled. *That's freedom,* he thought.

Swilling the last of their coffee, the three retreated to their cabin to prepare themselves for when they docked. They had to look as casual as possible. The FBI and other US government agencies were constantly watching the port in Nome. They were always on the look out for defector's, criminals, and other type's of riffraff that used the port as a gateway to the US and Canada. And they did fit into one of those categories.

The passports and ID's they got from Ellis had worked so far, but who was to say how the US would look at them? Hayden had to admit that Ellis did an exceptional job on them. He used photos that he somehow obtained from their personal folders. Hayden sat there thinking of the whole little ploy Ellis managed to contrive to keep Monique onboard and he wondered how he was feeling. He was hoping that he was sicker than a dog puking his guts out. Hayden wished upon him tenfold on how Monique would've been feeling had his plot played out. Chuckling softly, he looked over to Alex and Monique. "How do you guys figure our old friend Ellis is feeling today?"

"I was going to ask you what that was all about. Fill us in."

"That's right. I didn't tell you guys did I?"

"No. Now, that you mention it. It slipped my mind completely, I guess I've been preoccupied, so what was all that about?" asked Monique. He explained to them that he inadvertently came across a plan on how Ellis was going to make Monique sick. In order to have Red tag along instead, so that Ellis had some kind of assurance that they'd return. He filled them in also about the fact that Ellis was tripping out over the possibility that somebody with the initials of AF was onboard.

Alex began to laugh, "That's why he asked if I sent him a drink? Excellent, boy could we play with his head."

"Indeed we could, we should, and we will. I can't believe he was trying to make me sick. What an asshole."

"As long as we never let him know that we know what he's been up to and what he is afraid of then I think he'll be looking over his back for years to come. That in itself is going to wreak havoc with him." Hayden replied. "Let's talk about what lays ahead."

"You said you can get us some new arms once we get to Nome from one of our RRA contacts."

"Yeah, that's right. But only if the letter Pete sent is there. He didn't give me the location on the RRA's depot when I spoke with him. Instead, we decided he'd send a letter with the information to the Viscount Motel in Nome under the name of Ryce Lennskov. I'm afraid if the letter isn't there then we might be out of luck, Alex."

"I don't know about that. What kinds of weaponry do you suppose we should look into? I'm partial to Glocks especially if we can get them silenced or a few higher capacity submachine pistols. Maybe a couple of tear-gas grenades or something along that line. What do you two suggest?"

"I like the idea about the weapons you've mentioned but I think we better also pick up a sniping rifle. Not necessarily an M-40 but maybe a PSG-1 Heckler & Koch they are pretty much silent and are quite effective. I guess it's all going to depend on what's available. I say definitely small arms we don't need to cause a commotion. Or start world war three. Anything larger would be suicidal to our objective. Which is get on, get the cash, get off, and slip into the void. We want to be as silent and stealthily as possible."

"I'm curious to know, how many stacks of one hundred and five hundred-dollar bills equal sixty-four-million? We can't even figure it out mathematically without knowing how many of each there is. Could it be that half of it is in one-hundred-dollar bills and the other half five-hundred-dollar bills. Even if it is half and half that's a lot of cash to walk off with." Monique tossed into the mix.

"That's a bit off topic. But a good question, we haven't even thought of that." Hayden did some quick calculations. "I know this much it'll take three hundred thousand, one-hundred-dollar bills to make up thirty million and sixty thousand five-hundred-dollar bills to make up the other thirty million that doesn't include how many of each dollar will make up the other four million. We could safely say that it is sixty four hundred stacks. And that's a lot of paper. What we can't do is guess how much that might weigh."

"It's definitely going to take some doing but if we can pull it off we will." Alex replied. He was right, if they could, they would. They talked back and forth like that until the last three hours of the voyage was upon them and they crossed the International Date Line. Then they headed to the deck again to watch the horizon and land of the free come into view. As they approached the Bering Strait there were a number of other ships pulling in or pulling out heading in opposite directions and clouding the sky with exhaust and filling the air with the scent of diesel. Hayden's heart was jittery with anticipation as the Hilroy pulled into the Strait and headed north towards the Arctic and Nome Alaska. The jagged shoreline was scattered with indigenous trees and rock bluffs that went on forever. It was beautiful. Alaska was to their bow and Kivak would soon be at their stern. An hour later they approached the port of Nome and their freedom. They stood on deck and looked on as the Hilroy glided inland.

The port was full of people boarding while others were meeting their relatives and taxi's. The line-up to the docking terminals where their passports and other documentation would be looked at was backed up for an hour before they finally made their way to one. Hayden was nervous and beads of sweat formed on his brow he could hear and feel his heart as it beat faster and faster. Taking a couple of deep breaths, he proceeded over to one of the gates. Alex and Monique were behind him by four people. He wasn't sure how either one of them felt. If the Customs Officers suspected that their ID's were counterfeit, they'd be in deep. They wouldn't be able to explain who they were or what they were doing so far east of Russia with fake ID's.

"May I see your passport, sir? And what is your purpose for visiting Nome Alaska, in the United States of America?" The officer asked as Hayden reached for his passport and other pertinent information.

"Yes, sir," he began as he handed the papers to him. "I'm here on vacation to take some photographs. I hear the bear population this year is phenomenal?" The officer kept starring at his passport nodding his head as he spoke.

"The Kodiaks always seem to steal the show," he flipped to the next page of the passport, "there is more to do in Nome than take pictures of the bears." He looked up to Hayden. "How long are you expecting to visit the United States?"

"Ten to fifteen days."

The man continued to gaze upon him, "Enjoy your stay Mr. Lennskov." He said as he finally looked back to Hayden's passport and stamped it. Handing it back he smiled and nodded. Hayden's heart beat fast as he made it to the off ramp and onto US soil. Here he was in the good old U.S.A. with his passport stamped and freedom at his fingertips. He waited for Alex and Monique at one of the restaurants to the left of the off ramp. Streams of people milled around waiting for taxi's, friends, and busses to take them wherever it was they were destined for. It seemed like hours and he was getting a bit concerned when finally he saw Monique and then Alex. Exiting the little café, he met them outside.

"We've made it," he held out his hand for high fives.

"No present danger near or far shall leave upon me a single scar," replied Monique as she smacked the palm of his hand.

"Ooh-yeah." said Alex with a grin from ear to ear. The three of them stood there together for the first time in a free country. It brought tears to Monique's eyes, while all Hayden could do is smile. Alex inhaled deeply. "This is freedom friends. Doesn't it smell awe-inspiring?" Monique and Hayden nodded at him.

"That it does Alex, that it does."

"I can't believe we're here. My God we're here. We're as free as we want to be. It's totally exhilarating."

"I agree. I feel quite exhilarated too." Hayden inhaled deeply as though it would be his last breath.

"Let's get ourselves organised. The Viscount Motel is over one block. You should head over there and see if that letter has made it. Monique and I will try and scoop us a hotel room for the night say the one nearest the Navel Base I think it is called the Viewpoint." Alex began as he looked quickly through the pamphlet he had on hotels. "Yup, that's what she's called, the Viewpoint Hotel. That's where we'll meet whether or not we can secure a room. What do you guy's say?"

"Works for me." Hayden said.

"Perfect. Do you want us to take your gear?"

"Sure." He handed Alex his backpack. "What street is the Viewpoint on?"

"Hang on," Alex flipped to the page again, "okay its on Goldsmith and Naval Port."

"All right, I'll meet you guy's there as soon as I can." Hayden turned and walked away. A few minutes later he was walking up the walkway to the Viscount. He approached the lady behind the counter and asked if anything for Ryce Lennskov had arrived.

The lady looked at him. "Are you a guest in the Viscount?" She questioned.

"No ma'am I'm not. An associate of mine wrongly addressed a letter to me from Vuctin. I'm here in Nome doing research for a UN affiliate. It's rather an important letter and is quite relevant to the work I'm doing." He handed her his ID and passport.

"Say's here you got into port less then an hour ago."

"That's correct ma'am. The correspondences my associates and I have had were while I was at sea on the Hilroy. You see ma'am at first my UN Affiliates here in Nome were going to put me up here at the Viscount but a change of plans occurred that I'm not able to get into. It has nothing to do with the Viscount rather a location problem." Hayden explained hoping.

"The name this letter is addressed to is Ryce Lennskov?"

"That's correct ma'am."

"Hang on a second I'll check."

Thank you ma'am." Hayden watched as the lady entered a back room.

"How was that name spelled again?"

"That's Ryce Lennskov, spelled LENNSKOV, first name Ryce, spelled RYCE." He replied. A few minutes passed.

"Here you go." She handed Hayden the envelope.

"Thank you, ma'am. I appreciate it." Turning he smiled and exited the Viscount. He couldn't believe that the letter was there. Pete only sent it a week before they boarded the Hilroy. He walked the distance over to Goldsmith and Port. The Viewpoint Hotel was situated looking out over the Bering Sea and the Nome Navel Port. The port was probably a quarter of a mile away from the Hotel but you could easily see it from there. He found Alex and Monique in the lobby. With news that they managed to get a double room. It was one of the last available.

"Did Pete's letter make it?" asked Alex.

"It did. Let's head to the room and get this thing off the ground." Hayden followed Alex and Monique up a flight of stairs and down a hallway to room twelve. It was a spacious room boasting of a four-piece bathroom, two double beds, a couch, a desk, and a TV stand that held a twenty-seven inch coloured television. "Nicer then the cabin back on the Hilroy eh?"

"Check out the tub it's one of those fancy ones with jets. I can't wait to use it," said Monique. The three sat down on the beds and Hayden opened the envelope to reveal the location of their RRA contact. "It's at a warehouse on Billings and Seaside number 212. The name of the guy is Heneric Otto. Ever hear of him before?"

"Heneric Otto, nope. But if Pete says that's the guy's name then that's the guy's name. As for that address, it sounds to me like the same one the RRA has been at for the last while. I thought Pete told you the address changed?"

"He did. I don't know what's up with that why would he say that if it hadn't?"

"Hold on a second. You said Billings and Seaside right? The old address, Alex, was Bingham and Oceanway." Monique replied.

"That's right too. Good thing one of us remembered. I was thinking one of our own might have made mistake. Or was setting us up. You're right Monique. It was Bingham and Oceanway. As for Heneric Otto, I've never heard of him. The RRA and all it's associates are growing in numbers. I guess that's who we talk to."

"I say all three of us head over. I think I passed a street named Billings on my way here. All we have to do is look for Seaside. Are you guys into it? It shouldn't take us long then we can recoup here until our assault tomorrow night." Hayden said as he looked at his watch. "It's only going onto 4:00 p.m. What do you say?"

"Lets do it," they replied.

They exited the Hotel and headed back towards the port. Nome was a beautiful place at this time of year. The locals called it the land of the midnight sun and they knew this was one of the dilemma's that they would be faced with when the time came for them to strike. Whether the evenings got dark or not people had to sleep and that was their niche. They walked three blocks when they came to the street sign they were looking for.

Following the street westward for another block and a half, they turned down Seaside. The street led them along a steep grade that headed back towards the sea and to a bunch of warehouses and older buildings. It was in the old part of Nome and the streets looked a lot like the streets in Lengstin. Not to say that they were littered with garbage like Lengstin, rather they were built the same, made out of wood and above ground. They were built that way for the same reason in Lengstin and that was because of rain and mud.

The few people they passed smiled and waved as they happened by. Walking on those streets of freedom for the first time in his life, Hayden felt no remorse for what he did or saw in his past. It was the 'turning over a new leaf mentality,' that made him want nothing more than to get on with the objective and the freedom that waited.

A short while later, they approached the dirty building of 212 Billings and Seaside. It sat alone divided by an empty building and adjacent to a shoe repair shop. The dirty door looked cleaned compared to the dirty dark-age ridden building. The window in the door was covered with a piece of cardboard and it read, out of business. They knocked a couple of times until an old greying man answered their beckoning. The odour from inside as it billowed out was musty with a scent of gunpowder and oil, a smell the three of them were familiar with.

"Yes. Can I help you?" The old man questioned as he opened the door leaving it chained from the inside.

"Are you Heneric Otto?" The old man looked at Hayden quizzically and closed the door. They were made to wait a few more minutes until the door opened for the second time. This time they were greeted by a younger version of the old man, it was obvious he was the old man's son.

"What do you want with Heneric Otto?" He questioned the door still chained.

"Pete from Vuctin sends his regards." Hayden said. The young man continued looking at the three of them. Then he undid the chain and invited them in.

"Come in. If you know Pete then we're in business. You all ready know my name, before we go further what are your names?"

"I'm Hayden Rochsoff this is Monique and Alex Farell brother and sister I might add. We represent the RRA."

"I'll have to check on that. Excuse me and please help yourself to a seat. Beware that if you aren't who you say you are you'll have one chance to get out of here or you'll be buried at sea." Heneric slipped into an adjoining room.

"Nice guy." Hayden said.

"It's called business. Once he finds out that we are who say we are, he'll lighten up. You can never be too careful in this line of work."

"I know Alex. He's doing his job and I'm God awful happy he does it this tight. If we didn't have connections with guys like him we'd be screwed." The back door opened and Heneric approached.

"All right you guys are cleared. Follow me," he said gesturing to them. They followed Heneric to the furthest back room in the large warehouse. "What are you people in need of?"

"What do you have on the menu?" asked Monique as she looked at the rows and rows of shelving stuffed with boxes and crates that filled the room.

"Likely anything you might need. I have Glocks, M-40s, M-16s a few M-60s. I have inflatable rafts equipped with the best Mercury Outboard engines that they can be retrofitted with. I have grenades and pee shooters. I have a two man light assault helicopter that can be assembled between twelve and fifteen hours. It's equipped with one air to ground missile, an M-16 with over two thousand rounds and a grenade launcher boasting fifty impact grenades.

It's an early 1990's model but quite the little machine. It can hold as much gear as a modern SUV with two passengers. It's as easy as one, two, three to operate and quite dependable. It's also equipped with a reserve tank that can keep it in the air for almost a hundred miles after the initial tank runs dry. We did something near four hundred miles before we had to switch tanks when we transported it. All in all, it can remain in flight for five hundred sky miles on one refuelling. It is a bit unstable in traverse winds, but it is as easy as pie to land. It can be equipped with either floats or landing skids. That's about all I can say about the helicopter. Getting back to arms I have probably anything you want."

"That helicopter sounds like something else what does that run?"

"Near seventy five thousand USD. Are you interested?"

"No, no. Curious is all. What about Heckler & Koch PSG sniper rifles you got anything like that?"

"I have ten on hand, plus thirty thousand rounds. I have Glocks as well. I have six Calicos but not many rounds until my next shipment. Are you looking for something that's accurate and silent? If so your best solution would definitely be the PSG-1, I have a couple of silenced Desert Eagle's as well and they pack an unfriendly punch. The good thing about those is I have nearly five hundred rounds for them and they are all armour piercing."

They settled on two Desert Eagles and one hundred rounds of armour piercing stopping power, a PSG-1 sniper rifle, and ten clips with thirty rounds. They purchased three tear gas grenades, a GPS, rope, and one inflatable raft equipped with life jackets. The cost was $12,000.00 they paid with an RRA monetary resource that only Alex could activate. They paid an extra $2000.00 out of their own pockets to have the dinghy inflated and waiting for them at a designated area.

Heneric drew them out a map on where the dinghy would be located. It was near the Viewpoint Hotel not easily seen from land or sea. They'd have to descend a rock bluff. But it was easy going according to Heneric. As long as they picked it up before high tide the next night, it would stay docked on the rocky shore. If they didn't make it by then chances were good they would be out the cash they paid for the thing. Not to mention any chance of looking over the Navy Blue before they converged on it.

"What time exactly is high-tide?" asked Alex.

"She'll be here tomorrow night before 10:00 p.m. And gone again by 3:00 maybe 4:00 a.m. I suggest docking once the tides gone. Trying to dock a Zodiac while the Bering is clashing against the rocky shore would be suicidal to say the least. You either have to leave by then or be done with whatever it is you need to do.

The life jackets supplied with the vessel have homing devices that are activated by being in water for a couple of hours. If, you fall over or something like that rest-assure after a couple of hour's help will be on its way namely me. If you're dead all I retrieve is the jacket and you'll be buried at sea. In other words, if you're dead I don't retrieve your body. Nor do I notify anybody. If that is all then I'd say our business, is done. Gentlemen, ma'am, please follow me out."

Heneric lead them back to the door and handed them their purchases. The PSG was in a plastic carrying case and unassembled, the Desert Eagles were in shoulder holsters. The ammo for each was in another case as were the three grenades and GPS, along with the hundred and some odd feet of rope. Hayden looked at it all and wondered how they were going to cross town with it. "I don't suppose there's a taxi we can use? This is a lot to carry across town."

"Not to worry we already have a car waiting for you. It'll take you wherever it is your going providing it's in Nome." Heneric chuckled.

"Thanks a lot. You've been quite hospitable. I'll make sure Pete hears how well you treated us and if we ever have to do business again I'll look forward to it." Hayden said as he reached out his hand and shook Heneric's. Alex and Monique followed suit.

"Yeah it has been quite favourable Heneric, we and the RRA appreciate your support." Alex said.

Heneric nodded and opened the door. "The old man will take you from here. Be careful guys and I wish you well," he said as he closed and locked the door. They loaded up their gear into the back of the big Chevy Suburban then took up their seats, Monique and Hayden sat in the back while Alex and the old man sat up front. The old guy never spoke much other than to ask where he was taking them.

"To the Viewpoint Hotel." Alex replied.

"Ah yes, near the naval shipyard. That's a very nice hotel probably one of the better ones here in Nome. We, should be there in a few minutes." They arrived back at the Hotel five minutes later. "Here we are." The old man said as he pulled to the curb. The threesome unloaded their purchases and then thanked the old guy. He nodded and waved good-bye as he drove away.

"Let's get inside and out of view." Monique said as she turned and proceeded to the Hotel's entrance. Alex and Hayden followed close by carrying the few items. Once in their room they tossed the cases onto the bed and went through their purchases one last time.

Hayden put the PSG together— took it apart, and put it back together again. Until he was confident that he could have it put together and ready to fire in less than twenty-five seconds it was the quickest time he ever put a weapon together. It exemplified one of the things he liked about the PSG-1, simplicity. "I did it that time in under twenty two seconds," he boasted.

"That beats Alex's old time. Congrats."

"Twenty two seconds?" Questioned Alex in awe, "How long does it take you to disassemble it and then assemble it? Cause I've never been beat doing that. Go ahead time yourself." Alex dared him. He knew that Alex's time was somewhere between twenty-six and forty seconds for the whole feat chances were he'd never beat that. But, he was in a good mood and figured they could use some entertainment.

"All right. What should our wager be?"

"No wager I just want to see how quick you can pull that off."

"What, no wager. That's boring come on put something up." Hayden teased. He was prepared to offer whatever Alex did.

Alex smiled his unique smile and looking at Hayden, he said, "I've never gambled anything but my own life ever. If I'm going to I'm going to gamble big," he began smiling, "say one-million bucks from my share of the kitty or from yours. I'll even give you three chances."

Hayden smiled with amusement. "Wow, for a guy who has never gambled that's a big chunk but hey I'm up to it." He chuckled. He knew there was no way he could beat Alex's time but for a million bucks, he was going to give it his best effort.

"I want in on this little wager as well. I bet I can do it faster than either of you." Monique replied daringly. "I'll bet a million bucks too."

"Come on Monique you can't be serious?"

"Why is that?" She asked with humour. "You guy's aren't afraid are you?" She chuckled. Alex and Hayden looked at one another and shrugged.

"Okay. You're on. And since you're a lady we'll let you go first." Hayden handed her the PSG-1 already assembled. What she had to do was disassemble it and assemble it. She had three chances to beat her first time if she chose. She looked over the weapon for a few seconds then she nodded.

"All right, Alex are you ready to keep time?"

"Sure thing. On your mark, get set, go." They watched as Monique quickly took the gun apart and as quickly put it back together. Hayden was totally shocked at how fluent she completed the task not to mention at how little time it took her.

"Done," she said as she slammed the clip into place. Alex's eyebrows were raised as he looked at her time again.

"You did that in only forty-three point five seconds. That's amazing, I don't think I can even come close to that," replied Alex with sincerity.

"What do you mean forty-three point five seconds? Are you sure about that?" Hayden was dumbfounded.

"She did it in forty-three point five seconds. No fooling, can you believe that?"

"That's the quickest I've ever seen that done. How did you manage to pull that off?" Hayden asked quizzically.

"I don't know it seemed easy. Maybe all that training in the RRA is beginning to have an effect."

"Do you want to try and beat that time? Remember you're allowed three chances to beat your initial time." Alex reminded her.

"No, I'm happy with that. I figure forty-three point five seconds is going to be hard for either of you to beat," she said with contentment as she handed Hayden the rifle. She was right. Hayden tried three times to beat her but the nearest he was able to get was forty-seven seconds. Alex did it in a little less time something like forty-six point eight or some ridiculous decimal. She definitely out done them and deserved the million bucks a piece that Alex and Hayden now owed her. After all the excitement and name calling died down she retreated to the tub for a hot bath. Hayden headed over to the couch and stretched out in front of the big TV. Alex laid on one of the beds reading The O'Brien Series the book Hayden picked up on the Hilroy. "How is that book anyway?" He asked.

"Not bad. The characters seem real enough. You know they seem quite human. It lacks a few things. But, I guess that's why there is a second part. Which I'll definitely buy if I ever see it," he replied as he turned the page. Hayden looked back towards the TV and continued surfing. In minutes, he was fast asleep. Their first day of freedom had ended.

"Sixteen."

Saturday July 3, Hayden awoke from the couch his body aching from being twisted like a pretzel all night. He wouldn't have been so achy if the couch was another foot or so long. It was definitely not made for anyone over six-foot. Walking into the bathroom, his legs full of pins and needles he looked into the mirror. He needed a shave and his hair was strewn across the top of his head making him look like a punk rocker from Europe. Turning on the shower he reached for and gathered his toothbrush, razor, and shampoo. He then stepped into the soothing warm water. He was in the shower for a couple of minutes when he heard a tap-tap on the bathroom door.

"Hayden what are you doing?"

"What do you mean? I'm in the shower."

"The thing is it's only 3:00 a.m., man."

"What do you mean? The sun is out." He heard Alex chuckling from the other side of the door. "What's so funny?" he asked.

"Did you forget we're in Alaska. It's always stays light out in the summer."

He completely forgot about that. He opened the shower curtain and looked at his watch on the bathroom vanity. Sure enough, it was only 3:05 a.m. He burst out laughing at his stupidity. He couldn't believe it. He thought he was having his usual morning shower at his usual morning time of 8:00 a.m., when in fact it was five hours away. Alex was already back to sleep when he finished. He decided to take an early morning walk.

Stepping out into the early twilight, he proceeded around to the Hotels courtyard. He had a perfect view of the bashing Bering Sea as it collided banefully against the rocky shoreline. He could see a flock of sea bird's as they circled the dark cold water swooping down on schools of fish that were obviously near the surface. If he listened, he could vaguely make out their calls above the sound of crashing waves. Looking towards the Nome Naval Port he could see the big ship the Navy Blue. It's presence like a menacing temptation. Even from where he stood the ship looked extraordinary. He wondered exactly how colossal it would be up close and personal.

***

Back on the Hilroy, Ellis was changing his second pair of skivvies that he soiled. His gut gnawed and churned, his rectum contracted painfully every time he tried to move. He was cursing Hayden and the others now more than ever. It had already been 24 hours and the runs hadn't stopped, he was relieved the puking slowed, but he'd rather be doing that then constantly soiling his skivvies.

He wondered what Cookie put into Monique's linguini and how much longer he was going to feel that way. He had been ill before but never like this. He would take the most severe hangover he ever had—over the way he was feeling now. Lying back down onto his bed, he tried pitifully to fall asleep. He hadn't slept for more than five hours since being ill and now his deprived body ached for it but every time he got comfortable enough his gut burbled and wrenched making him careen in agony.

***

Hayden stood peering out at the sea and back again to the Navy Blue. He knew now what Heneric meant when he said that they had to be done with the Zodiac by this time and if they weren't to stay out at sea until the tide parted. The way the dark cold waves of the Bering Sea transgressed the shoreline a Zodiac dinghy could never withstand the Herculean force. Looking at his watch, he noted the time to be 4:30 a.m. The sun was beginning to cast shadows on the rocky shore below as it emerged fuller. It was weird how both the sun and moon occupied the pale blue sky at the same time and Hayden shook his head. It was only 4:30, *I guess that's why they call Alaska the land of the sun,* he thought. Winter would be something else the sun never shone then and Alaska was constantly shrouded in darkness.

Turning he walked back to the Hotel, the café was opening for breakfast and he stopped in. He ordered bacon and eggs, coffee, OJ and whole-wheat toast. The café was pleasant enough and the people seemed friendly. The smells emitting from the kitchen were that of bacon, and coffee, every now and then you'd get a whiff of tangy ketchup or cigarette smoke. There was an old AM radio station playing in the background hosted by an Inuit DJ. Hayden could tell by his accent. It was a good station.

The DJ who went by the call name of E.Skimo cracked jokes constantly between songs causing the few people who were seated in the café to laugh. Some of the music was focused on the Inuit people of the region, he didn't understand any of the words, but the beat was consolatory. He finished his breakfast and ordered another coffee so that he could sit and listen, to E. Skimo finish the program.

When he made it back to the hotel room, Alex and Monique were still fast asleep. He quietly slid onto the couch and turned the TV on. He watched the early morning news until 8:00 a.m., when Monique and Alex finally began to stir. "Good morning sleepy and dopey." he said.

"We might be sleepy but you definitely take the cake in being dopey, having a shower at 3:00 a.m.," Alex said as he chuckled.

Monique looked over to Hayden with her dreary eyes and raised her brow. "Oh do tell." Alex explained to her how Hayden got up and showered at 3:00 a.m. because it was light out and he figured it was later than it actually was. Monique broke out laughing looking at Hayden and shaking her head.

"What can I say? I truly thought it was closer to 8:00 a.m., it was light enough out." He joined them in laughing at his misadventure.

"Did you go back to sleep, or what?"

"Nah. I went out to the courtyard, had breakfast, then came back here and watched the early news."

"You must be tired?"

"Not really," he said. He yearned-for the day to go fast so that they could get on with their next task, checking out the Navy Blue and drafting their assault. There wasn't much to do until then. They spent the majority of the day in anticipation of what was to come.

At 8:00 p.m., they were descending the rock bluffs to where Heneric stashed the Zodiac. Climbing down the bluffs on occasion was treacherous but after a few minutes, they were standing next to the four-man dinghy. Their legs and elbows took a beating from the sharp jagged rocks they climbed down, but, other than that, they weren't any worse for wear. They uncovered the Zodiac from the bramble it was concealed with. After they managed to get it into the water it took one pull for the motor to fire up and seconds later they were out at sea.

The threesome coursed their way along the shoreline staying hidden as much as possible in the shadows cast by the enormous rock bluffs. There were a few other boats out and about none of them even gave them a second glance as they glided by. Coming around the last pinnacle before the Naval Base they could see exactly how prodigious the ship really was. Compared to it they were a mere dot in a world of large.

"That's a big ship." Monique said as Hayden opened the sniper rifle case to grab the 10X scope. He scoped in on the big ship and from what he could see, it was well guarded. There were four large towers. Two were at the bow and two at the stern he could only speculate that the men inside were armed. Each tower was probably the size of an apartment. How many men each tower housed was beyond him. There were gunmen strategically inserted at different viewpoints he could tell that they were armed with M-60s and surface to air missiles.

He looked along the top deck but because of the height, he wasn't able to see exactly what the deck consisted of. He could only see the helicopter pad and one chopper. "There are four towers that I can see as well as one whirlybird. There are gunmen posted all over the place and they're packing heavy heat. I'm talking M-60's and surface to air missiles. It's going to be difficult getting past all that."

He scoped back along the area where they saw the ladder in the picture of the big ship. It was there except five or six armed men were observing it. They weren't nearly as well armed as the others. "The ladder we noticed in that picture Alex is still there. The thing is five or six men guard it. I'm afraid though that's the safest and most feasible way onboard." He handed Alex the scope as he took the controls to the Zodiac so that Alex could have a look himself.

"Yeah, that is going to be difficult. I can't imagine the guards are on alert like that all night. I say we dock this dinghy near here somewhere and hold up until later. Maybe after the guards change over there will be fewer men. I don't know what else to do. There is no way we can get passed that many armed men."

"Let me take a look." Monique said as she reached for the scope. Alex handed it to her as Hayden slowly turned the dinghy and headed inland. "Hold up Hayden, hold up." Slowing the dinghy down he waited for her response.

"What's up?"

"Did you guys happen to see the cargo door that sits between the bow and stern down near the bottom of the hull? If we can get through that, we'd be in. It would also be an excellent spot to retrieve the goods."

"How would we get through a door like that. We haven't any C-4 to blast it. Besides, those doors only open from the inside." Hayden replied.

"If you can get us closer I'd be able to confirm that. It looks to me like there is a big handle on the outside. Check it out," she said as she handed the scope back. Hayden looked near the bottom and finally came across the door she was speaking of.

"It does to. There is a big handle on the outside. Maybe we can get in through there. Here Alex take a look." He took the controls again.

"Pull back Hayden. I spotted one of the ship personnel scope in on us. Make it look like were fishing or something," Alex put the scope between his legs. Hayden turned the Zodiac nonchalantly inland and proceeded in that direction until they were once again hidden in the shadows cast by the bluffs. Looking back through the scope Alex looked along the hull and to the big door again in time to see it open and another Zodiac approaching fast. "Jesus Christ we have company coming head for shore. We have to ditch this vessel and take for cover." Hayden gunned the Zodiac full bore and headed towards an inlet. The shadows from the bluffs obscured them and they were able to dock the dinghy two minutes later. The three of them used all their energy they could muster to carry it a short distance up the shore and ditch it behind some rocks. Then they headed for cover themselves. They could here the engine from the Navy zodiac that now began a constant vigil of regulating the shoreline.

"What now?" asked Monique.

"I don't know. What do you say Hayden?"

Hayden peered through the scope and looked towards the Navy zodiac that was afloat, a short distance from shore. There were four men onboard and they were scouting out the shoreline. He didn't know if they were looking for them particularly or if this was all part of their routine. Hayden looked again towards the Navy Blue and sighted in on the cargo door. It remained opened and guarded of course by half a dozen men in Navy Uniforms. "Want to go for a swim. The cargo door is wide opened." He said half joking.

"You might be onto something," Alex began.

"What? I was only kidding."

"Hear me out for a minute. If we could get them to come to shore we could subdue them and take their zodiac then head for the ship wearing their garb. It would get us close enough to get in that door."

"This can work we just have to think it out. It's brilliant Alex. We'd have to keep one of them conscious cause there is four of them and only three of us, and I'm sure those men guarding the door can count. Our cover would be blown and they'd be on high alert as soon as they saw that only three people were returning."

They discussed the idea for a couple minutes then acted. They decided Monique would be their best bet in getting the Naval Officers attention. She stripped down to her bra and panties, from a distance it looked like she was wearing a bikini. She walked the short distance from where they took cover to the shore and began waving at the officers and yelling. Finally, she was spotted, waving now more vigorously she hollered for help, telling the officers that she was stranded and that her dinghy capsized. It only took a few minutes before they approached. As soon as they docked their zodiac to offer help, Hayden sprung out from behind some cover and raised the PSG-1. "Step away from her and drop your weapons."

"What is this all about?" One of the officers questioned in defeat as they tossed their weapons to the ground. Hayden never answered. Instead, he slammed the butt of the rifle into the officer's skull knocking him out. Tying up the other officers and dressing in their uniforms, the three of them and the one officer Hayden clobbered boarded the Navy zodiac then headed towards the Navy Blue. As they skimmed across the open sea heading towards the cargo doors, they armed themselves. Hayden laid the sniper rifle on the floor where he could reach it quickly. Their plan now consisted of repressing those who guarded the cargo door.

As they drew closer to their objective, the men in the door began a military formation getting ready to greet their returning personnel. As the zodiac approached and they were close enough, they pulled out their guns. Hayden stood up erect holding the PSG-1, and motioned the men to turn around while Alex and Monique quickly boarded and secured them. They knew that the rifle Hayden pointed at them could saw them in half and would be virtually silent. They didn't even attempt a scuffle.

In the heat of the moment Hayden realised he didn't have the PSG-1 loaded he quickly pulled back the bolt and heard the audible click as a bullet entered the chamber, now it was ready. They pulled the Zodiac in and closed the door. Beads of sweat formed on their faces and foreheads as they unarmed the men and tied them up. Adrenaline coursed threw their veins filling them up with hunger and determination. There would be no turning back now. The element of surprise had worked. They were in.

"Seventeen."

Securing the six men, Monique kept her eye on them, while Alex and Hayden slipped through the exit that led them up to the foredeck. From there, they split up. They had to find a route up to the awningdeck nearest the helicopter pad and the Presidential Suite. It was there where the sixty-four-million-dollars awaited.

Hayden coursed his way along the foredeck staying hidden in the shadows and skulking behind pieces of navy equipment that was scattered here and there. It was 9:30 p.m. he noted. They had six hours to find the loot, retrieve it and make for shore. By then the tide would have dissipated enough so that the Navy zodiac they'd have to use could make it to shore unscathed. Once that took place the rest would be guesswork neither one of them had a clue on what their next move would be.

He was about to stand and dart over to some more cover near another door, when he heard the footsteps—his heart began to beat fast as he watched a set of six or so men pass him by. When he could no longer hear their footsteps he slowly peered above the forty-five gallon drums of fuel he hid behind. He looked towards the stern and back at the bow, there was a checkpoint between where he was now and where he needed to be and the men guarding it were heavily armed. He slowly began to crawl. There was a tarp a few yards away covering something up. For now, it was the best place to go. He stayed in the shadows crawling diligently towards his goal. It took him thirty minutes but he executed the task. The men were none the wiser.

Sliding around to the back of the tarp he peered down the deck again towards the door he was trying to reach. The checkpoint was behind him now. The foredeck also opened up and now there was very little cover. That door was still his destination and he knew he had to get there—one way or the other. He thought about simply standing and walking towards it. With Navy uniform on, maybe he'd get away with it. The problem was if he were questioned by someone he probably wouldn't know what to say bringing a quick surcease to their objective. If only it were darker.

Alex managed to slip passed every checkpoint in the opposite direction towards the bow and made it to the second deck. His heart was palpitating and he sweated. Opening a door, he entered a quiet galley. Here the cabins were much like they were on the Hilroy. He realised then that he was now in the personnel-housing sector of the ship. Still wearing the Navy uniform, he proceeded to walk to the end of the galley to another door. He passed two personnel who nodded at him as he walked by. At first he thought that would be it, the game would be over.

Adrenaline coursed through his veins and his heart skipped a beat. Continuing to another door, he entered. It led him to another flight of stairs and a bridge that coursed over to one of the big towers. From there, he could tell that they weren't guard towers as they first thought but were actually control towers. Still, there would be men inside and that could pose a problem. He decided to head back the way he came. Hopefully, the two men he passed were no longer about.

Making his way back to where he entered the galley, he decided to take a long hall that turned to his left. He followed it to another door, which lead him to the helicopter pad and the Presidential Suite. He stepped out in the shadows long enough to count how many men were guarding the entrance. He counted six. Then he turned and set out to find Hayden.

At exactly 12:00 a.m., the ship's decks were illuminated with big lights a loud horn blew and the ship became busy with the bustling about of what seemed like every person onboard. Then silence took over the evening sounds as a guard change took place. Only two men now guarded the checkpoint that Hayden passed. He was faced with yet another set back the floodlighting on the decks remained lit. It was for security purposes undoubtedly. The only thing that came to his mind was that the horn and lights were a signal for the last shift change of the evening and for the guards and other personnel to retreat to their cabins. It was a military signal for lights-out.

Good news for the three of them, not many personnel would be out and about other then the Navy sentries who walked the decks. Minutes later he heard the pitter-patter of running feet and then silence. He waited with his fingers crossed hoping it was Alex he heard. He looked at the checkpoint and noticed one of the men was looking intently in the direction of where the sound came from.

Hayden knew then that it wasn't Navy personnel he heard it was Alex. He found an old one-inch bolt lying on the deck near where he was hiding and he threw it behind the men into the shadows. They turned instinctively towards the sound their weapons drawn. One of them gestured to the other to go and check it out. Hayden hoped Alex had clued in. Sure enough, he had, as Hayden was watching the guards Alex came up to him and tapped his shoulder. "I found the way to the awningdeck and the Presidential Suite. We can get to it from the bow." He whispered.

"Good. I've been here three hours trying to make it to that door—way down there." He pointed.

"It must have been a bitch getting this far. Earlier there were six guys in every one of those check points and between here and where we entered, there a four check points."

"I know I crawled."

"C'mon lets head back. Follow me."

"Right behind you." Hayden followed Alex to the awningdeck and then they took cover behind the helicopter. There were now only four men guarding the Presidential Suite but they couldn't be sure how many were inside.

"How do we get past them, without having to kill them?"

"I don't know Alex I really don't want to kill anybody unless it is necessary. I have one of those tear gas grenades with me. I wonder if the smoke and sound of it going off would be noticed on a ship this size. Maybe it wouldn't? Or we can walk over. We're both dressed in Navy uniforms we can pull the same thing on them as we did to the men down below?"

"That is probably the best way. What about those lights they'll be shinning right into our faces."

"Can you shoot them out from here with the Eagle? They wouldn't hear a thing. After a few minutes we could likely prance right over to them and they wouldn't know if we were Navy or not. That is of course until we got closer."

"I'm pretty sure I could hit the lights from here but what about the glass if they hear it smash they'll probably check it out. Then again, if the lights don't smash, they'll probably think they blew out. It's a good idea I'm not too sure about the risk."

Alex had some valid points but they were running out of time fast. It was already 1:15 a.m. "We haven't got much time left. We got to do something fast, Alex. Either we walk down there with the lights in our faces or we take out the lights and then walk down. That's all we can do."

Alex nodded. "Okay. I'll take out the lights," he said as he removed the Desert Eagle. "But, if the glass smashes and falls to the deck it's going to be loud and I'll guarantee they'll be suspicious. The only thing we'll be able to do after that is mow them down and hopefully not alert anyone else. Are you ready?"

"Go for it." Alex beaded in on the lights holding the Desert Eagle in his right hand steadily like a piece of fruit hanging from a tree. There was a silent pop, pop and the lights went out. They waited a few minutes to make sure the men didn't radio ahead to question what happened to their lighting. Then they proceeded to walk over to them. The PSG-1 was slung across Hayden's shoulder not visible to the men they approached. The men milled around as the pair came into view. At first, they thought they were Navy and one of them asked why the lights had gone out.

"I don't know." Hayden replied as they walked closer. One of them looked at them and was about to pull out his revolver—realising the pair weren't who they thought they were. Alex swiftly planted the muzzle of his Desert Eagle against the man's temple, at the same time

Hayden swung the PSG over his shoulder and pointed it at them. "We are not here to hurt anyone so don't try to be a hero. Or I'll slew everyone one of you in under four seconds." The men looked at the PSG-1 and raised their hands voluntarily. "That's right you better do that. Be quiet and don't try anything brash or stupid unless you want to be splattered against the steel walls of this ship.

"You," Hayden said gesturing to one of the men. "Come here." The man walked over to him his hands in the air. "Without speaking and using only your fingers and nodding yes or no, I have some questions. Do you understand?" The guy nodded yes. "Good, is there anyone inside?" He asked. The man nodded, yes. "How many?" He counted to three. "There are three men inside?" He nodded yes. "Are they armed?" He nodded yes. "Okay. Here is where you get to speak anything louder then a whisper and you'll die understood?" The man nodded yes. "What are the men inside armed with?"

"Navy revolvers and M-16's," he said in a silent whisper.

There was something about the way he said it that made Hayden suspicious. He looked at him, his eyes turned cold and his top lip quivered—then he rammed the barrel of the rifle into the guy's mouth knocking out two of his front teeth. "You're lying aren't you?" The guys eyes watered with pain as shards from his teeth spewed out along with a mouthful of blood. "Now tell me how many men and what are they armed with?" He demanded again. As he pulled the three inches of barrel out of the guy's mouth so that he could speak. Hayden felt bad but he was protecting his own existence as well as Alex's and Monique's.

"There are no men inside," he began as he spit out pieces of his teeth. "If you're here for the cash that's onboard as I presume you are it is guarded by flash and tear gas grenades. Rigged to explode as soon as the crate is moved if they aren't disarmed. That's all I know." Hayden looked into the man's eyes again this time not as coldly. "All right. You shouldn't have lied the first time. You could have saved yourself a lot of pain, and a few teeth. Mosey on over to the others that my associate has up against the wall." Hayden said gesturing him to move. He and Alex tied and gagged the men then entered the Presidential Suite.

It was the third door in and to their left. Hayden opened it slowly and peered in. It was dark so Alex snapped one of the glow sticks and tossed it into the room. It landed in the middle of the floor beside a large metal crate that sat on top of a wooden pallet. Hayden was about to step through the doorway when Alex grabbed his shoulder.

"Hold it," he said as he pointed to a trip wire.

"Good eye." Stepping over the wire, they followed it along the wall. It lead to a switch that was obviously a silent alarm and then up the wall to a remote camera that focused on the crate. It wasn't anything fancy surprisingly. Not like you would expect from the US Navy. They decided the trip wire thing was something that probably the D.E.A contrived. Looking over the crate before they moved it they tried to find wires coming from it or some other tell tale sign that it was indeed rigged with teargas and flash grenades. But found nothing.

"It could be toothless out front was lying," Alex suggested.

"I don't know about that. He was in a lot of pain. I can't see him bullshitting not knowing what I might do to him next if I even suspected that he was lying. Then again, we're not dealing with the likes of Ellis and his people either. This is the US Navy. They're trained to protect and serve their country you know what I mean. I suggest we shoot the lock off and open this baby up. It could be the surprise is inside. We'll open it slowly and gently if we see any wires then we'll know."

"I agree. Let's get on with it." Alex said as he removed his Desert Eagle and fired at the lock blasting it opened. The sound of the gun was barely audible but the ricocheting bullet as it bounced around whirring made the pair drop to the ground and cover their heads.

"Whoa, that was interesting." Hayden said jokingly. But Alex didn't respond. Hayden looked over to him and saw the pool of blood that was forming. His heart dropped and he dashed to Alex's side. "Alex, Alex can you hear me?" He asked in desperation as he held Alex in his arms. Alex moaned then fell silent never to speak again. Hayden sat there with his friend on his knees sobbing quietly to himself. Then Alex moved ever so slightly, "Alex can you hear me?" His blood shot eyes looked at him and he nodded as blood trickled from his mouth and from his eyes like tears. His breathing was laboured and he gurgled a few more times. He gave Hayden the thumbs up sign and then fell silent. Hayden knew then that he had died. He was heartsick.

For what seemed like eternity, he sat in the darkness his mind racing with memories of Alex. At that point, he was tempted to call the entire thing off. Something told him though—that Alex wouldn't have wanted that. He'd want them to carry out the objective. He could almost hear Alex's voice. "C'mon Hayden get on with it. We haven't much time." As his eyes welled up with tears he slowly opened the metal crate and looked inside. There were no grenades, wires, or anything like that. It was simply full of cash, sixty-four-million-dollars of it. It would never take the place of Alex Farell.

He had no idea how he alone was going to move it. It dawned on him that he could use a lifeboat and lower it to the sea along with Alex's body. There was a lifeboat on the deck and it was just outside. He hurried over to it and removed the canvas. Returning to Alex's body he carried it to the boat and secured it. Forty-five minutes later the loot was loaded. Once that task was done, he forced the four men they subdued to rise and walk back into the room where the cash had been. Hitting each of them in the back of the head with the butt of the rifle, he exited and locked the door.

The pulley system, which, lowered the boat from the top deck to the water below was automatic and would land with a splash if he didn't slow it down. It took everything he had to slow it and when it finally hit the water his hands were bloody and blistered from the half-inch cable that ripped and tore at the palms of his hands. They burned with torturous agony. He could barely hold the oars to paddle due to the painful damage done.

As he made his way over to the cargo door, his thoughts were of Alex and Monique. How was she going to react? How could he explain her brother's death? Lining up the lifeboat with the door and ignoring the pain in his hands, he reefed up on the handle with all his strength. It was as though spikes were being driven into the palms of his hands as an agonising pain shot through them.

The door swung opened startling Monique at first as she spun around with one of the Desert Eagles, realising it was Hayden she lowered the pistol and rushed to the boat. Seeing Alex, she looked to Hayden for reassurance that he was only wounded. All he could do is shake his head and embrace her. "I'm sorry Monique. I'm sorry." They held each other close as tears rolled down their cheeks.

"I knew something like this was going to happen, I knew it…" she sobbed.

"Monique we have to get going. Come on." Hayden helped her into the boat.

"We should have chosen freedom. Just freedom," she sobbed into her still brother's chest. Hayden held back his own tears. He rowed the boat even stronger now trying to rid himself of the grievance towards Alex's death. *It should never have happened,* he thought. Monique was right. They should have chosen freedom.

Three months later, on October 27, Colleen and Hayden were married by a Justice of the Peace in Canada. Hayden managed to convince her to leave her job and travel with him. Monique and Hayden arranged with Heneric to have Alex's body buried. Then for three months Colleen, Monique and Hayden travelled under aliases until they were finally in Canada.

Monique was the only bridesmaid at their wedding and a picture of Alex was their best man. He was buried in a beautiful graveyard in Alaska that over looked the great Arctic Ocean. They spared no expense when they buried him. They managed to get fifteen million dollars to the RRA to help with the cause. Then, Monique and Hayden renounced all ties with the RRA—deciding to live the remainder of their lives in freedom. Eventually the road the three travelled, came to a fork and Monique headed for the Mexican coast and a life of her own. As for

Ellis, it was said that he ate the muzzle of his gun and died by his own hand driven mad because he never saw a penny.

"Eighteen."

Hayden leaned up against the cedar railing that skirted the cabin's deck. His dirty blonde hair gently blew in the pine scented breeze. His blue eyes focused on the view of the wooded village along the Arrow Lakes that he now called home. He and Colleen had been living there going on five years. A lot changed since 1997, and he was thinking back to that time now and how his friend Alex died from one of his own bullets as it ricocheted in a deadly whirr piercing his heart and lungs. It was a bad time for all of them. Now five years later he was living as free as the free world allowed. They were rich undoubtedly but his and Colleen's happiness wasn't the money. It was the love that they shared for each other, and the freedom he finally won.

Tapping his finger impatiently on the railing, he looked across the treetops down to the snow-covered village of Deer Brook. It was a quaint town along the Arrow Lakes and served him well as a refuge. Everyone living there was either retired or worked in the city. He scraped out his living as a hunting guide by choice. His clients were expected to reach him via mail, through other associates, or they showed up in Deer Brook and requested his services. He used no phone.

The hunting communities from Deer Brook all the way to the BC Rocky Mountains and into Saskatchewan knew about 'The BC Interior & Beyond Hunting Co.,' Hayden modelled it from his own ideas, blood and sweat, hard work and perseverance. There were a lot of legalities but he followed through. He got his Canadian Citizenship, his Firearms Acquisition Card allowing him to purchase and carry firearms. He studied the Canadian ethics of hunting and finally received his British Columbia Resident Hunter Number Card. Almost two years and $20,000.00 later he was set. What he didn't have was his Fur Bearing Trappers License but he was working on that.

Out of the three and half years he'd been in business none of his clients got skunked, everyone filled their tags. His keen sense for where the game was he credited this to his upbringing. When he and Colleen settled in Deer Brook they needed some kind of cover. A hunting firm was as good of a front as any in his mind. It also deterred people from asking why he owned so many firearms. It was something that the Canadian government was beginning to shun. Canada had a few quirks all right.

He managed a good living and rarely did they use the stolen cash that was concealed away in offshore tax havens and bank accounts. Out of the twenty-one million that he received, nineteen million was at his disposal as he added to Alex's donation to the RRA another $1.3 million. The other five hundred thousand was spent touring Canada and buying the property that they now owned. They both owned 4X4s, but you could never drive out of Deer Brook when the main road to the outside world was closed.

His was an old 1968 Dodge Power Wagon rebuilt from top to bottom. The 360 cubic inch high performance engine was blueprinted and stamped. He did the work himself including placing all the accessories. He added a winch to the front and back, a compressor, dual batteries, a lift kit, a roll bar. He even reinforced the door and side panels and added a few concealed cubby-holes where gear could be stored. The custom paint job was done by one of Colleen's girlfriends who lived on the outskirts of Castlebridge. She painted it midnight black and air brushed the head of a Siberian Tiger on the hood. It was the envy of all 4x4's in and around Deer Brook.

But not even his rig could plough through three to four feet of snow for a distance of thirty miles. The only means of distant travel during the winter was either by boat or snowmobile neither of which he owned or wanted to own. The town shut down during the winter months and all access roads were closed due to the unmonitored and frequent avalanches. Most of the townspeople returned to their homes in suburbia. Their hundred thousand-dollar cabin home was adequate for them to live in comfort. A large diesel generator pumped enough electricity to keep them in light with all the modern day conveniences of any modern day home in suburbia, excluding a phone. Hayden liked the solitude.

The beaches and homes that once held families were now covered in white and icicles hung precariously from all the vacant dwellings. Ice formed along the lakeshore and glistened if only briefly during the early morning then melted as the day progressed to only return again the following morning. It reminded him of the dew on the plush green lawns that grew vibrantly during the summer months. There were few people, who preferred living at Deer Brook all year around. As opposed to the hustle, and bustle of everyday suburbia. He and Colleen were two of the few.

An AG-Foods grocery store remained open during this time, where they bought their provisions once a week. A gas station supplied fuel to the many trawlers that fished the lake all year as well as the few snowmobiles that transported the true die-hard's of Deer Brook. Those that worked in the nearby city travelled by boat to and from their employment. It was the life and freedom he had always dreamt about. Now he lived it.

Today, something was different. Listening to the distant drone of an outboard he realised it was mail day and he was expecting a letter from Monique as he did every six months since their departure five years prior. Perhaps that is what was bothering him.

He walked down the wooded path and through the gate that led to the dock. "Hey Randy good to see ya. Anything special for me in all that mail?" He grabbed the bow of the boat and held it steady for the man inside.

Randy tended the main postal service that delivered and gathered mail from all the communities along the Arrow during the winter months. He lived his entire life on that lake and owned a big chunk of land and a nice cabin on the other side where not more than one other family lived. That side of the Arrow was called Little Brooklyn. It was a name one of the families dubbed the place. He never knew what the implication meant. Other than at onetime it was mined quite significantly for gold and silver. Most places along the Arrow were.

"Sure is. You got one here from Mexico and another from somebody named Ellis Leroy. According to the postmark it came all the way from Anchorage Alaska, didn't know you knew someone way up there." Randy handed him the letters. Hayden couldn't believe what he was hearing. Ellis Leroy was supposed to be dead. He reached out to take the two letters.

Randy noticed the glint of encumbrance in his eyes. "Looks like you've seen a ghost. What's a matter?"

"Ah, nothing. I was taken off guard at receiving this letter from Alaska. The last I heard the guy it is from swallowed the barrel of his .45." Turning he walked back the way he came his mind racing. *Could Ellis really be alive?* Stopping short of the wooden gate he looked to the dock and waved to Randy as his boat puttered out of the inlet and headed up the Arrow. Curiosity got the better him and he opened the letter from Ellis before making the last jaunt up the hill to home.

The letter was definitely written by Ellis's hand. It was in the same style and arrogant tone that he used to talk to people. It sickened him to think that he still lived. All the stories he heard about Ellis Leroy over the past few years that were relayed to him through acquaintances and such that he remained in contact with in Poski and abroad were false. It was a simple letter and it read:

Hayden,

'I have tracked you down in regards to one thing, my cut of sixty four million dollars. Like I told you five years ago, our paths would cross again. Let me take the liberty now to explain to you that I'm also in the midst of tracking down Monique. I stumbled across a very posh grave up here in Alaska that bears the name Alex Farell, I thought I'd look her up to give her my condolences about her dear brother's death. Once I have received confirmation on her whereabouts, you will hear from me again.'

There was no signature.

Tearing it up he tossed the pieces on the ground and cursed the day he met Ellis Leroy. He thought of Monique and how vulnerable she might be if he were able to track her down in Mexico. He wasn't sure if

Ellis could stretch his arm that far, but it was enough of a threat to prepare for the unexpected. The Arrow turned choppy and he could hear it in the background as it lapped at the rock bluffs their cabin rested on. Turning, he gazed out across the water. The Arrow was a majestic dark blue and was one of lakes that remained fresh and unpolluted in the British Columbia interior. He turned back toward the cabin and walked the last few yards to the warmth and his morning coffee. Opening the big oak door, he stepped in, welcoming the warmth. He dusted the fresh snow from his jacket and hung it up on the coat rack. Pulling up to the table in the dinning room he opened the letter from Monique and read it. She was doing fine and mentioned that she was fixing to foster a few children whose parents were accused of smuggling drugs and were now awaiting a fifteen-year jail term to end.

She invested a large amount of money into purchasing a five star hotel called 'El Tequila' which was on another island opposite her villa. She offered the two of them the opportunity run the place if they were ever up to it. Hayden chuckled. "If I could ever convince Colleen I might take you up on that," he whispered to himself. He was comforted knowing that she was doing well. He heard the front door creak open and the shuffling of grocery bags.

"Hayden are you in?" Colleen hollered from the foyer. Her long auburn hair dusted with fresh snow and her beautiful brown Egyptian eyes watering slightly from the strain caused by the glistening freshly whitened snow covered ground.

"Sure am, need some help?" He questioned as he entered from the back of the cabin where the dinning room was. Bending over he kissed Colleen on the cheek. "How was your day?"

Colleen didn't even answer. Instead she looked into his eyes and simply asked, "What's the matter?"

"What do you mean? I'm fine."

"Not according to your eyes you're not. What's up? You know you can't hide anything from me."

"It's nothing," reaching for the three bags of groceries he proceeded to walk away hoping she wouldn't ask again.

Removing her boots, she followed him. "Come here you." She wrapped her arms around his shoulders and looked him in the eyes. "Now tell me what's up?"

The two of them kept no secrets. Hayden was compelled. He explained to her about the letter from Ellis and how he threatened retribution. Colleen was dismayed and shook her head. "How did he ever find us? What are we going to do?"

She never met Ellis in person but saw him from a distance that time on the Hilroy five years ago when her and Hayden first met. What she knew of him was that he was a snake in the grass. Hayden always made it a point to describe him when he told her stories. Features he said that would always stand out were his deep green eyes, his bulk and foul mouth. "I need to think on it a bit. Here is a thought. We also got a letter from Monique. She's bought a hotel called 'El Tequila' and has hinted at you and I running it in Mexico. What do you think of that?"

Colleen stepped back with a look of surprise. "She did what. Bought a hotel? My God that woman is brilliant. And wants us to run it for her?" Hayden stood in front of her nodding his head. "I don't know if I could handle Mexico." She started, "If it ever came down to where we have no choice, I'd certainly contemplate it. That is one of the reasons why I wanted a phone."

Hayden nodded, "I know, I know. A phone would come in handy now wouldn't it? But who would of thought Ellis was alive. Last thing any of us heard about him was that he committed suicide. I'll write up a letter to Monique tonight and have it ready for when Randy comes by next week. That's all we can do for now. For all I know this is a sick joke." In the back of his mind, he knew this wasn't a joke. Ellis found him and his threats were as real as the choppy waters of the Arrow Lakes. All he could was send word to Monique and wait for correspondences from Ellis. It would be easy enough for he and Colleen to head to Mexico in a heated rush if need be.

Hayden held his eyes on the lake through the big picture window in the living room, the fireplace snapped and crackled and the radio in the kitchen played softly in the background. His mind raced with the last time he submitted to Ellis's ways and in a brief moment he relived the death of his best friend Alex.

He remembered how he thought he could hear Alex's voice say, "C'mon, get on with it. We haven't much time." He remembered how his eyes welled up with tears as he slowly opened the metal crate hoping for it to explode so that he wouldn't have to live with the pain of the death of his friend. There were no grenades, wires, or anything like that. It was simply full of cash, sixty-four-million-dollars of it.

He was jolted back to reality with a loud pop as one of the logs in the fireplace spewed an array of orange sparks across the hard wooden floor. Dashing over he pressed them out with his feet as he done numerous times before. He meant to have the fireplace screen replaced.

Looking down to the hard wooden floor that was once a beautiful birch, he realised his neglect. The floor in some places resembled craters on the moon. The floor was like his snowshoes, which he had still to repair, he wanted to do both but hadn't found the time or at least that was his excuse. Now the floor looked terrible and the frames for his snowshoes hung on a hook in his shop. He hadn't even ordered the leather strapping or resin he needed to repair them. *Boy,* he thought, *am I ever lagging.*

Glancing over to his gun cabinet, he remembered the vow he made five years ago to never submit to the likes of Ellis again. Nor to take another mans life unless in defence of himself or one he loved.

The last bit of sun glared in through the big picture window. Looking at its brilliance as it slowly slid behind the mountains of Little Brooklyn, leaving behind a sunset of vibrant colours of purple, pink, and saffron that looked to have been painted by the brush strokes from an artist's hand. He was surprised at how quickly the day passed. It seemed as though he only blinked.

The beautiful creature that now stood in front of him broke his gaze. She was dressed in her fuchsia lingerie. Her hair was hanging loosely and her bedroom eyes were pleading with him to make love. She looked to him and motioned him to follow as she headed teasingly towards their bedroom.

"Nineteen."

On Saturday he stepped out onto their deck and with a coffee in hand greeted the day. It was November 16, 2002. The rising sun warmed the mountain air as the icicles hanging on the eaves of the cabin began to melt breaking the silence with a constant drip. *Serenity at its best,* he thought. He recalled how cold it was the year before. Their generator broke down a few times leaving them shivering, until he could fix it or round up the parts. Thank God for his ability to tinker. This year though, it was mild.

Dumping the last of his coffee he turned and made his way inside. Colleen was sitting at the table eating her morning English muffin with huckleberry jam, her nose stuck in a book. "What's on your agenda today?" He asked.

"Not sure. Considering on doing some baking, but more than likely, I'll kick back instead and finish this book. What do you have planned?"

"I was thinking I would do some maintenance to the generator. If I have time I'll oil and clean the guns that I used this season. I might even curl up with you later on the couch. Maybe we can watch a movie or something."

"That would be great. We'll make our date for after dinner, say 7:00 p.m."

"7:00 p.m., it is." He answered as he turned and walked out to the foyer. Grabbing his toolbox he donned his coveralls then headed to the outbuilding that housed the generator. It would take him three hours to make sure everything was working without fault. Swinging open the doors he stepped in and switched on the light. His nostrils filled with the scent of diesel as he proceeded to the back and set his tools on the bench. The generator drowned out the silence from outside and caused his ears to hum. He hit the switch on their little generator and waited for it to kick down, before he turned the big one off. That way the flow of current to their cabin was not interrupted causing all their clocks to start flashing 12:00, he hated when that happened.

He couldn't know what was taking place in the cabin. Two men busted in on Colleen and were tossing her around the room like a rag doll. "Where is he? Where's Hayden Rochsoff. Start coming clean with me now or I'll throw you off those rock bluffs."

Colleen was terrified but she held her ground. "I don't know anyone by that name." The one man slapped her to the floor her lips were busted and she could taste the metallic of her blood as it trickled down her throat. The big guy grabbed her by the top of her head and threw her on the couch. Staring at her attackers in horror, she watched as they ransacked the cabin. Petrified, tears streamed down her face.

The big fat guy she realised was Ellis Leroy, Hayden's own flesh and blood. She could tell by his deep green eyes that she heard Hayden speak of. The other man was a brute as well not in width but in height. He was a good head and shoulders above Hayden, and Hayden was easily six foot four. Her eyes rarely left the men and she predominately took mental notes of her attackers, 'big and fat, green eyes salt and pepper hair. Tall, red hair, blue eyes.' The man with red hair approached her and put his hand on her inner thigh. "I can feel the steam," he said in a hissed breath. "Tell us where Hayden is. Or I might move that hand a touch closer."

With that said she found enough courage and strength to push the man to the floor. Standing before the man could, she stomped on his throat hoping to crush his jugular, larynx and whatever else was in there. Managing a few short strides toward the door the man grabbed her ankles and pulled her to the floor. With a solid thud, she fell forward with no time to brace her fall. It felt like all her teeth shattered as the right side of her head and face bounced off the hardwood. Ignoring all pain, she kicked her attacker off for a second time. Rolling over and onto her feet, she bolted for the door but there was no escape as the other man by now blocked any chance of an exit. "You bastard…" Colleen began with venom, as the man she kicked in the face approached and spun her around so that she was facing him, then rammed his hand down the front of her pants and grabbed her down below.

"You ever try something like that again and this hand," he said as he squeezed her even tighter causing her eyes to water from both the pain and the humiliation, "will demoralise you. Understood." He threatened with sick pleasure his hand still between her legs. Colleen remained strong and looked him in the eye with intent.

"By the look of you, this is probably the only way you can get it." She said as she spat in his face. The man withdrew his hand as though he was going to strike her again, but Ellis stepped in.

"Not now. She's our bait. You can make this a lot simpler if you'll tell us where he is."

She stared into the face of man with the green eyes. "I'm telling you the truth. I don't know anyone named Hayden."

"Funny, there are pictures of him and you all over this place. You leave me no choice… Red, knock her out." Colleen's eyes darted back to the other man named Red and she watched as he removed a vile from his inside jacked and poured a small amount on to a white kerchief.

"Wait, wait…" She began, "what are you going to do?"

"It's to late for questions now. You had your chance. Red, take her out." Red stepped forward. Before she could utter a word his right arm was around her neck and his left was brought up to her face. She struggled for a moment and then passed out.

Ellis retrieved a pen and jotted down five words for Hayden: 'Surprise. I'll be in touch.' He tossed it on the couch where a splatter of blood was most noticeable. Then the two men exited the backdoor carrying an unconscious Colleen wrapped in a quilt from their bed. Vaguely coming to a short time later she realised she was in a boat, too weak to battle or even lift her head she again passed out.

Deciding to get some fresh air, as the diesel fumes were beginning to take their toll, Hayden stepped outside. Inhaling deeply, he spat trying to rid the taste in his mouth. Walking over to the rock bluffs he looked out across the Arrow, and noticed a black and red boat that coursed its way south-east heading towards the city. It caught his eye because it was unfamiliar to him. He knew most of the fishers in the area and their boats. The one he looked at now was new to him. The way it slowed, sped up, and rocked this way and that told him that they were inexperienced.

Unaware of the horrors that awaited him at the cabin he made his way back to the generator and picked up where he left off. At it for a few minutes, the screaming engine of a snowmobile approaching fast interrupted him. Standing, he put the crescent wrench he was using in his back pocket, then wiped his hands with a rag and exited for the second time putting his chore on hold.

The yellow and red sled flew up the hill catching air as it crested. It was one of the O'Brien kids, he guessed. The kid passed him by and waved as he flew over the other side. Hayden shook his head and smiled. Looking towards the cabin, he half-expecting Colleen to come out and ask what all the commotion was about. When she never, he turned and went back to work on the generator. Thirty minutes later gathering his tools he cleaned them and put them back in his toolbox. He looked over the work he did one last time and made a few minor adjustments to the back up generator. Retrieving his toolbox, he exited into the cool afternoon.

Walking towards the cabin his eyes caught the first glimpse of two extra sets of tracks both coming and going. Rushing towards the footprints he dropped his tools and darted for the cabin. His heart was a lump in his throat as he threw open the cabin door. By the disarray of furniture, he knew something had gone on. Fear stricken, he dashed from room to room yelling for Colleen. Finally the piece of paper on the couch came into view and he took two strides to snatch it up.

Slumping to the couch and clutching the letter no tears rolled down his cheek. Instead, adrenaline coursed through his body like fires from hell as hate and anger poisoned his being. The boat he saw earlier was the key and he knew it. He tried to speculate the time at which he saw it, but his mind was blank. He knew one thing for sure, whoever it was had long since docked. Either in the city or at any of the boat launches that dotted the Arrow Lake shore. Ellis was obviously closer than he could have ever imagined. The letter he received from Alaska was one of Ellis's ploys to catch him off guard and it worked.

Glancing again at the five words Ellis left him, he wondered what Colleen was going through. How badly was she hurt? Had she been hurt at all? What was he supposed to do? How long would it be before he heard from Ellis again? These questions and others repeated themselves in his mind but there were no answers. Colleen was tough, he knew that, and if she were ever given the opportunity to escape from her captors she would take it and kill anyone who tried to stop her. It was a small piece of hope and he would hang on to it until she was safe and sound.

Standing slowly he walked to his gun cabinet and unlocked the door. He still had the two silenced Desert Eagle's, a Glock as well as the Heckler & Koch PSG-1 sniper rifle that he used in the '97 heist. They were stashed away in one of floors of the outbuildings. He put them there in hopes he'd never have to retrieve them. He looked over his hunting rifles. The one that caught his eye was the 30-06. With enough stopping power to drop a grizzly, it would make a mess out of Ellis Leroy.

"Whether, we're flesh and blood or not I'm done playing games…and as of right now I'm the winner," he said softly as he closed the cabinet door.

"Twenty."

Able now to open her eyes Colleen found she was laying in the back seat of a vehicle, her hands, ankles, and knees bound by plastic ties. Slowly inching her way up until she was sitting she looked out the window. Her timing couldn't have been better focussing her eyes she noted that they turned left off a main highway. What highway, she could not know. The fact that they were near one might mean the difference between life and death.

The driver was Red and the other man who she was certain was named Ellis was snoring. Red looked in the rear view mirror and smiled, bringing his hand up to his nose inhaling deeply. "Ah, the scent of a frightened woman." He was referring back to when he rammed his hand down her pants and grabbed her. It repulsed Colleen and she thought she would throw up.

"You're the type of sick bastard that would say that. Are you into necrophilia? Cause the next time you touch me like that you better hope I'm dead." Colleen gazed out the window looking for some kind of landmark that would tell her where she was. She knew now that the vehicle they were in was a Dodge Durango and that they were travelling north-west on a forestry road. As for landmarks or road signs, there were none. She could feel Red's eyes glaring at her through the rear view mirror. She kept her own eyes fixed on the window watching as pine trees passed by. "Where are you taking me?"

"When we get there you'll know. And when we get there I might get me some." He laughed. Colleen's heart was in her throat. Red's threats terrified her she could not imagine the things he might force her to comply to. An ordinary beating she could handle, but she'd rather be dead then live the rest of her life knowing that he had his way with her.

"Like I said you pervert. If you are not into necrophilia don't even try." Colleen was terrified at what her fate might be. She knew that if she were to show her fear then they had won. It was better she remained as cold as stone. Men like these two were nothing more than bullies. They took satisfaction and gained their power from the fear of others. She would never show them fear.

The truck finally came to a stop in front of a two-inch metal pipe gate. Red stepped out to unlock it. Colleen began looking for something she could use as a weapon. She opened the backseat ashtray hoping to find a poppy or anything that she could clasp in her bound hands until the time was right. She settled for a piece of sharp metal that she broke away from the inside.

It was flat and about an inch or so wide and about two inches long. It was used to put out cigarettes. She bent it up and down until it finally snapped off leaving a jagged edge like a serrated knife. Slipping the piece between her palms, she closed the mangled ashtray. Her heart seemed to beat a thousand times a minute from the adrenaline. She felt less vulnerable with the piece of metal, if thrust into someone's eye it could and would prove deadly.

Red returned and they proceeded up the road, the truck's tires spinning in the snow until finally they approached a log A-Frame cabin. "Here's home sweetheart until we can track down Hayden. Sit pretty until we get unloaded." Red reached over to Ellis and shook him awake. "We're here, c'mon get up."

Ellis opened his eyes and shook the cobwebs from his mind. "Good, good. We can finally question our friend in the back more thorough. What do you say to that darlin'."

"Whatever." Colleen said as she averted her eyes towards the cabin.

"Still being a hard ass eh? That' s okay. I like breaking people. Red, his forte is breaking woman." Ellis opened the passenger door and stepped out.

Red looked back at Colleen, a big smile crossed his face. "That's right. I think you and I will have a lot of fun together. I'll keep you alive long enough so you can enjoy it too." Snickering he turned and followed Ellis up the stairs to the cabin, leaving Colleen sitting in the backseat. She could no longer hold back her tears and broke down sobbing as her body began shaking due to fear and anxiety.

The cabin door opened and Red approached the truck reaching in he pulled her out. He tossed her over his shoulder and ascended the stairs up to the cabin, where he tossed her onto a bed in a back room. "This will be your room and my play ground," he said as he laughed and exited locking the door behind him.

He really wasn't the type of guy he was pretending to be towards women, but he knew how to put fear into them. If that entailed threatening them sexually, that's how he played the hand. He never raped a woman in his life nor did he ever intend to. He might be a mercenary but he did have a conscience. The incident where he grabbed her by the crotch was done in anger only to instil fear. Now impregnated with this fear Colleen was safe from that kind of harm. It was all part of the game.

Rolling to the side of the bed she carefully slid the piece of metal underneath the mattress. Lying on her back, she looked up to the ceiling. She felt like a mummy all wrapped up unable to move. Her head pounded from the chloroform or whatever it was that Red used to knock her out. She ran her tongue across her teeth for the hundredth time making sure they were all there. Her lips were puffy and swollen. She could feel the cuts inside her mouth along her bottom and top lip and her cheeks. Taking a deep breath she closed her eyes and drifted in and out of consciousness.

The sound of the unlocking door alerted her and she opened her eyes. It was getting dark out and the room was pitch black as big heavy curtains hung from the window blocked out what little sunlight was left. The door swung opened and the light flicked on causing her to squint from the brightness. The man in the doorway was Ellis and he held a cup in one hand and a sandwich in the other.

"Thought you might be hungry." Walking over to nightstand, he set the items down. "It ain't much, some chicken salad and a coffee. I'm going to undo these binds around your hands and knees but gonna keep those ankles bound." Ellis chuckled. "You're pretty quick with those feet and I don't suppose my partner wants another licking. But, you try to do anything stupid to me when I undo you, you'll be sent back to Hayden as a corpse. Understand?" Colleen didn't speak she only nodded. "All right, first let me get these hands undone." He reached into his pocket and pulled out a lock blade, bringing it up to her wrists he cut away the plastic tie. She felt relief as the blood that was deprived of coursing through her veins rushed to her extremities. "How does that feel? A bit better?"

She only nodded in appreciation. Ellis looked at her and smiled. Putting the blade between her knees, he thrust upward cutting the plastic bind. She held her breath as he mused over her body. Then he smiled and exited her room. Sitting up she slung her legs over the bed and reached for the sandwich. Removing the top piece of bread, she checked to see if the sandwich was safe. Satisfied, she ate it but left the coffee.

It would be easier to slip something into that…she thought. With some of her strength regained, she hopped around the room due to the binds that remained around her ankles. The window was barred on the outside and someone went to the trouble to stop it from opening. The closet held no coat hangers or anything else that she might be able to fight her way out with.

The room had obviously been secured. All she had was that piece of metal tucked beneath the mattress, hardly a weapon really. Even the plate that Ellis brought with the sandwich was paper and the coffee cup was Styrofoam. She was in a predicament no doubt, an unfavourable one, but she had been in unfavourable predicaments before. All she had to do was keep her wits and stay alive.

Ellis and Red sat around the table slurping coffee and reminiscing. "Hayden's little filly certainly left you with a few bruises, eh?" Ellis chuckled as he looked closer to Red' face.

"That she did. She's one spunky woman. Hell of a kick too. There's something familiar about her. I can't put my finger on it though."

"C'mon now think back. You're right about the familiarity. Think back to the Hilroy, five years ago. She's the waitress that worked at that restaurant, what was it called again…umm. It evades me."

"You mean she's the chick from the Pickled Onion?"

"Yeah, yeah, that's it. The Pickled Onion."

"I visualise her. You're right that is her."

"I didn't realise it myself until I got a good look at her. Then it became as clear as day. She even brought us coffee a time or two. Now if we could only track down Monique. Then we'd have the ball in our court, not that we don't already with that filly we got stabled in the back room. If we had both of them, this one and Monique, Hayden would submit twice as fast. Chances are he's sitting back at his cabin scheming on how he's gonna end my life." Ellis chuckled. "Only thing is he ain't gonna have a chance, is he?"

"Not with me around he won't. What's next?"

"I figure we'll let him stew for a bit. I'll get a letter to him telling him when, and where to meet. Then we'll go from there. Once he hands over the cash that he owes to get his little filly back, we'll blow his brains out." Ellis replied daunting a crooked smile as he took a long pull on his last Havana, forming smoke rings as he exhaled.

***

Hayden spent the majority of what was left of the day doing maintenance to the rifle and the three pistols he stashed under the floorboards of the fuel shed. One of the Desert Eagle's had suffered from being in the cold earth all this time and the firing mechanism continued to stick even after he oiled it. Noticing the handle grip he realised it was the one that killed Alex. Not wanting to remember the death, he tossed the pistol back into the box.

He loaded the other silenced Eagle and fired a shot, it discharged and ejected the brass casing as smoothly as if it were the first time it were fired. He emptied the remaining five bullets as fast as he could pull the trigger to make sure it wouldn't bind. Satisfied, he set the pistol down and retrieved his Glock submachine pistol. He fitted the pistol with the laser scope that he paid to have custom built years ago. It remained in the wooden case until now.

He had written two words on the box with a black marker, 'what if'. He thought about that Glock now as he held it in his hand for the first time in five years. It saved him on more than one occasion. The weight of it and the coolness of the blue steel brought a meek smile across his face as he thought about the relationship he had with it.

He tossed it from hand to hand, as one does with a baseball. The slapping sound against his palms became the only audible sound in the silence. He sat transfixed as if all that mattered now were how many times he could catch it. Realising finally that he had been sitting for quite sometime, he rose and grabbed the wooden box and retreated to the cabin. It was lonely and quiet without the presence of Colleen. Usually she'd be sitting on the couch at this time thumbing through magazines or reading a book from her numerous collections.

Bringing the box into the living room he set it down on the coffee table and slumped into the couch. Pulling the box of weapons closer he continued to check them. The Heckler & Koch sniper rifle was his preferred rifle. He loved the ambidextrous ergonomic design and how when fired it was virtually silent. He sighted through the 10X scope to a nail in the far wall of the cabin. Slowly he pulled the trigger. Surprisingly the gun recoiled and an audible pop sounded, startling him and he quickly stood, shaking his head at his mistake. He was so withdrawn he never thought to pull back the bolt to make sure it wasn't loaded. He sat in relief that he hadn't scoped in on something more cherished.

Picking up the spent casing from the floor he brought it up to his nose and smelled it. He would be able to tell if the gunpowder over the years was rancid or unstable if it emitted a more metallic smell then the sulphuric acidity that it would usually emanate. The smell told him that the powder after all these years was stable, saving him the time and effort in reloading forty or so rounds.

"Twenty One."

The chill in the air the following morning when he woke announced that the fire had long since burned out. It didn't matter. During the night, he decided that he was going to batten down the hatches and head to the city of Castlebridge. Perhaps he could track down the black and red boat and with luck a lead on where Ellis Leroy might be.

His best chance to make it to town in the least amount of time was to see if one of the many fishers would transport him, then again that might be a waste of otherwise valuable time. Hiking out he decided was his best option. Undoubtedly he'd have to spend one night out in the elements. Packing his wool underwear and an extra change of clothes, sleeping bag and items of food as well as a transistor radio he donned his Koflach hiking boots, grabbed the Glock, sniper rifle, and Desert Eagle then exited into the cool predawn of morning.

Together he and Colleen hiked that route once before but they took a week to do it. They swigged brandy from a wineskin, ate food cooked on an open flame, and kept each other warm by snuggling under candle light into the wee hours of twilight to be lulled to sleep by distant howls. They camped in the middle of the road at the summit halfway between Deer Brook and Castlebridge.

The road at that point even in the summer was single lane only. It cut into the mountainside not more than fourteen feet across. There were jagged and bone crushing cliffs on either side going straight down to the rocky shore some one hundred metres and straight up the other side for at least fifty. From that point, one could look for miles out over the Arrow. They spent two of the five nights camped there. Other than the howling wolves, their biggest threat was the possibility of a quick and sudden avalanche that could careen off the cliffs above and without mercy belt them to the rocks below to a certain gruesome death. That would be his goal for today, to make it to the other side of that summit and out of harms way in case this time his luck didn't hold. *It was all part of the thrill back then,* he thought as he stopped to take a break.

The wind carried with it the distant sound of crashing waves as the Arrow's hungry breakers reached out to the rock bluffs and shore to feed its ferocious winter appetite of driftwood, docked boats, and on occasion human life. Squinting from the bright sunlit snow, he looked onward up the road. For four hours he had been on the move and so far, things had gone well. The wind was picking up a bit he noticed and around this area he knew it could cause havoc. With hope it would pass. The downside to a winter storm was that it would slow him down. He had a minimum of one week before he'd hear back from Ellis, and in that time he was going to do whatever it took to find him sooner. Chances were he was going send him something in the mail and the mail only came once a week on Friday.

Poking around in a city sparsely populated as Castlebridge turned up a lot of inside information in most cases when information was needed. If nothing else he'd be able to find out if anyone else might have seen a red and black boat or for that matter who might own one.

***

In a windswept cabin in the suburb of Thurman, north-east of Castlebridge, Colleen was beginning to stir. She slept well under the circumstances with the constant thought of being assaulted, fortunately she hadn't seen either of her captors since Ellis brought her the sandwich and coffee the night before. *What would today bring,* she thought as she slipped the blankets off and stretched, hobbling over to the window she looked outside to face nothing but a stupid hill that rose up not a stones throw away.

Her ankles ached with numbness and pain from the tie locked around them. She looked at her feet to see that they were beginning to swell. Hobbling over to the door she banged on it until she heard the key being inserted and turned. The door swung open and there stood Red. "What is it you want?" He asked uncaring.

"It's my feet, you have to remove the binds. They hurt and are beginning to swell."

"Not my problem…anything else?"

"Can I use the bathroom." A sinister grin crossed Red's face as he gestured for her to go ahead and use it. Colleen hobbled passed him and over to door. Her mind racing with what his intentions were, as she opened the door.

"Don't close it."

"What. You're going to stand there and watch me do my business."

"Do you want to use the can or not? Cause I'm sure I can find something else you can use in the privacy of your own room like a five gallon bucket." Red snarled. Colleen was frightened and embarrassed all at once but her bladder begged to be relieved. She wouldn't look at him she decided. She undid and pulled down her pants quickly squatting on the toilet. It revolted her to have to sit there while he looked on. He even stepped a few paces closer while she wiped herself. He laughed and taunted her. "That's some nice pink you got there."

She felt like crying from the torment and fear as she stood and pulled up her pants. He even glared at her while she washed her hands for Christ sake. If she ever the chance, she'd kill him. She hobbled past him and back to her room not speaking a word or responding to his comments of perversion. The door closed behind her and then locked. She fell onto the bed and began to weep. She had been humiliated before never though to that degree. She didn't want to have to go through that as often as she knew she might. Perhaps it would be better to request a bucket and stay locked up until this whole thing was over or Hayden found her.

One preventable measure she would take would be to drink liquids but once a day and eat small quantities from each meal that Ellis and Red might offer. Colleen sat up rubbing the tears away from her face. Hobbling over to the window she brushed the curtain to the side and stared out. She tried to imagine the torment Hayden must be facing. Likely he was on his way into Castlebridge, on 'reconnaissance' as he would call it. This of course was all speculation entwined with her own hopes and wishes. Her bubble burst when she heard the door being unlocked. She darted a glance towards it as it opened up and Ellis stepped in. "There you are," he began as he looked over to the window. "How are ya this mornin'?"

"What do you care?"

"Little, if you must insist." He looked at her swollen feet and then to her eyes. "Hurts some, eh? I might consider cutting them loose. If you'd so kindly answer a question or two."

"And what would those questions be? Let me guess, one of them would be where's Hayden Rochsoff? Perhaps another might be, how much money do we have, right? Those would be the questions you'd ask aren't they. To answer them in order, I have no idea where Hayden is. I don't see a red dot between your eyes so I guess he isn't near. As for the money, that's none of your business." She said as bravely as possible. Ellis advanced closer until they were face to face. He looked down upon her as though she were dirt. She could feel his hot cigar breath being absorbed into her hair and skin. Her flesh crawled in repulsion and she almost gagged.

"Contrary to your last answer," he breathed at her. "It is quite relevant that I know your financial status. You see I'm looking for a ransom. If he can't come up with the sum that I'll be requesting, you'll be shot. Tell me, or for all I care, that tie around your ankles can stay there until your feet fall off. You wouldn't be so attractive then would you, with no feet. I'll give you one more chance. Finances, how are they, five, ten, fifteen million?"

Colleen looked at him, scared, unrestrained and repulsed, then spat on his lapel. He grabbed her by the top of the head and rubbed her face in her own gob. Then he threw her to the ground and kicked her. Rolling to her side, she clasped her chest in agony as she gasped for air. "Don't ever pull that again. Or I'll see to it personally that you live to regret it, understand." Ellis bent over grabbing her under the arm and dragged her back to the bed.

Colleen wrenched in pain as he tossed her onto it. "You've been in the presence of Hayden for too long my dear and it's gonna get you killed. I'm going to remove that bind around your ankles because I like your spunk. Likely it's going to hurt worse than when you got your first piece." He inched the blade of his knife between her two swollen and off coloured ankles. She hadn't recovered completely from the kick to the solar plexus and the pain in her chest surpassed the pain in her ankles as he cut the bind that bound them leaving behind an ugly imprint that for the next few days would scar her. Her feet tingled in relief as blood rushed to feed the starving vessels below her ankles. "There, that ought to make you more comfortable. The swelling should begin to dissipate by this evening. Since you're likely to be able to walk better we'll have some chores for you. Get well rested." Ellis stood and exited the bedroom.

His plan was simple and humiliating all at once. It was a plan that would ultimately cause heartache and despair. All the things he thrived on. He would make a video portraying rape and abuse. Then send it to Hayden with further instructions on what to do next and where to deposit a certain amount of cash. He smiled as he locked her door and walked away.

That evening, they forced her into one of the bedrooms. She was terrified that they were going to rape her and she tried to fight them off. Ripping away her shirt and cutting her bra for added effect they subdued her and tossed her on the bed. During this time, she promised herself that for every act they committed she would pay back ten-fold given the opportunity. She remained strong as they fondled her. They videotaped her spread eagle lying on the bed with her pants and underwear down at her ankles. Her tattered shirt and cut bra lay at her head, her bare breast and womanhood in full view of them.

The two men laughed with amusement and took only twenty minutes of footage out of a two-hour ordeal. The rest of the time was for their own sick pleasure as they forced her to pose. Ellis snickered. "That was good. Can't see any reason why I couldn't get a hundred thousand for her. What do you figure Red?"

"If I had a hundred grand I'd buy her myself. Then again, I might take her once for free."

"Don't even think about it Red, she's prime beef and no one likes their beef bruised."

Red chuckled, "I don't know, I kinda like a woman that's being around the block. Can't be the only man alive that likes his beef rare." Their taunts continued until finally she was given permission to go ahead and shower. The door to the bathroom had to remain open and both men sat in complete view of the shower. She knew they were watching but wanted nothing more at the time than to wash away the filth, the perspiration of fear and the feel of the men's unrelenting hands.

Even as she showered, she could feel their hands caressing her. Although they never raped her and only fondled and stared, the video would portray something else. Tears rolled down her cheeks as she scrubbed her skin with soap hoping to wash it all away. When the water ran cold she reached for a towel and dried behind the curtain, hidden except for her shadow from the prying eyes of the two men. She dressed in her tattered shirt and pants before stepping out.

Ellis and Red jeered and taunted her as she darted past them into her room giving neither the satisfaction of a retort. Red stood and approached her door his frame taking up the door space. "Your old man probably has a lot of fun rolling around with you." He commented sinisterly as he locked the door.

Colleen fell to her bed and wept. *What will Hayden think of me now? Will he believe what he sees in that video? He'll never know the truth until we are together,* she thought as tears streamed down her face. The harassment, demoralisation, and sexual advances she endured were certainly beginning to take their toll. She was not penetrated but they certainly took their time shooting the poses of perversion they demanded of her. It was rape of her spirit. Even after the hot shower as she lay there she wondered if she would ever feel clean again.

"Twenty Two."

Monday, November 18, 2002 chilled by the predawn freeze Hayden made for the road and Broadwater Provincial Park a fifteen-mile hike. It was swift going in the predawn due to the frozen snow that now held his weight as he progressed. By 9:00 or 10:00 a.m., he knew the snow would soften and again he'd have to fight with it. Off to a good start, the day was not, without incident. After two miles, he came across the destruction of a recent avalanche. The road was obstructed with debris and uprooted trees for a distance of fifty yards.

Making his way across he saw snowmobile tracks. He looked in all directions for any sign of survivors. Nothing moved or stirred, it was completely silent. Shaking his head in regret, he glanced up to where the avalanche came saddened to know that no one could have survived. Fixing to leave he caught a glimpse of a black glove sticking out of the snow. Running over he began to dig frantically with his hands as though there was hope that the person may have survived. He realised soon enough that he was digging out a corpse. Ice formed around the man's face and suffocated him.

Breaking away the ice from the dead man's face, he recognised him as the guy who broke trail every year for the local Snow-Goers of Kootenay West. He knew him as Snow-Goer George. Every year he broke the trail from Broadwater right on up through Deer Brook and into Granata some fifty miles further up the Arrow Lakes. There would be no way he could dig the body out with his bare hands. The ground was too hard and compact. Instead, his only recourse was to dig the body down to its shoulders, and flag it with the sapling and the dead man's glove. He took a compass reading in case another slide happened and wrote down the longitudes and latitudes. Making it easier for Search and Rescue to recover the body, once he got to Broadwater he would phone.

He squatted next to the frozen corpse of Snow-Goer George looking at him as if it were the first dead body he ever saw. He bowed his head in silence for a few minutes, then stood looking back only once he proceeded onward. The sun shone now and the audible sounds of indigenous winter birds that lived in the mountain thickets and along the shore below squawked, chirped and whistled. The birds it seemed were serenading him as he trudged on saddened by the death.

He couldn't think of that now. George was dead and nothing more could be done. The crunching sound of his footsteps across the frozen snow became quieter as the sun began to shine softening the virgin white snow. Every second step he took the snow gave way and he sunk up to his knees. Unfazed and completely withdrawn he walked as though hypnotised along the tree line where the snow remained shaded and frozen. Like a soldier sent to battle, he got closer to his destination with each step he took.

He squinted at the luminosity of the snow. The glare from the sun shot hot spikes of pain into his retinas. To him his eyes felt itchy and dry as though a leaf from stinging nettle was drawn across them or grains of sand were stuck in the corners. He brought a handful of snow up to them and patted his eyelids. The coolness took away the burn and finally he was able to focus. "Three more miles I figure..." he said quietly to himself still squinting. He continued along the now less shaded tree line avoiding the brightness as much as possible.

***

It was past 10:00 a.m. and Ellis was pulling out onto highway #3, going south-west towards Castlebridge. He decided to send the video he and Red made the night before to a little town called Elkwood which was in the north-east and about a four or five hour drive away. The letter was being sent to him in Deer Brook and would arrive that Friday. It was in the letter that Ellis mentioned the video and told him that for further instructions he was to pick it up in Elkwood. The video would be sent to the attention of Ryce Lennskov C/O General Delivery in Elkwood. It would be up to Hayden to retrieve it.

Ellis inhaled deeply from the White Owl cigar in his mouth. He hadn't been able to find a place where Havana's were sold, so settled for the White Owls. They weren't bad, but he'd rather have a Havana any day. He exhaled and smiled thinking about the reaction on Hayden's face when he finally saw the tape. *Damn I wish I could see that,* he thought as he inhaled another lung full of cigar smoke and exhaled into a fit of coughing.

Stopping at a nearby Shell station he filled the Durango with gas and checked all its fluids. He purchased a large black coffee and a dozen cake donuts, doused in powdered sugar. He devoured two of them before he made it back to the truck. It was near 10:30 a.m. when he pulled back out onto the road, coffee between his legs and the donuts on the dash. Today he felt like a million bucks. It would only be a matter of time before he'd have his hands on the ransom he was asking. *What could be better than twenty one million,* he thought.

The video was nothing more and nothing less than psychological trump card. He knew it would play heavily on Hayden's mind, and the wearier he was, the less likely he'd try anything brash to gain an upper hand as he done in the past, Ellis flipped down the sun-visor and smiled. *I can't wait to see him. He owes me that money and one way or another I'm going to get it,* he thought. Castlebridge was coming into view and he turned onto the bridge that would take him across the Columbia River and to the downtown core.

***

His trek slowed by the snow blindness he was plagued with, Hayden made his way to an outcrop of birch and he peeled a long strip of bark from the biggest tree and cut thin slits in it. Then he wrapped it around his head and fastened it with a piece of lace from his boot. Immediately he felt the relief. The coolness alone from the bark took away the itchy burning sensation he was fighting. He could look now across the shimmering white snow that caused him the discomfort. Squatting, he took a drink from his canteen, *another nine, ten miles and I'll be in Broadwater,* he reminisced.

With his eyes protected now he'd be able to pick up his pace and likely make the distance to Broadwater by early evening. Until then he wouldn't stop. Even now with the sun being out, the rest he took lowered his body temperature and he shivered uncomfortably. By evening, the mercury would certainly drop well below 0. It was best that he kept moving. Standing, he stepped out of the shadows and walked freely on the road no longer plagued by the brightness of the glistening snow.

***

Sitting at the table, Red poured himself a third coffee and was eating his second helping of eggs and toast. In the background, he could hear Colleen knocking on the door of her room, but he didn't care. He'd finish his coffee and food before he answered her. Whatever she wanted could wait.

He smiled at the thought of her spread out the night before. He loved the look of fear in her eyes and relished the fact that he ran his hands all over her. Her skin was warm and smooth and from what he could remember emanated the scent of some delicate perfume, her breasts were firm as any he fondled in the past. He compared them to his old girlfriend and hers were silicon. Colleen's were natural making them more desirable in his mind.

Finishing the last piece of toast he stood and walked over to her door and unlocked it. "What is it you want?"

"I need to use the washroom again if I could." She hated having to ask him that. Especially now since Ellis wasn't around. Although both of them were a threat, Red seemed to her to be the most likely candidate to do something barbarous. The only thing that gave her the confidence to ask was the piece of jagged metal from the Durango's ashtray that she broke away and now held clutched in her hand. If he tried anything, she'd lash out and go down fighting. She figured their game out. Both thrived on fear and intimidation. No longer would she feel either. She would turn stone cold until she was again in Hayden's arms.

Red held his gaze upon her looking her up and down. A creepy smile crossed his face. "As you wish. Will you need any help removing those jeans?" He asked as he gestured for her to go ahead. "And by the way the door stays open."

"I know the drill. Now, please excuse me." Colleen replied as she nudged between him and the doorjamb. She could feel his eyes burning her soul and degrading her in his mind as she squatted. Looking from the corner of her eye before she wiped herself, she was relieved to see that he was actually looking out the front window. Quickly she finished her business.

It wasn't until she turned on the bathroom sink to wash her hands that he finally turned back. Colleen wiped her hands dry and began to walk towards her room, when he stepped in her way. "How about some food? I'll even let you eat at the table. You and I haven't had the chance to talk alone. Are you hungry?"

She was hungry all right. She hadn't anything substantial since breakfast the day before. She studied his body language and wondered what the bottom line was. Did he want something from her? Was he expecting her to submit to his perversions? To prevent anything from taking place she kindly declined his offer. She knew that once Ellis returned later that afternoon she'd be fed something. "Please let me be." She commented as she sauntered by.

"That's fine. Be grateful I don't come in there and make you my whore." Red stammered as he locked the door.

Colleen fell to the bed her heart beating as loud as a drum. Now out of the sight of Red, her hands sweated and her body shuddered with anxiety as she put the piece of metal back in its hiding spot between the mattresses of her bed. Feeling a chill, she wrapped herself up with a quilt from her bed. She held it tightly across her shoulders. She hadn't seen sunshine for three days, except briefly on those few occasional trips to the washroom. She longed for the brightness and warmth of it. "Where are you Hayden?" She whispered as if sending him a subliminal message. One she hoped he'd answer.

Around this same time, Ellis was pulling up to the post office in Castlebridge. He parked opposite the red brick building nearest the liquor store, making a mental note to pick up some Vodka before he left town. Shutting off the truck he stepped out and headed across the street. The cost to send the two items seemed a little steep, but he held his tongue. Making his way back to the liquor store, he purchased a bottle of Vodka and a twenty-four pack of Kokanee beer.

He wasn't fond of beer but Red was. Tonight they would have a few drinks and reminisce. *It's only a matter of time before Hayden receives the packages and my demands.* The thought brought a smile to his face as he exited the liquor store. Stopping off at a local grocer, he purchased a couple of limes to go with the Vodka as well as party favours, and some real food. Then he headed back to Thurman.

He'd be back at the cabin in about forty-five minutes, his business for now done and the wheels of his plot in motion. Hayden would melt in his hands like butter in a skillet. Ellis contemplated yet another plot and that was to pry Colleen for information on Monique Farell. He needed information on Monique and Colleen was the easiest link to break. What he did know of her was that she settled in Mexico.

***

Hayden rested on a stump for the second and final time that day. He cast his gaze towards the final leg of his journey, the last steep incline before the road levelled off and descended into the broad valley below. It was close to 2:00 p.m., and his legs were wobbly from the day's hike. Being slowed earlier in the day with snow blindness and the search for George's body he calculated the time he lost to be four hours. *Four hours behind and stuck in the middle of an icy hell*, he thought as he rested. With less then two hours of daylight left he knew he would have no choice but to set up a camp one last time. When he set out that morning, he assumed he would have made the distances to Castlebridge by nightfall but that wasn't happening now.

The trek to the top of the steep incline was discouraging and slowed him down even more. The snow in places was crotch level and walking through it wasn't easy. He slipped and fell face first on more than one occasion. The cold steel barrel of the sniper rifle slammed against the back of his head each and every time. When the sun was only a memory he finally crested the top. The temperature dropped a few degrees he noticed, and with what little light remained, he sought shelter and rest. Tonight, he burrowed into the deep snow at the base of a large evergreen. Building a fire in the road he made coffee and roasted frankfurters on a stick.

Heat from the flames radiated across his chilled face as he sipped the hot black liquid and choked back the frankfurters. Tossing the last one into the fire he watched as it turned to charcoal. It was amusing to him how the wiener swelled to twice its size as little puffs of smoked ballooned upward from its charred remains. He was trying to keep his mind clear from thoughts of Colleen and the torment she was going through. But even the smouldering frankfurter couldn't keep his mind clear.

As darkness regained the stillness of day, he retreated to his burrow beneath the evergreen and draped his sleeping bag across his shoulders. Tonight he'd use the kerosene tent heater he stowed away in his backpack, it wouldn't emit as much heat as a fire but it would be enough to dry out his gloves, boot liners and sopping wet socks. He crouched close to the heater with his back to the tree absorbing as much of the heat as possible before the kerosene ran out. He brought with him a squeeze bottle full but it was possible he might need that at another time. The amount that was in the heater could carry him through until early twilight as long as he didn't keep it burning full bore. He stared into the hissing blue and orange flame watching until the heaters ceramic element began to glow. Turning the flame down he pulled the sleeping bag draped across his shoulders up and over his ears and face, leaving only his eyes and the top of his head exposed to the cold.

There was something about that night that made him feel uneasy. It may have been how calm, cold, or dark it seemed that night or the general concern he felt for Colleen's being. How was she being treated? Had she tried an escape? What were Ellis's demands? Obviously, it was money, but how much. Would he find Ellis and end the entire charade before it got out of hand? Who was the second man and what was the significant part that he played?

There were more questions than there were answers and he had less then a week to figure it out. If he couldn't upturn even a minute piece of evidence on where Ellis might be staying once he got to Castlebridge, he'd have no choice but to head back to Deer Brook and wait for further instruction. The return trip would take less than a few hours if he could hitch back by boat and a day's ride on a snowmobile. Either way the return trip would be a walk in the park.

He was confident that he'd get a lead from someone. Castlebridge was a small city. Any strangers bouncing about usually caught the eye of someone. Deciding to break the monotony of the evenings chilling silence, he turned on the radio surprised that he could tune into the local radio station. A ballad sung by Kid Rock and Sheryl Crow started. He didn't catch the name of the song. The radio went snowy and made an awful buzzing sound that echoed in the evening as the song ended. He turned off the eerie cackle and again all was silent and still.

Shivering beneath the warmth of his sleeping bag a chill ran up his spine. The hair standing up on the back of his neck was not, an unfamiliar feeling. Rather it was a feeling that warned him something was watching him. It wasn't the first time something watched him from a distance or in the dark. It was the feeling that he didn't like. Sitting with his back to the tree he listened for any audible sound but heard only silence in the still night air. He looked at his watch. It was 9:00 p.m. for nine hours he'd have to endure the evening cold. By 6:00 a.m., he wanted to be on the go and with luck finish the hike to Broadwater by early afternoon the following day.

"Twenty Three."

Rising at 5:00 a.m., he was surprised at how mild the evening had been as he slept. Now in the early morning, the air was chilled. *It'll be another clear and warm day once that sun begins to shine,* he thought as he rubbed his hands together. It was semi dark and the snow appeared pale blue in the early predawn. In the sky stars flickered and he watched as they twinkled out as the sun slowly rose greeting the new day. Before 11:30 a.m. that day, he made the distance to Broadwater.

Ducking into some undergrowth he dismantled the sniper rifle and put it in his backpack. The pay phone at the park entrance was out of order and he was unable to make the call to Search and Rescue. Once he got to Castlebridge, he'd head to the local R.C.M.P office and fill them in on the location and demise of Snow-Goer George. They could take it from there.

It was nice to be able to walk on a ploughed road for a change. Forty-five minutes later he was picked up by an acquaintance of one of his friends. He knew the guy as Catfish Sam. His real name was Rus. But when his buddy introduced the two of them, he had been introduced as Catfish Sam and he called him that ever since. "Nice of you to stop, Catfish. How you been?" He opened the door to the truck and sat down.

"Not bad Rochsoff. Did you hike in from Deer Brook?"

"You bet."

"Why would you do a thing like that?"

"Exercise, I guess. Got to get into shape for Bear season in April."

"How's the wife doin'? It must be pretty lonely for her way out there."

"She's used to it. She has a few friends that stop by to keep her occupied when I take off. Are you still with your old lady?"

"Sure am. She keeps me from getting into trouble don't ya know."

"I hear you. That's the thing about women, you can't live with them and you can't live without them."

"Ain't that the truth." Catfish replied as he drove across the bridge. "Whereabouts you want off?"

"Anywhere downtown will do."

Catfish pulled up to a curb opposite the local bar. "How's this?"

"Perfect. Thanks a lot. I appreciate the ride."

"I was going this way anyhow. No big deal, take care. See ya around."

Hayden nodded and waved as Catfish pulled out into the street and headed up town. The ride saved him a two-hour walk and he was grateful for that. Hurrying to the R.C.M.P station, he filled them in on where the body of George could be found.

"I can't believe you walked in from Deer Brook. That must have been a pain in the ass," Constable Miller said. All the RC's in the area knew who Hayden was. At one time or another, he guided a couple of them on hunts.

"It was nothing like the time you and I headed into Enterprise Creek."

Constable Miller chuckled, "Yeah, I remember that hike, but damn if you didn't lead me to the biggest elk I've ever shot. What brings you into town at this time of year anyway?"

He wasn't about to tell him the truth. "I felt the need. I wanted to see if I could do it."

"Are you thinking on hiking back as well?"

"Nah, I'll have one of my friends boat me back, or I might pick up a sled. We'll see how it goes. Here's those headings where the body can be found." He handed Al the piece of paper he wrote them on.

"Great, thanks a lot. We'll get S and R up there directly." Al looked over the bearings.

"Good enough. I got to get going. We'll talk again soon."

"Yeah, for sure. By the way, if you can't get a boat to take you back or you don't buy a sled let me know. I'll take you up in our boat, no problem, just stop by."

Hayden smiled and nodded. "Sure thing, thanks a lot." He exited the police station. *Now to get to the corner stone of this excursion,* he thought as he stepped onto the sidewalk. His second stop would be the local marina to find out if any one ever saw a black and red boat, and whom it might belong to. He made his way to the marina down by the old ferry dock. If anybody knew who, the boat might belong to he'd find the answer there. The owner, Rob, knew everybody in Castlebridge and had been running the Dockside Marina for five years. Rob was surprised when Hayden walked through the glass door. "Hayden, what brings you here. Deciding to buy a boat?" Rob questioned half jokingly.

"Nope. But, when the time does come rest assured I'll buy it here." He replied as he set his pack down and poured a coffee from the urn. "I was wondering if any of you guys might know who owns a black and red outboard? They were up at Deer Park a couple of days ago and left some fishing rods and a cooler behind on the dock. Since I was in town anyway, I figured I'd try and find out whose it was so that they can be informed that I have their belongings."

"Black and red eh?"

"Yep, it was an older boat. Do any of you know who owns one?" He took a sip from his coffee.

"Sounds like old man John's boat. Strange though, old John rarely goes up that far during winter. He lives down by the mill at two mile. I believe his fire number is 724. I'd phone him up Hayden, except he's like you and doesn't have a phone. He comes in here every now and again, I can relay the message if you like?"

"Sure, that'd be fine. I may walk over and let him know though. I haven't got much else to do and the walk would do me good."

"That works. He's a bit of an eccentric and forgets things, I might have to remind him. He'd probably enjoy your company and try to get you to join him in a few drinks. He drinks whiskey like it's soda pop." Rob chuckled. "You're sure I can't interest you in a boat. This year's Evinrude catalogue is in. It has some nice boats that are reasonably price."

"Always the businessman, eh?"

"It's what I do best."

"I'll tell you what, this spring you can try and convince me. Colleen has been hounding me to buy one anyway. What's the usual cost?"

"It depends on what you want. They can range from anywhere between twenty to thirty grand and above. That is of course if you buy it with the factory outboard. I could probably hook you up with a good motor for less than five grand. It would bring the price of the boat down a bit. A lot of my customers do it that way. If you were to buy a cabin cruiser, you'd need to add another fifteen grand to the total. For around here though all one needs is a pleasure craft."

Hayden sipped on his coffee and smiled as he scratched at the whiskers on his chin. "How about giving me a few brochures to take back to the little lady?"

Rob opened the drawer behind the counter and handed him a few. "Here you go man. That Evinrude on the front cover of that one will drop in price by spring, that's an insider tip for you. It's probably the best pleasure craft for the lakes around here."

"Thanks. That is a nice looking craft isn't it?" Hayden tossed his Styrofoam cup that held the coffee into the wastebasket. "I'll take these back to Colleen and see what she has to say. Thanks for the coffee and information, but I've got to get going. I'm going to wander over to old John's to let him know that the next time he's up and around Deer Brook to stop by for his gear."

"Make sure you say hi to him for me. That old codger probably gets lonely. A visitor will certainly brighten the poor bugger's day."

Hayden tossed his backpack over his shoulder and headed for fire number 724 down by the mill. Rob had been right. Old John was quite pleased to have company. He willingly told Hayden what it was he wanted to know. Apparently, he rented his boat to two burly men. He described Ellis to a tee. The other man who was with him was a big ox of guy with scraggly red hair. Hayden knew then that the other man was one of Ellis's henchmen that he met before, who went by the name of Red. He questioned John if he saw them return and what kind of vehicle they were driving.

"I have to tell ya, young man that I was in a drunken stupor when they arrived back. All I can remember is hearin' my old boat being docked. I didn't bother asking them how the fishin' was. That's what they said they wanted it for. I couldn't figure out why they didn't rent one from the marina, and didn't even bother to ask. I presumed there weren't any available is all," John said as he swallowed back the shot of rye in his cup. "Don't suppose you'd want to join me for another drink?"

Hayden felt obligated and agreed to have a shot with him. John poured him a drink and added an ice cube to his glass. "I don't mix my drinks, so I ain't got no soda pop to go with it. No sir, I drink it on the rocks straight up. Hope that don't bother ya none."

Hayden shook his head, "No, that's fine. You didn't happen to get a look at the vehicle they were driving did you?" He asked as he accepted the shot of rye.

"I sure did. Yes sir, I sure did. It was a fancy red Durango, even got a look at the plate to know they weren't from around here. I believe they were from up in Alaska somewhere. The fat guy even told me so. Said they were down here on some business trip and wanted to take the day to do some Kokanee fishin'. I told them the best thing to use for the Kokanee was a lure. They seemed not to know a whole lot about fishin' in these parts." John kicked back the rye and poured another. "Want another?"

"No thanks John, two is my limit."

"When I was a young man I drank no less then four for breakfast everyday. Keeps the pipes from rustin', you know." He chuckled as he tilted the glass to his lips.

"They wouldn't have mentioned where they might be staying. Did they?"

"We never conversed much. They paid me $150.00 US to take out my boat for the day and that's about it. I do recall the tall one sayin' they were going to be around for a couple of weeks. In a town the size of Castlebridge a brand new Dodge Durango, red in colour with Alaskan plates shouldn't be too hard to locate. What do you want with them anyway?"

"They left their gear on the dock at Deer Brook. I wanted to see to it that they got it back. But since they're from way up in Alaska, there is no point in me trying to locate them. I thought they might have been locals. Guess I'll keep their rods. If they happen by here again let them know that Hayden Rochsoff up in Deer Brook has their gear if they want it back."

"Rochsoff? You're the guy that runs that outfitters up there in Deer Brook, aren't you?"

"That's right."

"I'll be. Nice to meet you, I didn't realise who you were at first. You took my grandson up into the Selkirk's on a bear hunt a few years back and helped him bag a big brown. He told me you were one of the best guides he ever hired. Said you knew exactly where to take him for that bear, biggest bear he ever shot in these parts. Damn was he proud of that rug once he got it back from the taxidermist. You might recall him. He had the same name as me. My daughter named him after yours truly, when we were on talkin' terms."

Hayden was recalling the name and the hunt. "I remember him. How is he doing? Small world isn't it?

"It is a small world indeed…" the old man paused for a moment, "Johnathan was killed in a car accident last year around Christmas."

Hayden could hear the pain and sadness in his voice. "I'm sorry to hear that. He was a good kid from what I remember." That was all he could offer in way of condolences. "I hate hearing news like that."

"It's in the past, it's in the past." John downed his fourth drink, mulling over in his mind the death of his only grandson.

"I don't want to be a burden any longer. I best get going. I thank you for the info. If you're ever up and around Deer Brook, I live on the hill. Stop in. Once again, I'm sorry about Johnathan." The old man sitting across from him waved his hand in the air gesturing that life was life. And that all things must end.

"I do get up that way once in a while and I'll be sure to stop in," he said as he poured himself another whiskey. He walked Hayden to the door, glass in hand and bid him farewell. "If you ever want to stop in again the whiskey is always ready to be shared." Hayden smiled and shook John's hand. Then ascended the steep incline up to the road, his next course of action was trying to find someone who might have seen or knew where a newer red Dodge Durango might be holed up.

John was right. A red Durango with Alaskan plates shouldn't be too complicated to find. People had to eat, which meant they purchased food or ate out somewhere. It would only be a matter of time now. Proceeding northward towards town, he kept his eyes peeled in case he got lucky enough to spot a red Durango. It dawned on him as he walked that if Ellis were going to send to him further instructions he'd have to use the post office to do so. Perhaps someone at the post office could offer him another lead.

It was too late now, but it would be the first thing he'd do in the morning. For now he'd grab a room and rest his weary body. A hot meal was in order as well and he knew the best place for both would be the Monte Carlo Inn east of town. It meant another three-mile walk up town, but it would be worth it. The food there was home style and the rooms were quite reasonable. He could pry them for information as well. Perhaps they saw or served food to Ellis and Red, perhaps not. Either way that's where he was heading.

He walked the long hill that led up town when Catfish pulled over on the other side. "Where are ya headin' now?" He hollered across the road from the driver side window.

"The Monte Carlo." Hayden hollered back.

"I'll turn around and give ya a ride." Catfish rolled up his window and pulled a U-turn stopping beside Hayden.

Hayden tossed his pack into the back of the truck and opened the door. "You didn't have to do this."

"I have a great deal of admiration for anyone who walks all the way from Deer Brook. I'm surprised you didn't fire up the Siberian Tiger and plough your way into town." He was referring to Hayden's 4x4.

"I thought about that if only briefly. Besides, I wanted to see if I had the stamina to walk that far in snow six foot deep."

"Fenfawn always did say you were crazy. By the way have you seen him around, lately?"

"No, I haven't seen him in a few months. I've seen a lot of his old lady's artwork though. That is her art work painted on the Downtown Market's window, isn't it?"

"Sure is. They won't let her do anything as elaborate as she did on the hood of your truck. That there is some of the nicest work I've seen. Apparently, she works at the marina. Rob hired her to paint the custom boats he designs."

"Really?"

"Yep, interesting isn't it?"

They pulled into the Monte Carlo parking lot a few minutes later. "Thanks a lot for the ride Rus. I appreciate it." Hayden opened the door and stepped out.

"No problem Shotsoff," Rus said teasingly. "Say hi to the wife for me and don't be a stranger. If you're ever near Fruitmont, stop by and we'll drink some brew."

"You can count on it. I'll see you around." Hayden retrieved his gear from the back of the truck and waved. Catfish honked the horn, waved back, and sped out of the parking lot.

It was hard keeping things away from the people he knew and trusted but his training in the RRA taught him how. He didn't like it, however it was the only way for him to rectify the situation. Three days had come and gone and God only knew the condition of Colleen. He kicked the snow and mud off his boots before he entered the glass doors of the Monte Carlo. Walking up to the service desk, he rented a room. It was on the west-side and overlooked all the main streets going into the downtown core. He'd be able to see any vehicles coming and going from the three directions if he decided.

It was a comfortable room. The decor was saffron. Even the toilet and sink and shower were saffron. There was a wooden desk boasting a phone and a large coloured TV, as well as a vinyl high back chair and couch. He tossed his pack onto the large bed. Removing his boots, he placed his socks and boot liners on the register.

He was totally exhausted and although it wasn't quite 7:00 p.m., he needed to rest his eyes for what he thought and hoped would be a short while. Instead when he opened them again he realised it was past 9:00 p.m. Which meant the motel's restaurant was closed. It didn't matter a hot meal would have been nice but obviously, he needed the rest. Switching on the TV, he channel surfed. It didn't take long for his eyes to feel heavy and he strode over to the bed. Whatever tomorrow brought he wanted to be well rested.

***

Ellis and Red spent the majority of the day lounging and nursing their hangovers from the past night. They had looked in on Colleen once that night and left her with a bottle of water and a plate of cheese, sausage, crackers, and pickles. Then the two of them played poker and guzzled. Now, more than twenty-four hours later they were finally feeling up to par. Both of them looked like hell and smelled as bad. "It's 9:15 p.m., are you going jump in the shower first or am I?"

"I don't want to move. I drank too many beers last night. It didn't help either that I slept until 3:00 p.m., or the fact that we stayed cooped up all day. I'll grab a shower after you. Go ahead." Red waved Ellis on.

Ellis yawned and stretched, "All right. I'll try and save some hot water for you. You might want to look in on our stable mate, she hasn't been making much noise as of late."

"I'll check on her in a bit. Might as well bring her something to eat while I'm at it."

Ellis nodded and headed for the shower. Standing, Red turned up the thermostat and as the oil furnace kicked on he made his way into the kitchen. A slew of cans and bottles disgraced the table. A deck of cards sat precariously in a puddle of booze. There was an opened empty packet of White Owls with cigar butts and ashes inside. Obviously, it used as an ashtray. Two plates of drying pickles, soggy crackers, and hardening cheeses sat next to all this. There was an opened can of smoked oysters on the counter, the contents looked as though they were smashed or spit back out. It was like the frat house after a party full of college teens.

He shook his head at the mess and almost puked. “Sick.” He whispered beneath his breath as he went about cleaning. He tossed everything including the plates into the garbage. *Earlier it didn’t seem quite that bad. Probably because we were still drunk,* he thought. With the mess cleaned to a more desirable state, he brewed a fresh pot of coffee. He fixed a sandwich for Colleen and brought her a large glass of juice. “Here I brought you something to eat. If you want it come and get it cause I ain’t no waiter.”

Colleen stood from the chair she was sitting in and walked the short distance to take the offerings. “Thanks.”

He pushed the tray of food into her chest as she approached. “Here, go set it down and bring me the plate and cups you have. Bring back that tray too.” Colleen turned and swayed over to the dresser where she put the sandwich and glass of juice down. She retrieved the empty plate and extra cups from the top of the nightstand and returned them to Red. Nodding he didn’t mutter a word. He turned and closed the door.

Three hours later at 12:30 a.m., they entered her darkened room once more and roused her out of bed. “Get up. I have some questions for you to answer,” Ellis threatened as he pulled her covers off. Jumping up from her bed, she tossed the quilt over her shoulders. Frightened she held her ground.

“What kind of men are you? Busting into my room, your questions couldn’t have waited until morning?”

“Shut up or I’ll backhand you. Now sit down in that chair and listen carefully to my questions. Don’t squawk a word until I’ve asked them to you in succession. Firstly, whereabouts in Mexico does Hayden’s hometown acquaintance, Monique Farell live?”

Colleen knew exactly where he was going with question. “I haven’t a clue.” She answered smugly.

“Just as I thought. You’re a stupid broad did you know that. How about I have Red here throw you down on the bed. You know how he lusts over you. Perhaps a roll in the park with him will jar your memory? I’ll video it while he brutalises you for real and send that to my dear nephew Hayden. Do you think he might like to see that, huh, do you? I know Red here wouldn’t have a problem obliging.”

“You got that right. I’d love a go a round with her. Show her how a real man feels.”

“I’ll give you one more chance to answer. What part of Mexico does Monique live in?” Colleen’s heart was fluttering in her chest and she could feel it pulsating, she had to come up with a name of someplace in Mexico. "Are you deaf? Give me an answer and do it fast."

"First, I want you to promise me that you'll keep Red the hell away from me."

"I ain't going to promise you nothin', now hurry up with that answer."

"All I know is it's near San Lorenzo. Don't ask me the longitudes or latitudes cause I don't know."

"Longitudes and latitudes are pretty big words for a woman."

"Yeah, right. If you're a woman who lives in the city and the furthest from your home you've ever been is the City Park. Give me a break. Is it your opinion that women are stupid?"

Ellis stared at Colleen. He always liked spunky women. "It's the simple facts. Question number two, does Monique use her real name?"

"Of course. Not everyone in life lives on fallacy. She has nothing to hide."

"Is that right?" He quizzed as he turned to exit. Colleen answered his questions for now. He'd make a mental note of her answers and ask her again in a day or two. If she blabbed something different, he'd know that she was lying.

Red followed behind Ellis as he exited. Turning, he looked back to Colleen. "You're lucky you answered. I was getting anxious thinking about what I was going to do to you. Next time you might not be so lucky." He closed the door and locked it. Colleen sighed in relief and thanked God for being able to come up with what she told Ellis. Rising she returned to the bed. Staring up at the ceiling, she drifted back to sleep.

"Twenty Four."

The smell of food wafting up to his room from the restaurant below didn't force him to rise right away, but it sure teased him. Not able to take it any longer he sat up in bed and stretched, his watch read 6:15 a.m. Yawning he threw the covers off and headed to the bathroom and a hot steamy shower. Refreshed, he gathered his gear, exited, and walked down stairs to order breakfast. He wasn't surprised that knew the waitress who served him. "Hayden, what are you doing here?" the waitress started, "is Colleen with you?"

"Not this time."

"What in the heck brings you into town?"

"A crazy notion." He chuckled, "how have you been?"

"A crazy notion. Don't tell me, you guys finally bought a boat?" She seemed excited.

"Nope."

"A sled then?"

"If you can believe it I walked in."

"You got to be kidding, you walked in?"

Hayden chuckled. "I sure did."

"That's a little nutty."

"It's crazy what a man will do for a good breakfast." He winked at her. "By the way, you wouldn't have seen two foreigners here in the past couple days would you have?"

"What do you mean? I see different people here everyday."

"You would have noticed these guys. One of them has crazy green eyes, the other has a mop of red hair that always looks uncombed and is…well head and shoulders above me. Plus they would've been driving a newer red Dodge Durango."

"Sorry, I don't recall anyone like that. Why are you looking for them?"

"They rented a boat from an old guy down near the mill and left some gear behind on the dock up in Deer Brook. Ah, it doesn't matter. It was a couple of fishing rods and a cooler." He waved his hand through the air.

"If you like I can ask around. I either wasn't on shift or can't plain remember."

"That's okay, don't worry about it."

"All right. So are you ready to order?" Hayden nodded and ordered bacon and eggs, toast and a large coffee.

"Coming right up," the waitress pranced away towards the kitchen. He looked out the window into the chilly November morning. The post office was next, but that wasn't open for a couple of hours. If he couldn't come up with anything there then he'd have to head back. It didn't necessarily mean that Ellis hadn't sent him something via the mail on what he was expected to do next.

If he could track down Randy before he headed out with the mail for delivery that Friday he could retrieve whatever if anything was sent to him. The problem was after all these years he had no idea when Randy gathered the mail. If he gathered it every Monday and delivered on that following Friday or if he picked it up during the week or even the same Friday he delivered it. It never mattered before. All he knew was the mail was delivered every Friday. Contemplating this he was jostled back to reality when the waitress showed up with his breakfast order.

"Here you go, eggs, bacon, toast and coffee. Also, Natalie our cook said she recalls a couple of guys that fit your description. She said they were here this past Saturday, but she doesn't know where they might be staying."

"Thanks," he nodded. It didn't help him much, but if they ate there once, they might return. He didn't have time to sit around and wait, however, but he'd be sure to return before he headed back to Deer Brook out of curiosity to see if they had, that is if nothing else panned out. Drinking the last of his coffee, he paid his bill then stepped out into the cool morning. The breeze blew his hair and reddened his face with a chill as he strode towards the downtown core.

It was Wednesday, November 20. He wanted to put this thing to rest in two days, or that following Monday at the latest. By then, he knew if Ellis hadn't heard from him that he would start to get anxious and probably dispose of Colleen then slip into the void like a shadow from the past. Ellis wasn't stupid he already knew it would take Hayden a day or two to comply. It was part of the game.

He had no control over anything until he either found where Ellis and Red were holed up or he replied to further instructions sent by Ellis. The decision to hunt Ellis down might not have been a wise one. Time was definitely not on his side.

Hayden made it to the downtown core by 8:30 a.m., leaving another thirty minutes to wait. He walked over to a nearby coffee shop and by 9:00 a.m. was standing at the counter of the post office as the first customers of the day began to arrive. He heard one of the post masters call out to him, "Hayden Rochsoff. Well I'll be wasn't expecting to see you. How are things and what in God's green earth brings you into town?"

"To tell you the truth Wes I wanted to see if I could hike the distance from Deer Brook to here. I figured since I'm here. I might gather any mail that might be on its way to me. Can that be done?"

"It sure can. I'll go check and see if any thing is bound for you. I seem to recall that there are a couple of items. I best double check that before I say for sure. Hold on and I'll get right back to you."

"Thanks a lot. I appreciate it." Hayden leaned up against the counter, hoping and praying he intercepted something from Ellis. If he had, he'd be two days closer to his objective.

Wes returned holding an envelope in his hand. "There sure is something here for you, it's one letter. Here you go." Wes handed him the envelope.

Hayden looked to see who sent it. When no name except his own was on the envelope, his heart beat as though it was going to shoot out of his chest. "Thanks again. I'll be seeing you." Walking a short distance until he was out of view he tore into the envelope and removed the hand written letter which read: 'Seek a video sent to Ryce Lennskov, General Delivery, Elkwood. That is all for now.'

Hayden shook his head. He wasn't expecting any thing like this. The only way the post office would relay any information on something sent to a Ryce Lennskov in Elkwood would be if he got the RCMP involved. That was something he'd rather not do. If he did, Colleen would certainly disappear and so would Ellis and Red. He'd never have the chance to get her back into his arms again. He decided to rent a car and drive to Elkwood. He was struggling with two questions. When was the video sent? How long would the Elkwood post office keep the parcel in General Delivery before sending it back? It dawned on him it was unlikely Ellis even put a return address on the parcel in which case if he didn't retrieve it soon it would simply be, disposed of.

Elkwood was about a four-hour drive and the time was only 9:30 a.m. If things went as he hoped he could be back on his way to Castlebridge by 3:00 or 4:00 p.m., taking into consideration the amount of time he needed to rent a car. By 10:15 a.m., he was leaving the outskirts of Castlebridge.

He was glad that Castlebridge was small and he didn't have to wait in a long line up wasting precious time to rent a vehicle from the local car rental. He headed east towards the community of Elkwood. He had no idea how he would retrieve the parcel. He had no identification that named him as Ryce Lennskov that was from a time long past. That phoney identification was long destroyed and only Ellis knew it even existed. He certainly made the possibility of retrieving the parcel a difficult task.

With luck he would have enough time to change the rules and set him up, annihilating Ellis's threatening presence as well as the hired mercenary everyone called Red. With that done, he and Colleen could return to the way life was only a few days earlier. And the world would be less one Ellis Leroy and one mercenary named Red.

There were things, he hadn't considered and he thought of these as he drove. What would he do with the bodies? How could he dispose of the truck, or any evidence that might lead investigators to the conclusion, that he was responsible for the deaths of the two men? How could he and Colleen get away with out leaving a clue?

"We'll cross that bridge when we come to it," he repeated to himself. "Until then, stay focussed on today."

It was always best to remain focussed on one objective at a time. One mistake could end it all, and he would be the loser. An hour later he was held back by avalanche control on the Kootenay Pass, only three hours away from Elkwood. It took crews two hours to reopen the highway and to get the traffic moving again at a fair pace. It annoyed him that he was slowed down by two hours. Anymore set backs would likely see him get into Elkwood after the post office closed for the day, leaving him with no other choice but to spend the night there. Something he wasn't keen on doing.

He wanted to be back in Castlebridge that evening and continue his pursuit of Ellis and his henchman. The only way that was happening now was if he travelled like a bat out of hell the remaining distance to Elkwood. Once he made it to the bottom of the Pass he sped the car up and travelled at speeds between 110 and 120 km/h, when the road conditions allowed him. He made it to Elkwood before 4:00 p.m., and closing. The postal clerk never even gave him a second glance as he asked for the parcel. "Excuse me ma am. Would there be a parcel here in General Delivery for Ryce Lennskov?" Hayden asked with a slight Russian accent. The postal clerk turned and walked over to the General Delivery isle. She looked at a few different items and then finally returned with the parcel.

"You say Ryce Lennskov?"

"Yes ma'am."

"You're in luck. Here you go," she said as she handed him the parcel.

"Thank you ma'am."

"We wondered about this one. There was no return address on it, it was scheduled for disposal beginning next week on Monday in the a.m. Good thing you came by."

"Yes, indeed. Thank you again." Hayden turned and exited clutching the parcel as though someone was going to try and steal it from him. He walked the short distance to where he parked and tore open the large manila envelope that held the tape. There was no letter, only a video. His mind raced as a rage greater than any he ever felt built up deep inside his being.

"If you have hurt her Ellis I will torture you until you die." He slammed his fist into the steering wheel. He needed to find a place quickly where he could view the tape. He rented a room at the Elkwood Motel. He had no intentions on staying there. Once he viewed the tape he'd head back to Castlebridge and proceed with his next objective.

Hayden opened the door to the room and directly turned on the TV and VCR. In the first minutes of the tape, he was repulsed at what he was viewing. He watched as Ellis and Red fondled Colleen as they taunted and pointed at her.

His heart and mind were livid and he quickly fast-forwarded it to the end, where Ellis sat in a chair in the middle of the room with Colleen's naked body spread out on the bed behind him. A smile crossed Ellis's face and he chuckled as he began to speak. "There you have it, Hayden. Your woman is very firm. She will be an asset to the Russian sex trade unless you come up with $21,333,333.

This of course would have been the equal amount divided between the three of you out of the $64,000,000 you, Monique, and Alex took from me. Have you forgotten it was because of me that you have that money now? I'd like all of it but three million to be deposited in a Russian bank account on the Komandor Island under the name of Wilhiem Deboskoff account number 1103567 at the New Bank of Vladivostok. Three million in large bills is to be handed over to me at a designated location.

First though, deposit the difference into the account I mentioned. Once that is done you will dial 504-555 -2728 and confirm the deposit. Then you will be given the location on where to meet me with the three million and to retrieve what may be left of your little playmate. Don't even attempt dialling that number until you have made the deposit. Or I will send pictures to you in the coming months on how well this tasty morsel of a woman behind me is being treated by her whoremasters in Russia. You have until midnight November the 29th, after which time expect those pictures. With that said, I wish you luck."

The video ended there. Hayden removed the video, refusing to watch the whole thing. The few minutes had been enough. Tossing the room key onto the bed, he exited into the early evening. He had to get back into Castlebridge as quickly as possible. It was only from there could he continue with the objective. Somehow, he was certain that Ellis and Red were holed up somewhere near there. He tried to erase the scenes of the two men fondling Colleen, but the images were to real for him to forget.

As he drove back to Castlebridge his rage burned like fires from hell, as did his fear for Colleen's life. He would kill Ellis Leroy no matter what. Nothing would stand in his way. Even, if he had to hunt him down until his dying day. Tears of fury welled up in his eyes. He felt helpless. What could he do? How could he find that bastard and his henchman and exact the revenge he swore in his mind?

"Twenty Five."

Arriving back in Castlebridge that evening at 9:30 p.m. and although the car rental place was closed, he parked the car amongst the others in the lot. Retrieved his gear from the trunk and slipped the key and other pertinent information through the mail slot in the glass front doors of the rental office. The entire time it took him to drive back from Elkwood he couldn't put the vision of what he saw on the video in the back of his mind, it sat right up front playing over and over again.

He contemplated what his next move ought to be. He had a good friend who sold cell phones. Perhaps he could track the signal of Ellis's cell phone without alarming Ellis. It was a possibility he needed to investigate. If he could get the location of where the signal was coming from, he'd have a good chance in finding Ellis before long. If it couldn't be done then he'd have no choice but to comply with Ellis and arrange to do the transactions. He didn't have the entire amount but he'd rally the rest if he needed. If he was short a few hundred thousand, chances were Ellis wouldn't care.

Renting another room for the evening downtown at a Hotel called the Arlane, he settled for the evening. Sleep took him quickly as he lay down on the bed, but he was awake soon as animated visions from the video haunted him. Sitting up in bed, he shook his head trying to erase the dream. He was shivering in a cold sweat. He felt so useless, so unreliable. If he'd only paid more attention to what had been going on when Colleen was abducted. If he'd only sat with her, rather than trying to fix a problem that didn't even exist yet. Sure the generator needed maintenance but it could have waited. He felt guilt. It made his heart thump as though it was going to explode.

Thursday, November 21, 6:30 a.m., he splashed water on his face to wash away the cobwebs from the past night. He checked out of the Arlane before 7:00 a.m. and proceeded towards a coffee shop. His mission was to head over to the Columbia Cell Phone Co. and find out about tracking the signal from Ellis's cell phone. He knew Stacy opened at around 9:00 a.m. and he wanted to be there when he showed up to open shop.

Stacy was a loud man when he talked with friends, but, behind the counter he was a gentle salesman and well spoken. He came from a rich family that at one time owned a window and doors outfit, they also dabbled in custom-built cabinetry and framing work. Stacy's older brother took over operations of the outfit and Stacy soaked his money into the cell phone business. Hayden met him in the first year he and Colleen moved to Deer Brook and he considered him one of his most trusted friends.

Arriving at Stacy's shop before 9:00 a.m. he watched as he pulled up. "Hey what brings you into town? Where the is that pretty old lady of yours?"

"Hey Stacy how's it been going?"

"Pretty good. Some things have changed. I'm heading to Puerto Rico to open up shop down there. Business sucks up here right now, but it always does at this time of year. Come on let's get our asses inside and have a coffee. What brings you into Castlebridge before spring? Finally pick yourself up a sled or boat?"

"Nah, not yet. Considering it though, I hiked in. So, you're heading to Puerto Rico? Good for you, you're expanding then. Figure business will be better down there?" Hayden questioned with excitement.

"I don't know if it'll be better or worse. It's an opportunity that recently came about. But back to you, Jesus, you better check yourself into the mental hospital. That's one helluva hike. Here I'll dial the number for you." Stacy jokingly reached for his cell phone.

"You know they wouldn't have me."

"I suppose you're right. You'd be like a caged animal with rabies if you were locked up."

"Or worse. Anyway what I wanted to ask, is it possible to trace a cell phone signal without dialling the number?"

"That can't be done. I could find out whom the number belonged to. Perhaps even in what location the phone was last used. All private cell phone companies have locals. For instance, mine is location 41-50, which covers Castlebridge and most of the west Kootenay region. If I plugged in someone's cell phone number and the last local it was used in was 41-50, I'd know that the cell phone was last used in my general local as well as the date and time. If it were to say local 54-01 for instance, that'd be the east Kootenay region, you know Creston and east towards the Alberta border." Stacy brought his coffee cup to his lips and took a swig.

"So what you're saying is you could tell me where the phone was last used and at what time, that sort of thing, but you couldn't pinpoint the signal unless you dialled the number?"

"If you got a number give it to me and I'll find out where and when it was last used. I'd be curious to know why you'd want to do that, you and Colleen didn't pick a cell phone up from one of these other companies trying to cut my grass did you?" Stacy chuckled.

"If we were going to buy a cell phone package it'd come right from you. A friend of mine is down from Alaska and should have been near Castlebridge by now, except we haven't heard from him yet. He was scheduled to get a boat ride up to Deer Brook yesterday, which was one of the reasons I hiked in. I wanted to be here when he arrived and surprise him. I don't want to phone cause then he'll know I'm in town and that would ruin the surprise. Haven't seen him in almost five years and I'd hate to have to give away my intentions on surprising him." Hayden wasn't sure Stacy was falling for that line of crap. He was trying to bullshit a bullshitter but it was all he could offer for an explanation.

"Most people don't even realise their cell phones are going off until the second or third ring. We could dial the number and let it ring only once. You don't need to talk to him. I'd be able to tell you exactly where he is then."

"You could get the location on one ring?"

"I suspect so, once the line is open it shouldn't be a problem."

"Well then how about we do it that way?"

"No problem. What's the number?" Stacy plugged a tracing device into the back of his office computer.

"It's 504-555-2728." Stacy dialled the number and as soon as it rang he hung it up and pressed a key on his keyboard.

***

Ellis looked over to Red. "Did that cell phone ring?"

"I didn't hear a thing. There is no way Hayden would be calling already is there? It's only Thursday. Doesn't the mail get delivered to him on Friday?"

"That's what I understood. I was probably hearing things, getting anxious I suppose. I don't expect him to call until early next week. I figure that once he gets the letter it'll take him at least a day to arrange transportation into Castlebridge. Then another day to retrieve the video. I wish I could be there when he viewed that." Ellis began to laugh. "You know what, that's the funniest part of this whole charade."

"It is funny. It's also mean and that's what I like. Poor Hayden, once he sees you and me fondling his precious Colleen he's going be so distracted that he isn't going to know which way is up. His mind will be racing," replied Red as he and Ellis both broke out laughing for the second time at Hayden's expense.

***

"Got it. According to the trace your friend or at least his cell phone is in Thurman, my local as a matter of fact."

"Thurman?" Hayden questioned, "that's only a forty five minute drive away. Thanks. I best get down to the dock and wait for his arrival." Now he knew where Ellis was. Now he could follow through with his next objective.

"No problem. See you in the spring." Stacy called after him as Hayden exited into the pale grey morn.

"For sure, and good luck down in Puerto Rico if I don't see you before you leave. Take care. We'll get together soon." He half walked and half ran to the end of town and crossed the bridge that would take him to the highway that lead into Thurman. He couldn't be seen, not now and especially not on the highway, or in Thurman. He could leave no trace that he'd even been there. He decided to make his way to the little town along the main power line that was cut into the mountain that separated Castlebridge and Thurman. Thurman was a bit bigger then Deer Brook, finding a red Dodge Durango with Alaskan plates wouldn't be too difficult.

There were no hotels or motels in Thurman, but there were a number of rental cabins available all year around. A few were off the main highway ten to fifteen miles. These were ones that cross-country skier's, those wearing snowshoes or those on snowmobiles rented. The ones that were five miles from the main highway would be the ones to check out first. It was obvious that Ellis and Red rented one of these and he would seek out every one if need be. It was going to take him no less than five days before he'd have hiked the forty-five or so miles into Thurman. If he could do it, he'd be in Thurman sometime on Tuesday at the latest. He'd have to force himself to hike between ten and fifteen miles a day providing the weather allowed him. It would be quite a feat to pull off but he couldn't turn back now.

"Twenty Six."

Ellis sat across the table from Red. His eyes focussed on the snow falling. The wind blowing outside caused the evergreens to sway this way and that as though they were dancing. The local weather channel warned of a severe snowfall for in and around the Kootenay West region. With it temperatures were suppose to drop significantly and the weatherman was suggesting that record lows could be expected overnight. Ellis brought his hand to his chin and ran his fingers over his whiskered face.

"By the look of what's coming down outside I'd say we're in for a snowstorm. Have you check out the furnace fuel? I'd hate to run out cause I'm bettin' we aren't gonna be able to drive out of here in a day or two. Might end up snowed in for a bit if she keeps snowing."

"I checked the fuel yesterday. I think we'll be okay. You're right though about getting snowed in. One of us ought to head into town and pick up some supplies before it's too late?"

"What's left of the grub I picked up the other day?"

"The cupboards are pretty much bare and the fridge is empty."

"I guess so then. You go ahead this time. Pick up some Vodka and limes too would ya? And try not to be noticeable. The last thing we need is to blow our cover. Make it quick. Get into town and get out. You should be able to do the round trip in a couple of hours. That's allotting you the time to pick up the grub. Fill the Durango up as well and top it off on your way back. That tank has to remain full at all times. It's near noon now so you best get going."

"Anything special you want?" Red asked as he stood up from the table.

"Nothing special, just be sure to bring back some Vodka and limes. And grab me a couple of packs of White Owl's."

"Will do. See you back here around dinner time." Red grabbed the keys hanging from the wall and exited into the afternoon. God he was glad to get out of there. He'd been cooped up for too long. He needed to breathe. To get away from Ellis for a bit, and to be alone. This particular job was becoming monotonous. He felt as though he himself was being held captive. Red swept the Durango clear of snow then headed to the main highway five miles away. The forestry road was ploughed beyond the big gate but the road to the gate was sheer ice and topped already with a few inches of snow. Minutes later he pulled up to the gate and unlocked it. He proceeded to the main highway. Signalling he turned south-east and headed towards Castlebridge.

The highway was ploughed, sanded, and clear. There was little traffic and the drive to Castlebridge was pleasant even as the snow fell like down from a feather pillow that burst open. He shook his head.

"Damn snow," he muttered to himself. It always seemed to last so long and here it was only the early part of winter. He decided that once this deal was done and he got his cut he'd head to some place down south where it was warm.

Ellis owed him at least a brief holiday away from all the crap he'd been hired for and did in the past five years. Ellis could even join him if he wanted. Chances were though that Ellis would disappear into the void for a few years after this charade ended. Their partnership might even end after this score. And he'd be free to seek out his own action. That is of course if it went as planned. If it did, they'd both be sitting on a lot of coin, eight to ten million each. It was enough cash for them to retire or at least go their separate ways. *If it comes down to that, it comes down to that I guess,* he thought. *Maybe a retirement from all this wouldn't be such a bad thing.*

Ellis was pouring himself another coffee. He too was feeling the call of retirement. He was in his mid fifties and did a lot in his time. He liked the thrill of it all but lately it wasn't the same. He was running out of options in his life. He was hated and not trusted by a dozen different government organisations that would rather see him shot dead or skinned alive. Undoubtedly there was a hefty price put on his head by a few syndicates in Russia, but that didn't matter. Russia would never be his home again. He'd do business there with a select few but only from a distance. No way would he ever step on Russian soil again. Ellis shook his head. "You've burned a lot of bridges old friend," he whispered as he returned to the table and sat with a coffee in hand.

His mind drifted back to the time when he accepted the handshake and manila envelope for divulging the RRA's plan to over take the CPA. Sure, some of the CPA died but so did five RRA members. He received a healthy sum of fifty thousand dollars for that in formation and with that he disappeared for a year.

It was only by coincidence that he ran into Hayden and was able to force him to steal and kill. Hayden definitely had the last laugh back then. With the ransom, he was hoping to collect for Colleen his intent was to slip into Mexico. Not necessarily to hunt down Monique, that was only if Hayden didn't abide. If he did, which Ellis was most confident he would, then Mexico was where he was going to seek refuge, it was another reason why he wanted to know where Monique now resided. He didn't want to be near, where she could identify him.

All Colleen revealed to him about Monique was that Monique resided in San Lorenzo. He knew that the information might be false, but he couldn't be sure until he questioned Colleen again. If she stumbled with what she revealed when he first questioned her in regards to Monique then he'd know for sure. He brought the cup of coffee to his lips and slurped at the hot brew.

***

Castlebridge came into view and Red felt relieved that he wouldn't have to drive in the snow much longer. Hopefully by the time he picked some things up the snow might have slowed. He pulled up to the liquor store first and purchased a 60.oz, bottle Smirnoff as well as a twenty-four pack of Kokanee for himself. His next stop was the local market. As he walked the isles, he picked up on a conversation being discussed by two older women, about a dead man who was discovered by Hayden Rochsoff from up in Deer Brook.

An avalanche killed the man and Hayden reported it to the RCMP that was all Red made out. Hurriedly he finished with the shopping. He had to fill Ellis in. For all he knew Hayden was stalking the two of them right now. They had to prepare for what might come. Red quickly paid for the groceries and headed out of town long before he wanted to. It was snowing like a bugger and it slowed him down. He cursed the weather, but thanked his good fortune for hearing what he heard.

If Hayden already retrieved the tape then chances were things were going to turn out differently. The chance that things weren't going to go as planned went up 99%. He pulled up to the cabin shortly after 4:00 p.m. He told Ellis what he heard and all hell broke loose. "What do you mean that he may be on to us. Do you have a clue on when that might have taken place was it this year last year or what? Did you pick up a newspaper to find out?"

"Why are you freaking on me for? No, I didn't pick up a newspaper and no I don't know when he found the body. I heard conversation and that's all. Beats me when it happened. I can only speculate recently. Open that Vodka and have a drink will you. Damn, settle down a minute. I suppose I should have picked up a paper but it was the furthest thing from my mind. I might have fouled up a bit, but I might not have as well. Say I was still in Castlebridge and out of the blue, Hayden stood in the doorway. What do you think might have happened? He'd have filled you with lead and you know it. So don't go spouting off to me about why I didn't pick up a paper."

Ellis looked at Red coldly then adverted his eyes to the window, "One thing is for sure, if he's on his way the snow will slow him down for a day or two. I know he isn't going to drive here. He can't risk being spotted. He'll hike in and use the element of surprise. How long would you say it would take a guy like him to hike forty-five miles at this time of year through all this snow? Figure six, seven days?"

"Couldn't say. I haven't a clue. Maybe he could do ten miles in a day. The only one who knows for sure is Hayden," Red replied with a bad taste in his mouth from the screaming match.

"All right let's say four maybe five days. Today is Thursday, say he arrived into Castlebridge on the third or fourth day after we grabbed his sweetie, what day would that have been?" Ellis tried to calculate the past few days.

"That would have been Tuesday or Wednesday."

"If he received the letter on either one of those days we can estimate that he ain't going to be near us until Tuesday. When I put this charade together, I wasn't counting on hearing from him so soon. We best keep our eyes peeled. We'll be ready for him. We just have to come up with another plan for when he arrives. If we don't hear from him by Tuesday then we'll be all right and he's playing by my rules."

"Let's hope." Red replied. He and Ellis nodded at one another and then put away the groceries. Neither one spoke much to the other. The tension between them was thick enough that it could be cut with a knife. It was probably only the second time in their business relationship that they screamed at each other as they did that day. By late evening, feeling the effects from the beer and Vodka they made amends.

"Red. Sorry about t'day. I didn't mean to rag at ya like I did."

"Not to worry. I figure I yelled right back anyway…" the two started to laugh.

"That you did. That you did. You put me in my spot too, you did."

"You made me feel a bit incompetent and I was retaliating."

"That's one of the reasons I like ya. Ya ain't never afraid to speak your mind." Ellis tilted his glass in cheer. "To becoming rich," he said. The two clanked their drinks together.

"To becoming rich."

Colleen trained her ear to the door when she heard them arguing earlier in the day. Now she sat on her bed, ragged and hungry. Neither one of them brought her anything to eat or drink that entire day. Her stomach ached for food and her throat felt dry and raspy. She was comforted knowing that it was possible that Hayden was closing in on her whereabouts. At the same time concerned that Ellis and Red also knew. How could she warn him? Was it even possible? Was Hayden on his way? These questions bounced around in her mind and she began to tremble. "Hayden, please be careful…they will kill you," she whispered to the silence in her room as tears welled up in her eyes. Colleen buried her head into the pillow and sobbed. She had been at the mercy of Ellis and Red for six days already and she wasn't sure she cold last another six without having a complete break down.

"You have to stay strong, it won't last much longer. Hayden is coming," she wept.

And he was.

In fact, he was fifteen miles closer. He travelled the fifteen miles he set out to do that first day as he headed to Thurman. He was surprised that he did it too with how badly it snowed during the day. Now he was bedding down for the evening and preparing himself for another strenuous fifteen miles that he'd force himself to do the next day. If he could do it he'd be thirty miles closer by late evening the following night and with luck and determination, he'd be in Thurman by Sunday evening. Kneeling close to the fire, he warmed up his hands. His body ached from the long day's hike. Finally wrapping himself up in his sleeping bag, he closed his dreary eyes.

"Twenty Seven."

Rising the following morning chilled to the bone, he scavenged in the near brush to gather dry wood to light a fire. It wasn't light yet but the sun was slowly rising although obscured at times by passing clouds. Finding enough deadfall, he scurried to where he spent the evening. Tossing the dried branches onto the snow covered ground he rubbed his hands together trying to take away the numbness of the cold morning. Feeling to his cold hands finally returned and he quickly lit a fire.

The fire warmed his hands and face as he knelt next to it. *Making a shelter this evening, there's no way I want to sleep under the stars tonight,* he thought as he reached for his canteen of water, looking to the darkly clouded sky he took a swallow. His destination was another fifteen miles north. Warm enough now to continue he doused the fire and gathered his gear then took up his journey. He walked for six hours sipping from his canteen when he was thirsty. Looking back the way he travelled he finally rested.

Ahead were two more inclines not nearly as steep and then the mountain range that the power line was carved into levelled out for a distance. He guessed by memory to be about twelve or fourteen miles. After that, the power line began the long descent into the town of Thurman his final destination close to thirty-five miles away. From where he rested he could faintly make out the Kootenay River as it snaked its way south to meet up with the roaring Columbia. The highway below or what he could see of it looked like a trickling creek as it travelled along the banks of the river.

Four hours later he was shrouded in pea soup fog and it slowed his pace down until finally there was no choice but stop and wait until it dissipated. Wet and miserable he sought shelter in the dense forest that skirted the power line. He was glad for the forest's density as it protected him from the freezing rain that pelted down. Even the fog didn't seem as thick in the dense bush. Finding a big enough tree, he built a shelter at its base. He had walked non-stop for ten hours already and only travelled eight miles. The weather and the steep terrain certainly toiled his plans at making fifteen. Making himself comfortable, he sat down on the cedar bows he gathered and spread over the ground. A fire flickered and snapped as puffs of smoke billowed into the still evening. Looking at his watch, the glowing hands told him it was 6:30 p.m. Ahead of him, was a twelve-hour wait before first light.

***

Colleen sat upright on her bed when she heard the door to her room being unlocked. Ellis's big bulky size blocked the doorway as the door flung opened. He held in his hand a paper plate full of crackers, cheese, pickles, sausage, and for a change a quartered red tomato and fruit juice. "I'm guessing by now you're getting hungry. Here, I brought ya few things."

Rising weakly from her bed she approached the plate of food. "Yes, I am hungry. Thank you for bringing it to me." She accepted the plate and juice then turned and walked back to her bed. Ellis stared at her as she traipsed back and sat down. For a brief moment, he felt compassion. He didn't hate her, how could he? He didn't even know her. Had she only played by the rules when they busted in on her things for her might have turned out different. Now though she was nothing more than a piece of meat on a fisher's hook.

"It ain't much. Seems whilst Red was gathering groceries yesterday he came across two broads talking about Hayden."

Colleen's heart sped up at what he was saying. If it were true then she knew Hayden was definitely looking for her. She looked back to Ellis as though what he was saying was old news. "Red claims he heard them talking about Hayden finding some frozen body along the road coming from Deer Brook. I don't suppose you know when this might have taken place. Red seems to think it happened recently and of course if it has well you know what that means."

Colleen shook her head. "I have no idea when that might have happened. Last year though we found a frozen corpse along the shore between Deer Brook and Broadwater. That's all I know. Maybe your brilliant sidekick heard the old ladies talking about that? It was around this time of year." She returned her eyes to her plate. She was hoping that answered Ellis's question and that he'd leave. But instead he continued.

"I'm not so sure at what you're saying has any truth. I'll tell you this much, today is Friday if I don't hear from Hayden by Tuesday either by the number I left with him on that video," Ellis snickered. "Or if he stands in front of me, either way, we don't hear from him by then you'll be waking up in Russia greeted by a few of my comrades." Ellis turned and exited her room.

Frightened and panic stricken Colleen sat on the bed the last words Ellis said echoed in her mind. She set the plate on the nightstand and curled up on the ragged bed, sobbing.

Red was sitting on the couch in the living room of the cabin his feet up on the wagon wheel coffee table. He was watching TV although most of the time the TV flickered and became snowy as the satellite continued to fade in and out. He heard Ellis approach. "What's new with our stable mate?" he asked as Ellis swung into the easy chair next to him.

"She says that crap you heard yesterday happened last year. Said they found a corpse last year tits up on the shore between Deer Brook and Broadwater. Says that might be what the old ladies you heard were blabbing about. But I doubt it. I think she was bullshitting me. I think, Hayden is on his way. I think he managed to get that info I sent him earlier than I expected.

Course, I can't or should I say, we can't be sure. However, I'm a bettin' man and I'm bettin' he's on his way. Don't know where he's comin' from or when he'll be getting' here. We best get prepared for anything. Tomorrow we have to board up her window, in fact, we'll board up all the windows someone can look in or come through. I don't know what to do with the Durango it stands out like a sore thumb. Maybe we should park it out back?"

"I say we definitely board up the windows. As for hiding the Durango, I don't think there is a reason for that. If we need a quick get out then she's parked exactly where we want it. It might be a good idea though to rig up those cheap surveillance cameras we brought along? They ought to be good enough for a quarter of mile or so?"

"That's brilliant. That's what we'll do.

"I think we got six cameras in all. We'll train two on the gate an another halfway up the road coming to the cabin, others we can set up around a perimeter outside. Thank God for Radio Shack." Red chuckled.

"No kidding. You and I make a good team. You know that?"

"I suppose we do, but it certainly gets depressing at times. You know how I hate being cooped up. This job has certainly kept me cooped up. I hope the wait is worth it."

"C'mon, five to eight million plus or minus each will certainly be worth the wait as well as the want. I guarantee it. Think about it. Think about what you can do with that kind of money. It's a lot more than I'll ever see before I'm dead. Of course had things gone my way in '97 when Hayden and his two friends screwed me, I was guaranteed fifty six million but no that nephew of mine had to cross the line. He'll pay now. He'll pay now." Ellis pulled a White Owl out of his shirt pocket and fired it up. He knew that if Hayden was on his way they were definitely in for a surprise. He knew what Hayden was capable of.

Although he never knew it, Ellis had been watching over him for years. He knew exactly how many times he tried to escape from the Communism that he was forced to live with back in Russia. He knew that each time he was picked up for jumping the borders that he took his beatings, stood up, and tried again. It was a wonder they hadn't simply killed him. Nothing ever deterred Hayden when he made up his mind. Not back when he was a teen and definitely not since. He would definitely be a force to reckon with.

***

Hayden's boots and liners were dangling over the flames like pots of stew being cooked. His woollen socks stretched out on the circle of rocks he gathered to go around the fire pit. His sleeping bag wrapped around his shoulders like a big shawl. The Desert Eagle and Glock were at his side. He hadn't assembled the sniper rifle yet and decided that now was as good of a time as any. Selecting a piece of wood he tossed it on the fire, then reached around to his pack.

As he swung back around with the pack in his hands the contents spilled out and into the flames. The fire he knew would ignite the rounds of ammunition he stored in it. Without a moments hesitation he reached for the two pieces of the sniper rifle that also fell into the flames. Then with cat like reflexes he leapt up and sought protection behind a large tree as rounds of ammunition exploded like fireworks in an array of pops and bangs.

He waited a few minutes for it to be safe before stepping out from behind the tree, hoping that not all the rounds were spent. His hopes were dashed once he realised there was only one bullet left for the sniper rifle. He cursed the day shaking his head, "One shot, two kills," he whispered as he stared blankly into the flames. The good news was that both the Glock and the Desert Eagle were loaded with thirty-three rounds and two six round clips respectively. He'd have to be close for the rounds to count.

Shrugging his shoulders, he reached for the unassembled sniper rifle. He looked it over closely in the light from the fire. The scope cracked so he removed it and tossed it into his pack. The rifle itself hadn't suffered other than the stock being scorched lightly. Rubbing snow on the burn mark, he wiped the soot away with one of his socks.

After attaching the stock and fitting it for his shoulder he slowly slid back the bolt and loaded his only remaining bullet for the rifle into its chamber. The silver casing and its black and white Teflon tip glistened in his hands like tinsel draped across a Christmas tree. The audible click as he let loose the bolt seemed louder than the fireworks only moments before when all Russian made 7mm silver jackets but the one he held exploded in his evening fire. The PSG was loaded and ready and so was he.

Before sleep found him that evening he removed the laser scope from the Glock and retrofitted it to mount on the PSG-1 Heckler & Koch. It was as if he were in a trance and perhaps he was. Standing, he retreated to the darkness not illuminated by the fire. Pointing the rifle at a sapling that he guessed was 50 yards away. He adjusted the red dot of the laser scope from its original configuration of 30 yards for the Glock. He could have left it without a scope, but if he had to use the rifle, it would be more precise and deadly with the scope.

If he used one of the smaller calibre handguns, it would be up close and personal and no scope would be needed. The PSG was capable of penetrating two bodies with deadly results. The Teflon tips didn't break up or mushroom. Teflon tips held their shape as they penetrated flesh and passed through bone leaving a consistent sized entrance and exit wound with enough velocity and punch to do it all over again. Satisfied that the scope was true he retreated to the fire and shelter.

Staring deep into the flames his mind played back every moment of his life it seemed, and each scene got faster and faster as they swirled like a vortex to finally erupt in a splattering of blood. *Come on old boy don't be losing it yet. We have a ways to go,* he thought.

He was trying to avoid the feelings of hatred and vengeance. It felt as though he no longer controlled those emotions and to be out of control or otherwise distracted could ultimately kill him. The fear he felt for Colleen's safety didn't allow him to forget so easily the reason for this trek or the horrors he saw on the video days earlier. It was these thoughts he knew that would drive him mad if he succumbed to them. He had to clear his head of all thought and feeling. *Think back to what the RRA has taught you. Become that killing machine you left on Russian soil all those years ago,* he thought to himself as if he were trying to keep his own soul from faltering. No matter how hard he tried to convince himself the machine was no longer. What guided him now were the two things mankind could not be without, love and hate.

"Twenty Eight."

Saturday, November the 23, seven days had passed since Ellis kidnapped Colleen and for seven days, he planned Ellis's death. No matter what awaited him when he finally tracked the two down, no matter what. In his mind, they were dead. Not wanting to waste any time he loaded up his gear and headed again northerly towards Thurman. Before the sun even peaked in the east he walked three miles guided only by the illuminating white covered ground and the hum from the cables above that vibrated with mega watts of power in the stillness of the predawn.

It was uncanny that only now he heard the sound for the first time. At times it seemed so intense he thought he felt his fillings rattle. Why now was the humming so loud? He speculated that WK Hydro let one of the dams loose due to everyone cranking up their thermostats, leaving no option but to kick in the hydroelectric turbines to boost the available electricity. Whatever the reason, today in the early twilight the cables buzzed with an unnerving drone.

Self-indulged with memories of his past he sauntered on until the hands on his watch read 8:00 a.m. before he rested. The sun shone in the pale blue sky warming the chilly morning air. He took a swallow from his canteen and looked in the direction of Thurman. Calculating distance he guessed there was another twenty to twenty-five mile hike before he'd be in Thurman. Looking to the sky and observing how clear it was he knew it would be a good day. He figured he walked at least five miles before taking the break, if he could do another fifteen he'd be only ten miles, give or take a few from his destination. He added snow to his canteen and swished it around. Standing with confidence and determination, he set off.

***

Ellis and Red were beginning to stir. It was 9:30 a.m. Colleen had been awake for what seemed like hours. Today as she rose from her bed, she felt stronger than in the past week. She felt nothing. No fear, no humiliation, no pain, and no hunger. She was no longer herself. Had she gone completely mad? Seven days of hell squandered away from her any compassion for life she might have and the only thing that was going to change it would be when she was again in Hayden's arms. She knew there were only three days left before Ellis and Red were going to change plans and move their operation somewhere else, sending her to meet her fate in Russia. Could Hayden do it? Could he find her in time?

She walked around the little room following a daily routine she had been doing. In seven days, she had not been outside her room except to use the bathroom on that rare occasion. The last shower she took was the one directly after the phoney video shoot. It was all one of Ellis's sick ploys and tactics that he used to convince Hayden. *Did Hayden fall for it? Did he believe what he saw?* The door to her room unlocked and both men stood in the doorway. Red was carrying five lengths of board, and Ellis held a hammer and a can of four-inch spiral nails. "What's going on?"

"What does it look like? We're boarding up your view to the outside world."

"Why?"

"Never mind the questions and sit down," Ellis replied as he stood at the doorway and watched Red nail up the boards.

Colleen walked over to her bed and sat down. She knew why. These two thugs were afraid. They knew Hayden was on his way and they were preparing for an unwelcome outcome. Was it not enough though that the window was barred? Now they didn't want anyone looking in and at the same time block the little amount of sunlight the window let in. It could only mean that, indeed, things were expected to change. It added hope to her desperate situation and she smiled to herself.

Before Red finished with his hammering, she took the opportunity to ask if she could use the bathroom. Ellis simply nodded and waved her on by.

"Don't try anything stupid or brash. Use the can and toddle back before Red finishes hammering. We have work to do and we don't want to be slowed down because you're in the shitter, kapeesh. Now get going."

She slid past Ellis's fat body that continued standing in the doorway causing her body to rub against his. He smiled as he slightly pressed his body into hers and the doorjamb. His rancid breath beat down on her like thick smog. Finally he tilted back on his heels and let her past.

Colleen darted into the bathroom and splashed water onto her face then rinsed her mouth. Ellis's breath coated her skin like a thin layer of grease. She almost threw up. She returned to her room as Red was pounding the last board into place. Ellis let her by but not without sniffing loudly as she passed as if he were trying to smell her womanhood. It was a vulgar attempt to humiliate her but she never gave it a second thought as she slid by and took her spot on her bed and waited for them to leave.

"There, that ought to keep prying eyes from prying." Red picked up the hammer and nails.

"Good, now let's get the others done."

"Right behind you." He looked back to Colleen. "It'll be a damn shame if the power goes out. The only light you have left is the sixty-watt bulb glowing in the ceiling and stuff happens in the dark." Laughing sinisterly he closed the door and locked it. Another attempt by the two to humiliate and frighten her. Colleen wasn't going to let it affect her. She was a slab of cold stone.

Ellis and Red met at the table in the kitchen after pouring themselves a coffee.

"Looks like the weather may be tolerable today. Should be able to rig up the cameras later, first let's finish with these coffees and get the other windows boarded up," Ellis gestured. The two slugged back their morning coffees rarely speaking each of them in their own way preparing themselves for the furies of hell that Hayden would be bringing. If indeed, he was coming at all. As for now neither one was certain.

The two walked from room to room slapping up boards across the most likely and vulnerable windows Hayden might try to gain access through. He wouldn't get the drop on them. Finally finishing with the last window the two men returned to the kitchen where the aroma of freshly brewing coffee filled the damp kitchen air.

***

Hayden figured he walked another three miles when he could hear what sounded like a half a dozen snowmobiles blasting in his direction from Castlebridge along the same route he was walking. He tilted his head and cupped his hand around one ear to listen. He wasn't sure if they were getting closer or turned back. It was hard to tell with the terrain moving up and down so drastically from time to time. He didn't welcome the idea that they might be travelling towards him for obvious reasons.

Bolting into forest he continued onward as the snowmobiles whined getting closer. After a half of a mile breaking his own path, the snowmobiles finally passed him. Waiting until it was clear he worked his way back to the road and followed in the tracks left by them. The snowmobiles he noted travelled ahead of him by a mile or two. Stopping for a brief moment he pulled out his extra pair of woollen socks and stretched them over the outside of his boots.

He was taught the technique a long time ago. The socks prevented any real identifiable indentations in packed snow and soft ground, virtually disguising the tread mark from his soles. Satisfied any footprints he may leave behind would not be spotted by untrained eyes he set off. The din from the snowmobiles was distant and he walked until he crested over another hill where he rested for the second time. It was 1:00 p.m. according to his watch.

Looking he could faintly make out the snowmobiles as they capped the last steep hill before heading down into Thurman. It was only a good day's hike before he too would be descending it. Not wanting to lose anymore of the encouraging day, he ascended the hill from which he rested. He wanted to make it to the bottom and perhaps the half-mile distance to where the final hill began its brutal rise up to the sky. Once there he'd set up an evening camp. In the early a.m., weather permitting, he'd set off to reach the top by noon. If he could do that, he'd be well ahead of his schedule.

***

Ellis and Red were adjusting the surveillance cameras they set up along the road and near the gate leading up to the cabin a few hundred yards away. They had a great view of the gate and two approaching views of the road. Outside the cabin one was planted in a tree and rotated every three seconds to another view of the perimeter. The remaining two were mounted at both the front and back entrances of the cabin. "Not bad for the price we paid," Ellis commented as he looked at the twelve inch monitoring screen.

"Let's hope they can withstand the weather. I have those two along the road mounted on a couple of trees and they are protected from rain and snow but I don't know how well they'll fair if it turns cold. I imagine they'd be good for below freezing. How much below freezing I couldn't guess. For six hundred bucks, I don't think we can complain. They'll serve their purpose." The two nodded approvingly.

"They'll work. We'll have a few-minutes warning if someone unwanted shows up. Enough time to prepare a welcome." Ellis snickered.

"Unless of course they manages to slip by and stick to cover. In which case we better be able to react quickly cause we'll only have a couple of seconds to get the drop."

Ellis could feel the tension in which Red spoke and he questioned him. "Sounds to me like you have some apprehension. You ain't afraid of him are you?"

"I wouldn't say so much afraid as a bit uneasy."

Ellis looked at him hanging on to every word. It was true they may have started a fire that they couldn't control. Ellis turned and looked at the monitor. Was it better to pack up and head for higher ground, glaring at the black and white screen his mind raced and he swallowed hard fearing that an unfavourable outcome was in his future.

"Twenty Nine."

Ellis was awake most of the night, he sat transfixed staring at the black and white monitor, zooming in and zooming out the surveillance camera views. Hoping to sight in on Hayden but the night of vigilance proved to be uneventful. Nothing moved and nothing stirred. It was 4:00 a.m., when he finally decided to try to close his eyes. He lay on his bed half a sleep and half a wake, his mind muddled. Rolling onto his side, he put his arm under his pillow to double check that his .45 was there. Then thoughts of his past danced in his head until finally sleep found him.

Hayden was doing the total opposite. Today he would make the distance to the final mountain range he'd have to cross before descending into Thurman. By evening, he might be in Thurman itself. He wondered as he walked if his efforts were justifiable. He could have easily reported the entire charade to the Mounties and perhaps by now the entire ordeal could be over. Then again, he also knew that if Ellis managed to get wind of something like that Colleen would become a victim of the worst kind.

Twelve hours of steady walking finally brought him to the crest of the last mountain range before descending into Thurman. From where he stood he could look to the horizon and faintly make out the glow of the town itself. He wanted nothing more than to continue walking. He knew, however, that it would be best if he settled in for the evening and was rested for what lay ahead. He would burn no fire on the hill that night for obvious reasons. Where he sat overlooked Thurman and a fire flickering in the dark evening on the power line of all places would undoubtedly be spotted.

Instead, he wrapped himself up with his sleeping bag, if he needed he could light the kerosene heater for warmth. He stared across to the yellow glow of Thurman. Down there somewhere, was where Colleen was being held. Somewhere down there, she waited for him. So too did bloodshed and death. The eerie sound of an owl in the distance brought with it the howling of coyotes, and in the distance even further away he could make out the barking of dogs, as if answering the mournful call. He felt as though he was being hypnotised by the sounds. It seemed as though he could almost reach out with his arm and touch Thurman. The reality was it was a good half-day hike away.

He looked blankly at the flickering lights that dotted the evening sky like thousands of tiny Christmas tree lights. "Funny, that's not far away." He whispered to the silence. He returned his gaze to the yellow glow of Thurman in the distance. *Hang on Colleen. I'm on my way and I'm bringing the furies of hell with me. We'll be together soon, I promise.* It was a solemn oath.

As he sat there looking in the direction of Thurman he felt little regret for what his intentions were. Men like Ellis Leroy and Red were minions that fed off other people's fears. They were nothing more than dictators of the worst kind. *Am I any better? What does that make me if I kill them?* He thought.

"Thirty."

In the silence of dawn he rose. Today he'd make the distance to Thurman and by early evening, he'd have a good inclination on where Ellis and Red were holed up. He already decided on which cabins he was going to check first. Obviously, they would have rented a cabin that was accessible by four-wheel drive. There'd be no way Ellis wanted to be way out in the middle of nowhere. He'd want a place far enough out of the way not be noticed but close enough to the main highway for a quick retreat, that was a given.

There were three cabins that were on the west side and only a few miles from the main highway. It would be these three he'd check out first. Continuing his descend along the switchbacks that would lead him to the outskirts of Thurman, he knew that once he was within a half a mile of the town he'd have to use stealth. He couldn't be spotted.

Losing his footing on the steep grade, he fell headfirst into the snow, and slid on his stomach for about fifty feet until he finally found his grip. Stopping, he got to his feet and dusted himself off. Blood ran down his face from where a rock or bush scraped him. He received a wallop from the barrel of the rifle as it slammed into the back of his head and now there was a good size goose egg forming. He wasn't sure if he should laugh or swear at his blunder. He brought his hand to his face to feel the severity of the wound. It was below his left eye and along the bridge of his nose, then it ran its course down to the top of his lip. It wasn't bad, but it was enough that he knew he should receive a stitch or two.

His eye too would undoubtedly turn black and swollen. As for the bump on the head, he could expect to have a headache. He took the opportunity now to take a well-deserved break. He drank from his canteen and looked over his gear. All of it remained intact. Positioning the backpack and his rifle before setting off again and as the cool air bit at his wound causing him to squint he walked on. He lost his peripheral vision in his left eye because of the swelling. Luckily for him, it was his left eye. If it was his right he might have a bit of a problem trying to scope in on his opposition when the time came, if he had to scope in on them at all. That was the beauty of the laser scope. If he could see the dot, he knew where the bullet was going. *Only need one eye for that*, he reminisced.

***

Colleen rose unaware of what time of day it was as her room was pitchblack. She stood and walked over to the light switch and flicked it on. Since her window was boarded up she was constantly wondering what time of day it was and she wondered that now.

Was it early morning? Was it noon? What time of day was it exactly? She had no way of knowing. Not until one of them looked in on her. Sitting down she brought her knees up to her chin and wrapped her arms around them. In the stillness of her room, she felt like she were a caged animal waiting to be slaughtered. Would she ever be free? Filled with self-doubt and fear, tears welled up in her eyes. She did not cry aloud, instead the salty tears rolled down her cheeks to her expressionless lips and mouth where she simply wiped them away. She wanted it all to end. The worst part of the whole ordeal was when they videotaped her and how the two men touched and fondled her.

She was humiliated. She didn't even have the good sense to signal Hayden in the video, somehow letting him know it was all a farce. She wondered if that would have made a difference. The outcome would be the same she'd be stuck in the room until it was all said and done. *I could always use that piece of metal I have tucked under the mattress to slash my wrists.* She shook her head. "Don't be foolish girl, calm down. No need to even think like that. Shame on me," she whispered. Taking a few deep breaths she stood and walked over to the door.

Raising her hand to knock on the door for one of them to come to her, she heard the audible ringing of a cell phone. Her heart sped up and she put her ear to the door. She heard them speaking on occasion that Hayden, was suppose to call a cell phone. It was her hope that this was the call. Her hope turned to fear when she heard Ellis's voice talking. "I have her here now. Come on lets be reasonable. There is no way I'd let her go for that. One hundred thousand in US currency is what I want. If you can't meet or beat that take a hike."

She knew exactly what the conversation was about. Ellis was putting in motion his plan to sell her to the Russians. Trembling with fear and emotion she hardly made it to her bed with her wobbly legs, overcome with sheer terror her body convulsed as she cried into the blankets uncontrollably. She dreaded what might become of her if Hayden didn't soon come.

Reaching beneath the mattress, she grasped hold of the only hope she thought she had. Clasping the metal piece in her sweaty hand helped her feel less vulnerable. It was her security blanket. Now more than ever she was willing to use it, either as a means to protect herself from what might come or for the unspeakable. She didn't favour that option. She would not die by her own hand. She would force them to kill her or die themselves when it came to that point.

Ellis and Red already concluded they weren't going to flee that Tuesday. They weren't going to flee at all. They chose to wait for Hayden to call or show up in person. Probably the worst decision they could have made but they couldn't know that. Each of them held their own reservations on waiting but when they were that close and held negotiating power they were certain they'd come out on top. Nothing was further from the truth. Ellis flung his heavy body into one of the chairs at the table. He was pissed off at the call he received and his heavy breathing was confirmation.

"Those idiots in Kamchatka are a bunch of muzhiks. That idiot Conkov tries my patience. I'll tell you that much."

Red shook his head. "What the hell is a music's?"

"Means, Russian peasant is what that means. Conkov says to me, no way would he pay more than fifty thousand for a woman like we have stabled, says she'd be more of a headache than a money-maker. Canadian women are too crazy he says. Can you believe that imbecile? I guarantee she'd be the best money-maker out of all them horrid wenches in Russia."

"We can't deny she wouldn't be a pain. We also know that she is crazy. I've never met a woman who could withstand as much crap as she has. You can bet that she'd slit our throats from ear to ear given the opportunity. She's a feisty wench, can't deny that. Conkov is probably right."

"Ivan Conkov is nothing but a mealy mouthed puke. He's an idiot as sure as your hair is red. Fifty grand, who does he think he's dealing with? Remember that name. Put it on your hit list."

Ellis turned his attention to the coffee perking away on the stove. He had three more associates in Russia that he intended on contacting in regards to the price he could get for a Canadian woman in her mid thirties. His best bet was and had always been, with Ivan Conkov. If he didn't want her for a hundred thousand, it was unlikely anyone else would either.

He would simply tell the others that Ivan offered him at least that much. It would be a blatant lie, but the results could be favourable. Colleen was a true beauty. In Ellis's mind there was no way he could be doubted a hundred grand for such a hard-bellied woman. He glanced up to the clock hanging on the far wall. He was surprised that it read only 11:00 a.m. "I can't believe it's only 11:00 a.m. Seems it should be later."

"Are you going senile? That's been the same time on that clock since the first day we got here, the battery is obviously dead. It's actually 12:15 p.m. and to keep you straight it's Monday the twenty fifth." Red chuckled as he stood to fetch himself a cup of coffee. "Can I bring you one?"

"Thanks. To retort to your previous comments, I'm not sure if I'm going senile or have a case of cabin fever. I know one thing for sure and that's I'll get a hundred grand or millions or I'll die trying."

"I prefer the millions myself. However, having a good contingency plan which, obviously you do won't hurt the outcome. We'll get some kind of coin, I'm hoping for more than fifty thousand."

Ellis averted his eyes to the window as he sat in self-contemplation. "Tell me something, ever think of death."

"Think of it. I live with it. If you're asking me if I fear it, damn straight I do. Some say they don't. I on the other hand am scared of it. Once a man closes his eyes for the last time, it's forever man, and that's a long time. Here's your coffee." Red set the steaming hot brew on the table in front of Ellis. "Now tell me what's with all these out of the ordinary questions?"

There was a long pause as Ellis turned his head back to the kitchen table. "It ain't nothing. Was curious to know how you felt on the subject. And you're right, once our lids are drawn closed and we've breathed for the last time...that's the end." Ellis brought his coffee to his lips and slurped, his gaze again averted to one of the only windows that they hadn't boarded up.

Red sat across from him staring at his own cup of coffee, he wondered what got into Ellis? "C'mon you know better than that. Tell me what's up?"

"Truth is I think my time dancing with the devil is about to end and I don't mean Hayden. I mean everything in general. This time I think the devil is going to win. If he doesn't and we walk away, I'm going to head down south. This is the last game old Ellis Leroy is going to play even if I end up being a peasant myself. This is the last show I'll star in."

"In the five or so years I've been acquainted with you, I've heard some of those exact words come out of your mouth more then once. The only way the game will ever end with you is like you said, when your lids are drawn closed. No, this isn't going to be your last trip into the beloved hall of sin. You don't know any other way, and like me, you gamble with your life everyday. We have scars here or there some have healed over time and all that's left are faded memories. Your time isn't up yet, old boy. You owe me some coin and I aim to collect." Red said with humour as he stood and exited into the living room.

"Punk kid," Ellis murmured beneath his breath as he stood and poured himself another coffee. Red was right of course he wasn't done yet "Not until my lids are drawn closed," he repeated softly as he smiled and shook his head. Returning to the table he sat down with a heavy sigh not completely convinced that he'd walk away from this charade unscathed. *If I breathe my last breath here, at least it wasn't on Russian soil.* There was a fate a lot worse waiting for him there.

He rose again and poured a coffee into a Styrofoam cup. He slapped some honey and jam, on a couple pieces of bread and brought them to Colleen. He had to keep her healthy. No one would want a sickly looking woman. She was sitting on her bed when she heard the door being unlocked. Clutching the piece of metal, she tried to look as inconspicuous as she could. The door swung open and Ellis approached her.

"Got coffee and some bread for you. I suggest you eat every piece. I'll bring you some other stuff later. For now, eat this. There's going to be some changes around here and you need to be in tiptop shape when it all boils down. When you're done eating come to the door and I'll let you shower. It's been a while obviously and for a woman you stink."

"Gee I wonder why that is?" Colleen retorted.

"Don't get smug. Keep that trap of yours closed for the time being." Ellis turned and left her room.

Colleen looked over the food and picked at it sparingly. Although hungry, she wanted to avoid the humiliation of having to shower especially since Ellis and Red would undoubtedly watch. There was no way she wanted to be without the security blanket that she continued to clench in her hand. It would be hard concealing it as she showered. Her mind raced with ways that she could hide it. The most feasible method was in her mouth. It took a few tries before she was able to place it finally between her cheek and gums. Repeating the procedure until she could do it without too much difficulty she approached the door and knocked on it. "Can I have my shower now? I'm done eating." She waited for what seemed like forever before Ellis answered.

"Hang on a second." He unlocked the door and gestured for her to go ahead. "I suggest you wash those clothes as well. Use the shower water if you have to. I don't care. Just clean them up. I'll grab you a couple of towels. Get going. Don't be shy pretty lady and remember the rules the door remains open."

Colleen never spoke in fear he'd notice the piece of metal she held in her mouth. She only nodded and proceeded to the washroom. God she hated them. The entire time she showered she felt their glaring eyes. It nauseated her and frightened her all at the same time. For twenty minutes, she withstood their glances and perversions.

As she dried herself, Red managed to glimpse something metallic clenched between her cheek. Without warning he darted forward in only a few short bounds and grabbed her cheek from the outside with his forefinger and thumb, the way a mother grabs a child. There was something there and he knew it. His vice like grip on her cheek caused Colleen to scream in agony as blood spewed from her mouth. "Thought you were pretty smart huh? What you got in there?" He squeezed harder causing her to almost pass out from the excruciating pain as the serrated piece of metal cut deeply into her cheek and gums.

"Spit it out now you dumb broad." He swatted the back of her head with a blow that seemed hard enough to knock out a lesser woman. Colleen spit the piece onto the bathroom floor and it skidded across the linoleum leaving a trail of blood behind. Her body quivered with fright and blood trickled from her mouth. "That hurts don't it? Grab some paper and stuff it in your mouth. That was a stupid thing to do. You're lucky I didn't shoot you."

Colleen could only nod as tears streamed down her face. There she was not a piece of clothing on and Red standing directly beside her. Even now, as blood spewed from her mouth, he stood there looking at her like a hungry wolf. "Hurry up. In fact here, take this shit paper with you. Grab a towel and your clothes and skidaddle back to your room."

She quickly gathered her belongings and roll of toilet paper then hastily made a beeline for the room. "That's a damn good eye. What was it she had in her mouth?" Ellis wanted to know.

"Some kind of metal piece. Don't know where she got it." Red held the piece up. "It'd definitely cause a bit of hurt." He tossed the piece into the garbage can on the front porch. "That was a bit of excitement to start the day. Can't wait to see what the rest of the day might hold."

"How bad you figure she's cut?"

"It's in her mouth. It'll heal in no time. She isn't going to be able to lip off for a while though," Red replied. "We'll check in on her in a bit. Rest assured the merchandise ain't going to spoil."

It took only a few minutes for the first wad of paper she stuffed in her mouth to become a sopping bloody mess. Removing it, she threw it into the wastepaper basket beside her bed. It sounded like a mammoth spitball as it splattered against the side and slid down. It took four wads before the bleeding slowed. She ran her tongue gently along her cheek and gums. She could feel the two large gouges and a lot of swelling. The cuts to her cheek and gums felt as though someone used a razor to try to skin her alive from the inside out.

Bringing her hand to her cheek, she caressed it. The greatest pain was in the inside of her mouth. Every now and again, she could still feel and taste blood as it trickled down her throat. She had no security blanket now. Just regret.

"Thirty One."

His head pounded mercilessly and he had been struggling with the pounding since the rifle smashed him in the back of the head when he lost his footing. The pain he realised was to the left side of his face. At times, it made even walking unbearable, but he pushed on. He was close now. A little headache wasn't going to slow him down. Finally making his way to the bottom of the steep incline he turned back and looked at what he struggled his way down.

The ground before him now levelled out and became as flat as the plains. It would be easy going from there. He rested briefly and looked at his watch. He'd been awake since early morn and trekked easily ten miles in the nine hours he was at it. Now, a little past 1:00 p.m., he knew he'd make the distance to Thurman within the next four hours. It would be dark. Depending how he felt when he finally located them would be the deciding factor on what he would do next.

To make a move while being impaired by any ailment including lack of rest would be foolish. He'd have to be completely rested and alert. Anything less would be ignorance and would cost him dearly. He walked another half a mile when oddly enough the left side of his face went into a fit of muscle convulsions. His eye blinked uncontrollably and he felt dizzy. Stopping, he swayed back and forth before falling to his knees. His head felt as though it were going to explode. Finding the strength to stand he shook his head, *I must be more fatigued than I'd like to think,* he thought as he continued onward.

For two hours, she sat on the bed too afraid and too sore to want to move. During that time, neither Red nor Ellis looked in on her. Then again, why would they? It wouldn't matter to them if she bled to death. Her face was an agonising mess of pain and swallowing became a feat in itself. It hurt her every time. Red was right, she wouldn't be able to speak clearly until the wounds healed. Reaching for the cold coffee sitting on the nightstand her hope was that some liquid would ease the pain. Tilting the Styrofoam cup to her lips, she took a drink. It hurt, but it was tolerable. At least she could drink liquids.

Returning the cup to the nightstand, she stood from the bed for the first time since her shower. She did her daily routine of walking from here to there and back again. It was all she could do to keep herself from going completely mad. For eight days, she had been locked up and for three of those, she didn't even see the sun. She had no idea what time it was, she never got a chance to ask. The boarded up window gave her no clue nor did her captors. She knew it was daylight and that it was Monday.

"Figure we ought to check up on the broad?" Red questioned.

"Haven't heard too much commotion coming from her room, probably wouldn't hurt." The two men stood and moved over to her door. Unlocking it, they found her standing. Her cheek resembled a big blood blister. Her face was swollen and blood caked the corners of her mouth.

"What's the lesson we learned today?" Red mocked her with disdain.

"Let me guess you ain't able to talk?" Ellis interrupted. Colleen looked at him with hatred and nodded. "At least you're still standing," he continued. "Be grateful for that. Your wounds will heal in a day or two. Who knows, maybe this time next week it'll only be Hayden's funeral that you and his friends will attend. Then again, it might all end right here. In which case the local authorities are going to need two body bags, one for each of you."

Red snickered, "With her mouth shut she sure does seem appetising." He glared at her and Colleen glared back. If she wanted to she could tell him where to go. "Told ya she'd be all right." The two men returned to their usual places in the living room where the surveillance monitor was set up.

"Anything showing up Red?"

"Not a thing. Even if we missed something the lights would be bleeping."

"With the events of the day coming to a halt we best keep vigilant. He ain't going to pop in with a big smile." Ellis looked at the black and white screen of the monitor paying close attention to the six views they had. He felt like he was in a submarine and was looking through a periscope. There was nothing out there except a pallid sun and the shadows it cast by its fading rays. It wasn't a dispiriting view it was just the same thing they had seen for the past few days since setting the cameras up. It was like they were the only people that were left on earth.

***

Hayden battled with a few more bouts of dizziness as he trudged on. However, the headache slowly faded to a constant twinge in the back of his skull. The bouts of dizziness he blamed on fatigue, the lack of substance, and constant worry. Soon that would all be over. Soon he and Colleen would again be in each other's arms and they could continue to live their lives. He slowed enough to reach back and retrieve his canteen. He was parched in a way he had never been parched before. There was a metallic taste in his mouth and no matter how many times he spat it remained constant. It seemed as though it was his sinuses, bringing his thumb to one nostril he blew the other one out.

Blood and mucus splattered the snow down by his feet and his ears rang. He did the same to his left nostril with totally different results.

It felt as though he had blown air through his tear duct in the corner of his left eye. The pain caused him to squint and he instantly brought his hand up and touched the corner of his eye. He felt a warm tacky liquid, which turned out to be a blob of goo and blood. Blinking a couple of times, he felt relief in his eye.

The metallic taste was gone, and for now, he felt ten times better. Swishing a mouthful of the cold water around inside his mouth, he spat it out. He inhaled a few times through his nose as deeply as he could. Whatever was going wrong seemed to be fixed now. Finally, he could breathe through his nose. His eye sighed with relief and the throbbing gnawing pain at the back of his head was completely forgotten. He tilted his head to the left and back to the right stretching his neck as he did so. Not much further and he'd be on the outskirts of Thurman. Repositioning the backpack and rifle, he set foot once more.

Ellis was glued to the monitor staring blankly at its screen. He could smell his own sweat as he sat there. He hadn't showered he guessed in three or four days and his own perpetuate stink was nauseating him. He ran his fingers through his hair and it felt greasy and uncombed. Scratching his scalp like a dog ridden with fleas he called over to Red who sat on the far side of the room riveted to a Times Magazine that he read easily twenty times.

"There ain't nothin' new in that zine. I'm heading for a shower, keep your eagle eyes on this screen. You see anything that might resemble Hayden before I'm done, holler."

"Yeah, yeah, will do. Don't play with your tally whacker for too long." Red stood and took up Ellis's position in front of the monitor. If their calculations were right about how long it would take a man like Hayden to hike the distance from Castlebridge, then it would be in the next twenty-four hours that they'd know if he indeed sniffed them out. Red was beginning to train his eyes again on how everything looked so different on the monitor when Ellis's cell phone rang. He looked towards the sound, stood, and retrieved it. It wasn't the red phone that Hayden was suppose to call, it was Ellis's private one.

"Hello." He answered.

"This isn't Ellis."

"You got that right. This is Red. Ellis is busy right now. Who is this?"

"You got to be joking. Is this Red Ironside?"

"What is it to you? Who are you?"

"It is you. This is Mckendric, Mckendric Povoff. I can't believe you're still working with that SOB. I figured by now you'd be doing something of your own."

"Mckendric. How have you been?"

"Same old, same old. When's the old boy gonna be available to take his own calls?"

"He's in the shower right now steam cleaning the Crisco off his bod. I'll definitely let him know that you buzzed. Are you down on the Pacific west?"

"Victoria BC to be exact. I heard through the grapevine Ellis was trying to pawn something off that I might have an interest in. I hear she's in her mid thirties and is cocky as hell. Just the kind of woman some friends of mine in Asia are into. You guys are up near the Kootenays is that right?"

"I don't think it makes a bit of difference where we are, Mckendric. I'll let Ellis set you straight on all that. As for the merchandise, I know I speak for Ellis when I say we want nothing less than one hundred thousand in US denominations. It sounds like a lot for a piece of meat, but she'll double your investment in less than a year and I'm betting she has at least five good years left. Depending, of course on how well your friends take care of her."

"I knew he was asking at least that. All right. Let him know I called. I might ring him later. If not tell him to ring me back in a day or two if things don't work out with her sale. I'm sure he's got my number. I'll be in Victoria until the end of next week, then I'm headed back to Australia."

"You bet, I'll pass the message on." Red shut off the phone and returned to his seat in front of the monitor to the same view and the same old bullshit. He hadn't heard from Mckendric in well over five years. Hadn't even heard Ellis speak his name, except maybe three times. He and Ellis both knew the kind of business Mckendric ran, and chances were he was one of the business associates that Ellis was eventually going to contact anyway. He probably wasn't Ellis's second choice. It seemed to Red though that Mckendric was shooting straight, and that indeed his little Asian friends were interested in doing a deal.

Red didn't care who paid that much for her. He hadn't sat around for two weeks planning and travelling with Ellis to the beautiful Kootenays to get stiffed. He either wanted half of what Hayden could come up with or half of what they could get for his little plaything on the black market sex trade. So far, Mckendric was the only one willing to pay. Red held his stare on the monitor as he reminisced. It seemed like hours when finally Ellis returned. Red laid out to him what transpired while he showered and that Mckendric did sound sincere.

"He's another mealy mouthed puke. Says things all the time but never has the balls to follow through. We'll definitely keep him in mind. I have some issues in pawning her off in Canada. I'd feel better if the Russians take her then I know without a doubt that she'll never be found and that's how I want it if we have to go that route. It's good to have the feelers out though. Are you going to be able to handle sitting there in front of that screen for a couple more minutes? I want to go fetch something from the kitchen to eat."

"You sit here and keep your eyes peeled. I'll throw us something together. Your cooking sucks. What do you say to those T-bone steaks and some spuds?"

"I say I can't smell them cooking. Get on it then and make a big pot of spuds. And throw some mushrooms on them steaks. We got a few cans of Money's up in the cupboard. You might even consider throwing a can of pork 'n' beans into a pot."

"That's all I need is for you to be shitting you're pants all night. I think I'll pass on cooking the beans."

"You're a big baby. What kind of man can't handle another man's flatulence?" Ellis snickered.

"A man that's got to live under the same roof as you. You may have had a shower and might be clean on the outside, but you're rotten in the inside. You got a cesspool for a gut and every time you eat your Libby's you stink for a month."

"Get on with the meat and potatoes then. Make enough for our house guest, it'll be entertainment later watching her eat solids."

"That's funny," Red snickered, "what better way to spend a drab Monday evening."

Ellis sat facing the monitor. His gaze strained on the Durango's view and the road up to the cabin. As dusk settled the view of the Durango became less visible but he could make out the silhouette in the background.

The two views, which, led along the road to the cabin remained good although he did have to adjust the night vision more than once. The front and back entrance views to the cabin itself were aided a great deal by automated lighting. Anything that passed within a certain distance triggered the automated sensors, which, in turn switched on a floodlight. It was impossible to enter the cabin without this light illuminating the entire front or back-entrance. The sensor could be outsmarted easily enough, but fooling it or simply smashing the bulb would alert them.

Ellis sniffed the air as the smell of cooking steaks wafted his way causing him to salivate. He could hardly wait to sink his teeth into one. Red finally hollered from the kitchen that the fixings were ready. Ellis rose to grab a plateful. Ten minutes later he was finishing up the last piece of steak on his plate and scooping the last of the potatoes into his mouth.

At the same time that was going on, Hayden made the distance to Thurman. He was crouching behind some bramble along the road leading to one of the houses that sat off the main highway. He had to cut across the yard and over a hill to reach the first road that led to the first cabin. He watched the house intently until he figured it was as good of a time as any to dart through the yard and over the little null.

The road he stood on now even in the darkness of evening, he could tell that it hadn't been used. Still he wanted to be sure that the cabin at the end didn't hold the two men. It was only a quick four-mile jaunt up the road, if they weren't there he would cross through the bush to the second cabin. If he didn't find the two men in the first or second cabin then hopefully, he'd run into them at the third, which, if he remembered correctly was only about three miles from the second and on the other side of a ridge. Looking at his watch, he noted the time to be 5:45 p.m.

Ellis scraped the leftovers into the kitchen garbage. He put one of the remaining steaks onto a paper plate and the other into the fridge. There were no potatoes or mushrooms to add to Colleen's plate so he added some cheese, a quartered tomato, and a couple slices of bread. He poured a Styrofoam cup full of juice and scooped a pad of butter onto her plate then proceeded to her room.

"Hey Red, can you step away from there for a minute and open the door. My hands are full." Red stood up from the monitor and walked over, unlocking the door for Ellis.

Colleen braced herself for what was coming, thinking the worst. "Like I said I'd bring you some more food. Got for you here a T-bone steak, a tomato, some cheese, bread, that sort of thing." Ellis sat the food down on the nightstand. "How's the mouth feeling?" He asked with a half chuckle. Colleen was about to speak but he raised his hand. "Nothing needs to be said. Enjoy the food." Colleen tapped her wrist gesturing for the time. "It's evening." That was all he said as he turned and walked away.

The food sitting on the nightstand looked scrumptious, it was too bad she wouldn't be able to eat any of the steak. It was obviously another sick joke. She could barely open her mouth wide enough to speak or drink let alone try to eat meat. She'd be lucky to be able to chew the tomato or cheese for that matter. Reaching for the plate, she sat it on her lap. God the steak looked good. She brought the plate up to her nose and inhaled deeply. It even smelled good.

For the past couple of days, she was fed nothing but crackers. Now that she was unable to open her mouth wide enough to chew they served her meat and a T-bone at that. They were plainly being bastards. She nibbled at the cheese, bread and tomato but didn't dare try to chew a piece of meat. The little amount of chewing she had to do to eat the thin slices of bread caused her a great deal of agony. It would be a few more days before she'd be able to eat anything more substantial then bread and liquids.

"Thirty Two."

He stood a short distance away from the cabin. From there he could tell that cabin number one was completely vacant. He jogged most of the way and now he panted, gasping for air. He tossed the pack and rifle off his shoulder and squatted to catch his breath. *Nothing like a brisk jog on a snow covered trail. Man I'm not as fit...as I use to be. That little jaunt wouldn't have even made me break into a sweat a few years back*

Twisting the lid off his canteen, he took a long healthy swallow of the snow water inside. Glancing at his watch he realised it took under one hour to reach the first cabin. At 7:00 p.m., after a short break he stepped into the forest that separated the first cabin from the second. It was at least a mile to the other side. The forest luckily for him was sparse and he commuted the mile hike in less than thirty minutes to only be disappointed again. It, too, remained vacant. Things turned from bad to worse when the metallic taste he had in his mouth earlier in the day returned as did the pain in his left eye.

What was going on? The pain shooting spikes of fire into his eye was obvious, but the nauseating dizzying spells couldn't be contributed to the wound on his face. He tried blowing out his nostrils as he did the first time but nothing seemed to be blocking them. He wondered then, if maybe he picked up a parasite from the snow water, he had been drinking. The only thing he could think of that might make him feel as he did was the dreaded Beaver Fever.

Reaching around back and retrieving his canteen, he added a couple of iodine tablets that would purify the snow water. It would make the water taste like crap but if it wasn't too late and he didn't already have the fever he'd rather be safe then sorry. *Should have done that from the beginning.* He reminisced. If he did have the fever within forty-eight hours he'd feel the brunt of it, and between now and then he could certainly count on the trots. Running around like he was on this cold winter night wasn't going to help him either. He decided that he'd continue over the ridge regardless and check on cabin three. If his luck hadn't improved by then and it too was vacant, he'd call it a night and likely break in to sleep.

If door number three held his prize, he'd finish up with the objective before dawn's early light. He wasted the remainder of the hour gathering his thoughts and resting. Ahead of him was a three-mile hike up and over Lookout Pass in the north-west Selkirk Mountains. He knew the Pass. It wasn't nearly as bad as it sounded the worst part was the first part. The other side was an old farmer's field. Beyond that another road led up to the cabin. He could vaguely remember that there was a cattle guard across that particular road and a big pipe gate. Once the gate came into view, it was only a short distance to the cabin. It sat back along the tree line and up against a knoll which protected both the south and west-side of the cabin from the day's glaring sun. It was also probably the most modern of them all.

Can't rest long with the temperature dropping, got to keep the blood pumping, he thought as he proceeded. *If I rest too long, I won't be as limber.* He only walked a few hundred yards when his equilibrium gave out. His head pounded with vengeance and it caused him to spew. Dry heaving a couple of times he held his gut in wretched agony and broke out in a sweat. Flopping to the ground on the seat of his pants, he moaned. "Wha...what the fu..." he couldn't burble a word. His whole world was spinning. Finally, the ride ended his body quivered from the rush. "What is happening, to me? Am I dying?" He managed to blurt as he slowly rose to his feet. Running the back of his hand across his forehead, he wiped away the sweat that was causing the wound on his face to sting.

Whew, good to be standing. C'mon old boy let's try to get moving. He coaxed himself. Two hours later he was crossing the farmer's field. It was a struggle to get that far but he managed. It was a little past 10:00 p.m., and the evening air was turning cold. He felt good considering he had been walking since 5:00 a.m. In only a few minutes he'd know for sure if the eighteen hours of exertion he forced upon himself that day would pay off. His hope was heightened when he made it to the road that snaked its way to cabin three.

He could tell it had been travelled on and he made an educated guess that the same vehicle travelled it each time. It snowed once since Thursday when he began the forty-five mile hike across the three mountain ranges that separated Castlebridge and Thurman. Therefore, he could be certain that no vehicles had come or gone since then. *Could be it's empty too. Or whoever is there hasn't moved,* he thought as he walked around a bend. At that point, the single lane road became completely overgrown on either side with cottonwood and pine.

It was like a tunnel made up of saplings and overgrown trees. It looked eerie in the darkness. The twisting branches of the cottonwood were completely bare their leaves gone since fall, and they resembled arms and hands reaching out to the stars. The evergreens in the back looked like giants with their arms outstretched. Thirty minutes later his heart sped up and adrenaline coursed through his veins. The closer he got the faster it beat. The gate was coming in view. Jogging now he approached and ducked under the gate, up ahead was the last and final cabin. Hardly able to contain himself he breathed in and out trying to gain his composure. He removed his backpack and tossed it under a tree. He double-checked his firearms and made sure they were loaded. The Desert Eagle he tucked into his shoulder holster, the Glock in his waistband and the sniper rifle he carried in his right hand. He still had to use caution. It was likely that there were booby traps maybe even surveillance cameras somewhere along the road. Ellis was no dummy. But in the darkness Hayden couldn't see one.

He focussed his eyes on the road, looking ahead and then back again. He could only make out the gleam but there was something hanging from a tree less than twenty feet away. Whether it was a camera or not he couldn't be sure nor did he want to take the time to find out. Crouching he darted to the undergrowth. He wasn't going to risk walking along the road. Following the bush, he made his way to the cabin keeping his distance from the road at about twenty yards to his immediate right. Finally, the cabin came into view.

He stood staring at what had been Colleen's home for eight days. He could see that the majority of all the windows were boarded up. *Afraid of something or someone are we?* He thought as he darted next to the large oil tank behind the cabin. Taking refuge, he focussed his good eye to the back entrance and as quick as lightening he felt dizzy. An excruciating pain shot from behind his head to his left eye, numbness followed the pain and so did shallowness of breath.

He fell to the ground his world spinning faster than any ride at a fair. His head felt as though it was going to implode from the inside out and his face contorted unwillingly making him bite down on his own tongue. He lay on the cold ground his eyes staring blankly to the stars above. He couldn't move. All feeling to his body it seemed rushed away with his last breath before falling to the ground. The few seconds that he laid there seemed like eternity.

He felt no pain even as the blood from his tongue wound trickled down his throat did he feel a thing. Wrestling with unconsciousness, he found the strength to rise. Sitting upright and clutching the rifle, he slowly stood on uneasy legs. Leaning up against the oil tank, he fought to prevent himself from falling again. He was completely blind in his left eye he couldn't even discern colour with it. Bringing his hand up he felt to see if the swelling blocked the view. To his dismay, it hadn't. He was still breathing though. He knew where and what it was that he was supposed to be doing. He wasn't dead yet. *I might be close to death, but I don't intend on dying first.*

Standing, he looked at the cabin. At the gable end of the back porch there was a floodlight and below that was another light. It was hard for him to tell from that distance and especially with only one good eye. Chances were he the light was automatic and anything passing by would turn it on. He confirmed this when he tossed a snowball. The floodlight illuminated instantly revealing not a second light but a camera.

Crouching in the shadows he watched as camera lens extended and rotated. Ellis sat in front of the monitor curious as to why the light turned on when nothing came into view. "What do you make of that Red? Red, Red are you awake over there?" Ellis asked as he turned to the couch where Red was opening his eyes.

"Yeah, yeah, I'm awake. What's up?"

"The floodlight out back switched on. But not a thing walked by."

"Anything could have triggered it. If you want I'll go take a look."

"Do that and smile pretty for the camera too. I want to make sure its working properly." Red sat up from the couch and headed through the kitchen to the back door holding in his hand a .45. Opening it he stepped out onto the back porch and glanced around. He saw nothing. Walking down the back stairs and out to where the camera could view him. He waved his arms in the air a few times.

Sitting in the shadows Hayden watched. He wanted right then and there to storm the cabin and take Red out. Finally Red turned and started back to the door. At the precise moment, Hayden bolted behind him pulling up to the outside wall of the porch out of view from both the light and camera. He could only hope that whoever was watching the camera hadn't seen him. Adrenaline surged through his veins with velocity and strength. He had no idea where all the stamina came from. Only minutes earlier he was a quivering mess of incoherence.

He waited only a few brief seconds before he crept up to the door and slowly opened it a crack to peek in. He could see Red standing inside the kitchen, but far enough away that he knew he could slip into the porch virtually unnoticed. "Did you see me do the dance?" Red hollered from the kitchen. He hadn't wanted to lock the door yet in case Ellis hadn't seen him and he'd have to go back out.

"Sure did. You didn't see anything did you?" Ellis knew he hadn't but he certainly had and he knew that right about now Red was in for a big surprise. Ellis quickly stood up and slid behind the living-room wall, his .45 unleashed and in his hand.

"Probably a bird or something flew by. I didn't see any tracks anywhere and no bullets echoed. I'd say it is nothing to worry about. If anything walked up that road we'd have seen it." Red replied as he turned to lock up. It was too late though, as he turned he was staring at the muzzle of a silenced Desert Eagle pointed to his skull.

"Unless of course they didn't walk up the road," Hayden hissed as he released the safety. "Don't speak a word old friend. Turn around and lead the way." Red was taken by total surprise. The last thing he would have ever expected was Hayden to be standing there when he turned to lock the door. But there he was in the flesh with a

Desert Eagle. Red smiled but didn't speak. Hayden gestured for him to get moving. Slowly Red turned about-face and walked a few paces ahead. He was elated as he drew close to the front room and noted that Ellis was nowhere in sight. He obviously saw Hayden's brazen attempt to take them by surprise.

As Red stepped over the threshold into the living room he tried to dart to one side but Hayden fired the pistol knocking him to the ground as he wounded him above the knee. Then all hell broke loose. Ellis stepped out from behind the wall firing his pistol. The .45 echoed with a boom, boom. Hayden fell to the ground knocking over the kitchen table as he returned the fire. It was a miracle that Ellis missed him.

He glimpsed Ellis diving behind the couch, and from the corner of his eye, he could see Red sprawled out clasping his right leg as blood spewed from between his fingers. He was trying to get hold of a pistol with his other hand, but it was out of his reach. Hayden stood and bolted into the living room kicking the pistol he was reaching for. And with the same agility and speed he kicked over the couch that, Ellis took cover behind. Ellis had no time react before Hayden pressed the cold steel of his Desert Eagle into his temple. "So we meet again." Hayden said with hate and hostility. "Stand up you fat pig. Where's Colleen?" It was then that he heard the knocking. She was alerted when the first gun shots echoed and hid under the bed. Her mouth was to sore for her to be able to call out. Instead, she resorted to banging on the door. "Lead me to that knocking right now, if you've so much as hurt a hair on her head I'm going to splatter your brains all over the place. Now get going." Ellis slowly led him to the door.

Hayden was in rough shape and Ellis could tell. He was waiting for the opportunity where he could side step him. Ellis saw him falter and almost tumble. He turned quickly to try and subdue him. However, Hayden got the drop on him and fired his Desert Eagle into Ellis's knee knocking the big man down. Ellis tumbled backwards grasping his knee as he fell to the floor screaming in agony. "You, you've blown off my knee."

"Now you and Red got a matching set." Hayden said as he reached down to pull him to his feet. He managed to get both men tied up with their backs to one another. The task made easier because of the fact neither were in much of a position to fight back, they both lost a lot of blood and were as weak as new-borns. Other than their cries of pain as Hayden tied them neither one spoke a word. They knew the game was up. Hayden wanted nothing more than to execute them. However now they looked more like pathetic excuses for men than the bullies he wanted to kill.

He walked back to the door. Putting his hand on the knob he tried to open it, but realised it was locked. "Colleen, can you hear me?" There was only a knock on the other side. "If you are gagged knock twice." There was no knock. "Colleen, I want you to step back from the door as far away as you can." If you understand, knock once." Colleen did so. "All right sweetheart step back." Hayden waited a few seconds giving Colleen time to step back and out of the way. Then, he fired two rounds into the doorknob and the door swung open revealing the woman he loved. She ran to him and jumped into his arms. Hayden couldn't remember a happier time in his life. Embracing one another, Colleen burst into tears. She pointed at the wound to her mouth and it was clear why she hadn't spoke. Then with all the pain tolerance she could muster she simply said, "Hayden I love you." Hayden held her tightly, kissing her face and head.

"I love you too. God how I love you too..." Then he slumped to the floor his eyes rolling to the back of his head. Numbness again consumed him and he convulsed uncontrollably. Overcome with fear Colleen cried out, "Hayden what happened." she cried as pain tore through her mouth like a thousand glass shards cutting away at her. Hayden moaned that he'd be all right and that what he needed was a place to lay down, and he feebly pointed at the couch. From there, he could keep his eye on Ellis and Red while he rested.

Colleen helped him over and he slumped into it. Every ounce of energy he had was spent. His head pounded again with sheer agony and the metallic taste in his mouth returned. Colleen sat next to him until he was content. Then she rose. As she did, he vaguely came to. He watched as Colleen approached her captors and with eight days of rage she balled up her fists and punched each of them square in the mouth.

Ellis was the only one out of the two that remained coherent and he was working on trying to get loose. He taunted Colleen trying to keep her close so that he could pounce on her. "Is that all you got for eight days of hell. Show me how you really feel. Think of these hands all over that tender sweet smelling body of yours and lest we forget how my tongue felt on your breast."

Hayden watched all this as it unfolded. Bits and pieces missed because he kept slipping in and out of consciousness. It played out in front of him like a slide show. He was too weak to warn Colleen and too weak to help. One moment she was backing up away from Ellis and the next, he had his arms around her waist trying to pull her in close. She managed to kick him in his knee and he crashed backwards, falling onto the floor with a thump as the big body of Red landed on top of him.

Hayden remembered Colleen standing over both men, the sniper rifle in her hand. Ellis started to rise. Like the coward he was he was holding Red up in front of him by his armpits. Red's head slumped forward. He was like a rag doll in Ellis's hands. Ellis began yelling something. Then Hayden heard it, the audible pop of the PSG 1 as blood splattered the kitchen wall and Ellis and Red fell for the last time. "How's that for eight days of rage, asshole." Colleen tossed the rifle onto the floor next to the bodies. Now it was over. Now she could forget.

It took three weeks for Hayden to recover from a serious concussion and exertion. Colleen was treated for the cuts in her mouth that shredded her gums and lacerated her cheek. Two days later, she was finally able to open her mouth without too much pain. The entire incident was classified as self-defence as it was noted that Hayden didn't pulled the trigger.

Ellis and Red were buried in a local Cemetery and only their names were carved into the crosses. There were no prayers or pieces of poetry, only their names. On December 20th, Hayden and Colleen boarded a plane bound for a little villa in Mexico and a Hotel called, 'El Tequila'.

Printed in the United Kingdom
by Lightning Source UK Ltd.
125586UK00001B/73/A

9 781894 936712